THE LAST SUN

THE LAST SUN

THE TAROT SEQUENCE | BOOK ONE

K. D. EDWARDS

an imprint of Prometheus Books
Amherst, NY

Published 2018 by Pyr®, an imprint of Prometheus Books

Cover illustration © Micah Epstein
Cover design by Nicole Sommer-Lecht
Cover design © Prometheus Books

Inquiries should be addressed to
Pyr
59 John Glenn Drive
Amherst, New York 14228
VOICE: 716-691-0133
FAX: 716-691-0137
WWW.PYRSF.COM

22 21 20 19 18   5 4 3 2 1

Library of Congress Cataloging-in-Publication Data

Names: Edwards, K. D., 1971- author.
Title: The last sun / K. D. Edwards.
Description: Amherst, NY : Pyr, 2018. | Series: The tarot sequence ; book 1
Identifiers: LCCN 2017040881 (print) | LCCN 2017050831 (ebook) |
    ISBN 9781633884243 (ebook) | ISBN 9781633884236 (softcover)
Subjects: LCSH: Atlantis (Legendary place)—Fiction. | Missing persons—Fiction. |
    BISAC: FICTION / Fantasy / Urban Life. | FICTION / Gay. | FICTION / Fantasy /
    Paranormal. | GSAFD: Fantasy fiction. Classification: LCC PS3605.D8875 (ebook)
    | LCC PS3605.D8875 L37 2018 (print) | DDC 813/.6—dc23
LC record available at https://lccn.loc.gov/2017040881

Printed in the United States of America

Ground Zero of Dedications: For Mom and Dad

CONTENTS

CONTENTS

PROLOGUE

My name is Rune Saint John.

I am, before anything else, a survivor: of a fallen House, of a brutal assault, of violent allies and complacent enemies, of life among a people who turned their back on me decades ago.

Among those who matter I am known and notorious. I am the Catamite Prince; the Day Prince; the Prince of Ruin. I am the last scion of my dead father's dead court, once called the Sun Throne, brightest of all Arcana, now just so much ash and rubble.

These are my accounts.

THE HEART THRONE

"—said 'What do I look like, your *talla*?' And then I said, 'You must be mad—go live off someone else's income, you wrecked parasite.'" The rich man pronounced *wrecked* in the old Atlantean accent, cleaving it into two waspish syllables.

I flicked a shrimp tail into a potted plant and wiped my mouth on my tuxedo sleeve. I caught the rich man's girlfriend giving me a raised-eyebrow look and thought, *right, manners*.

I re-circulated through the ballroom, where snarls of people mobbed a football field's worth of parquet flooring. Two-story, majestic windows rose toward a baroque cathedral ceiling. What wasn't window was gilded mirror, facing each other and reflecting the gala's light and motion in an infinite loop. It was pretty, but I couldn't help thinking the effect was wasted on this self-indulgent crowd, like a gold filling in a rotted tooth.

A glance at my watch showed there were still thirty minutes before the raid would begin. Smoothing my impatience into an expression of moral vacuity, I wandered.

There was plenty to look at. Ice blocks sculpted into nude satyrs. Banquet tables supporting crystal bowls that brimmed with jewel-colored pills, and slender bottles of bizarre substances—not so much drinks as the idea of drinks, filled with oils and aloes and meaty twists of smoke. There was a forty-man chamber orchestra; a woman with flames dancing across the enamel of her teeth; a young page who chilled people's drinks with a spell that left frostbite on his palms.

Servants saturated the crowd, delivering tray after tray of champagne. They were young, drugged, and blankly beautiful. I banked my distaste at this, and said nothing. It would be over soon enough.

Missing Brand, I gave the back of my ear a sharp tap. He'd probably want to kill everything in sight too.

"It's working," he snapped, his voice a tinny echo inside my head. "Calm the fuck down."

I hid a smile, flicked the transmitter with a fingernail, and moved on.

The surge of the crowd pushed me off course, which was how I found myself in the last place I'd intended to go—by the windows that faced the ocean. I stood there and stared at the familiar stretch of shore that abutted the Lovers' property. The gray night tide was lit by the sweep of a decorative lighthouse. In my memory, though, it was daytime; I saw a long white beach, and sand as soft as campfire ash.

I turned away from the window.

A woman's nasal soliloquy caught my attention. She was dressed in handfuls of lace cinched at the waist by a samite belt. Her sagging breasts strained against the material as she pointed out the window and spoke to a crowd of young people.

"It's true. You must have heard the stories, dearies. That is the old Lord Sun's estate over there. I was here that night, when he was murdered. None of us knew what was going on at the time, of course—the enemy had set stealth wards. We never heard the fighting, never heard the screams. It was a slaughter. Almost to the man. And the one who lived, the heir scion? Taken to a shed." She leaned closer at this, her voice lowering. "Taken there by seven masked men, and, by gods, the things they did to that poor boy. They had him for hours before he escaped. He was the only survivor. You still see him around, every now and then. A very, very pretty man, but rank with darkness. It precedes him like a fog. I can sense such things; I have seer blood. They call him the Catamite Prince, owing to his . . . relationship with the Tower—which I certainly wouldn't repeat in mixed company. You must have heard—"

"It's been said my family has seer blood, too," I interrupted.

"Shit," Brand said.

The woman turned toward me. Her ears and neck sparked with sigils in the shape of sapphire jewelry. Ten, no, twelve. She wore *twelve* sigils. That's just what was in plain sight. A million dollars' worth of magical firepower, and all of it probably used to store nothing more serious than spells to hide her flatulence, or make her eyebrows look plucked.

"Truly?" she said, warming to the interruption. She narrowed her eyes suggestively at my forehead, where my disguise spell placed my eyes. The disguise made me taller and blond—and, apparently, not rank with darkness.

"Yes," I lied. "Yes, it is."

"Then tell me my future, you lovely man."

While her young relatives humored her with expressions just shy of eye rolls, I took one of her hands. "I see you crawling on a field of blood and char, with bone shards in your hair."

Her eyes went wide, an oil spill of mascara.

"Rune," Brand said in my ear, but I was already walking away.

To hell with her. To hell with her sigils, her fat fingers, her crowd of stupid boot-lickers. To hell with the Lovers and their Heart Throne and their drugged slaves. To hell with nine men in animal masks in a carriage house, and all the other stupid details people got wrong.

"Don't fucking make me come down there," Brand said.

Our Companion bond thrummed with his concern, no matter how gruff he sounded. So I stopped, closed my eyes, and took a breath. Then another. I wasn't the only survivor the night my father's court was destroyed. Brand had survived, too: my Companion, born human and bonded with me in the crib, raised and trained to protect me. And he had. He'd saved me—saved us both—that night.

I ducked my head and whispered, "I hate seers."

"Well aware," Brand said.

"Especially fake seers. She's a fake seer. I hate fake seers."

"Still fucking aware."

"Isn't it time yet?" I asked.

His low, drawn-out *umm* had me on guard instantly. He said, "We've got a hiccup. I've got Julie on the line to fill us in."

"*Julia*," a woman stressed.

Brand paused, very possibly to count to ten. He said, "Message received. Rune, you remember Julia, our uptight raid liaison. Apparently Julia dropped the ball and forgot to mention the lab wing is under a secondary security system."

"I didn't—!"

"Julia, please, just focus," Brand said. "Finger-pointing accomplishes nothing. I'm sure Lord Tower will be very understanding about your monumental fuck-up."

The woman took a sharp breath. "Lord Sun, please listen. It's true the lab wing is on a separate security system, but we've still got a few minutes before the raid begins. I have the security book for tonight's party, and I know which of the Lovers' people are on plainclothes duty and where they're stationed. I've identified at least one high-level security director with an access card that should get you into the lab."

She directed me to an archway by the chamber orchestra. Past it, every other archway on the first floor was lined up so you could see a dozen adjacent richly appointed rooms in shotgun procession. Julia told me to narrow my search to a man just under six feet, with ginger hair and hazel eyes.

"There's three," I whispered.

"Three what?" Brand asked.

I put my mouth against my sleeve as if to cough and said, "Three tall red-haired guys."

"Of course there fucking are," Brand said.

Julia said, "Check all their pockets after the spell blast goes off. Take any key cards with the Heart Throne logo on it. It's the best we can do. They won't hold the raid on our account."

I glanced back at the red-haired men. One was staring at his fingers with a dreamy expression. He had primary-colored smears around his mouth, probably from the rainbow pill buffet. The remaining two were standing by the wall, watching the antics of the crowd.

I went back into the crowd and found the loudest, most offensive drunk in eyesight. "Is it true?" I asked him.

He turned unsteadily from a beleaguered group of people, who took advantage of my interruption to slip away. He glared at me blearily and said, "Is what true?"

"That you did that thing. With the horse."

"What thin' with the horse?"

"The redheaded guy by the doorway—right over there—he said you blew a horse in the stable on a bet. He's telling everyone. How did you keep the horse still? I've got some Tic Tacs if you need one."

The drunk swung through the crowd. He got confused when he saw two redheads and picked one at random. He made some blah-blah tough guy sounds and started shoving. The redhead shoved back.

You can learn a lot about a person by the way they fight—profession, temperament, sometimes even ethnicity or nationality. This particular redhead had no training, no balance. While he was shoving the drunk away, he wasn't thinking ahead to strike, let alone about the next counterstrike. But the *second* redhead was watching the altercation with calm and assessing eyes. He stood with his right side facing the shoving match to minimize body target, knees loose and shoulder-width apart, weight shifted to the balls of his feet.

"Rune, it's starting," Brand said sharply. "Stay safe."

It happened at once.

The spell smashed through the room—not quite an explosion, more like heat rising from asphalt in fast-forward. Nearly everyone in eyesight collapsed. Just collapsed. The only sounds were the hiss of fabric; the clatter of orchestra instruments; an overturned pill bowl that scattered drugs across the parquet.

When it was over, there were only four of us on our feet. We picked our way through the tangle of bodies, exchanging nods and clipped greetings.

A large group of Arcana had banded together to attack the Lovers in the raid; and now that the Lovers' guards were immobilized, each had their own part of its corpse they wanted to pick clean.

"You okay?" Brand asked.

"Countercharm worked fine," I said. I went and rifled through the security guard's pockets for his key card. I found it on the first go.

Once upon a time, the Heart Throne had been the archetype of sex and love and shiny, happy fluids. They'd been *important* to Atlantis. We're a society, after all, that embraces the idea of group marriage, that finds pure heterosexuality as abnormal as pure homosexuality. We flaunt our appeal as a matter of breeding and survival.

But after the fall of the Atlantean homeland, the Lovers, like so many of my people, changed. They started making ventures into unwelcome, even forbidden practices. Worse, they crossed borders to do it. They compromised our treaties with the human world and put all of New Atlantis at risk.

And so a decision was made. No less than twelve Arcana banded together under a legally sanctioned raid. In exchange for tactical strength and manpower, each Arcana would get a share of the spoils. They would divide the Lovers' people, assets, precious metals, real estate, bank accounts, magic, artwork, heirlooms, technology, sigils . . . Termites were less effective than a formal raid.

I was there at the behest of my sometime-employer and former protector, Lord Tower. Which was what took me toward the lab, where I might finally get to stab someone.

Other members of the raid ghosted past me as I made my way to the west wing. They were dressed as guests, servants, slaves, valets, bartenders—whatever it had taken to get them through the door and in position for the attack.

The key card got me past every door. The main building's decorative knickknacks eventually phased into an office area's utilitarian gray carpets and humming fluorescence.

I shook my wrist. My sabre, now in the form of a scuffed gold wrist-guard, stretched and slid over my knuckles. By the time it was in my palm, it had transmuted into a swordless hilt, which I held facing outward like brass knuckles. It was a powerful and adaptable tool, built from fire magic. It was one of the few weapons that had survived the fall of the Sun Throne.

"You don't call; you don't write," Brand said in my ear.

I smiled. "What's happening downstairs?"

"The main raid just broke in. Fun for all."

"And all of the Lovers' people are still knocked out?"

"Yeah, but keep sharp," he said. "Knowing you, you'll get surprised by the one guard who happened to pass out in a lead-lined shitter."

"I can handle myself."

"Sure you can," he said, "but you're wearing my fucking jacket."

"Is Julia still on our channel?"

"I'm here," Julia said.

"Just curious—any sign of Lady Lovers?"

"Negative. We can't even confirm she's on-site. Another team is tracking her."

I was coming up on the entrance to the lab wing. Bulletproof plastic blocked the corridor. A door of the same material had been fitted with a card reader. Seven mercenaries waited for me. It would be their job to tie up the unconscious scientists and lab workers.

The merc in front, shouldering a shortened assault rifle, stepped over. "It's a different security system, my lord. We're going to have to blow through."

"Or," I said, and flashed the key card in front of the scanner. A panel burped green, and the door slid open. Without another word, the soldiers crouched low, sifted through the opening, and dispersed in different directions.

I followed a memorized floor plan with some occasional guidance from Julia. My destination was one of the chemical labs. If intel was right, it was one of the least-fortified spots with terminal access to the Lovers' operating system. The operating system was reportedly the closest thing in development to an actual artificial intelligence; the Tower had cashed in a lot of favors to stake it during the raid.

I entered the lab with my sabre raised. Two men—two *conscious* men—were huddled on the other side of the room.

They were pale and shaking. In their white lab coats, they resembled the sickly mice they experimented on. One of them, a young guy, held a stapler; the other, an unplugged desk lamp.

I said, "Two scientists, an entire lab full of nasty chemicals, and that's the best you came up with."

The older of the two dropped the desk lamp and snatched a stainless-steel letter opener off the desk. He grabbed his young colleague and shoved him in front as a human shield, then pressed the tip of the letter opener to the boy's jugular. "I'll kill him," the scientist said breathlessly. "I swear, I'll kill him. Stand aside and let me go."

"Am I missing something?" I asked.

"Do you want his death on your conscience?" the man demanded.

"He's a slaver. *You're* a slaver. I'm still missing something."

"He's an *intern*. And we're not slavers!"

"I see," I said, and shot his hostage in the thigh with a bolt of fire. The young man screamed and dropped and curled in a vomiting fetal position. The older man started gibbering in panic. He dove into a corner of the room and pulled himself into a ball.

I went to the nearest computer terminal and stuck a flash drive in the USB port. It was programmed to do all of the work for me, which was just as well, since my computer skills were limited to dodging the spyware on porn sites. When the red light stopped blinking, I pulled the flash drive loose and headed out.

"This is wrong," the older scientist moaned.

I stopped. "Excuse me?"

"This is not right."

"Do you even know what's going on?" I asked.

"Scapegoats," he spat. "You've made us scapegoats to human law. We are *Atlantean*."

"Are you part of Project Laius?" I asked.

The scientist shut his mouth, surprised.

"You are, aren't you?" I said. "That's so awesome."

I shot him in the head with a sabre blast. He tipped and convulsed for the whole two seconds it took him to die.

The stuff that began with projects like Laius had ended with the mind-fucking of underage kids, who spent the rest of their miserable lives in dog collars as someone else's property. So I did what I did, and my conscience whistled.

Brand was in mid-shout as I left the room. "What are you going on about?" I asked, starting down the corridor at a light jog.

"What the fuck happened to you!"

"I downloaded the program. You didn't hear all that? Two of them were awake."

"Hear what? I couldn't even feel you through our bond. Julia, what the fucking hell is going on? Why did we lose him?"

A moment of static and Julia said, "I've got similar reports from the other mercs in that wing. The rooms must be shielded. Not everyone was dropped by the spell blast. We need to plan your extraction, Lord Sun."

There were some additional noises on the line. Julia said, "Wait! We're— Yes. Yes, we're also getting reports the spell blast is wearing off sooner than we expected. I don't know if a team has had time to secure the roof. Abort roof exit."

"No," I said. "It's the quickest way out, and I'm ready to leave."

"I don't know if it's secure. Abort roof exit."

"Well, since you repeated yourself," I said, banging through the metal fire door that led to a stairway that led to the roof.

"I'm mission coordinator; you're required to follow my lead. Shall I make this an order?" she demanded.

Brand laughed. "Look, Julia, I'll handle it from here. He's my partner. We planned on a roof exit."

"You serve your partner poorly," she said in a tight, clipped voice. "If you want him out of the building alive, the safest route—"

"Mind your fucking manners," Brand said, all humor evaporating. "He's not one of your mercenaries; he's a scion of Atlantis. If it was a question about needing safe routes, I'd have him turn the entire side of the mansion to slag and gingerly fucking tiptoe through the puddles of plasma. Get off the goddamn line. Rune, fuck, this is why I hate teamwork."

I proceeded with my exit as Brand disconnected Julia.

The roof was flat and strewn with gravel. My line of sight was crowded with HVAC units and elevator machine rooms.

The fire-exit door swung shut on a slow spring. I tilted my face into a humid ocean breeze, letting it tangle my bangs. "I'm out," I said.

"Have a nice flight," Brand said distractedly.

"Yeah, about that. I was thinking maybe instead, I can just drop down to the lawn and—"

A man stepped around a corner in front of me. He had an assault weapon. Its barrel jerked up. I barely had time to think *I should have activated my Shield spell a few minutes ago*, when something cracked and the man fell down. A red mist floated where his head had been.

When I could breathe again, I said, "I especially liked it when you didn't warn me. That part was fun."

"Fucking ingrate," Brand said in my ear. "I was lining him up when you walked outside."

I squinted at a water tower some two thousand feet away. Brand was an excellent marksman. It was one of the reasons we'd lasted as long as we had. That and my magic. Because the cool transmitters, and spell bombs, and the squads of mercenary backup? Those weren't resources we normally had. A normal job went like this: I went somewhere I shouldn't,

I tried not to get caught, and if I did, Brand shot someone in the head. It was a good day when the corpse had pizza money.

"Any more surprises?" I asked.

"You want warning?"

"That'd be nice," I said.

"Duck."

A dragon rose behind the mansion on wings as long as a tour bus. It spat out a stream of nuclear fire and demolished a guard tower. I could feel the heat from half a rooftop away, but hopefully not the radiation. I'd heard Lord Chariot had summoned one of the remaining dragons for the raid, but seeing it was something else.

Just as the dragon glided out of sight, panic—genuine panic—suddenly buzzed through my Companion bond.

Brand said, "Rune. Get out of there. *Now!*"

I dropped behind a heating duct and reached for my ankle sigil just as Elena—Arcana of the Lovers, head of the godsdamn Heart Throne—swept across my line of sight.

She lifted an arm toward a seamless limestone wall. A dark archway rippled into visibility. She went through.

"Rune," Brand warned after a few seconds. "Move."

All I could think was *Secret. Bloody. Room.* Her House is falling down around her, and she heads here? I couldn't even begin to imagine what kind of things she must have stashed in there.

"Don't you do it, Rune," Brand said without having to ask what I was thinking. "Don't you fucking dare."

"I'm just going to wait. Over there."

"I'm fucking serious. Get the fuck out of there."

"Right over there." I pointed innocently.

"I will shoot you in the ass, the goddamn ass! I will shoot you in the ass, and you'll be shitting through an inner tube for weeks!"

"I'll be right back," I said.

"In! The! Ass!"

I headed for the secret room. Elena had to leave eventually. She was being raided, for gods' sake. Visions of gemstones the size of goose eggs danced in my head.

I got within arm's reach of the archway when a spell I hadn't seen yanked me into oblivion.

When I came to, I was chained in a corner. Heavily stylized panels of amber glowed dully under electric light. Elena stood in front of me.

Lady Lovers was not a striking woman. Her nose was too small, her eyes close together, and she had the faint jut of an overbite. She was also covered, absolutely covered, in sigils. They were shaped as earrings, as a forehead circlet, as necklaces, lip piercings, rings, bracelets, hair clips, and discs strung into a belt. Assuming all of them were charged with spells, I was well and truly fucked.

"Hell," I whispered.

"Indeed," Elena murmured. She started to say something else, but the words hitched as she peered closer. She'd recognized me—which meant my disguise spell was gone, along with gods knew what other of my abilities. I tested the manacles with a yank.

Elena said, "Your presence is . . . unexpected. Yet not unfitting, I suppose. Stranger things have passed down the River. Faith, but you are a very pretty thing, Lord Sun. Hasn't it even been said that you are the most beautiful man of your gener—"

"That'll be enough of that, thank you," I said testily. Then, in a burst of sanity, I added, "Ma'am."

"As you wish. Are you a part of the raid, Lord Sun? This *is* a raid, I assume?"

"It is. I'm sorry."

"Tell me. How many of my dear fellow Arcana turned hand against me?"

There was nothing to gain by lying. I sighed. "Twelve, ma'am."

Her mouth tightened, and she stared at her feet. The average, sanctioned raid usually involved half that number. She gestured at my left arm. The cuff snapped open. She did the same for the right.

I moved away from the wall. Almost immediately, I sensed the presence of my sigils again. It gave me a couple aces up my sleeve if I needed them.

"With all respect, Lady Lovers," I said carefully, "are you surprised?"

"At what?" she asked. "At being vilified? At bearing witness to the mortality of my court? I would have expected you to understand how I feel. We are not dissimilar. Our Houses, both raided. Our courts, gone. Our people, scattered and abused and stripped of everything for which they've labored."

I flushed more angrily than I'd have expected. My father's murder and the fall of my court was not anything like this. Not that I argued the point. It wasn't worth the effort.

Elena went to a mirror. She pressed a fingertip against the surface. Images rose, blistering her reflection. Her body blocked most of the images, but I saw blood, fallen bodies, a mass of activity.

She wiped the mirror clean with a gesture and said, "To each age, a magic ascends. Death magic ruled the final days of the homeland. Hearth magic ruled the rise of New Atlantis. I had thought, perhaps, the Lovers' time had come, that the age of heart magic was upon us." She stopped. Grimaced. "I don't know why I'm wasting what time remains defending myself to anyone. It's a useless exercise. Worse, a fundamentally dishonest one. I know things went ill; I should have yielded the court to another couple when my Gerard died. The Heart Throne was ever meant to be ruled by a pair." She looked at me over her shoulder. "Did you know I had but one consort? My Gerard. Very unusual, yes? He was my *talla*." Her soul mate—though, in Atlantean terms, soul mates weren't always a cozy and romantic concept. Hatred was just as strong as love, in terms of a metaphysical catalyst.

"I didn't know that," I said politely.

"He was. But onward to a more pressing matter." She straightened and faced me.

Red flags snapped open in my head.

She said, "Look upon my face, Rune Sun."

Power crashed through the room. I bit my tongue and barely acknowledged I'd fallen to my knees, even as my forehead banged down in front of them. My dick swelled, an erection so painful I stuffed my fist in my lap. She had assumed her Atlantean aspect—she'd called on her deepest magic—like opening the door to a furnace the size of an ocean liner.

"Look upon my face," she repeated. Her voice reverberated, an unnatural echo.

There was no room for resistance. I raised my head and looked.

She had skin that moved with gemstone color, the way fingertips will whiten when pressed against a hard surface. She had translucent hornet wings, a dress made of rose petal, and a scent—a musk—of honey and semen. I tried to laugh, because I wanted to seem brave, but the moan in my throat strangled it. I tried to get up. Fell. Scuttled back against the wall.

"I would beg a favor, pretty Rune. I swear by the River your answer will be your own." That was an old way of saying she wasn't going to mind-fuck me for compliance. "I ask that you deliver, and protect, a package of mine to a safe destination. It is nothing that will intrinsically bring you harm, and it breaks no laws. It is a very, very personal request. I speak the truth. I swear by the River. In exchange for your service, I will give you a sigil."

A sigil. She was offering me a sigil?

My mouth went dry with greed.

She walked over to me. Her magic moved with her, each footfall rimmed in damp grass cuttings. She placed something on the ground. When she drew her triple-jointed fingers away, a sigil, shaped as a ring, remained behind. It was a gold band with an ellipsis of emerald chips across the top.

"It is a good sigil," she said. "I've had it many years. I will give it to you if you accept the task."

"I don't . . ." I swallowed. "Nothing illegal?"

"I swear by the River, no."

I had so few sigils of my own. It represented far, far more than monetary gain.

"I agree," I whispered.

"The package will be waiting at your home. You'll want payment in advance, of course. And so I give this sigil freely; your Will is now its Will."

The bond between me and the ring snapped into place. Just like that, it was mine. I had a seventh sigil.

Elena raised a hand toward the mirror on the wall. Her eyes flashed bright, and I felt the release of a spell. In a breathy voice, she said, "There. It is done. You should leave now, pretty Rune. You owe me a task and I'd not have you caught in the fire."

"Fire," I repeated. Reality ran a step ahead of tact. "No way. You did not just set a—a what, a bomb countdown? Did you set *a bomb*?"

She bent and kissed the word *run* against my ear.

Across the room, the archway shimmered back into visibility. I leapt and ran. My ears popped as I raced through the archway and nearly twisted my ankle on roof gravel. Brand's voice swore to life over the earpiece. I drowned out his shouting by yelling the word *bomb* nine times with no punctuation.

He notified the rest of the raid team. Things happened quickly. People jumped out windows, trampled through doors. Others ran onto the roof and used flight, levitation, unassisted gravity, even a bloody winged horse.

I sent my willpower into my gold ankle chain to release its stored spell. Buoyant magic shivered through my body. I pushed off the roof, and my body didn't stop moving. Wind broke against me as I spun midair and flew.

The actual art of flying is not a comic-book experience. It is scary and dangerous as fuck all, and clumsy, and intemperate.

You get sunburn during the day and freeze your ass at night. It's hard to breathe. You can't see straight—especially if you forget your goggles, as I always do. Gravity pulls strangely at your limbs, turning you into a marionette with snapped strings. Oh, and bugs. You get bugs in your teeth. A bee stung me in the throat once.

But in this case, with a bomb's timer set, I embraced the spell wholeheartedly. I soared to the water tower, grabbed Brand, and we made a bum's rush off the property. I set Brand down at his motorcycle a half a mile away. We both stared back at the mansion, waiting for the climactic finish. Nothing happened. After a few minutes, we called it a day.

Brand was mad as hell and kept all his comments clipped when I filled him in on what happened with Elena. Then he got on his motorcycle and left, a dramatic exit as loud as the arc of a chainsaw.

I sighed, got in my beat-up old Saturn, and drove home.

Three streets before my final turn, I heard an almighty *CRACK*. In the rearview mirror, the horizon turned black and gold.

Brand was still unlatching his rifle case when I pulled into the cul-de-sac where we lived. He opened the lid to make sure the contents hadn't shifted during his ride. "You're a fucking dumb-ass," he said.

"I know."

"You know that, right?"

"I *know*."

"No, seriously, it was a stupid fucking dumb-ass move. You don't mess with Arcana; they're all deadly, even the queen of the fucking love faeries. Now you're stuck doing a favor for her."

"But I got a sigil out of it," I said, holding up the emerald ring I'd had zipped in my pocket. "Pretty cool parting gift, yeah?"

"Gift? I have this image in my head of exploding cigars. Or flower boutonnieres that squirt water. Peanut cans with snakes."

"Big word. *Boutonnieres*."

He snapped the rifle case shut and spun the combination lock. I was pretty sure this conversation wasn't over. The episode with Lady Lovers had rattled him, which wasn't an easy thing to do.

We headed toward the front door of Half House, our home. As I fished for my keys, Brand said, a little hesitantly, "That woman. The fake seer. She didn't bother you too much with what she said, right?"

"Nah," I mumbled.

He watched my face closely. "'Nah'?"

I gave him a little smile and bumped his shoulder.

"Don't smile at me," Brand said. "You're still a dumb-ass."

We piled into Half House's nine-foot-wide living room—which was the sum width of the entire building. I swept a gaze across the coffee table and frowned.

Brand squeezed around me, then pointed to the table. "But . . . ?"

"No cookies," I said.

"She always bakes cookies when we have a job," he repeated, as if I was arguing the point.

He went in search of our housekeeper, Queenie, who lived in a tiny cottage in the backyard. Normally she laid out fruit drinks and snacks after a successful job, her small way of celebrating the fact that she was still employed.

I dropped into a puffy chair and wrenched off my boots. They were among the most expensive things I owned: so finely cut to the shape of my foot that I didn't usually wear socks. I reached for a jar of powder I kept in a nearby wicker basket and sprinkled some to absorb the moisture. Impact and endurance wards, etched into the leather, tingled dully against my fingers.

The back door opened, and Brand came back through the house. He stopped in the doorway and didn't say anything.

For a horrible second I thought something was wrong, that Queenie was hurt, that our work had finally followed us home. Then Queenie came up behind him. Her plain face swung side to side in a nonstop headshake.

She said, "You took a seventeen-year-old boy?"

I said, "Um. What?"

"For a sigil? You took a seventeen-year-old boy to get a sigil?"

"Funny thing about that package you have to deliver," Brand said.

My mouth opened. My mouth closed.

"No, no, it gets better. Guess what," he made air quotes, "the 'safe destination' is."

"Please tell me Elena didn't send us a seventeen-year-old boy. Please tell me a seventeen-year-old boy is not the package."

"Oh, she did. And, oh, yes, it is. But, again," he said, "it gets better. Guess what the destination is?"

There was no sand to stick my head in. So I just closed my eyes as Brand said, "His age of adulthood—his twenty-first fucking birthday."

Well, shit, I thought.

HALF HOUSE

No one has ever been arrested or convicted for the slaughter of my father and our people. It has become one of New Atlantis's enduring mysteries.

The assailants had been circumspect, of course. In the absence of a legitimatized raid, the response by the Arcanum—the formal, collective body of all Arcana—would have been implacable. The unplanned destruction of a court lessens all of New Atlantis, when other courts don't get fat off it.

I don't remember what party I was sneaking back from; I just remember being fifteen and carefree and drunk and stoned, and trying to avoid Brand and the household security force. I think I got as far as the solarium—at least, I can dimly remember something rushing up at me in the solarium—before I was hit with a stun spell.

I woke up in the carriage house, in the custody of nine men wearing animal masks. My hands and feet were bound. Brand was there, but he was not conscious. He would not return to his senses for hours yet to come.

They kept me there while the rest of the estate ran with blood. Eventually Brand woke up. He surprised them. We escaped. No one else did.

Over fifteen people died that night, the entire live-in staff. Their bodies were burned beyond the point of recognition. Most were identified only by the simple elimination of who didn't show up for work the next day.

Media exposure was inevitable. I was very young, handsome, and disgustingly over-privileged. It was a lurid and sensational crime, and I was photogenic in my disrepair. Consider also that Atlantean society does not protect its victims: it exposes them, it uses them as moral lessons on fitness and survival.

Two decades later—*two decades*, significant even among a people who aged slowly—the story just. Won't. Fucking. Die. It gets me a lot of sidelong looks on the subway. Truth be told, I suppose I do my best to earn them.

I woke to the sounds of fighting, which tricked me into thinking that I was still asleep, because I'm always fighting in my sleep. Rubbing my eyes didn't make the noise go away, though.

I arched my throbbing back and stretched, the tips of my fingers and toes brushing the edge of the custom king mattress. I crawled to the foot of it—the only way off, since there was less than an inch of clearance on either side—and swung my legs onto the floor.

After yawning a cantrip, a honeyed ball of light appeared above me, chasing back the narrow room's shadows. I padded to the air-conditioner and used pliers to turn the broken dial to the off position.

"Rune?" Queenie said from the stairwell. She hesitated half a landing below my eyesight.

"Someone's yelling and I haven't had coffee," I said.

"That's why I came up? It's Brand. And, um, your seventeen-year-old?"

"He's not my—" I glared at the ceiling. "I'll be right down."

I dry-swallowed two Percocet to ease the soreness in my shoulder, and did a one-legged hop into dirty jeans and a clean t-shirt. The pants were tight. Noticeably tight, especially across the backside, and wasn't that just great. It had been a frigid winter, a cold spring, and a cool early summer. I'd spent too many months hiding in sweaters.

I tugged at the waistband and freed up an extra half inch while jogging down the tight spiral stairway. The second floor was split into a guest bedroom and full bath. The disturbance was coming from the bathroom. The first thing I saw when I entered was Brand holding Matthias Saint Valentine's head in the toilet. Matthias was wearing just a towel.

I pointed at Brand.

He gave me a look. That was it. I waved an impatient arm at the toilet. Brand sighed and loosened his grip a little, and Matthias's head lifted out of the bowl, spitting water. His white-blond bangs dripped over his face and hid his expression.

"Allow me to explain," Brand said. "Apparently, our Queenie tried to unpack Little Lord Scion's suitcase while he was in the shower. Not her job, of course, but she's just that kind of person, isn't she?"

"Brand, really, I'm not ups—"

Brand raised his voice over Queenie's. "In the midst of her friendly efforts, Little Lord Douchebag comes trotting out of the bathroom, takes one look, and asks our Queenie whether she'd be able to do it right, or whether he'd need to do it himself. Upon her recounting this criticism to me shortly thereafter, I hastened upstairs to inform him that, yes, he would need to do it himself. I took offense to his dismissive response. Further discussion ensued. Eventually it appeared that the most diplomatic solution was to stick his fucking head in toilet water."

"Let him go," I said.

Brand's hand, hovering just above the smooth, pale skin of Matthias's neck, flipped up.

Matthias glanced over his shoulder to make sure that Brand had complied. He gripped the towel tight at his waist and stumbled to his feet.

Whatever he saw on my face must have reassured him. I could almost read his reaction like ticker tape. *Rune is a scion like me. He'll understand.*

I went over and put a hand on Matthias's shoulder. When I had enough leverage, I shoved him into the shower stall. He tripped over the low lip and fell. I turned on the cold water, and he scrabbled noiselessly at the side of the fiberglass stall in shock.

Then, to my vague unease, the fight went out of him. He pulled his towel into his lap to cover his genitals and turned his face from us. The cold made his body shake like hard sobs.

Queenie said, "Must be tough? Losing everything? I wonder if he even knows who survived last night, or which of his family is still alive. Do you think . . . Well, do you think maybe he just finds it easier to act high and mighty—maybe it's, I don't know, his armor? How was it with you, Rune, the day after you lost everything?"

Brand and I exchanged guilty looks. Brand shut the shower off. Matthias stopped shaking but stayed where he was, knees and face drawn into a ball.

Brand leaned over Matthias's prone body and said, "Sorry about that. Rune's got anger issues."

I shot Brand a dirty look. But for the first time, a really unpleasant thought occurred to me. At best, I'd been a part of the raid that had dismantled Matthias's home life. At worst, his father had been a lab chemist.

I cleared my throat and said, "Matthias. This is a bizarre situation and . . . It's just bizarre. Your grandmother tricked me, and we need to talk about that. But until then, we'll treat you like a houseguest, and you'll act like one. Okay?"

He hesitated so long that I didn't expect an answer. When it came, it was soft and hoarse. "Yes."

"Excellent," I said. "Great."

I turned and punched Brand in the thigh, hard enough to give him a charley horse. He *motherfucker*ed me through gritted teeth while grabbing the spot.

"Anger issues," I told him.

I spent the rest of the morning in my sanctum on the third floor, studying Elena's emerald ring.

There were many types of magical disciplines, all of them as unique as the willpower it took to quicken them. But the most common type of power available to Atlantean scions came from our sigils.

Sigils allowed us to store spells for later use. They were generally shaped in the form of jewelry or piercings, the finite product of a lost art, which made them all the more precious. In giving me a sigil, Elena had dropped close to a hundred thousand dollars in my lap. Selling it wasn't an option, though. The one time I'd suggested selling one of my six meager sigils to pay our cable bill, Brand had put a knife through the television set, ironically ending the discussion. Each sigil, in his eyes, was a chance for me not to get killed in a firefight.

Now I had seven sigils. I fooled around with Elena's sigil, trying unsuccessfully to figure out what kind of spell she'd already stored inside it.

Just when I was ready to drain the spell from the ring, Brand came into the sanctum. He was in a t-shirt and running shorts, sneakers and no socks. For all that, he still had about five weapons on his person, right down to a silver garrote threaded through his shoelaces.

He kicked off the running shoes and sat down on the floor in front of me.

"I did some research on Little Lord Asshat," he said. It lacked any real heat, though. I'd overheard him earlier giving money to Queenie to buy Matthias "a razor, a toothbrush, and a fucking clue."

Brand said, "He's definitely Elena's grandson. His father was one of her sons. Him and his mother are alive—or at least they were before the raid—but it looks like his uncle had custody of him. No siblings. Did you know he's nearly a full-blooded fae?"

"A changeling?" I asked, surprised. Full-blooded fae had the ability to alter their appearance—not as dramatically as were-folk, but it came in handy.

"Don't know. Fucking ask him. Anyway, he hasn't gotten in trouble, nothing in the gossip rags, he hasn't run up any debts. He's just a birth certificate and a guardianship filing. That's it."

I asked the question that had been bothering me most of all. "Why him? Why did Elena save *him*?"

Brand shrugged and asked the question that most bothered him. "Do we have to let him stay here?"

"I don't know. If I screw with my oath, I screw with my magic. Lord Tower wants to see me this afternoon—maybe I can find a way to ask him without actually asking him."

"The Tower called?" he said, a little suspiciously.

"Maybe he wants to give me a big fat check."

"Why does he need to see you to pay us? Do you think he's got another job for us?"

"I don't know," I said. "If we've got to feed and water this kid, then I hope so."

THE TOWER

Among modern cities, New Atlantis is a precocious freak.

The expenditure to create it—in terms of money and magic—was incalculable. Hundreds of abandoned human buildings from all over the world were bought and teleported to Nantucket: sanitariums, madhouses, churches, palaces, hotels, skyscrapers. Taking possession of these ruins wasn't as difficult as it sounded. Humans never appreciate what they've allowed to fall into disrepair.

New Atlantis now occupies half the acreage of Nantucket, just a little over the size of Manhattan. The former topography of the island—scrubby trees, sand dunes, wide-open spaces—lasted as long as it took us to strip it clean and slap on a coat of asphalt. Don't even get me started on the west end of the island. The Westlands were the poisoned magical backwash of the translocation magic; a deadly mess of monsters, pocket dimensions, and heavily warded Arcana compounds. I had as much interest in taking a Sunday drive into that countryside as I did in getting a colonic with jet fuel.

The human world never figured out the phenomenal expense it took to create New Atlantis, or the unlikelihood that it would ever be possible again. To them, it looked as if we pulled our Gotham out of a cereal box. They saw their abandoned buildings turn into craters overnight, and assumed that that was the sort of thing we would always be capable of doing.

Not a bad rep to have.

I spent much of the morning in my sanctum, filling my sigils with a balanced blend of defensive and aggressive spells. Brand did his own preparation in the basement, only with knives and Kevlar. Our experience with the Tower had taught us well. A job offer and the actual beginning of the job were very often simultaneous events with Lord Tower.

That said, Brand wouldn't come with me to meet Lord Tower; he'd just join up if I needed him. I kept him and the Tower in separate rooms as much as possible. They didn't get along, which, when you're talking about two personalities like that, was like mixing an oil spill and a tidal wave.

A few minutes before I was about to head downstairs, Brand poked his head up the spiral stairway. "The fuck?" he said.

"What the fuck what?" I said.

"Queenie is outside, fussing over Matthias."

"He's coming with me. I thought I'd bring him along, get a feel for him."

Brand came up the stairs. "You're taking him for a walk? To get a *feel* for him? You know he's not a dog you picked up at the fucking pound, right?"

"Aw. Look who's worried at being replaced. It's okay, you're still my best friend."

Instead of swearing some more, Brand rolled his eyes. He was a master at eye-rolling. He used facial muscles and forehead wrinkles for the whole effect.

I picked up the sigils I'd laid around me, refastening them around my ankle, fingers, and neck. The ivory cameo had a pain-in-the-ass clasp, so Brand came around and helped me with it.

He said, "Look six ways before crossing the fucking street."

"I will."

"Don't forget down. You always forget to look down."

"I *will*," I said. He was always uneasy when I left the house without him. If I ever got hurt when he wasn't around, I wouldn't even be allowed to the bathroom without an escort for the next six months.

I went downstairs, put on my boots, then met Matthias on the front stoop. Queenie had all but packed him a bagged lunch. She hemmed and hawed her way back inside, while Brand pretended not to look at us from the upstairs window.

"Ready?" I asked.

He stared at the ground. "If you insist."

"Only in a friendly sort of way," I said. When that didn't get a rise out of him, I shrugged and set off.

Half House was on a cul-de-sac in a quieter part of the city; but, in a sold-out housing market, that only meant the quiet parts were two streets away from the loud parts. I made a beeline toward loud, where there was a coffee shop on every corner.

I ordered a triple-shot and bought Matthias a black iced coffee, which he indicated he'd prefer after a series of one-word answers to my questions. Then he made me wait while he dumped three inches of raw sugar into his coffee, packet by packet by packet. When he was done, I led us outside and away from the shop.

I snuck glances at him as we headed toward a nearby plaza. He was a good-looking kid. More pretty than handsome, but at his age you could still grow out of that. He had the strange fae coloring that managed to be pale yet luminous, and hair so blond that it was almost white.

At that hour, the streets were hopping with lunchtime activity. We passed the mundane and the miraculous. Rolling vendor carts steamed with cashews, a pair of lounging werelions stretched their bellies toward the sun; there were people in business suits and hair shirts, iPod armbands and cilices, high heels and webbed toes. A hunchback in silk swept by, three asphalt golems in her wake. Their pebbled arms were looped with pink shopping bags.

Matthias watched all this, and I watched him watching.

He touched his ear twice when the light turned from white to amber on a crosswalk; went blank when a werelion teased a crooked finger over his passing thigh; bit hard on the corner of his lip when the hunchbacked matron called him 'grandchild' after we stepped aside to let her pass.

I tugged my sunglasses out of my breast pocket with one hand. A brass translocation plaque in front of us stated that the nearby statues were from the ruined Kopice Palace in Poland's Brzeg County. I said, "Is that an elk?"

Matthias didn't so much as glance.

"They never go into enough details on these plaques," I said. "I always have to look them up online. It's a hobby of mine." I waved at the antlered animals. "I'm thinking elk."

Matthias offered the ground a tight smile and raised his drink to his mouth. My polarized sunglasses gave the lid of his cup a petroleum sheen, so that it looked like he was sipping rainbows.

I sighed, and we started walking again. "Is the guest room okay?"

"Yes. Thank you."

"Good. Queenie did a run on our closets, by the way. To find you more clothes. You'll probably get better stuff from Brand, if you don't ask too many questions about the stains. You're better off just thinking they're blood."

"I'll make do with what I have."

I let the ensuing pause stretch, then stuck out my ankle and tripped him. While he recovered from a windmilling stumble, I said, "You're making it real hard to talk, Lord Saint Valentine."

A brief surge of heat mottled his cheeks. To my delight, he didn't check himself before he said, "What is it we need to talk about, *Lord Sun?*"

"Matthias, this isn't an eighties sitcom. I can't casually accept an orphan into my house for comic relief."

"I just need a place to stay until I get on my feet. That's all. Just a room for a couple weeks. Then I'll leave and you can keep my grandmother's sigil."

"It's not about the sigil. There's—"

"So I can have it?"

"It's not *completely* about the sigil," I said. "There's also this whole issue about my promise to watch you until your—"

"Age of majority? No. Her words were vague in order to get you to make a promise. There's no way she expected that much from it."

"It's not what she expected that counts. It's what I expect, and what the laws of magic expect. You burn an oath, it comes back at you threefold."

"Her words were vague," he insisted. "Give me safe harbor until the worst of this is past, and the price will be met. I'll acknowledge it. That makes a difference, right?"

"There are still bigger issues. I know you can't see them, but they're there."

"Bigger issues like how I feel about the raid that killed my court? The raid you participated in? Those issues? Or issues like people wanting me dead, people who'd like nothing more than to take a parting shot at my grandmother? Or issues about what people will say when they see you in the company of a seventeen-year-old male minor? Issues like how we're going to live in a small house on top of each other? Or about how much you're responsible for me? Whether you need to get me educated, buy me clean underwear, make sure I drink enough dairy?"

He wasn't stupid, that's for sure.

"No one will recognize me," Matthias insisted. "I didn't . . . I wasn't in the public eye. I was not . . . popular. I served other purposes." When I didn't say anything to that, he finally raised his head and met my eyes. It was the first time we'd really looked at each other, and it seemed to startle him. The word *please* slipped out of his mouth as a mumble.

A crow-black limousine slid to a nearby curb. "Our ride," I said.

I let the conversation die, because it felt like I was kicking a dead horse, and Brand was better at kicking things. Plus, part of me remembered Queenie saying, *How was it with you? The day after you lost everything?*

I didn't recognize the driver, whose gaze traveled up my body as she held the door open. It was a safe bet she wasn't admiring me so much as mapping my pressure points and joint weaknesses. Most of the Tower's people were like that. Even his housecleaners knew how to balance a throwing knife.

Inside the limo, I fiddled with the temperature controls until the vents weren't whooshing air, and turned on the radio. We had plenty of time to kill. Rush-hour snarls had reduced the two-mile distance to wagon speed.

"You a shapeshifter?" I asked Matthias.

"Yes."

"Are we talking full-on animal form, or just cosmetic?"

Matthias held up a hand. The sleeve of his shirt slinked toward his elbow. He concentrated, and green whorls ran around his flesh. The fingernails turned shell pink and grew a couple inches into pointed tips.

"*Functional* cosmetics," I amended. I hadn't expected much more— though claws would have been nice. True animal shapeshifting was rare outside the Beast Throne, which was how Lord Devil preferred it.

"I can hold my own," Matthias said.

"We'll see. Do you have any sigils of your own?"

Matthias broke our gaze. "No."

Not important enough for sigils, but important enough for Elena to save. To be singled out as her court fell around her. Curiouser and curiouser. "Have you met many Arcana, other than your grandmother?"

"No."

"When we get to the Tower's penthouse, you're to stay in the antechamber. I need to figure out what to say to him, and how to introduce you. You were right—there are people out there who wouldn't mind taking a grievance against the Heart Throne from your hide."

Matthias' eyes lit up with an unidentifiable emotion, but he kept his lips pressed shut. The skin on his arm returned to its usual paleness. His nails receded to a normal length.

The car stopped at the canopied front of the Pac Bell. An armed concierge opened my door. I got out and gave the area a quick three-sixty along both the x- and y-axis; then got bored of pretending I was Brand and just stared at the beautiful building. Once, it'd been the Pacific Telephone Building, built in San Francisco back in the mid-1920s. Twenty-six stories of art deco limestone magically restored to brand-spanking-new, right down to the eight terra-cotta eagles glaring at me from the parapet.

Matthias got out of the limo and we headed inside. The day's heat gave way to the sterile coolness of a lobby. When I pulled out a key card to activate the private penthouse elevator, I got a startled reaction from Matthias. I wondered how much he'd heard about me and the Tower, or if he thought the rumors were true.

Lord Tower owned the entire building but kept the penthouse floors as his personal residence. In the entire time I'd known him, I'd never seen so much as a maid upstairs. He kept it clean with either magic or the things that magic could summon, and I wasn't in a rush to learn which.

I stuck Matthias on a spindly-looking chair in the antechamber. Hoping that neither of the Tower's children were about—his daughter wasn't so bad, but Dalton was a monster—I headed toward the living room on the other side of the floor.

The Tower was waiting for me by the window, his face blurred by a ray of sunlight. It was a homey image, as if he'd been peeking out the drapes to follow the progress of my arrival.

"Rune," he said.

"Lord Tower."

The Tower was—or appeared to be—a not-too-tall man in his early forties, with waxy, black hair and cocoa eyes. He had constant five o'clock shadow, fingers like a surgeon, and a swimmer's build. I'd once thought him the most beautiful man in all creation.

He stood before me barefoot in silk pajamas. The vulnerability was an affectation. The clothes buzzed with powerful wards. He probably could have bounced bullets off his chest or survived a jump from the patio ledge.

While some Arcana still existed on dangerous fringes, like the Hanged Man or the Fool, most had learned to mimic humanity. Arcana like the Tower mimicked it flawlessly. They had embraced and flourished in their exposure to the human world.

The Tower was a renowned artist, a politician, and an entrepreneur. He had been the old monarchy's spy and executioner for centuries, and he held our people together when the royal court failed. The Emperor died in the last days of the Atlantean World War, and the Empress, in her unhinged grief, vanished into the wilds of America. Now and then there's a tabloid sighting, largely at truck stops and waffle houses. Every culture, it appears, has an Elvis.

Lord Tower was the head of the Dagger Throne, and I had made promises to him at the age of fifteen in a desperate bid for protection. While my term of service had ended years ago, I remained on speed dial for projects he didn't trust others to handle, which always made our visits interesting.

He led me to a sunken area on the other side of the room and sat on a sofa with his back to the doorway. I couldn't have done that without fidgeting. Then again, I wasn't wearing clothes that could deflect napalm.

I took the seat against a wall, facing the windows. They had the shape and height of doorways, which always made me feel like I was one stumble away from a suicide attempt. Still. Pretty view. I folded my hands in my lap and waited for the Tower to speak.

He'd just started to open his mouth when Matthias stuck his godsdamned head in the doorway.

Matthias's jaw dropped when Lord Tower turned to stare at him. He stammered, "I—I—I wasn't, I was, I needed to . . ."

I gave him another moment. He didn't move or complete his thought. I said, "You're two inches away from a trip wire that will melt your face off."

Matthias retreated so fast that his footsteps sounded like applause.

"Must you make me so terrifying," Lord Tower sighed.

Shit. I ground my palms into my eyes. "He's a houseguest, Lord Tower. He wasn't supposed to leave the foyer. I was going to talk about him. I'm sorry."

"I know who he is," the Tower said.

"You . . . know who he is?"

"Lady Lovers' grandson. Matthias Saint Valentine. He's been with you since yesterday. Quite a bold move, picking up side work for Elena on the eve of her destruction."

He already knew everything. My brain scrambled for a diplomatic response. "We crossed paths on her roof. She asked a favor. It's nothing against you or your interests, and it didn't compromise my assignment for you. I promise."

"I'm aware." He gave me a small smile. "Such a big favor, though, even for such a nice trinket. It'll be amusing to see how it plays out."

It was hard to tell if he was secretly upset. Most likely, he just enjoyed seeing me squirm. The Tower loved to set off intrigue as if it were a firecracker, scaring the hell out of everyone around him.

He said, "Would you like me to learn more about Matthias's immediate family? I could make enquiries to see if they survived the raid."

It was a very generous offer, and I had no idea if it was wise to accept. While I thought it through, I said, "I heard Lady Lovers was being held by the Convocation."

"Elena is allowing herself to be held by the Convocation. Not that she could do otherwise, I suppose, unless she wanted the Arcanum to step in. I expect she'll be exiled. I'm not really sure. It's a situation without recent precedent."

"If . . . Yes, if you could find out about Matthias's family, I'd appreciate it. Thank you." I chewed on my lip. "Do you know anything about Matthias himself?"

"Such as?"

"Such as why he is important to Elena."

The Tower took a few long moments to consider that. He finally shook his head. "I know that, when Matthias was born, his grandmother had high hopes for his magical potential, and she spent much time with him. As Matthias grew older, that magical potential never manifested, and he was given into the care of an uncle for other uses. Marital alliance, I believe. I'm not sure. It's possible that Elena was simply fond of him."

The Tower's pocket began buzzing. He pulled a slim phone up to the light, and his expression went still. He relaxed it into a shallow nod for me, and stood up to walk to the edge of the room.

I tried not to stare, especially when I heard Lord Tower say, "Handle it, then."

It'd taken years, but I'd come to learn some of the Tower's poker tells. Mostly, it wasn't a specific reaction that gave him away, but the empty place he retreated to when he was trying not to react. For instance: I was able to recognize the face he made when he ordered a man's death.

After another moment, he came back to the sofa but didn't sit down. I pretended to stare up at the ceiling and whistle. He narrowed his eyes, and then made an exasperated sound.

"I know nothing," I said.

"You'd be a wonderful liar if you took any pains whatsoever to not joke in the same breath."

"Sorry. Was that anything for me to worry about?"

"It's entirely unrelated."

I shrugged it off. It wasn't the first time I'd heard the Tower taking care of business, nor the fiftieth, nor the last. New Atlantis is not a democracy. Our elected Convocation only resembled representation. At the heart of everything in our city were the Arcana; they weren't only the kings on the hill, they were the hill itself.

The Tower made a dismissive gesture. "You did very good work the other night, in case I didn't mention it. The operating system you downloaded from the Heart Throne has been most instructive."

"Good to know."

"If you have time, I have another assignment."

Ah.

He said, "There's a person I'd like found. Come. We'll have coffee outside."

I headed to the patio while he prepared the coffee. The outdoor resin furniture had been soaking in sunlight all afternoon and was warm against the high-altitude chill.

I could barely see twenty blocks into the distance. The city smog was denser than usual. On a good afternoon, from this height, you could see the forest line of the Westlands through the careening alley of skyscrapers.

The Tower returned and set a cup of coffee in front of me. He slid a check and a manila folder underneath a ceramic ashtray.

"Do you know Addam Saint Nicholas?" he asked.

"Saint Nicholas. Justice family name."

"Yes. Addam is Lady Justice's middle son."

"Can't say I've ever spoken to him, but I think I can place the face."

"He's missing," Lord Tower told me.

I took a second to absorb that. "That's . . . not insignificant news. Why haven't I heard anything about it? How long has he been missing?"

"He failed to appear at a business meeting yesterday morning. He was last seen by his assistant just after seven o'clock the previous evening, in the offices that he and three other scions let. When his assistant left for the day, he was alone. It's unclear if he made it home from there."

"How can that be unclear? Lady Justice must have a manned gate."

"He doesn't live exclusively at the family compound. He owns a private residence in Edgemere—an apartment in a converted church."

"Does he live alone?"

"Yes. No consorts. A confirmed bachelor, much like you."

I ignored the jab. He'd mentioned more than once that I could increase my power base through marriage. I said, "I'm still confused. I'm assuming the private residence has security. Why hasn't the guarda been able to confirm if he ever made it home?"

"The guarda, at this time, is not investigating."

"Should I take this to mean they don't consider him missing?"

Lord Tower dipped his chin at me. "Addam has disappeared before, usually for a day or two at a time, never much longer. He calls them his 'walkabouts.'"

"His *walkabouts*," I said, with heavy sarcasm. "How strange. It's so unlike rich kids to bastardize meaningful aboriginal customs. Tell me, do his *walkabouts* take him anywhere near drugs, whores, or malted spirits? Those are usually the best ways to lose a day or two."

"It's doubtful. Addam is a very . . . spirited young man, but well-grounded. He has great potential. I've prepared that folder for you. It has the names of close acquaintances, basic biographical data, and information on his company."

I pulled the folder out from under the ashtray and flipped through the first few pages. One of the printouts listed Addam Saint Nicholas's business partners. A name jumped out. I whispered, "Fucking great," and turned the page before I could start brooding.

After a bit, I said, "Would I be crossing a line if I asked why you're interested in finding Saint Nicholas? If the guarda—or his family—isn't raising hell over his disappearance, why are you?"

He fixed me with an unusually serious expression. "Rune, I know that questioning assumptions is part of your process, but in the interest of time, I must ask that you operate as if something has happened to Addam."

"Okay," I said slowly. "Foul play."

"Addam is also my godson. It's not an unusual practice. I have many godchildren in other courts. But Addam is special, and I worry. Additionally, he's the son of an Arcana, in particular Justice, and Justice—along with Temperance, Strength, and the Hermit—form a strong power bloc. How Addam's disappearance could cause larger problems, I can't yet say. That's why I need you."

"What sort of larger problems, in particular, could you see in relation to the Moral Certainties?" I asked, using the collective noun for their power bloc.

"They have their fingers in many pies. They're brokering peace talks between the werewolves and werecats. They're heavily represented in the Convocation. Justice is the traditional patron of judges; the others are patrons of religious leaders and the guarda. And let's not forget their businesses interests—they net over a quarter trillion a year. Do I think Addam's disappearance is related to any of these things? Not really. Is it a possibility? Of course. The connection may not be obvious yet." He took a breath. "Will you help, Rune?"

I snuck a peek at the check. There was one more zero than I was used to. Well, for fuck's sake, what more did he think I needed to understand?

"I'll get started right away," I said.

LEPERCON

Back at Half House, I checked in with Brand to catch him up on the situation. Then I headed to my room to dry-swallow a couple painkillers, change, and go on my daily tour of Half House's defenses. It's possible I also took a small nap.

The primary house wards were kept in a decorative holder by the front door, humming with a sputtering intensity. Even the meanest Atlantean home had wards protecting their hearth from the usual suspects: allergens, odors, humidity. Half House, like those mean homes, couldn't afford the best on the market. Our wards still did their jobs, just less . . . aesthetically. The freshness ward smelled like pine needles and tar pitch; the anti-allergen ward gathered dust into gritty pebbles that crunched underfoot.

The strongest of my defenses was buried under the house.

It was the single surviving mass sigil from the Sun Throne, an artifact of great, great power. I'd been charging and recharging the same defense spell in it for years. Its sole purpose was to protect us during a siege. I had never used it for anything else, despite the temptation. As a defensive measure, it was a safety net not just for me but for Brand and Queenie as well.

When I was done checking the wards, I took the spiral metal stairway down to the basement, where Brand had claimed his bedroom. He kept it perpetually dark and cool, which made the room's moldering mess seem almost exotic. The décor consisted of weapons, dirty clothes, empty water bottles, PowerBar wrappers, porn, and vitamin pill bottles. He was a very organized person in every other part of his life; the bedroom was the one place he let his chaos show.

He was on the futon. I slumped next to him. The painkillers had started to kick in by then. Everything—the room, my clothes, the blanket on the chair—settled against my nerve endings like flannel.

"Did our bond just go dopey?" Brand asked.

"Aspirin," I said.

"Are you telling me that aspirin theoretically exists, or that you took nothing but aspirin?" he asked.

"This is why I never play poker with you," I said. "Stupid Companion bond."

"What hurts?" he asked.

"My shoulder. I think I wrenched it when Lady Lovers manhandled me. It'll be fine."

Brand got up and rummaged through his pint-sized refrigerator, then filled a plastic baggie with ice. He banged it against the cement floor until it was slush and came back to the sofa. Carefully, he pressed it over my shoulder.

"Fucking dumb-ass," he said.

We were quiet for a while. The ice pack took away whatever ache the painkillers hadn't. I finally said, "I think we need to do some research on this Addam, get some more background."

"Like finding out what the guarda knows about Saint Nicholas's disappearance? Maybe checking into his company, learning more about his business partners? Contacting some of his friends from that list the Tower gave you? That sort of research?"

I gave him a look.

He said, "You and your fucking naps."

"If you looked up Addam's business partners," I said, "then you know Geoffrey Saint Talbot is one of them."

Brand summed up his feelings with, "Douchebag."

"We have to talk to him. Him and Addam's other two partners. The last place Addam was seen was in their offices. What did you learn about the company?"

"Addam founded it with Geoffrey and Geoffrey's brother, Michael, and with Ashton Saint Gabriel, from the Iron Hall. They pooled their trust funds and invested in it. That's what they do—they invest in start-up companies, use the influence of their courts to push through red tape. Think about it. The Moral Certainties own judges, church leaders, guarda officials. That's a lot of grease for a lot of sticky fucking wheels."

"Where are their offices?"

"LeperCon."

"Ooh, street cred," I said with a fake sound of approval. LeperCon was the nickname for one of the more run-down city areas, a mishmash of buildings and streets translocated from Boston's old Combat Zone. "LeperCon" was wordplay on its Irish heritage. I was more familiar with the area than Brand would suspect; I've had reasons to visit it on my own.

I said, "Let's go check them out."

Twenty minutes later, I remanded Matthias into Queenie's care and set out with Brand.

I dressed for the outing in a fancy shirt I'd found in the ruins of Sun Estate, on one of my semiannual forays onto its haunted grounds. Between the shirt and a pair of black slacks, I wouldn't embarrass myself in a business setting.

Brand was in his work clothes, a high-end mix of tactical apparel. He shopped for them on a website that also sold guns and crossbows. The loose black shirt had many pockets—holster pockets, pockets for ammo, hidden pockets up the sleeve designed for handcuff keys or pepper spray or small knives. He covered it with a custom-made chest rig lined with knives.

As we walked to the subway, Brand lapsed into his vigilant body-guard mode. I mirrored it to a point—I paid attention to our immediate vicinity, oncoming alleys and doorway openings, open windows, rooflines.

Brand took that state of awareness to depths I couldn't even imagine.

He didn't just assess the danger level of approaching pedestrians, he *assumed* they were a threat and mapped out how they'd attack, how hard they'd hit, the spots he'd be most vulnerable, his best chance to counter. Every time we turned a corner, he planned new escape routes. He was very, very good at what he did.

When the subway terminal was in sight, he fractionally relaxed. He said, "I talked with Lord Keaton, Amy Beige, and Fiddler Blue. Addam isn't into anything dirty that Keaton knows of. Fiddler doesn't know the family well but suggested we arrange a meeting at the Enclave later. Amy Beige called me an asshole and hung up. I think she's still sore about the wyvern."

"Why the Enclave?"

Brand's eyes swung to a roof, down the side of an adjoining building, across a sewer grate. "There's a regatta. The Moral Certainties are hosting it."

"Maybe we can get an audience with Addam Saint Nicholas's family there. I'll put in a request with Lady Justice's people. It's been a while since we went to the beach."

"Aren't you going to feel a little self-conscious in a bathing suit?" he asked.

"Stop making fun of my weight," I said. "And while you're at it, pay better attention. Matthias is following us."

Brand gave me a perfectly blank look. I loved catching details before he did. I said, "He's got on that purple t-shirt that Queenie gave him. He's two streets back. By the pretzel vendor."

"Are you being smug? Is that a smug look?"

"Of course not," I said.

"Do you feel smug because you just spotted Matthias by the pretzel vendor?"

"Not at all."

"Because he's been following us since we were half a block away from Half House. He went out the second-story bathroom window and down the drainpipe. He's let us keep a two-block lead except when he ran into Starbucks to get an iced coffee. You noticed none of this."

When I wisely said nothing, Brand glared at me. "Rune. He's going to get himself killed, following us around. It's fucking bad enough we have to feed him, do we need to be responsible for funeral expenses, too?"

I sighed. "Do you want me to go grab him?"

A slow, dangerous smile spread across Brand's pressed lips. "I've got a better idea."

My phone buzzed. I pulled it out and saw it was from an unlisted private number. "Hello?" I answered.

"Isn't it time for us to meet yet?" someone asked anxiously.

"Excuse me?"

"It's not, is it? I'll leave the motor running, though."

The caller hung up. I stared at the phone, unsure what to make of it.

The aboveground entrance for New Atlantis's main subway hub was a building translocated from Spain. The Canfranc Station had been built in the early 1920s, ambitiously linking France and Spain along the side of the Pyrenees. Three stories tall, seven hundred and ninety feet long, over three hundred and sixty-five windows.

The subway itself was a throwback to the earliest days of underground systems. They were literally trains, albeit powered by sigils that moved the linked cars without noise and pollution. New Atlantis Transit was a joint venture between the Magician and the Chariot, part of a city contract worth close to nine digits.

We bought tokens and moved to the platform for the northwest line, which would drop us off in the heart of LeperCon. Brand waited until we were boarded before he excused himself with an evil chuckle.

I people-watched. It was that weird stretch of travel time that existed between the morning and afternoon rush hours. Robes and shorts, suits and hemp sacks, messenger bags, briefcases. There was a group of beggars loitering by the emergency exit. They had the dead, waxy skin of the Bone Hollows, Death's court.

The conductor made a public address over the intercom system, sternly reminding passengers that windows were to remain closed at all times. Fifteen seconds later, Brand came back to the seat with Matthias in tow. Matthias's hair was windblown and sticking up in all directions. He looked like he was about to cry.

Brand shoved the young scion into the seat and said to me, "Play good cop."

I slid across the facing seats so that I was next to Matthias. Brand dropped into my abandoned spot and began to clean one of his blades. I said, "Off the top of my head? Purple is a bad color for stealth."

"I'm supposed to say I'm sorry," Matthias whispered.

"Sorry for what?" I asked, wanting to be clear.

"For disrespecting you," he said.

"As nice as it would be to live with someone who showed me respect, that's not the point."

Brand stopped fake-buffing the knife and gave me a level look.

I said, "It's not me you shouldn't disrespect, it's my orders. Our orders. You're not trained to follow us into the kind of places we go. If this is going to work, Matthias, you've got to understand that. That shit you pulled this afternoon at the Tower's? And following us on an assignment? This can't happen again."

"I . . ." He flushed. "I needed a bathroom. At the Tower's. I didn't think you'd mind. And today, I was just, I was curious. You're . . . I was just curious. You've been . . . nice to me. I was just curious."

"If you want to say thank you, let me be the first to suggest baked goods. Maybe a nice muffin basket. But don't follow us on a job. After everything you've lost, you don't need the aggravation, Matthias, trust me."

"Everything I've lost," he repeated. He smiled at his lap. I couldn't tell what type of a smile it was, either, other than it being far more complicated than any teenager's smile ought to.

I'd been catching glimpses of emotion that derailed most of my hunches about Matthias. I was starting to think that, rather than being important to the Lovers, Matthias had been somehow damaged by them.

Since I didn't have any better ideas, and I was nosy, I decided to fish. "I forgot to tell you. I asked Lord Tower to find out about your family. Did you live with your parents or grandmother before the raid?"

His eyes widened, and his skin went ash gray. "I was. No. No, I was . . . kept by an uncle. Until the arrangements were made. I didn't— I haven't—I haven't seen my parents in years." White wrinkles pinched the sides of his eyes and mouth. He cleared his throat and said, "Did you ask Lord Tower to find my uncle?"

"What do you mean by *arrangements*, Matthias?"

"What?"

"You just said you lived with your uncle while arrangements were being made."

The stammer redoubled. "M-marriage. That was. What. M-my grandmother, Elena, that was w-what she was going to do with me. M-marry me off to someone. Please. Please, you don't need to find my family, or tell them about me. They don't need to know where I am."

"I only asked the Tower to find out about them. He wouldn't make contact without asking me first."

I exchanged a confused look with Brand as we all settled into an uneasy silence.

Brand pulled out his smartphone. I replayed recent events in my head. Ten minutes shy of our stop, Brand slid over and angled his phone screen at me. I took it, hit a button, and promptly shut down the web browser. I'd never been very good with technology. I tried to find my way back to the screen. A message popped up asking me if I wanted to begin a factory reset.

"For fuck's sake," Brand said. "It's like watching Gilligan try to make a radio out of coconuts. Give me that." He snatched the phone back and tapped some keys.

He'd surfed to the website for Moral Confidence, LLC. The "Contact Us" page had photos of the principal investors. I let my eyes slide unhappily over Geoffrey's bookish smile. Brand put two fingers on the screen and zoomed in on the picture of Addam. A handsome man.

"Have you learned anything else about Addam's family?" I asked. Then I pointed at Matthias. "Don't pay attention. Don't remember anything we say. Don't talk to anyone about what you don't remember."

Brand said, "Big court. Small immediate family. Lady Justice only has four surviving children—the rest died in the war. Oldest is Christian. Addam is next. Then comes Ella and Quinn. Not much info on the two youngest, but I did learn something about Christian. There was an Eyes Only memo in the folder the Tower gave you. He's been ill."

"Really?" Scions didn't get sick. They were swimming in sigils and healing magic; they had ways to eliminate almost any illness or injury.

"Hospitalized, even," Brand said. "I didn't get the sense that it's a big fucking deal—it's not like they're flying healers in from across the world. But still."

"Still. The heir scion is in the hospital. Addam, next in line, is missing. Do you know if Addam and his siblings are close?"

"Not sure, but there are a bunch of press clippings about Addam and his brothers volunteering at public concerts. Free concerts. Like, for the dirty masses. Some of the press clippings even made it sound like Addam wasn't full of shit."

"Lord Tower seems fond of him," I said absently.

"So? I could go my entire fucking life without that seal of approval," Brand said.

There wasn't time to say more. The train whistled as we slid into LeperCon.

Unlike most major cities, New Atlantis was not designed to evolve.

It wasn't built on the assumption that it'd go through development cycles—that today's run-down streets would become tomorrow's coffee shops and art galleries. Rundown streets were built into the city's design; and luxury towers would always be luxury towers.

LeperCon had been pulled from the worst of Boston's old Combat Zone. It was now a good place to find cheap apartments, ethnic grocers, and reliable blue-collar drug dealers. The land under the translocated buildings had once been a bog, and the smell persisted, giving the three-street neighborhood a strange whiff of car fumes, crumbling cement, and old weeds. I knew the area well, but I hid my familiarity from Brand. It wasn't something he needed to know.

Addam's office sat on a slow intersection, kitty-corner to a gas station and bodega. Their building was protected with embarrassingly strong wards. I pictured a team of Moral Certainty magic-users scuttling into the neighborhood in advance of Addam's arrival, making it scion-proof by sticking plugs in electrical outlets and a gate at the top of the cellar stairs.

An anxious female voice buzzed us into the building, giving us directions to the second floor. To get there, we passed through what I grudgingly admitted was a beautiful old foyer—soaring ceiling, exotic wall murals.

The woman with the anxious voice met us at the doorway to Addam's offices. Lilly Rose was plucked straight out of Technicolor 1950s. Sweet and blonde and hand-wringingly upset. My presence knocked her off-balance—if a person had heard of me, it usually did—and I decided to keep her that way.

"I've been asked to look into the whereabouts of Lord Addam Saint Nicholas," I said. "Are his business partners on the premises?"

"Yes, they are; they're in a meeting with a client right now. I'm so happy that—"

"Do not disturb them. We'll speak with them later. For now, I'll need to see Lord Saint Nicholas's personal space. Immediately."

"His office? I should let the others know that—"

"I'd rather you not speak to anyone until you and I talk," I said ominously. "According to my records, Lord Saint Nicholas was last seen in your presence."

Her mouth worked for a moment, as if it wanted to start having three conversations at once. Brand sighed, shoved past me, and put a weightless hand on Lilly Rose's arm.

"Hello, Lilly. My name is Brand, and that back there is Matthias. We're helping Lord Sun try to find Addam."

When Brand used *Lord Sun*, it was for one of two reasons. Either he wanted to remind the person we're speaking to that, as the last of the Sun Throne, I was technically in charge. Or he was irritated because I was acting like I was.

"Really, I'm so glad," she said sincerely. "I'm sorry if I seem flustered. No one else seems to be taking it seriously. Addam has—well, that is, he's done things like this before. Taken spontaneous trips. He's even done it without telling me. I don't know why I'm so sure that this time is different, but it *is*, and no one will do anything. What if he's hurt?"

"We'll find him," Brand assured her. "We're very good at that. You said you spoke to him the night he disappeared?"

"Yes. Like Lord Sun said, I'm probably the last person who saw him. He was working late and I left before him. He told me he was going to burn the midnight oil, and then go home to a good book."

"Was that strange?" I asked.

"For him to stay late? Oh, no. Not for the middle of the week, at least."

"Does Lord Saint Nicholas have an active social life?" Brand asked. "Was it unusual for him to go straight home from work?"

"Again, in the middle of the week, no. Or at least it wouldn't be strange for him to go straight to his condominium or to the Justice estate. His weekends are more relaxed. He does a lot of charity work with his brothers. He enjoys music and arts festivals." She held her hands, knotted into a single, squirming fist, to her chin. "Please, be honest with me. Do you think something is wrong?"

"I think he'll be fine," Brand told her. "Lilly, was anything different the day—or in the days before—Lord Saint Nicholas disappeared? Was he upset or worried? Did he do anything different from his normal routine?"

We followed that with our other standard questions: What was Addam wearing? Did he have any known medical conditions? What was Addam working on when she'd left him? Was there anyone strange outside the building when she left? Where does he keep his passport? Her answers were negative: nothing strange, out of the ordinary, outside routine.

Brand said, "Have you checked Lord Saint Nicholas's condo yourself?"

"Oh, yes," she said. "I went there the morning he didn't come to work. Then in the evening, and twice yesterday, and again this morning. I even spoke with his building superintendent. They said he never showed up that first evening. They have cameras that monitor that sort of thing."

"Is Addam the type of person to make enemies?" I asked.

Lilly smiled for the first time. "Not even his exes are enemies."

After that, she showed us to Addam's office—without, thankfully, alerting the other business partners.

Addam had a modest corner office, decorated with expensive furniture built with the specific purpose of not looking expensive. Addam had made a fair stab at modesty, I'll give him that; but the truth was in the ceramic toilet-brush holder, in the expertly warded locks on his desk drawer, and in the not-imitation leather seating arrangement.

As soon as we were alone, we began snooping.

The key to a really thorough search is to take the room apart with your brain first. It's not just a matter of glancing behind artwork and opening drawers. You need to look for hiding places built into the structure of the building: crawl spaces, vents, loose flooring, and drop ceilings. You need to look in the hollow part of furniture and fixtures, and behind electrical plates—especially if you spot any wear on the screws. You need to look for seeds, bent spoons, ash, and tile discoloration. You have to look in CD cases and battery compartments; in toilet tanks; in the cardboard cylinders of toilet paper.

When half an hour turned up nothing more than a waste of half an hour, I released a psychometry spell from one of my sigils. I'd stored it special just for this trip.

The world flashed in color-negative until the spell settled into a humming balance. Psychometry was a potent, tricky bit of tactile magic. Recent events leave short-term psychic snapshots in our reality. Psychometry allowed me to connect with those snapshots. The spell was potentially overwhelming, even disabling, so Brand had to help, guiding me to various spots he wanted me to examine.

From Addam's desktop, I felt excitement. A business venture in the works? Something to do with music patronage.

From the marble sink in his private bathroom I got a generalized sense of lust. Addam had stood there and put on cologne while talking on the phone.

From the doorknob, I suffered a vivid, thirty-second scene between Addam and Lilly regarding the death of her kitten, Lady Jiggles. Addam thought he'd buy her another kitten a week or two down the road. Something genetically rare with long hair. Lilly would like that.

From the rug in the center of the room, I got music. Music and dancing. Addam liked to dance as he walked around and read paperwork.

On the sofa I got the idea that he occasionally and discreetly . . . *amused* himself after everyone went home and he still had a few hours of work remaining. I didn't get an actual mental playback of the act, just the idea of orgasm as coffee break.

And then Brand was shaking my shoulder and saying my name.

I had no idea what was going on.

Why was I on the ground?

I'm on the ground?

I tried to bat Brand away and climb to my feet, but he wouldn't let go of me. My eyes squeezed shut in embarrassment.

"Did I faint?" I demanded.

"What the *fuck* happened!" he hissed. Matthias hovered at his shoulder, equally alarmed.

I felt sick. Confused. I said, "I fainted because of the sofa? That doesn't make sense. It wasn't really scary. He's not an unattractive man."

"What the fuck are you talking about! Are you okay? It happened after you left the sofa, next to the door!"

The . . .

It came back in a roaring, messy rush. I'd left the sofa. I'd gone to the door. I'd knelt in front of it and touched the rug and—"Gods!" I swore.

"Rune, *what?*"

"Something got him. Something bad. Something really, really bad. Holy shit." I looked around me, still dazed. Dancing and masturbation and Lady Jiggles and ceramic toilet-brush holders—and then this, in this single spot, a tiny concentrated memory of . . . of desiccation and rot and barely restrained violence. Something *wrong* had been in this room.

"It didn't hurt him," I said. "It took him. That's everything. Everything I saw. Whatever it was, it took him, and it was powerful."

A glass of water appeared in my peripheral. Matthias. He also had a damp washcloth. First I put on thin, black gloves I kept in my jacket pocket, to keep from triggering more psychometry flashes. Then I buried my eyes in the washcloth.

"Just what the hell was Addam Saint Nicholas involved in?" Brand said.

The door opened hard, and someone said, "Stop whatever you're doing *at once.*"

I lifted my face from the washcloth, and saw Brand's expression darken—at himself, because he'd missed the approaching footsteps, and at Geoffrey Saint Talbot, whom he simply didn't like.

Geoffrey, an armload of books against his sweater-vest, eyeglasses crooked on his nose, said, "Follow me to the conference room. Now."

Geoffrey Saint Talbot was the second-oldest child of Lady Temperance, the ruling Arcana of the Temperance Galley.

When we were younger, we'd been peers. As teens we'd became something more. Geoffrey was well-schooled and handsome, and a few years my senior. I suppose our relationship was a sort of rebellion. Lady Temperance's intolerance for same-sex relationships was extremely unusual among Atlanteans. She preferred to pair her children with scions they could breed with.

Fumbled kisses had led to other fumbled stuff—and then to a night in a cheap hotel near a human neighborhood in Nantucket Town. Geoffrey had charged his sigils with trinket magics to amuse me. Naked on the polyester bedspread, he'd filled the air with firework sparks and tulip petals and a brief, genuine snowfall.

When the Sun Throne fell, Geoffrey turned his back on me. He found someone with ovaries and a clean name. I could still remember his rejection, the night I accepted that's what it actually was. It had been several weeks since the massacre, and the first time I'd snuck away from the Tower's—and Brand's—protection.

I'd made my way to the Bowers, a gated retail community that young scions snuck into at night. Twenty or so were scattered across the lawn, in small, drunk groups. Whispers flared as I passed. No one said my name, and no one stopped to welcome me. I wasn't close enough to see Geoffrey's expression as I approached, but his entire body jerked. He took the hand of the girl on the bench next to him, whispered something in her ear, and led her off into the bushes.

I'd slunk back to the Tower's penthouse in shame. Brand—furious I'd snuck out—took one look at my face and never asked a word about it.

People thought I shut down after the attack, but that's not completely true. That night in the Bowers? That was a turning point. That's when I realized that everything was different and always would be.

The thing you must never forget about Atlantean culture is that we don't coddle our victims. Victims are quarantined and cast out, their defeat viewed as a genetic defect. In turning his back on me, Geoffrey hadn't done anything the rest of society hadn't.

Then again, I hadn't been fucking the rest of society, and I held a grudge.

We left Matthias with Lilly Rose, and followed Geoffrey. The conference room he stalked into was a blatant show of force: loud metal-and-glass furniture, a mass sigil bolted to one wall, with smaller wards set around it in a starburst pattern. Addam Saint Nicholas's two other business partners were standing around the table.

Ashton Saint Gabriel was the son of Lord Strength, the Arcana of the

Iron Hall. He was pimped out in the season's latest—a spray of iridescent snake scales along one of his cheekbones. He had his family's signature trait: reflective, gunmetal-gray irises. An unfortunate genetic quirk, all things considered. Made it hard to hide their bastards.

Geoffrey's younger brother, Michael Saint Talbot, was dressed in baggy cargo pants and a short-sleeved polo shirt. An old rugby scar cut through the side of his lips, and, if I remembered correctly, two of his slightly-discolored front teeth were fake. Since he could have easily corrected them with magic, the lack of affectation was in itself an affectation.

And then there was Geoffrey. Soft brown hair; lanky build; penchant for sweater-vests. He had the same square-lens glasses he'd worn as a teen. They were a sigil. He liked to store scholarly spells in them, such as short-term didactic memory or the ability to read in the dark. I glanced at the books in his arms: rare herbology and Mesopotamian arena fighting. Typical Geoffrey.

Ashton said, "Rune Saint John. So. This is what you're up to these days. We hear such interesting stories, off and on."

Michael, who was juggling a foam football from hand to hand, glared at me. "You broke in here. I was going to call the guarda. You're damned lucky I didn't."

"That's refreshingly brave of you," I said.

His glare blurred into confusion.

"Admitting that someone overruled you," I said.

Michael's face soured back into a glare, but his eyes darted toward Ashton. I said, "And I didn't break in. I'm here on a legitimate enquiry regarding Addam Saint Nicholas's disappearance."

Ashton frowned. "We've been concerned that Addam hasn't checked in, of course, but *disappearance* is a strong word."

"And yet, apt. Why don't we sit down and talk?"

Ashton opened his arms toward the conference table. We all took seats, except for Michael, who stayed at the window and tossed that stupid football from hand to hand. The humid sky behind his head was now mottled gray and white with rainclouds.

Brand didn't say a word, so I took the lead. While it would have been great if they launched into suspicious villain dialogue, it was boring stuff.

I asked many of the same questions we had of Lilly, and got mostly the same replies. Ashton did go deeper into the details regarding Moral Confidence's investment portfolio, and Geoffrey did list some of their recent successes. They'd funded a joint venture with the Chariot to develop an electric cart that might work in the Westlands (which actually was interesting; technology went bugfuck as soon as you left city limits); a for-profit beach-blanket music program; and an information-exchange program with a Switzerland think tank. Geoffrey was proud. He almost relaxed and met my eyes as he spoke.

Ashton, on the other hand, kept constant eye contact. Like a blustery handshake, textbooks called it *forced kinesics*. Ashton controlled his body language in order to control first impressions. The only time he slipped was when one of his partners said something he disagreed with, at which point they would be met with a silent stare.

Things got interesting again when I asked why they'd felt the need to form their own business.

Michael's face darkened and he said, "My and Geoff's mother is strong, but she doesn't have ambition, she doesn't want more then she's already got. She's frugal. This isn't Atlantis, though. It's New Atlantis. There are different opportunities here. If our mother won't seize them, then why not us?"

Ashton stood, pulling the conversation back to him. He made as if to stretch his legs and lean against the nearby wall, but the nearby wall contained the mass sigil, and Brand would have none of that. I didn't see the exact look he shot Ashton, but Ashton stopped moving. "My, Rune. Such impressive, professional questions. I hope you get paid well for all this work."

"I get by," I said. "I think we've covered enough for now. I may need to follow up with you again, or with Addam's clients. Thanks for your time."

The conversation had only been a starting point. Or, better yet, bait. I wouldn't have to wait long for someone to tug on the hook.

Brand went to fetch Matthias from the waiting room, and Michael and Geoffrey followed, but Ashton placed a hand on my shoulder to keep me back. He said, "I was hoping to have a brief word without your junk-yard dog in attendance."

It was so wonderfully, openly hostile. I actually smiled at Ashton.

He said, "As interesting as it is to see what fallen royalty such as yourself does for kicks, this is my business. If you fuck with it, I will shred you."

"You don't seem very worried about Addam, Ashton."

"If I'm worried about anything, it's whether we need to assign someone more . . . official to find him. See here, Rune. I'm not looking to embarrass you. It must be hard being ostracized from your peers."

"It's like you know me," I said.

"While you're brainstorming your next quip, let me summarize this entire wrecked situation: I don't know if Addam is in trouble, I surely hope he isn't, but either way I've got idiot partners to manage, a company to run, and clients I don't want upset. If there's anything I can do to assist, and I have the bandwidth to help, I will. But learn some fucking discretion. Here's my private number." He tucked a business card into my shirt's breast pocket. His hand lingered.

"Hey, Ashton?" I said.

He waited. Then he said, "Hey, Rune?"

"That's twice you've put your hands on me. If you touch me again, I will hurt you. No lie. I'm that much better than you. You should learn some discretion yourself."

As I spoke, my glowing eyes reflected in his mirrored corneas. It was my Atlantean Aspect, a sign of my power, stretching awake and popping its claws. Ashton's smile faded.

"Thanks for the card," I said, and left.

The psychometry magic had long since dispersed, so I stripped the leather gloves while we headed downstairs, now able to touch things without triggering visions. Brand shot me a look but asked no questions about my conversation with Ashton.

We were halfway down the stairs when we heard footsteps coming after us. Brand cocked his head and said, "Geoffrey." Don't ask me how he was so sure. Brand was a crazy good Companion. For all I knew, he'd mentally translated the floor vibrations into poundage.

I said, "Go on ahead. I'll meet you outside."

"That's gonna happen," he said sarcastically.

I huffed at him.

"Fine. Don't blame me if you get killed while I'm gone." He started downstairs. When Matthias didn't move with him, Brand gave the young scion a cool look. Matthias smacked into the railing in his rush to scramble past.

I stayed where I was as Geoffrey came into view. His body language hadn't changed. He was still holding his books defensively across his chest. Since we had history, I suppose his nervousness could have meant anything.

"Can we talk?" He took a deep breath. "I know we haven't spoken much lately."

"*Lately?* Did you really just say that? Go back upstairs, Geoff."

"No. No, we need to talk. I don't know what's happening—I don't know what you *think* has happened to Addam—but I feel like a lot of this is about me."

"About you."

"About us."

It wasn't even worth swearing about. I said, bluntly, "What happens to the company if Addam is gone?"

"What?"

"Easy question."

"Rune, I have nothing to do with Addam's disappearance. If it really even *is* a disappearance. None of us would hurt him. If we lose him, we lose his connections. That's worth more to our future than anything the company is worth right now. And how can you be so sure he's in trouble? What did you find in his office?"

"Something that shouldn't have been there. Geoff, am I going to find out you guys are into bad shit?"

"Absolutely not. Nothing we do here would get Addam in trouble."

"So I'm not going to find out anything bad?" I asked again, like I was talking to a small child.

Geoffrey's face hardened. Like most adults who'd been bullied as kids, he hated being mocked. "If I can help you locate Addam, I will. I've got nothing to hide. But, Rune, I swear, if I find out this is more about your grudge against me than in actually helping Addam—"

"Are you shitting me? My grudge? The only thing you need to know about me is that I'm doing this for someone you don't want to mess with. I hope you're being straight with me, because I've got no interest in protecting you."

I turned my back on him—and imagined Brand giving me a furious look because you *never* turn your back on a hostile body. So I continued the momentum of the spin until I was facing Geoff again. To my surprise, the smirk was gone. He looked lost and uncertain.

It was not the first time I'd seen an expression like that on a scion's face. When something went so wrong that I needed to become involved, scions were usually in over their head. Most of them had little ability to handle a true crisis.

The knot in my chest loosened. My anger drained away. "Geoff. Something pretty damn bad was in your office, and I'm pretty damn sure it left with Addam. You need to take this seriously. Call me if you learn anything, or if you have trouble. Okay?"

He stared at me for a couple beats, then lowered his head in a half-nod.

When I went through the lower stairwell's door, the first thing I saw was Matthias, alone, on the bottom step in the building's foyer.

"Where's Brand?" I asked.

"Checking the street. Where are we going now?"

"I was thinking we'd—"

There was a sound. A loud sound. In an empty marble vault like the foyer, every noise amplified into an ominous echo. What gave me pause was that I couldn't place it. It wasn't a footstep or talking. It sounded like a falling or pattering. And crackling? I sniffed for smoke but smelled none.

"Matthias, get up," I said, skipping down the stairs.

"I feel funny," Matthias said, pressing a hand over his stomach. "Do you feel funny?"

Fae were sensitive to magic. I had my own skills in that area and could tell that someone was most definitely working magic nearby. I said, "*Up!*" and snapped my fingers at him. The sound was louder now—a definite rainfall, small bits of material against the stone floor. Someone breaking through the ceiling or wall? I shook my wrist and transformed my sabre into a sword hilt.

I moved us away from the open center of the huge foyer, hugging the wall. I spared a glance at Matthias to make sure he was following and alert—and saw his eyes go wide. I turned back around as something staggered into view.

The monster was unaccustomed to its legs and lurched into an antique brochure stand. Wood shavings spiraled up under glistening red talons. Plaster chips flecked the ground around it like dandruff, and fresh oil paint dripped from its fangs like saliva.

Born out of a wall mural; driven by high-end summoning magic; forced into a three-dimensional reality. *Gargoyle.* Atlantean gargoyles are not the stone guardians of human invention. *Gargoyle* is a catchall name for any object imbued with sentience—like the animated plaster mural stalking toward me.

It stretched its neck and made a sound like the breaking of a book's spine. When it had as much geometrical life as it needed to balance on two legs, it shrieked.

"Go!" I shouted at Matthias, and shot a bolt of fire. The gargoyle roared and stumbled. I distracted it with another firebolt to let Matthias get a lead.

Since the firebolts were barely slowing it, I brushed a thumb across my white-gold ring, then touched my mother's cameo necklace. Both sigils released their stored spells, creating an overlapping surge that made my stomach acid pop. I turned the Shield spell into armor that shimmered over my body in fractal facets before sinking into my skin. I sent the Fire spell into my sabre, to buffer its own innate fire magic.

My next round of firebolts glowed like road flares. They staggered the gargoyle, but even as I watched, the burn marks lightened into brown and turned into brushstrokes, becoming part of the muralled skin.

I ran to the exit. Matthias was already pulling on the closed door. When he saw me, he shouted, "Locked!"

Fists began pounding on the other side. Through my Companion bond I felt Brand and his sudden alarm.

Locked doors. A gargoyle.

Strong, strong magic.

This is an ambush.

I glanced up the stairs and saw that the second-floor door had slammed shut. Sealed too? There was an archway leading deeper into the first floor, the only open exit.

"There, go there!" I said, pointing. As the gargoyle went from a lurch to a sprint, I grabbed Matthias and ran.

The archway led to a fluorescent-lit galley that broke off into offices. The doors on the right, facing the interior of the building, were shut. I heard people pounding on them to get out. I yelled for them to stay the hell in.

I checked the doorways on the left, the ones facing the front of the building. The first was a custodial closet; the second, a learning center crowded with desks and older-model computers. At the end of the hallway was another closed door, so I picked the computer lab, which at least had a bank of windows on its opposite wall.

"Get a chair; break a window," I told Matthias. "Hurry!"

Plaster claws in the hallway had me whipping around. I concentrated and sent my willpower—my magical essence—into my sabre. Molten metal boiled upward from the hilt, cooling into a glowing, garnet sword. I stopped the blade just short of bastard length, which made it manageable with one hand while keeping my other free for spellwork.

I'd already transferred Fire into the sabre; now I stretched the spell up the length of the blade. The sword burst into flame and cast rust-colored shadows on the polished wooden floor.

The gargoyle lurched into the doorway. It still retained a semblance of its mural image: a generic demon drawn to tempt generic saints. It assessed the room with careful, reptilian interest, and crept at me.

I eased my posture; relaxed my knees; and leveled my breathing. I drew a map of the room in my head so I wouldn't trip into my opponent's arms. There would be enough room for a good first swipe, and the first swipe is everything. A skilled strategist can see the end of a fight in that first swing.

When the gargoyle was in range, I sprang, lashing out with a horizontal cut that bit into its shoulder. It flinched and roared as fresh paint spilled down its chest. I followed that with more slashing cuts, putting as much strength behind them as I could without sacrificing my guard or overextending my arms.

The gargoyle's claws swiped for the inside of my thigh. I blocked it with a downward parry. The gargoyle tried it again, liking that move, which would either tear into a major vein or rip my balance out from under me. The urge to jump back was strong—but leaps only looked good in movies. You can't change direction midair.

Then I screwed up. I went for a center thrust that opened a tear in the gargoyle's chest but left me vulnerable for a gutting. I barely managed to bash away its arms as claws raked my abdomen, taking a handful of fabric and flesh.

I backed off to rebalance. My belly was hot and wet, blood ribboning across my ribs. It wasn't hurting yet, but blood loss would cost me quickly.

The gargoyle's wounds had already dried and become part of its painted surface. Worse, the spots where I'd torn or chipped it had become another danger, with edges as sharp as broken glass.

It came at me again. I ducked a chest-high swipe, spun around it, kicked it in the back of its knees. It stumbled. I slammed the flat of my blade across the back of its head. It went down on all fours.

Across the room, Matthias was surrounded by pieces of cracked chairs. The windows weren't broken. I could almost feel the magic that sealed us in—a strong, strong spell. I had to assume all exits were blocked. We needed to find a more defensible spot. If I couldn't go out the first-floor doors, maybe I could get to the roof?

"The main hall. Back to the main hall!"

Matthias ran along the left of the struggling gargoyle. I moved a step behind him, stopping at the doorway. I brushed a thumb over Elena's emerald ring. Its stored spell released. Magic branched across my vision like frost on a windowpane, giving everything a momentary bluish tinge.

The gargoyle regained its footing. I held out my arm, and a globe of sluggish ice thrashed and formed in my palm. Before the gargoyle could leap at me, I pitched it.

The Frost shattered against the gargoyle's painted surface. The gargoyle didn't stop moving, but its joints began making snapping, splintering noises.

I raced to the lobby. Matthias was futilely banging on the sealed front doors.

"Where do we go?" he asked in a panic. "It's still lock—" He caught sight of my stomach. It must have been more of a mess than I thought. He raised alarmed eyes to meet mine—and then, with even more surprise, lost balance, tripped into a pillar, and cracked his head against it. I reached down, fisted his shirtfront, and yanked him back to his feet.

"Your eyes," he gasped.

My Atlantean Aspect was rising, a sign of my strength among other scions. I could feel the heat from it on my face.

The gargoyle roared into the lobby. Abandoning its graceful economy of motion, it now stormed past the marble pillars, arms wide, claws extended. Gouged chips of marble flew in its wake.

I didn't have time to touch the sigil on my ankle, so I concentrated on the feel of the loose gold links. A Wind spell sprang loose. The initial rush of magic left my skin feeling tight and inflated.

I raised an arm and pulled the lobby's air currents toward me. With a skill that came from years of limited sigils and cornered desperation, I infused the Wind with Frost's frigid temperatures. I redirected the gale toward the gargoyle.

It staggered and slowed, but kept on coming.

I threw everything I had into the spell, reducing the gargoyle to all fours. But between my sabre use and the spells and blood loss, the edges of my vision were going dark.

I said, "Run for the stairs!" I grabbed Matthias's arm and my right leg collapsed under me. A lot of blood loss, then.

Matthias divided a petrified stare between me and the gargoyle. I didn't understand why he wasn't running, until I saw that his fingernails had grown two inches, the tips drawn into points.

He jumped between me and the monster.

I got my second wind. I stumbled up, grabbed the collar of his shirt, and hurled him in the direction of the stairs. In the process I missed the worst of a claw swipe I hadn't seen coming. The cheap magical wards in my jacket saved me from a gash, but the pressure of the blow still knocked me off my feet. I let my sabre blade crumble into glowing sparks until just the hilt remained. I thought I could force more firebolts, buy Matthias a few more moments.

A car drove through the front of the building. The heavy front doors flew into the marble lobby with a bang. The moment the driver's side door was clear, it opened, and Brand dove out. "Distract it!" he shouted.

I didn't think I could come up with a distraction better than a bloody car, but I put everything I had into my sabre. With the aim of the desperate, I shot a lava-bright firebolt into one of the gargoyle's eyes.

It shrieked and reared. Brand ran up behind it. He had something that looked suspiciously like a strip of duct tape in his hands. He slapped it against the gargoyle. A grenade pin dangled from his thumb.

"*Down!*" I shouted at Matthias, and either fell or slid behind a pillar just as the teen landed next to me.

The concussive blast sent a crack through the marble. Pebble-sized bits of wall mural bounced off my upraised arms. The violence of the action settled into an immediate silence, punctured only by the rain of plaster.

"Holy shit," I whispered. I brushed blue paint chips out of my hair and crawled out from behind the pillar.

Brand was inching his head from behind another pillar. I said, "The car?"

"Stole it from the gas station." Brand squinted at the bent, smoking hood. "I hope the Tower has us on a fucking expense account."

The guarda arrived. I was hastily bandaged by emergency technicians. The lobby was now a busy crime scene.

"My lord, just to be clear," one of the uniformed men said, "the gargoyle entered the premises from over here."

I said, "*Entered* the premises? It pulled itself off the wall. Right there. In the spot with the monster shaped cut-out."

"My lord, I—"

I walked away from him.

They'd take the easy way out, and chalk it up to wild magic. New Atlantis—not to mention the Westlands—was lousy with unstable energy. I didn't have the luxury in believing that, though. The gargoyle had shown too much sentience. Plus, the doors and windows had been warded shut to prevent our escape. That showed skill. It showed purpose.

Brand was waiting on the other side of the room with Matthias. Some people got the shakes after an adrenaline surge. Brand got pissed.

He leaned into me and said, "If those bastards upstairs—"

"Not them. Or maybe? I don't know. It takes time to do a summoning like this. Or a hell of a lot of power. I don't know if they *could* do this, or even had time to do this."

I looked toward the stairwell, which was now unsealed. None of the scions had come downstairs. The guarda had sequestered them in their offices while they sought witnesses.

"Could whatever was upstairs—whatever you felt in Addam's office—have been a gargoyle?" Brand asked.

I shook my head no. The gargoyle wasn't even a little like the nastiness I'd sensed in Addam's suite.

My own adrenaline ebb was weakening me. My bad shoulder ached. The bandages on my stomach had already soaked through. I'd refused a trip to the hospital, wanting to spare the bill and heal myself.

"You saved me," Matthias said to me from behind Brand. I couldn't quite identify the expression that lit up his face, but it wasn't nearly as comfortable as plain gratitude. "You saved my life."

"If we get you killed your first week, people will make fun of us," I said.

Brand said, "Rune, if we find out the Tower knew Addam was into some shit he didn't tell us about, I'm heading to the Pac Bell with a whole fucking roll of duct tape."

I pulled out my cell phone and dialed a private number. Vivaldi began playing in the background while the call connected. The Tower answered by saying, "How's your stomach? Shall I send my healer?"

I didn't waste time being surprised he knew what had happened. "Did you tell anyone you hired me to find Addam Saint Nicholas? Or that you were *going* to hire me?"

"I may have mentioned it in certain circles," he said.

"I see. Just out of curiosity, did you introduce me by name, or just call me Bait?"

I could almost hear his smile. "For what it's worth, only anyone involved in Addam's disappearance would have understood the significance of your association. Based on that, and given the people I spoke with, I now suggest you focus on his siblings and business associates."

"Excellent information, Lord Tower. I would never have suspected them."

He said, "I have every confidence in you."

The call disconnected.

THE ENCLAVE

I woke to another hot morning. Moaning my complaints, I got up, turned on my old, rattling air-conditioner, then lazed on my bed for nine more snooze alarms.

Before I could hit the tenth, Brand poked his head over the edge of the spiral stairway. "Will you get the fuck up already?"

"I'm reviewing the case in my head. I'm strategizing."

"Strategy doesn't give you fucking pillow creases," he said. With a snort, he stomped the rest of the way into my bedroom and went over to the window. His baggy white bathing suit turned translucent against the roaring sunlight.

"Can you get me some vitamin water from Queenie?" he asked.

"Why can't you?"

"She's mad at me. I think she hid them."

I opened my mouth to ask the obvious, but he waved me off. "I may have used the dishwasher without asking her."

"Bullshit," I said. "You put your socks and underwear in it again, didn't you?"

"The washing machine is broken," he said defensively.

"Oh, wonderful." I threw a forearm over my eyes. We'd have to take turns schlepping to a laundromat until I could call a repairman. Between that and property taxes, the Tower's two checks would all but evaporate.

"Stop that," Brand said. "You're going to give yourself frown lines."

"And that bothers you because . . . ?"

"Because you'll get old faster than me, which means you'll get rejuvenation treatments before I need them, and through the wonder of the Companion bond, I'll fucking end up looking twelve."

"Did you come up here for a reason?"

"The water. And to tell you I pulled the research on the idiot scions."

I'd asked Brand to look into their school records. Most scions were educated at the Mangus Academy; and Brand and I had a backdoor into their servers. I'd hoped it would give us an idea which of them might have the ability to summon a gargoyle—let alone to summon whatever had taken Addam from his office.

"I got their grades and course loads," Brand said. "You already knew about Geoffrey. Top of his class, lots of academia and theoretical magic—as opposed to those practical courses that support the idea of theoretical survival."

"Geoffrey has what it takes to work a summoning," I said. "What about his brother?"

"While it's possible Michael's spent his life masterminding the image that he's dumb as tar, I'm betting that's just an insult to tar. He's got some training in aggressive magic—enough to fucking cheat at rugby—but the chance he'd be able to pull off a big ritual? No."

"What about Ashton?" I said.

"Ashton did post-grad work in Poland."

Well, that snagged my attention, as Brand knew it would.

Two of the biggest human casualties of the Atlantean World War were magically radioactive zones in Poland and America's Pacific Northwest, both sites of battlegrounds. Very little lived in the fading blast radii, which made it perfect for spell training. The camps had very good PR staff. I knew this because the human world never asked what they were training *for*.

"Okay," I said slowly. "Ashton's father is old guard. He'd expect his kids to do tours of duty."

"So maybe he's not the useless fucking dandy he wants us to believe."

I thought about Ashton's parting words and said, "Maybe he's not."

The Surfside Beach Enclave sat at the western end of Nazaca Road, the priciest real estate on the island. The Enclave was originally part of a ruined resort built in the 1920s for pampered French colonials looking to escape the crushing poverty of Cambodia's Phnom Penh. Thousands of Cambodians lost their lives building Bokor Hill Station, not to mention those that died during the resort's final abandonment at the hands of the Khmer Rouge. The building was baked in their misery.

The jungle's rust-red moss still clung to some of the stonework, giving it a decrepit allure. Brand, Matthias, and I entered through one of the side doors and worked our way through carefully extravagant security points. My footsteps got heavier the higher I climbed, until finally we stopped before the doors of my father's suites.

I raised my hand toward a stylized sunburst emblem. Sealed wards within the doors recognized my presence and opened on oiled hinges.

The Sun Throne's rooms were decorated in wicker and driftwood, with powder-blue walls and lots of windows. The living area led to an outdoor terra-cotta balcony. Off the balcony, a narrow stairway merged with other narrow stairways, down to a private, heavily guarded beach.

It'd been years since I'd been back. I'm not sure what I'd expected. There were no cobwebs. No haze of dust. No sheets sagging off furniture like folds of dead skin. The rooms were so close to memory that my father may have just stepped outside to have a drink, or to watch me hunt for sand dollars in the tidal pools.

In some ways, it was easier to look at the ruins of Sun Estate than it was this deceptively whole memory.

I closed my mind against the images.

"We could spar," Brand said.

I frowned at him.

"It'll make you feel better. We could go outside and spar, if you want."

"Sparring means something different for me than it does you," I said. "Sparring is getting hit in the face a lot." But I smiled and started unpacking my beach bag with a little less morbidity.

We had a couple hours to kill before I was due in Lady Justice's suite, so Matthias and I changed into two bathing suits from a supply kept in the suite. I didn't like the speculative looks Matthias was giving me, though. Especially when I took off my pants.

Matthias squinted at me and said, "Is that a——?"

"No."

"But it looks like a——"

"It isn't," I said.

Brand started to open his mouth, so I pointed at him.

Not all sigils were lucky enough to be shaped as jewelry or weapons. Sigils are tools for the manifestation of our magics, and our magics are driven by human appetites—aggression, sex, defense, shelter, and so on. Considering that, it's not outside the realm of possibility that some sigils would be shaped as marital aides, like the one threaded through a leather strap and tied around my thigh.

"It's a cock ring," Brand told Matthias.

"Godsdamnit," I said. "It's a sigil. I have a Shatter spell in it. Do you know how few scions can pull off Shatter?"

"His magic cock ring," Brand said.

Almost none of my sigils had been given to me. Most were scavenged from the haunted ruins of Sun Estate. I tried, on a daily basis, to forget I'd pulled this one from my old seneschal's nightstand.

"Lord Tower makes his Companion work in a basement office all day," I told Brand. "I take you to the beach."

"Mayan's basement office is an armored vault with a hundred security personnel," Brand told me. "You probably won't be able to tip the towel boy."

I lifted my long-suffering gaze to the ceiling and said, "Let's go swimming."

I got some sun. Brand threw wooden practice knives at seashell targets. Matthias spent most of the time standing and staring into the ocean, moving his eyes from one point of the horizon and back. After a while, he came over to us and said, "Are there really krakens out there?"

"Young ones," I said. "The adults hang out near the whirlpools off

Smith's Point in the Westlands. The babies are dangerous as hell, though. Don't go swimming past the wards."

Brand said, "Every year there's at least one stupid American college that tries to make New Atlantis a spring break destination. The newspapers have a field day when they get eaten."

Max spent the next fifteen minutes splashing in the shallows—the only part of the cove protected against predators. When a wave knocked the back of his knees, he fell on his ass, swallowed ocean water, and burst into laughter.

"So how is it," Brand asked, "that the grandson of an Arcana is acting like it's his first day at the beach? What the hell is his story?"

Later, a servant invited us inside for refreshments. I was sweating heavily by then. It soaked my hair, beaded my sunscreen, pooled in my ear canal. I tilted my head and shook it out while Brand and Matthias piled into the room around me.

Enclave staff swept through the doorway and deposited sandwiches and frosted pitchers. The last one to leave stood rigidly at attention, waiting for a tip. I said, "Do not remove a fly from your friend's forehead with a hatchet." The young man hesitated, bowed, and departed.

"You're not as funny as you think, Lord Sun," Brand told me. He grabbed a soft drink, went out on the balcony, and slouched into a chaise lounge to take a nap.

Matthias wandered, snooping in drawers and cabinets. He was wearing a pair of my old flip-flops, so thin that he looked barefoot. It made me think about his wardrobe, and everything else he needed to become a normal person again.

What was I going to do with him? Did he really have a way to land on his feet? Nothing I'd seen yet had shown me that he had friends, contacts, support networks, funds—anything.

"I wonder what'll happen with the Lovers' rooms," Matthias said. He was staring up at an arbor watercolor. The Tower had painted it for my father, well before I was born. Matthias said, "They have rooms here too, right? All Arcana do? Will they save them, like they did with your rooms? Will someone else come along and run the Heart Throne? Or will there be no more Heart Throne? Is that even possible?"

"I don't know, Matthias. The old rules don't apply. Things are so different since the Unsettlement. The world is so different. Did you spend much time here growing up?"

"The beach? Never."

"I'm surprised you didn't come with your grandmother. I read somewhere that Elena loves the ocean."

"That . . . wasn't the type of relationship we had. I didn't spend much time with anyone in my family."

"Except your uncle?"

Matthias was by a mirror, and his reflection was at an angle to me. As I watched, his face transformed. For a second I thought the emotion was grief; but the thing about genuine grief is that it can look an awful lot like fear. Matthias was afraid. Glassy-eyed, pale-skinned, lip-trembling afraid.

Cold realization swamped through me. I was beginning to suspect what sort of life Matthias had lived. I was beginning to think maybe he had some experiences like mine.

I closed my eyes and put the worry away for the moment. "Matthias, I've got to change, and then go see Lady Justice. Do me a favor and stay close to Brand, okay?" I glanced over at Brand. He was dead to the world. He'd curled into an *S*, dimpled ass cleavage sticking over the side.

Matthias wiped at his eyes before turning around to face me. He nodded and went to the lounge chair next to Brand. In that awkward way that teenagers have, he took a minute to get situated, ultimately positioning himself in an exact imitation of Brand's casual slump.

Shit, I thought.

Lady Justice's rooms were in the middle section of a divided second floor. She shared the space with the other Arcana who formed the Moral Certainties.

It would be impossible to enter one of the residences undetected—

they were too heavily warded. But security in the hallways was a little more lax, which I exploited.

Just off the second-floor landing, I bent to tie a shoe. While squatting behind a plant, I rubbed a finger over my gold ankle chain, and its sigil spell released. Magic dripped down my body in vaguely electric trickles. When I stood, I had turned the color of the speckled white walls. Camouflage was a thrifty magic—not as intensive to store as a genuine invisibility spell, but just as resourceful if you knew how to use it.

The Moral Certainty wing was a short, fat corridor that opened into four sets of rooms. Three of the four suites were thrown open. Servants made their way in and out with food, drink, towels, and toiletries. I hung around for the better part of ten minutes, spying on what I could.

Ashton Saint Gabriel was in Lord Strength's rooms. He was dressed in boating shorts, with bare feet propped on a coffee table as he reviewed the contents of a manila folder. There were several piles of paper spread on surfaces around him.

Michael Saint Talbot and his younger sister, Lucie, were throwing a Frisbee inside Lady Tolerance's rooms. Michael laughed, while his sister glanced around anxiously and cast apologetic looks at the servants. The servants dodged to and fro to pick up overturned vases and straighten tilted portraits. After a few minutes, I realized Michael was using a sigil spell to make his sister fumble the Frisbee.

Thing was, Michael wasn't even a particularly bad example of a scion. Most scions were just as wasted and wasteful. Few appreciated the power they had at their fingertips, or how lucky they were to have a family armory. They stored priceless, irreplaceable sigils with spells that cleaned cigarette smoke out of their jacket, freshened their breath, or made their eyes glow in black light—or to make their lips slide over their teeth into constant smiles, to increase the size of their dick, to throw laughter behind them when they told bad jokes. I'd even known a scion who regularly stored a spell that made the snap of his fingers more crisp and sharp than he could make them sound on his own.

After a while, I got bored and angry with spying, and moved toward Lady Justice's quarters. I had to step aside to avoid a departing group of men and women. They were young and beautiful, and they appeared to be familiar with each other. Justice's consorts, maybe. I'd heard she had a sweet tooth for pretty and politically disinclined spouses.

I stood in a nook and dissipated the Camouflage. My skin pinkened to normal. I finger-combed my bangs and headed to my appointment.

Justice's apartment was now empty except for two people. The first was a middle-aged woman dressed in comfortable robes cut low in the cleavage. She stood by the side of a much younger woman.

The younger woman had the makings of a phenomenal beauty—honeyed hair, gold-green eyes—but she was thin to the point of disfigurement. I could have circled her biceps with my thumb and forefinger. Her cheeks were so concave that her entire face shuddered when she swallowed.

As soon as the older woman registered my presence, she released a spell from a sigil pendant. The girl became plumper, face fuller, hips more shapely. The older woman turned on me and said, with glacial and imperious disapproval, "Sir."

"Rune Saint John to see Lady Justice."

She hadn't recognized my face, but my name made her blink. "Preposterous. Your name isn't on today's list."

"Really. I spoke with one of Lady Justice's assistants earlier. I'm here to ask after Lord Addam. Excuse me, but I don't believe we've had the pleasure?"

The nudge for manners put her on autopilot. "Apologies. This is my niece, the Lady Ella Saint Nicholas, daughter of Lady Justice. I am Diana Saint Nicholas, Lady Justice's sister."

Addam's younger sister said, "You're here about Addam—*why?*" She had a high voice sharpened with a Slavic accent. I'd read somewhere that the Justice clan had strong Russian ties.

"Regarding his disappearance, Lady Saint Nicholas."

Ella dropped to the sofa. I didn't get the idea it was from shock; she was just so damn unhealthy. "Addam hasn't returned calls. Mother said we may have to make enquiries if he doesn't contact us soon. Did she ask you to make enquiries?"

"Actually, I'm looking into Lord Addam's whereabouts on behalf of a colleague. Do you mind if I ask you some questions?"

"When you say *disappearance*," Ella went on, "what does that mean? We assumed Addam flew off on one of his whims. That's not uncommon."

"Nothing would make me happier if that was the case," I said, because, honestly, the Tower didn't pay by the hour. "Consider my efforts a precaution."

There was a pause while Diana and I waited for Ella to speak again. Ella closed her mouth, tucked her feet under her, and began fretting with the hem of her blouse.

Diana took a seat next to Ella and weighed down Ella's hand with her own. It did not strike me as a kind gesture. She said, "Lord Saint John— or is it Lord Sun? I'm sorry, I should know that."

"I haven't officially picked up my father's mantle, so neither will offend me. Actually, please, call me Rune."

"What sort of questions did you have?" she asked, dropping my name entirely.

"Just some general questions. Lady Ella, you mentioned Lord Addam is away a lot. What sort of places does he go?"

"Oh, where doesn't he," Ella said, exaggerating the *doesn't* with an eye roll. "He has a man or woman in every port. Addam is very handsome. Very energetic. He always needs to be doing something. He likes to dance and listen to music. Does that help?"

"At this point, all information is useful. When he goes away, does he let you or the rest of your family know?"

Ella considered that, biting down on a chapped lower lip that hadn't been prettied by her aunt's glamor spell. "Not always, no. But if it's more than a couple days, he'll let his assistant know. Have you spoken with Lilly Rose?"

"I have, actually. Has Lord Addam been upset lately?"

"Addam doesn't get upset," Ella said with a dainty head shake.

"Do you get along with Addam?"

Ella smiled and looked toward Diana. Diana leaned into the conversation and said, "Is there reason for us to be concerned?"

"Not at all," I lied.

There was a certain way people had of dropping their jaw to fake a smile. Ella had done that. She was evading my question. So I asked, again, "Lady Ella, do you get along well with Addam?"

"Everyone gets along with Addam," she said.

"When was the last time you spoke with him?"

"I believe . . . a week? Yes, a week, to the day. We were taking photos in the Iron Hall with the other Moral Certainty scions. It was a public-relations event."

"You must know Ashton Saint Gabriel, then. I've spoken with him and the Temperance brothers. Did you know they're Addam's business partners?"

"Of course I did." Ella shifted her gaze to Diana. "Shouldn't we offer refreshments?"

I scooted forward on my chair, startling her. "Can you think of any reason why someone would want to hurt your brother?"

She faked another smile. "If I had to guess?"

"Sure."

"A jealous husband. A jealous wife. The jealous boyfriend or girlfriend of one of Addam's girlfriends or boyfriends. Addam is very amorous. I will admit, he tends to stay on remarkably good terms with his old flames . . . but their flames might feel otherwise. I really do think this is a silly line of questioning. Perhaps Addam's made a new little love nest for himself somewhere? He's due for another infatuation."

Ella glanced at her aunt. Diana stood and said, "I'm sure my sister is expecting you."

Lady Justice had turned one of her Enclave apartments into a sanctum. Diana left me at its door and beat a dignified retreat to the living room.

I went inside and had no time whatsoever to prepare for the sledge-hammer impact of Justice's Aspect.

It was like a furnace door had been opened in my face. Through teared-up eyes, I glimpsed a silken web crisscrossing the roof of the chamber. Something hallucinatingly arachnid descended from it. The image lasted a second, too quickly for my mind to sift meaning. I just had that brief impression of fluttering strands and multiple eyes, and of a nightmare dropping to my level.

Then Lady Justice hit the kill switch on her performance. Her Aspect vanished. She stood in the middle of billowing drapes, not a web. She wore a feathery, white cape. Her hair was drawn into a single elaborate braid. She resembled a woman in her fortieth year, maybe younger, but it was hard to tell on account of the stretched agelessness that came with multiple rejuvenation treatments.

Lady Justice's eyes were not normal. I'd heard this before.

They shifted and changed, their shape and color stolen from nearby memories. Even more unnerving was my implausible recognition of all the variations. I saw first my father's flame-colored eyes, and then the squint of the last person I'd embarrassed myself in front of, and finally the glare of a critical neighbor.

"Hello, Rune Sun," Lady Justice said. Her accent was thicker than Ella's, the *R*s as slick and sharp as ice picks.

I dropped my chin and kept a civil tongue, even though her drama irked me. "Lady Justice. Thank you for the invitation. I apologize if it's an imposition."

"It's not, if it involves Addam." Unlike everyone else I'd met, she said Addam's name with the ancient Atlantean pronunciation: *Ahd-dahm.* "If I understand correctly, you are in the employ of Lord Tower, and you suspect Addam is the victim of mischief. I must assure you: that is not the case."

"You know he's okay?" I asked, surprised.

"He's my child. A long time ago, I took certain measures to know if he—if any of my children—were in true danger. I sense nothing of the sort from Addam."

For a second, I was thrown. I'd convinced myself that Addam was in trouble.

Then I remembered the results of my psychometry spell. Even in memory, the *wrongness* of it, like unwashed skin, like necrotic tissue, made my stomach turn.

Lady Justice said, "I'm more curious as to why Lord Tower thinks my son is in danger."

"I wouldn't presume to speak on Lord Tower's behalf, Lady Justice."

"A prudent response," she said softly. Her eyes shimmered from Brand's crayon blue, to Ashton Saint Gabriel's reflective silver, to Geoffrey's rich autumn brown.

I decided to unbalance her. "I've heard that your oldest is sick. Christian."

"Christian is indisposed," she said after a pause.

"Isn't that unusual, Lady Justice? You must have access to the best healers on the island. In the world."

"And once they diagnose Christian's illness, they'll eliminate it. Until then, they are simply being cautious."

"Are his symptoms serious?"

"Are you here about Christian, too, Rune Sun?" Her eyes shifted into the pale lilac of my first nanny; and then a bloodshot green—eyes I'd seen on a man wearing an animal mask, once upon a time.

I swallowed something too bitter to be just anger. "Do you know much about Addam's business partners?"

"Some."

"Is it a friendly relationship?"

"They seem amiable. They are successful."

"They've made a lot of money?"

"I've never asked for the particulars. Addam is very clear that it is his project, separate from my interests."

"But," I said, "it's a project that still depends on your influence. From what I understand."

"To a degree. In a very real way, though, it's his influence, too. No one, however powerful, *is* Justice. I lead the Crusader Throne. I am not the entirety of it."

"Do your children get along?"

She went very still. "They do."

"Do you know of anyone who would hurt Addam?"

"Your second question steps closely on your first. I would hope you're not accusing my children—accusing anyone in my court—of something untoward."

"I'm just asking questions, Lady Justice."

"Yes. You seem very good at it. Asking questions."

Her smile deepened into something less stable. She circled to my left, and her gaze deliberately slid down the front of my body. She said, "I'd thought rumor might have exaggerated your beauty. It didn't, did it? I think perhaps you *are* the most beautiful man of your generation."

Waves of heat rose under my skin. My fingers tightened into fists.

"I see why Lord Tower favors you." Her eyes flicked up to my clenched jaw. "Ah, now. So serious. Is it horrible, to be called a beautiful man?"

I did what I always did when someone too powerful pushed too many buttons. I turned very, very formal. "Lady Justice, I'm embarrassed to have to remind you that with the death of my father, I became the voice and the will of the Sun Throne. I would ask that you afford me the semblance of respect, if you cannot manage the real thing."

To my surprise, she blinked.

The color of her eyes faded to a plain burgundy. "Forgive me, brother," she said, grimacing. "I overstep."

One day, I'd have the power of my father. It was in my blood. It was my legacy. But that day wasn't today, or next year, or probably even next century. There were many, many boxes of mac and cheese between me and a seat on the Arcanum. For her to call me brother was, as far as concessions went, one hell of an apology.

Lady Justice sighed. "I admit: I suspect Lord Tower is playing some unknown game. I would like to know why. Yet it is wrong to try to obtain that information in a manner I find so distastefully reminiscent *of* Lord Tower. I should have simply asked you, Lord Sun. Has Lord Tower sent you into my house for a reason?"

"Lady Justice, Lord Tower doesn't use me as a pawn in the affairs of other Arcana." Not without a much larger paycheck. "He knows how I feel about politics. I really do believe he's just concerned about Addam."

"Lord Tower is . . . fond of Addam. Addam is his godson."

"He mentioned it. Lady Justice, if I may ask—and please don't take offense—are your spells or wards really that good? Are you sure Addam is okay?"

"I am sure he hasn't been hurt. It would take a great deal of ability to hide that from me. I do not know where he is, though. I have not—I do not—interfere. Understand: I am loathe to involve myself in my children's affairs, even in matters of harm or peril. They must be strong if they are to survive outside my walls. New Atlantis would pull my children down. It is the nature of ruling." She paused. "I would also have you understand this: if you discover someone did hurt my son, you are to tell me. While I am sparing in my protection, I am very generous in my reckoning. Such is the nature of Justice."

Behind her, her shadow twisted into something with multiple legs that thinned into sharp points.

An Atlantean Aspect is a difficult thing to describe.

A particularly powerful magic-user can look different—distorted—when strong emotion is upon them. My eyes, for instance, glow orange. But Arcana—real, ruling Arcana—are the closest things to gods on this planet. They *must* have fearsome Aspects—it's a survival mechanism, like a predator's coloring or the ruff of a wolf. There are stories of Arcana becoming burning bushes, scorpions, and F5 funnel clouds. I saw Lady Lovers turn into a faerie with hornet wings and overactive pheromones. I've heard that the Hanged Man's aspect has made brave men piss blood.

I saw the Aspect of my father only once, and even then just out of the corner of my eye. The only thing I remember was a pillar of light so bright that it left an afterimage for hours.

Many scions of the newest generation don't have Aspects. A lot of academics cite this as evidence that the Atlantean race is in decline. I disagree. Just because most scions don't turn into jabberwockies or lightning bolts when they're pissed doesn't make them weaker, it just makes them children of a different world.

Younger Atlanteans can't afford to have one foot in Atlantis's past. We are no longer separate from the human world. Blending in has become our survival mechanism.

The attack came as I returned to my rooms.

It was a clever, twisted bit of spellwork. The magic wound its way past all my adrenaline responses and sent me into an immediate, drowsy trance. I changed course in a daze and wandered in a direction not of my choosing.

The soles of my shoes scuffed the tiles as I passed through well-appointed, heavily guarded hallways. None of the guards stopped me or acknowledged my fugue. I climbed a set of red-stone stairs, which ended in an arched hallway flanked by empty suits of armor. The armor, scored with blade marks and mace dents, lacked the spit and polish of pampered antiques.

At the end of a hallway, a man called to me.

I went toward him and smiled when he reached his hands toward my neck.

"It shouldn't be this easy to influence you," Lord Tower said. "You need to practice your resistance techniques."

Then his face froze and he looked down.

I poked my sabre, transmuted into dagger shape, into his belly.

"At least you didn't banter before the killing blow this time," he said lightly.

I transmuted my sabre blade to wrist-guard form and shook it over my fist before it firmed. "For the record, I even knew it was you doing the influencing. You're too proud. You need to muddy up your magical signature with mistakes and flaws."

"Indeed. I have sangria upstairs. Will you join me?"

I followed him through a set of rooms that were twice the size of mine. The Enclave owners famously parceled out Arcana apartments equally, but the Tower's old job as the monarchy's chief spy and torturer gave him unspoken privileges. The things he did in private produced unsettling acoustics, which were best kept to their own wing.

A cool, dark stairway opened onto an unshaded rooftop terrace. The Tower had summoned—literally summoned, ripped right from the ocean in big, messy chunks—seven water elementals that served as his security. They prowled the rooftop, glistening and rippling under the strong summer sun. White sand, plant life, and shell fragments swirled under their skinless surfaces.

One of them handed me a glass of sangria, and I saw a tiny fish dart up its forearm. It left behind fingerprints made of wave foam.

"I'll have your report now," the Tower said. He sat down on a reclining patio chair—the word *perched* also came to mind. He was barefoot again, but he had traded in pajamas for a bathing robe made of Atlantean grass silk.

"I guess this means you're aware I saw Lady Justice?" I asked.

"I am," he said. "Was it productive?"

"Instructive, at least." I took a minute to bring the Tower up to speed. He was a master poker player with very few tells. Except for a stillness when I mentioned the psychometric impression in Addam's office, I didn't know if any of my investigation was news to him.

"What will you do next?" he asked.

"Talk with Christian Saint Nicholas. I want to learn more about his illness. Him being sick, and now Addam missing?"

He peered at me. "You suspect Ella Saint Nicholas."

"She raised some flags."

"You're aware it is very unlikely that she'd be able to dispose of both her older brothers without being discovered."

"At this point," I said, "I'm more aware that whoever took Addam is someone who has the resources to send a gargoyle after me. Back when you made me bait. Without telling me."

"In my defense, I had no prior knowledge of the gargoyle."

"You said you were trying to flush someone out. And then you said I should focus on family and business associates. Why?"

The Tower stared at a lump of fruit in his drink, then eyed me over the rim. "I suggested your involvement in a social setting. Addam's partners were present."

"You mentioned that I was looking for Addam?" I asked.

"Not quite. At one point, I mentioned that you did odd jobs for me. And at another point, I mentioned that it was strange that Addam hadn't returned my call, and I was concerned. It occurred to me that someone with a guilty conscience might put those pieces together."

I tried to think if any of the scions had seemed surprised to see me, or had been unsurprised that I was looking for Addam. I blew a raspberry through my lips, unsure. "Is this political, do you think? Some sort of break in the Moral Certainties? Is Addam splash damage?"

"I'll certainly be paying attention to that possibility," he said. "I'll leave it to you to decide if there are more personal reasons at play."

"Ella Saint Nicholas was in the social setting, wasn't she?"

"She was," Lord Tower said. "Be careful, Rune. The Moral Certainty courts are known as devout, which is a short step from fanatical. They dislike scrutiny. Be very careful."

He opened his mouth to say more, stopped, and frowned. That was as much warning as I had.

A wave crashed over me. Foaming water tunneled up my nose and past my lips. It caught me on an exhale, which is all that kept me conscious. I was too confused to understand anything except the boldest of sensations—salt; the clear, sharp bite of cold water; Brand's distant, sudden alarm; the painful squeeze of deep-sea pressure.

The pressure got worse and worse, a building cramp that turned my belly concave. Air bubbles seethed out of my mouth in a gasp. I flailed upward for air, but the water followed, an unbreakable, melting curtain between me and sunlight.

Just as quickly as it began, it ended. I collapsed into a choking kneel, surrounded in hissing mist. There were patio flagstones under my hands.

Hindsight came at a limp. I was still on the roof. I'd been attacked by a water elemental.

"The hell?" I coughed, shaking my head and staring up.

The Tower stood with both arms extended. Writhing streams of liquid gloved his hands. He turned to his remaining creations—which were not attacking—and preemptively turned them into explosive clouds of vapor.

I did not like that I hadn't been able to protect myself. I did not like being saved.

"It was as if it was drawn to you," Lord Tower said, staring at the rapidly drying puddles.

"Or," I said, "we were just attacked."

"Through the Enclave's defenses? Through my own control? Impossible."

"I see. So we're blaming wild magic? Twice? In twenty-four hours?"

It didn't get a rise out of him, but he did stare back at the destroyed elementals with sharper contemplation.

I crawled to the patio edge, grabbed the railing, and hoisted myself upright. It didn't surprise me in the slightest to see Brand climbing the terraced walls between the beach and the roof, largely ignoring walkways and stairways while keeping me in his panicked line of sight.

Behind me, the Tower said, "Rune."

I looked over my shoulder.

Lord Tower said, "Find Addam."

NEW SAINTS

That evening, Brand and I left Matthias in Queenie's care and headed to New Saints Hospital, where Christian Saint Nicholas had been admitted ten days prior.

Brand took us by motorcycle. Early-evening rush hour hadn't thinned enough to make it a quick commute. I took the time to review what we'd learned about Addam Saint Nicholas's disappearance—which was a much quicker task than reviewing everything we hadn't learned.

Addam was removed from his workplace by, or at the command, of Person Unknown. Person Unknown took Addam without any visible signs of a struggle.

Lady Justice said she'd have known if any of her children were hurt or in peril. So either her spell was defunct, or Addam wasn't hurt or in peril, or Person Unknown was powerful enough to override or mask Lady Justice's spell. Person Unknown also, presumably, had the magical spit to summon a gargoyle, as well as break through the Enclave's and the Tower's defenses to wrest control of the water elemental.

The problem was that our list of suspects didn't exactly ring with masterminds. Between Ashton, Geoffrey, Michael, and Ella, there were more than enough red flags to warrant a second look—but none of them had what it took to break through Lord Tower's safeguards. They just didn't.

So how does someone without the aptitude to best Lord Tower, best Lord Tower?

They contract with someone who *is* powerful enough.

I couldn't shake the memory of what I'd sensed in Addam's office. That tinfoil-aftertaste sense of corruption. A stench like that usually came from a What, not a Who. There are plenty of evil beings in New Atlantis ready to barter away their power in service of others. Our history is full of greedy Atlanteans whose eyes were bigger than their souls.

The bike slowed. Brand parked two city blocks away from New Saints. Since there was a coffee shop on the corner, I made no protest.

As Brand eyed the surroundings in a slow three-sixty, I pulled out my wallet. It was upside down and sent loose change clattering to the pavement. When I straightened from picking it up, I saw that Brand was staring at my ass. I decided to feel flattered.

He said, "I know you've been bitching about your weight gain, but, honestly, I wondered where it was all *going.* Now I see. That is one magnificent ass. But maybe you should start jogging with me."

I stalked into the coffee shop. Brand caught the swinging door before it hit him in the face. He said, either oblivious to or disinterested in my pique, "I overheard someone the other day say that people didn't need to do cardio because people three hundred years ago didn't have treadmills and they got along just fine. Can you believe that shit? People three hundred years ago also didn't have dishwashers, laundry machines, grocery stores, or running water. Their entire fucking day was a little more complicated than moving their fat fingers toward the remote control. We—"

"Stop talking," I said.

He caught the look on my face. "I called it magnificent."

I placed my order and elbowed toward the barista counter. "What I don't understand is why one of Addam's business partners would want to harm Addam," I said. "Geoff was right. Even if Addam is arguing with them about their investments—even if they want to take bigger risks like Michael Saint Talbot does—Addam is still far more valuable to them alive."

"If he dies, his shares revert to the surviving partners. That's a lot of money."

"Sure," I said, "but the value of those shares isn't even close to what Addam's continued contacts and influence are worth. Addam is their link to the Crusader Throne. It doesn't make sense that any of them would want to remove him."

"Unless something's going on we don't know about. And maybe it's not them. Maybe Addam's sister is involved. She's third in line for the throne, and now Addam is missing and Christian is in the hospital."

"But how does she think she'd get away with it? Justice may not *protect*, but it *reacts*. With a mother like hers, how could Ella get away with killing both older brothers?"

"Because Ella's confident that no one will be able to prove anything," Brand guessed.

I thought about that.

If Person Unknown had a way to screw with Lady Justice's spell or Lord Tower's control, then it wasn't a huge leap to say they could cover their tracks—at least enough for plausible deniability.

I said, "Here's another thing. Say they've hired muscle. Say Ella, or whoever, has hired a practitioner very skilled at magic—or contracted with some*thing* skilled at magic. If this hired muscle has the power to break through Lord Tower's controls, why the hell am I still alive?"

"Because they weren't trying to kill you," Brand said. "Think about it. Lord Tower didn't even believe at first that someone seized control of the elemental. He thought it was an accident—that the elemental just went haywire. And the guarda blamed the LeperCon gargoyle on a fluke of wild magic. Maybe someone is just testing boundaries, or checking how well protected you are, or seeing how annoying you're going to be."

"Oh, I'm plenty annoying."

"You are," Brand said.

"Maybe this isn't hopeless. We know more than I thought we did."

"Rune, we just tried to eliminate seventy-five percent of the suspects, leaving behind an anorexic woman whose aunt has to cast a glamor to keep flies from settling on her. We know shit."

I pulled the wrapper off a straw and said, "This is why most of our assignments don't involve anything more complicated than you shooting something and me setting fires."

The barista handed me my iced mocha with raised eyebrows. I took it, and we headed to the hospital.

New Saints had been translocated from North Brother Island, off the coast of New York.

Built in 1885, the former Riverside Hospital spent much of its existence as quarantine for the mentally ill and contagious. Riverside had been the home of Mary Mallon, an immigrant cook and asymptomatic carrier of the typhus virus. Riverside was also the site of the 1904 *General Slocum* disaster, in which a remarkably stupid sailor snuck a smoke in the ship's linen closet, starting a fire. The burning steamer foundered on the shore of North Brother. Of the eleven hundred souls lost in the tragedy, many died in the hospital's wards as doctors and nurses pulled burn victims from the wreckage.

Psychic residue is a potent, tangible source of power. And power isn't good or bad, just like one body of water can't be wetter than another. Healers are just as able to plug into the remains of tragedies as death ritualists are.

Atlanteans are, by large, a practical people.

Brand and I headed down a corridor whose diamond-shaped tiles were white and red. Around us, the hospital's magical imprint flickered in and out of existence. Brand couldn't see it, but I could. Translucent gray bars appeared on windows; ghostly cages sprang up around hospital beds; shoelaces vanished and reappeared on passing nurses' shoes.

"Did the Tower say anything about Matthias?" Brand asked.

I blinked. "Do you *want* the Tower talking about him?"

"He told you he was going to look into Matthias's family. I know Matthias wasn't close with his parents, but he talked about that uncle. The uncle might want to know he's okay."

I thought about the look on Matthias's face when I'd mentioned his uncle.

"What?" Brand asked, almost a growl.

"I'm not sure Matthias's uncle was . . ."

"Was what?"

"A good part of his life."

Brand stopped. I passed him. A ghostly mental patient in a straight-jacket flickered into existence between us.

"What does that mean?" Brand asked.

"Just that . . . I want to know more before we contact Matthias's family. Okay?"

"Sure," he said.

"We'll talk about it later."

"Sure," he repeated, but slower.

We stared around us, realizing that we weren't quite sure where to go next. Brand said, "Wait here. I'll get the room number."

He strode away. Annoyance simmered through our Companion bond. He'd guessed that I'd guessed that Matthias was hiding something pretty damn bleak from us. And since there weren't many taboo subjects between Brand and I, he'd soon realize I suspected that Matthias had been abused.

Someone *psssst*ed me from a nearby hallway.

A young man curled his fingers around the corner and leaned into view. The teen had cowlicked blond hair and wore a music festival t-shirt that was two or three sizes too big for him.

"Can you come with me?" he asked.

I said, "Probably not. Do I know you?"

"Maybe? I can't remember. I'm Quinn. I think people are going to die if you don't come with me. It's not far. I don't know why we can't talk here, but we can't. The floor's not right."

He smiled at me as if what he said made perfect sense.

I said, "Quinn? Quinn Saint Nicholas? Are you Addam's brother?"

"Come on!"

He took off at a trot, without even looking over his shoulder to make sure I followed. He hit a fork, frowned at his feet, and darted left.

Brand was still out of sight. He had his cell phone with him, though, and he'd know through the Companion bond that I wasn't in trouble. "Shit," I decided, and ran after Quinn.

I transmuted my sabre as I jogged. The metal wrist-guard stretched taffy thin and scraped over my knuckles, then hardened into hilt form as I flipped it over my palm. On top of that, my sigils were freshly loaded. If the boy was leading me into a trap, I'd roll into it like a tank.

The corridor opened into an acre of white marble ringed by Corinthian pillars. Overhead, a domed crystal roof was flushed with sun, producing an overall effect more like snow-blindness than illumination.

Quinn stood in the middle of the rotunda, looking around with a baffled expression.

"Why did we have to come here?" I asked. "Who is going to die?"

"We come here because this is the floor where we talk. Blood looks really-really red on it."

"Did you just threaten me?" I asked softly.

His startled gaze snapped toward me. "Why would I do that? I'd never hurt you!"

"You'd . . . This is nuts. You *are* Addam's brother, aren't you?"

"I am. Haven't we met yet? And I'm not sure what's wrong. Or—well, I mean, *many* things are wrong. I just don't know what's going to go wrong *now*." He gave me a helpless look.

Was he a half-wit? I hadn't heard that Justice had a half-wit son, which was strange, because scion gossip was parasitic and pervasive and loved to find weakness in Arcana courts. I said, "Quinn, does your family know you're here?"

"Why do you say it like that?"

"Like what?"

"Loud and slow, like I don't speak English. I don't think they know

I'm here. They don't much care where I am, unless Addam makes them care. I thought I came to see Christian, but it wasn't about Christian at all, it was about you. You're why I'm here. Aren't you?"

All of a sudden, I realized I'd heard Quinn's voice before. "You called me yesterday. You asked me if it was time for us to meet. Then you told me the motor was running."

"I did?" he asked me. His face split into a grin. "I did! I remember now. Did you find the duct tape? It was very clever of me, wasn't it?"

Brand had found duct tape on the dashboard of the car he stole. The car that was outside the gas pump, across the street from where I was attacked. Had Brand told me the engine was running? The skin on the back of my neck began to itch.

"Did you know a gargoyle was going to attack us?" I asked. "Did you leave the car there?"

"*Clever*," he stressed.

"Quinn, how did you know that?"

"Well, I didn't know for sure, not always, just most of the time. You almost always need my help, so that Brand can find a way in and save you. It takes too long for you to do what you need to do, otherwise."

I said, "You're a fucking seer."

I have always, always mistrusted seers. I have always had reason to.

It started when a female seer made a prophecy. She was friends with my father; there was a party with lots of alcohol; and over my crib she pronounced: *"He will be the most beautiful man of his generation."*

Other people were in the room. Word got out. I've tripped over that godsdamn prophecy time after time after time. It made it so easy for people to mock me.

I had other reasons to dislike seers, too. They almost never saw the future clearly enough to do more than cause it. The ones with limited ability prostituted their talent or outright lied; and the ones with a true gift were smart enough to hide from you when you came looking for them.

It wasn't obvious where Quinn Saint Nicholas fit in the spectrum, but I had a feeling the universe was going to make me find out.

My cell phone vibrated. Brand had texted, in all-caps, "THE FUCK."

I held up a finger to Quinn while speed-dialing Brand, who answered by saying, "I'll put a fucking bell around your neck. See if I don't."

I told him where Quinn and I were. He got quiet and professional, and snapped his phone shut without a response.

"That was Brand!" Quinn said excitedly. "I miss Brand. He'll make me laugh. Why did you never try to kiss him a second time? Is it because he pushed you into the water?"

"Oh," I said, more of an exhale than a word. I'd once gotten drunk and kissed Brand, the day after my thirteenth birthday. He'd kissed me back, shoved me into the swimming pool, and never spoke of it again.

"Are you mad? You look mad," Quinn said, nervously.

"You really don't want to read my thoughts, Quinn Saint Nicholas."

His face fell. "Oh. I forgot. You don't like seers." Then he burst into another delighted smile. "But you like me anyway. You kissed me on the eyebrow once. And you'll hit the bully with a barstool after he calls me a freak. Or at least you do most of the time. Sometimes Addam grabs the stool first. Once I was very brave and kicked him in the shin myself."

He's seeing probabilities, I told myself.

And because it was such an unlikely thing, I repeated, *He is seeing probabilities.*

A moment ago, I was wondering if Quinn was sane. Now I was thinking he wasn't insane enough.

"Quinn," I said. He'd known about the time I'd kissed Brand. He'd left the car outside the scene of the gargoyle attack. "If you're a seer then . . . Do you know where Addam is? Do you know if he's hurt?"

"No. I don't. I can't—" His eyes went glassy, and he rubbed his nose onto the shoulder of his t-shirt. "I can't see him. But that's what I think I'm supposed to tell you. That's what I remember telling you. I remember that you're standing right here, on this floor, and I tell you that you're asking all the wrong questions. You're too caught up on the *What* and *Who.* The reason my mother can't find Addam is a *Where.*"

Where?

There were places on the island that interfered with everyday magic; places crazy with wild magic and null zones. The Westlands. The prisoner cells in the Convocation building. Anything to do with the Anchorite's court. Now there was a mad fuck.

Quinn's face twisted in concentration. "I can only see a little. I think there are . . . ghosts. And a dried river. And a desert. I definitely see a desert filled with sand and broken glass. Ciaran will tell you more. He's waiting for you at the bar with the ice cubes. Make sure you bring Max."

"Wait, what? *Ciaran?* I have to talk to *Ciaran?* Godsdamnit. And who's Max?"

"But," Quinn said, and looked upset. "I could have sworn you'd meet Max by now. It doesn't make any sense otherwise."

"Do you mean Matthias?"

"Oh. No. He'd rather be called Max. He'll tell you." Quinn smiled, as if it were a perfectly normal thing to clear up.

My head started to hurt. A bar with ice cubes? What kind of bar didn't have ice cubes? And there were no deserts on the island. And *Ciaran?* I didn't want to share a city block with the principality known as Ciaran, let alone a conversation.

I reached out and touched Quinn's shoulder to make him focus. The collar of his t-shirt was frayed, and the tip of my finger brushed his bare skin.

A rush of power arose, so potent that it manifested as a spiraling breeze. I jerked away from Quinn, furious at myself, because nothing ever good came from touching a seer. Damn my eyes if I'd triggered a prophecy. I already had enough of those in my life.

A look of horror spread across Quinn's face. While his hair blew into his eyes, he hid his mouth behind a hand and said, "Oh gods oh gods oh gods, what *is it?* It's like a hole in reality. It will want to touch your *face*, because you are *food* to it, and then everything will start in the middle again, and oh oh oh *oh* there are storms, and they're alive, and there are waves as big as buildings, and we're all a school of fish trapped in a bottle, but none of this happens at once. And . . . and . . . and . . ."

He went still. A bright bead of red appeared under one of his nostrils. It grew like a soap bubble, then burst and ran down his lip. I said, a little dazed, "You have a nosebleed. Quinn. You need to—" I mimed tilting my head back.

There was a handkerchief poking out of his jeans pocket, scored with drops of dried blood. I tugged it out and waved it in front of his eyes. When he didn't respond, I covered my fingers with my shirt sleeve, and stuffed the handkerchief in Quinn's hands.

After a few seconds, Quinn started to blink and shake his head. He touched his bleeding nose with the tissue. He whispered, "I've made a mess again, haven't I?"

"It's okay."

"Are you very mad at me?"

"Why would I be mad?" I asked.

"When I have nosebleeds, sometimes, it means I told people things they don't always want to hear. If Addam were here, he'd take me to another room. He'd stay with me until I was okay. He gets upset when people are angry with me."

"Addam sounds . . . like a good brother."

Quinn's eyes filled with tears. He balled up the handkerchief and cleaned the rest of his face with efficient, practiced swipes.

He said, in a harder voice, "Animals kill their runts. I saw it on a TV show about birds. The baby runt bird gets shoved out of the nest. The runt's brothers and sisters won't waste food on the runt, because most of the time a runt won't survive. I'm a runt. I take food from my brothers. I make them weaker by being alive. But they've never blamed me. *Never.* Especially Addam. I'm so scared." Quinn took a step toward me so that his face was close to mine. His breath smelled like grape chewing gum. "If Addam dies, I won't make it."

"It'll be fine. You'll be fine, Quinn."

"You don't understand. It'll either be with rope, or in a bathtub. I don't know why I don't just steal Ella's sleeping pills. I'm much less scared of swallowing pills than I am of cutting myself. But all those times that Addam dies and leaves me, all I see are ropes and bathtubs. But . . . of all the ways that Addam can be saved, it's *you* on the path."

He blinked. "Oh. Brand is coming now. We won't be able to talk alone anymore. Don't tell him I almost cried."

I turned just in time to see Brand stalk into the rotunda. Ashton Saint Gabriel dogged his footsteps, and Brand didn't look so happy about that.

"We're okay?" Brand asked me.

"We're fine," I said. "Ashton Saint Gabriel. What a coincidence."

The scion had on a tight, shimmery gray shirt that complimented his reflective corneas, and cologne that was presumably trendy given how awful it smelled.

He said, "It's not a coincidence at all. Your visit was unsettling. I thought I'd talk with Addam's brother Christian to see if he knew where Addam was."

Quinn was frowning. When it came to real seers, even I had to admit that it paid to study their nonverbals. I said, "Why don't we see what Addam's brother Quinn has to say about it."

"Of course," Ashton said, and turned an uncomfortable look on the teenager. "Good day, Quinn. It's a surprise to see you without an escort. Does your family know you're alone?"

"Why don't I know why you're here?" Quinn asked bluntly.

Brand blinked and gave me a look. It made me blink, too, but for different reasons. "Quinn, what does that mean?" I asked.

"I'm not sure," he said. "It's hard to figure that part out right now. The attack is too loud. Oh. We're about to be attacked. They have grenades."

"He's a seer!" I said, but Brand had already drawn a knife.

While Ashton stared at us dumbly, I ran a thumb across my white-gold ring. The Fire spell I'd stored flushed through me like a fever. I siphoned the magic into my sabre hilt to bolster the firebolts. "Are you armed?" I said. "Ashton! Are you armed?"

"But there's no one there," he said, gaping at the rotunda exits.

I touched my mother's cameo. A Shield formed a crystalline light-construct over my free hand. I kept it there, rather than draw it across my body. You can't stab grenades; we needed another strategy. "Quinn, are you armed?"

"I have a Shield spell, too," he said. "And I can make a Door."

"Open one," I ordered, just as a grenade skittered into the rotunda.

It slid glassily along the marble floor. I sent my Shield outward, and slammed a small dome over the grenade. It jerked, and the dome lit up like a small white sun.

Two more grenades slid toward us. I threw a Shield over the first. Brand ran forward, grabbed the second, and fast-balled it back into the hallway. It vanished into an unnatural curtain of shadow that had billowed up to hide our attackers.

"We're in a bloody hospital!" I shouted at him. "Bystanders!"

"Don't *even*!" he snapped back, because he was my Companion, and he'd let the entire building fall around our ears as long as he could keep me safe.

A fourth grenade was lobbed. I shot it with a firebolt. It made a crackling sound and caved in on itself like melting plastic.

There was still no sign of our attackers behind the black mist. Ashton was standing there like a trauma victim. We were in a godsdamn hospital with patients in the crossfire.

And then bullets began firing from a second corridor. The first barrage clipped Ashton in the arm and coughed powdered marble at my feet.

"Quinn, the Door!" I shouted, using Fire to superheat the air in front of us. Molten sparks blossomed as the bullets incinerated.

Ashton had fallen when he'd been shot. He staggered to his feet, blood droplets splattering against the ground. They were obscenely red against the snowy white.

The bullets were quickly devouring my Fire's duration. To buy time, I divided my Shield and sent it whistling across the rotunda in two separate directions. Semi-visible blockades rippled into life at the mouths of both corridors, pinged with pinpoint flares as they absorbed gunshots and grenades or whatever the hell else they were throwing at us. The shields would not hold long.

Quinn still hadn't released his Door. I yelled, "Do it!"

"But I can't go!" he cried. "I can't! I'll die! Every time, I die, because I'm not good enough to fight them, and they're always there. And you can't stay here, because if you do you may die, which means Addam dies, and I need you to save him. So take this! I give it freely. Your Will is now its Will."

He'd pulled a small disc from a slot on his decorative belt and dropped it into my hands.

One of my Shields vanished with a static popping sound. A grenade came at us. I took it out with a firebolt, and then filmed the hallway opening with the last dregs of my Fire. The crackling edges of a flaming barrier blackened the white walls.

Looking down, I saw the disc was a sigil. Quinn had given me a sigil.

I thrust it back at him, but he danced sideways and said, "A lot of times, you give it back. Go! Hurry!"

"I can't just leave you here!"

Brand wrapped his fingers in the collar of my shirt and said, "Activate it. You," he said, glaring at Ashton. "Get your fucking act together!"

Ashton stared at his torn shirt and bleeding arm. Numbly, he raised a hand and touched his copper-colored necklace. As the barricade on the south wall unraveled for good. Ashton held up an arm and unleashed a roar of Wind. Bullets met the gale and ricocheted, scoring the wall.

I closed my fingers around Quinn's sigil and released its stored spell.

The Door manifested as a black circle in mid-air, rimmed by a narrow band of yellowing light. A twisting funnel trailed behind the circle.

I'd need to give it a direction, and fast, or risk corrupting the spell—which was a good way to translocate your ass into the middle of a wall. "Quinn, there's got to be a direction that's safe. *Think.*"

Behind me I heard the wail of Ashton's Wind. A stun grenade was deflected the way it came, filling the unnatural black veil with a flash of lightning so powerful that, for a moment, it revealed men in black clothing. The men went down like bowling pins.

Quinn said, "Outside? Through that wall?" He turned, and just as quickly shook his head no. "The roof? No, not the roof, most of the time it collapses on the babies. I can't—it's hard to—" Fresh blood began to trickle over the crusted streaks under his nose. He dropped his gaze. "Steam tunnels! They'll come for you, even down there, but you can run. You need to find Ciaran and let the ghosts eat first and run toward the people on the corner and leave the bug alone. And tell Addam I love him!"

I didn't catch him quick enough.

He dropped to the ground while projecting his Shield into a dark semi-sphere that covered him. Just like that, he was as good as lost to us.

"Finish it!" Brand demanded, pointing at the unanchored Door.

I gave the magic a direction. The funnel end whipped around and sliced into the ground. Brand kicked Ashton in the ass, shoving him through. Then he grabbed my arm and pulled me with him.

The light went crazy.

Gravity went insane.

A slope became a vertical fall.

I smashed into concrete. Dust swirled into my nostrils, heavy with mold and age. Brand was already on his feet. I had time to see that we were in a narrow brick corridor before the portal closed. It took the last shred of light with it, leaving us in unrelieved blackness.

Ashton, who'd landed under my legs, croaked a light cantrip. It manifested as a scotch-colored flame above our heads. Like Quinn had said, we were in steam tunnels, built to house the massive iron pipes that heated the hospital. The pipes had long since rusted with disuse.

"Who," Ashton tried to ask, but his voice shook so bad that he couldn't finish. He cleared his throat and said, louder, "This is outrageous. Who in their wretched mind would attack sons of the Arcanum? It's an act of war."

"Hey!" Brand said, poking Ashton's chest. "Dial it the fuck down. We're not safe yet."

Ashton knocked Brand's hand away. "Touch me again and I'll have you whipped."

My vision went red. I grabbed Ashton's jaw before he could say anything else, and slammed him against the wall.

I said, "You're a scion who took over a minute to release his spells in an ambush. He's a Companion who grabbed a grenade with his bare hands and threw it at our enemies. Who do you think needs to be whipped? Shut up and follow orders. There will be plenty of time later to bleat about your hurt feelings. Brand?"

Brand had pulled a black skull cap from his back pocket and was tugging it over his bangs. "Let's go that way. Ashton, keep the cantrip going. If we get in trouble, stay the fuck out of Rune's line of fire."

We headed in the direction Brand had chosen.

Ashton's face kept working like he had something to say. Finally, in a grudging tone, he said, "Addam has really been kidnapped, hasn't he? Someone tried to kill us because of it."

"Not kill," Brand said. "Not right away, at least. They were using stun grenades and darts."

"Darts?" I said. "Not bullets?" I thought about it, and drew together a few other puzzling details. "I think the grenade fragments were rigged to self-destruct. It was a nonlethal trap."

"Maybe," Brand said. "And maybe they would have rigged an accident, once we were down. Something that explained our deaths. But now they messed up, and they messed up in front of witnesses."

I said, "They've compromised themselves. Which means they're going to get a little more blunt in their attentions. They can't risk letting us leave."

On cue, wind surged around us. It was so cold that at first I thought it was a blast of heat, burning my nostrils and lungs. Worse, it carried the taste of carrion and death magic.

Brand said, "Everyone on your toes. Rune, spells ready."

We turned a corner and entered an untended section of the subbasement. Cobwebs, crusty with grime and desiccated insect corpses, broke against my outstretched sabre hilt. The tunnel opened up into a massive room with stone arcs and a vaulted ceiling. There were channels on the ground for floodwater. Old crates lay in splintered piles.

We were halfway across the room when they attacked.

Two men wide and six men deep. They had skin like spoiled milk, and their seeping, gangrenous flesh was stuffed into black turtlenecks and jeans. They wore holsters filled with knife blades. Some had guns. They made no noise, exchanged no words. Their feet whispered over the cement floor as they ran.

Brand wiped his free hand over his chest harness. A blade slid into it, made of volcanic glass inlaid with strips of coral. A special blade for a special enemy: he'd already figured out what they were. I said, quickly, "Ashton, they're recarnates; they can see in the dark. Don't let the light go out."

"And stay out of our way," Brand added.

I punched the first recarnate, my shoulder shrugging up to cover my face. It ducked and stabbed at me. I blocked its forearm, jabbed, caught it on the chin. Brittle bone crunched.

While it was off-balance, I nailed it with a spinning backfist. It staggered back, nearly falling. I kicked it into another recarnate, then shot a firebolt through its eye.

Three recarnates swarmed past me. Brand engaged two; Ashton paired off with the third. The bulk of them were in front of me.

I ran a thumb over Elena's emerald ring.

A Frost spell shivered loose. I sent a frigid gale howling toward the dead men, freezing the pus on their cheeks and hardening their joints. I spun, punched, kicked. Decayed tooth enamel spit from a broken jaw; a jagged arm bone sliced free from cadaverous flesh. I stopped one recarnate with a close-range firebolt strengthened by the last gasps of my Fire spell. The overpowered firebolt created an entry wound so large that my arm almost slipped through it.

A lull—measured in heartbeats—gave me enough time to look for Brand and Ashton. Brand was surrounded by corpses, and his two knives dripped with black gelatinous blood. Ashton was attacking recarnates with showy, epic blows that completely left him open to ripostes.

In front of me, two recarnates dropped to their knees. A third loomed over them. Some sort of scoped gun rested on its shoulder. I spun to the left as it fired, and the bullets made a pneumatic hissing sound. Darts.

The three of them were lined up, so I pulled the remainder of the Frost magic into my hands and sent it outward in a cone. Dead skin whitened in hideous, flash-frozen patterns.

I jumped them. Fingers snapped off on triggers; a jaw caved in; one of them lost a hand. I focused my willpower on my sabre hilt, and a blade began to boil outward. I lengthened it into a garnet katana and cut the rest of the recarnates to pieces.

It was over in seconds. My last swipe divided a recarnate in half. Its skin, covered in tattoos from its human life, split like old parchment, revealing a mess of organs and black, oily blood.

"Some of them are still moving," Brand said in the silence that followed. There was a gash on his forehead, bleeding freely.

"Put them in a pile," I said.

Brand and I kicked body parts toward the center of the room while Ashton stood around uselessly. The upper half of one of the recarnates stared at me with sentient eyes that burned with rage at its desecration.

Someone had pulled their bodies from the ground and done this to them. Someone had raised them. It was a magic so unpalatable that I couldn't name a single court that still engaged in it.

I sent willpower into my thigh sigil. The magic slid out like the pin of a grenade. My Shatter spell turned the corpses into bits and vapor. Pieces caught fire, making a sound like fat popping on a hot skillet. I felt it when their souls feathered past me, returning to wherever they'd been torn from.

"This is an abomination," I said softly.

"We're not out of this yet," Brand said. "Let's find a door."

"I bet if we—" I started to say, and my stomach spasmed with nausea. I dropped to my knees as Brand's outstretched hand slipped off my shoulder.

Through a daze of illness, I saw a hooded man standing on the other side of the room.

Brand started to speak. Ashton was saying something. Everything was dulled to distortion.

Then a wave of power washed from the man, thick with death magic. The world came loose. Literally loose. A huge bite of reality tore free around the man—slats from the crates, chunks of the cement floor, the dust and dirt that our fight had churned up—and began to spin around him.

He flung it at us.

The nail of a board dug a wire-thin slash across my cheek. A chunk of stone scraped the skin off my knuckles. Another chunk smashed the bones in my left elbow. My arm dropped, useless, as Brand pulled me to the ground and covered me with his body. Through the *V* of Brand's armpit, I saw Ashton dive behind a pillar.

Debris pattered. A moment passed. My ears were ringing so bad that I couldn't hear a thing. Brand was a dead weight on top of me. I felt warm liquid drip off his head and onto my eyebrow. He was alive, but unconscious, which didn't make me any less terrified for him.

I pulled Brand off and crawled between him and our attacker. My sense of peril was a small, living thing; it scraped and clawed up my throat.

The man walked closer to me. I think I shouted. When he was near, I realized that he was dead. He was an *it*, a recarnate. A raised body. Which was not possible. A recarnate could not fling magic around like that.

It wore a plain brown cowl, pulled deep over its head. It reeked of over-ripe citrus and unwashed flesh. Laid over that smell was the crisp and incongruent odor of new linen.

It lifted a bone-white hand. A band of parasites crawled around one knuckle in a parody of a ring.

The creature spoke in my head. It said, in fascination, *What are you?*

Which was just too fucking funny. What was *I*? I tried to cough a reply, but it made no sense. Blood and spit speckled the backs of my hands. My smashed elbow hurt so much that I nearly passed out.

The thing said, *You smell like abasement. You smell delicious.*

It reached for my face.

Suddenly, Brand grabbed my shoulders and threw me backward. He was covered in blood. My panic solidified into strategy. I showed him my fist, the one with a rarely, rarely used sigil. Brand went pale and dove to the ground behind me.

I don't know if the creature read my mind. Maybe it was only its instinct for self-preservation. But just before I was about to unleash Exodus, it stepped backward and held up its arms in a type of surrender.

It said, *I have missed so much, if things such as you walk this world.*

Rotting waves of power washed from it. What I'd thought was surrender became something else, as it pulled the roof down.

There was a parking lot above our heads. An entire section of it— painted asphalt, cars, a cement bench—fell down into the basement.

Dust mushroomed. The creature vanished behind the blockage.

We got the hell out of there ourselves, before a car could drop on our heads.

CUBIC DREAMS

I was sprawled across the floor of my third-floor sanctum, riding out the exhaustion from storing and casting not one, not two, but *three* healing spells. It had taken three healing spells to patch us up after our fight with the recarnates. Since Brand and I needed to be mobile in addition to able-bodied, I'd doctored each spell with the magical equivalent of caffeine, at the cost of occasional junkie twitches.

Sleep would have to wait. Matters had moved beyond our caution. Ashton—who'd bailed on us as soon as he could back at the hospital—would talk, which meant our investigation had moved into the open. The plan now was to dress like slumming scions; trawl the clubbing district for the principality known as Ciaran; and see if Quinn's hints could lead us to Addam Saint Nicholas.

Ciaran wasn't answering the phone number I had for him. According to sources, he had been holding court at a bar called Cubic Dreams in the wee hours of the morning. Brand had headed downstairs to gear up and prep Matthias. Against whatever meager shred of paternal sensibility I may have had, I was listening to Quinn and bringing Matthias along with us.

"I talked with Amy Beige," Brand said from the stairwell.

Amy Beige was a contact who worked in city healthcare. "Quinn," I said.

"I apologized about the wyvern. So she told me he's alive. That's all I know. His Shield went down, but hospital security showed up."

Brand walked barefoot over to his corner of the sanctum and opened the trunk where he kept his special knives. I stared down at the white-gold sigil in my hand—newly minted with a Fire spell—and wondered why I was so grateful that a kid I'd just met was unharmed.

"You kissed me on the eyebrow once. And you'll hit the bully with a barstool after he calls me a freak."

"You okay?" Brand asked.

"This case is getting weird."

"No shit," Brand said. "Were you able to get Lord Tower on the phone?"

I shook my head. "Went to voicemail."

I put the ring back on my finger and made a fist around it. "I can't figure out what happened in that basement, Brand. A recarnate using spells? And leading other recarnates around?"

"Have you figured out what kind of magic it was using?"

"That's just it. There is no *figure out*. It's like asking where the fourth side of a triangle goes. New magical disciplines just don't pop up. I get that the Dead Man was using a variation of death magic. I get that he had no sigils on him, or at least none that I felt. I get that he was using spells, actual spells. But I can't see the line that connects those dots."

"People can cast spells without sigils."

"Sure, after they've spent their lives studying how to do it. Even then, they'd never get the range and strength that the Dead Man did. He should have burned out after that first telekinetic blast, forget what he did with the roof."

Brand said nothing while he lined up knives. He'd broken into his most expensive arsenal. All of them black volcanic glass, inlaid with coral and vulcanized coal. Obsidian, coral, and coal were three substances that had a very adverse effect on the defenses of magical creatures. It had to do with their elemental nature—coral formed in the ocean, obsidian in lava flows, and coal deep in the earth.

Brand muttered, ". . . knew how to fight."

"Who? Ashton?"

"Ashton's a douche. Did you see all those fancy flourishes? He's lucky he didn't get gutted on the first counterattack. No, I meant the recarnates. The fucking zombies. They knew how to fight, and at least one of them knew how to use a firearm." Guns were anathema in our culture. You didn't bring bullets to a magic fight; it bruised our sense of spectacle. You needed a special dispensation to even own guns, like Brand had.

Brand said, "So it begs the fucking question—*whose* bodies were they? There were twelve of them, including the guy you've so cleverly tagged the Dead Man. How can twelve fucking bodies go missing and get raised on an island? And recarnates don't just appear, do they? They get summoned, right? Which leads us right back to the question—who really kidnapped Addam?"

"I hate that we have to bring Matthias with us."

"Don't tell him that. He's going to ask you to slow dance." When Brand saw the look on my face, he rolled his eyes. "What? You didn't know he's crushing?"

"On me? Why me? Maybe he's crushing on you," I said, somewhat panicked.

"I stuck his head in a toilet. You straddled his body and fought off a gargoyle."

"Godsdamnit," I said.

Brand's humor faded. "Do you really think it's a bad idea to bring him with us?"

I shrugged. "I think . . . Quinn is the real thing. I really think he's got the gift. And I don't think he's lying. If he says Matthias has a role to play, then Matthias has a role to play. I just don't like it."

"I'm pretty damn sure that before this is over, we'll have plenty of other things not to like. We haven't even talked about Ciaran yet."

I couldn't hide a flinch. Arcana were bad enough. Take away any sense of rules or purpose, and what you had left was something much like Ciaran.

"Oh, and I pulled our clubbing clothes out of storage," Brand added, and ducked his face before I could fire a look at him. Brand liked us to dress for our environment; but when it came to his capacity to show skin, he was far more Atlantean than I was.

It was going to be a long night.

The first thing I did after looking in the mirror was to grab an ankle-length duster and button it all the way up. The clubbing outfit consisted of a black, mesh shirt and sheer, translucent black slacks. Very translucent.

Matthias came running out of the guest bathroom as soon as he heard my footsteps on the stairwell. He was wearing a short-sleeved bowling shirt with three buttons open, and his pale chest swirled with a fae sheen of dark greens, blues, and purples.

He held up a tube of medicine. "It's heat rub," he said. "I found it in the cabinet. I was thinking that I could put it on your shoulder. You hurt it, right?"

"Um," I said. "Maybe later. We're heading out. See you downstairs."

Brand was waiting by the car, dressed in a leather gladiator harness and tight, gray pants. The first thing he said was, "A coat? A fucking tweed coat?"

"Have we met?" I asked.

"Ladies and gentlemen: Rune, the other white meat."

I glared at him and took off the coat. I opened the door of our beat-up old Saturn and threw the coat in the back seat.

Five minutes later, Half House was locked up, and we headed out. It was drizzling by then, and dagger-shaped clouds drifted past the face of the moon. The moisture stirred up the smell of salt from miles away. I turned out of our cul-de-sac and merged into city traffic.

Matthias said, "Maybe I should borrow a gun?"

"Maybe fucking not," Brand said.

"Just stay close to us," I said to the rearview mirror. "And, hey, should we call you something other than Matthias?"

"Like a code name?" Matthias asked.

"No, Matthias. Not like a code name. I never asked you if you had a nickname."

"Oh," he said. His mouth opened and closed, as if the invitation baffled him. "I suppose . . . I once had a friend. She called me Max. I liked that."

He said it like the idea of a friend was just as unusual as picking his own nickname. It made something inside me twinge—pity or conscience, I'm not sure which.

"Max," I said. "Max it is."

Cubic Dreams operated out of a five-story building called the Otis. Translocated from Washington State, it was once a skid-row hotel frequented by drug addicts and sex offenders. It must have been beautiful in its prime. It still had the bone structure of a great beauty, weighed down by decades of bad choices.

The bar was on the top floor, and it vibrated with music and energy. If I hadn't known in advance it was a human bar, I would have spotted it the moment I walked through the door. The management catered to tourists with glaring displays of parlor tricks. The air was filled with will-o'-the-wisps and mist, and magicked bubbles that burst into showers of random debris. In the minute we lingered at the doorway, I suffered spatters of beach sand, snow, green glitter, and inchworms.

The bartender gave us a glance as we approached, and he swiped his way toward us with a dirty rag. He was very handsome and not wearing a shirt. He said, "Hey, love. What's your poison?"

"Something with an antidote," I joked, lamely, because he was handsome and not wearing a shirt. Brand rolled his eyes, so I cleared my throat and said, "A bottle of diet raspberry ginger ale for me. Spartacus will have bottled water. Matthias? Max?"

"A beer?" Max suggested.

"Nope."

He sighed. "A virgin daiquiri."

The bartender slapped our bottles on the counter. As he turned to make Max's drink, Brand and I watched like hawks. It was never a smart idea to get anything without a seal in a New Atlantis bar.

When I was convinced that he hadn't doctored it, I let the bartender pass it toward Max. To Max's delight, the bartender said, "On the house, cutie. Love the skin."

In due course, I installed Max and Brand at a corner table, then went off to find where Ciaran was holding court.

117

A procession of rooms was packed with drunks and dancers. In one room, I passed a group of pale, young humans giggling in a corner and trying to speak Atlantean, which I'd heard was the new Klingon. In another room, a delirious woman had doused herself with the contents of a glow stick and was doing lopsided pirouettes. Radioactive-looking drops flew from her arms and speckled the crowd.

By the time I had gotten to the last room, I still hadn't spotted Ciaran. I took a stool at a heart-shaped bar and ordered another soda, to see if he'd come to me on his own.

A middle-aged human ignored my scowl and sidled up. He didn't peg me as an Atlantean—and I wasn't sure how I felt about that. In a distressingly short amount of time, I learned that he was on a business trip; that he ran the Atlantean fan club for the Hierophant; and that he liked wine coolers.

He started talking about the days that led up to the Atlantean World War. "It was my Where-Were-You-When moment," he said. "Like how people used to talk about JFK? I still remember the moment I heard. God, everyone was so scared. Vampires and faeries were *real*. There was an *Atlantis*. I was in daycare, and the ladies who ran it were crying and talking in the corner. And then all of our mothers came and grabbed us, and took us home. My mother made us turn off the lights and hide in the basement. Can you believe that? She actually filled old milk containers with water, and made my father stop and buy as much canned food as he could afford. It was crazy. Like I said, it was my Where-Were-You-When moment."

"Was it?" Ciaran whispered in his ear.

The man stiffened.

Ciaran said, "What about this: Where were you when you came to the attention of something far outside your comfort zone?"

The man's thinning hair roots stood out against a now-pale scalp. Ciaran smiled and slid into a chair. He didn't smile *at* the man, he smiled at parts of him: at the pulse on his neck, at his earlobe, at the dent in his lower lip. Ciaran said, "My, but what *dreams* are in your head, Gregory Roberts. They beg a closer look."

The man's hand went slack. His martini glass fell over without breaking. He stumbled away from us.

I said, "You just about done?"

Principalities were freelance powers, occupying a niche somewhere to the left of a sitting Arcana. But unlike Arcana, principalities were not bound by etiquette, rules, or predictable motivations. They were beings of indefinable power, amassed over centuries, who answered only to their own whims.

Ciaran had eyes that rippled with the appearance of light, like sun on moving water. He had dark-blue hair, lips as red as carnage, and an affinity for wild magic. Colors and texture had a nasty habit of changing around him, depending on his mood. I've seen him mess with wallpaper, portraits, and even, on one memorable occasion, a theater usher's eyes.

As long as I'd known—and known of—Ciaran, he had profited in the service of secrets, selling them to those in need. He had a host of innate mind-fuck powers that aided his business, not the least of which was a touch of true seeing.

Saying I was eager to know why Quinn had sent me Ciaran's way was a grim and curious understatement, like wondering if your microwave was hot enough to cook your cat, or whether a pair of scissors was sharp enough to cut off your finger.

"Bars and banks," Ciaran swore, leaning away from the table so that he could get the full effect of my outfit. "Look at you, showing off your bits and bobs."

"That's just what I need to sleep at night, a compliment from you." I tipped my chin at him. "Hello, Ciaran."

"Rune. I was getting bored waiting. Quinn thought you'd be by sooner."

If I hesitated, it wasn't for long. I'd known the Tower too long to be shaken by people trying to startle me with unexpected information. "How is Quinn, then?"

"Just the way you left him. In a coma."

Okay, maybe I had one or two startles left. "A coma? Quinn is in a coma? Brand talked with the hospital earlier. They said he was okay."

"Ah, like magic!" Ciaran said in delight, just as I felt the warm, familiar presence of my Companion at my shoulder. "Speak his name, and he appears! And how are you, better half?"

"Quinn is in a coma?" Brand asked.

"Yes, he is, and I'm sure Rune will fill you in afterward. Shouldn't you be watching that little blond thing you scarpered in with? Be a dear and give us some space."

Brand said, "We're on the Tower's business, Ciaran, and fucking impatient about it. How did you speak to Quinn if he's in a coma?"

The red, lacquered bar top turned coal black under Ciaran's fingers. He smiled tightly at Brand and said, "Careful with your tone, boy."

"*Ciaran*," I said.

"All friends, all friends!" He widened his smile again. "My apologies, Companion. I didn't mean to be rude. But, truly, I've never been very comfortable with threesomes. Someone always gets left out. Why don't you go dance? Go *dance* and be *merry*."

I felt the release of a sigil spell. It was directed at Brand.

I was half a second away from transmuting my wrist-guard when Brand simply turned and walked away.

"You mind-fucked him," I said in a very quiet voice.

"Embarrassingly easy."

"You're scary, Ciaran," I whispered, "but I can be scarier."

"Oh, relax, Lord Sun. It's only a trifle. You have my word—no harm has been done. He'll simply enjoy himself."

I didn't care about his word. My rage was a real and growing thing. There were some lines you couldn't easily cross with me, and mind control was one of them.

Ciaran said, "You *are* in a mood, aren't you?"

"You're going to want to paint between the lines for the rest of this conversation, Ciaran. I'm trying to find Addam Saint Nicholas, and I act on the Tower's authority. Quinn Saint Nicholas sent me to you. Tell me what I need to do my job, and the Tower will compensate you."

Ciaran waited a good ten seconds. Then he raised a hand for the bartender—a short Atlantean with Japanese mythology in her genetic cupboard—and said, "Parched."

Since he'd blinked first, I humored him while he ordered absinthe. It was delivered in a tulip-shaped glass with a small tray of accoutrements. Ciaran separated out the slotted spoon, the chipped china saucer holding a large sugar cube, and a tiny carafe of ice water. The smell of anise clogged my nostrils.

"Addam Saint Nicholas," Ciaran finally said. "I know him through Quinn. Quinn and I share certain gifts. I'm aware of your prejudices toward those of us who see, but even so, you must admit Quinn's ability."

"I do."

"He's the rarest type of seer. He can see probabilities. Now, I would hesitate to call his talent *unreliable*, but it *would* be apt to say that he sees so much that he's not always able to make out the forest through the trees. I tell you this by way of disclaimer so that you don't accuse me of riddles."

"Ciaran, how did you talk to Quinn? How long has he been in a coma?"

"Since you left him. His Shield went down and the bad guys used concussion grenades. He has not regained consciousness. Quinn's not exactly *alarmed* by his condition. He says, and I quote, that *most of the time* he wakes up, and *sometimes* there's even cake."

"How did you talk to him?" I growled.

Ciaran sucked absinthe off his thumb. "Dream-walking."

"You dream-walk."

"I have many hidden depths, little Arcana. Quinn, who is in a coma, reached out to me through the dream world. He and I had quite the chat, and then we put our heads together to see if we could get a better *impression* of where Addam is being kept."

"Quinn said Addam was in a desert. Something about sand and broken glass? A dried-up river?"

"Put your thinking cap on," Ciaran said. "I'll even spot you more clues. Addam is within city limits, but he's not on Nantucket soil. He is not in a pocket dimension or a phase."

"Not on Nantucket soil, but in the city?" If he hadn't mentioned pocket dimensions, it would have been my first guess. "Not on Nantucket soil, like, *legally*? Like embassy grounds?"

"Warmer. And Quinn tends to speak in metaphor. He didn't *say* Addam was in a desert."

I remembered something else. Quinn had said: *You're too caught up on the* What *and* Who. *The reason my mother can't find Addam is a* Where.

A metaphor.

Sand and broken glass.

"An hourglass," I said. "A broken hourglass. Farstryke Castle. Gods-damnit, they're keeping him in Farstryke Castle."

Ciaran clapped without making a sound.

I said, "Wonderful. Just great. I need to find Brand. I'll talk to Lord Tower about your compensation. And please answer your bloody phone if I call."

Ciaran waited until I'd gotten out of my chair before he added, "Oh, and if Brand comes with you, he dies."

I stopped.

I turned my head.

Ciaran said, with petty relish, "Every time. Quinn says that if Brand comes with you, he dies every time."

My heart began skipping beats. I had accepted Quinn's gift as real, and I didn't think Ciaran was lying, which meant that this was real—it was real, it was real, and the *what-ifs* began to tear great, meaty strips out of my brain. *What if I'd figured out where Addam was on my own? What if I'd never had to meet Quinn or speak to Ciaran, and never heard the warning? What if I'd taken Brand? What if I'd lost him?*

The shock began to prickle and itch, then it woke into rage.

My Atlantean Aspect burst to life. Whatever was in my eyes was nothing as simple as a glow, though. A light flared, as bright as burning magnesium. Ciaran's pupils dilated, and he threw up his hands. The people closest, the people who could see whatever had become of my face, backed away in a dramatic spill of drinks and chairs.

"Tell me," I whispered, and the words carried like rifle shot.

Ciaran squeezed his eyes shut and made an open-handed gesture of compliance. He said, only a little shakily, "Quinn told me to pass along the warning. I'm not sure what rosy future Quinn prefers to see, but in the one he likes best, you and Brand are dear to him. He said that if Brand accompanies you into the castle, he will not leave it alive. Quinn was very clear about the parameters of his seeing: Brand can't come into the castle with you."

The light died. My Aspect fled.

I turned and left.

I stood in the hallway for a long time.

There was a bulletin board with personal adverts for used futons, roommates, and anonymous sex.

There was a lithe, brown-skinned fae with corn silk for hair, waiting outside a closed bathroom door.

A human rocked back and forth on the ground. He was dressed in an expensive suit and had shallow cuts crisscrossing the tops of his bare feet.

I stood in the hallway for a long time, watching everything and nothing, until I remembered how to breathe again.

Max was slumped at a corner table. Brand wasn't with him. His slack-jawed attention was on Cubic Dream's dance floor. I'd started to look that way myself when he whispered, "Brand's dancing."

The dance floor was tiny, but, even so, a space had formed around my Companion.

Man and woman alike watched him move. He was aware of neither. His eyes were closed in something not unlike rapture, as his head swung in and out of rays of colored gel lights. He danced like he was under attack—like the world was coming at him from all sides.

Tears bit the back of my eyes. There was a word for a death prophecy.

It was called a Grim Omen. Brand was going to be furious as hell, but there was no way he was setting foot near Farstryke Castle.

Next to me, Max noisily sucked up the last of his daiquiri. He propped his chin on top of the straw, and the straw crumpled. His face smacked the table. He started to giggle.

"Matthias?" I said. "Max?"

Out of the corner of my eye I saw Brand swing to a stop and look toward us.

Max said, mock-serious, "Rune?"

I pulled his glass toward me and sniffed the dregs. "Max, have you taken anything?"

"You think I stole from you?" he demanded in outrage.

"No. Have you taken anything. Tonight. Are you bloody smashed?"

"No, I am not! I am perfectly sober. Don't be such a . . . a . . . a salty cucumber." He frowned. "I have no idea what that means." He burst into laughter.

Brand came back to the table. He gave me an uncertain look and said, "I was dancing."

"Ciaran mind-fucked you."

Brand's lips went straight, the corners pressed tight. Then he blinked and looked closer at me. "What's wrong?"

I wasn't ready to talk about the Grim Omen. And something was wrong with Max. "Look at him. Is he high?"

Brand stopped looking suspiciously at me long enough to look suspiciously at Max. "Oy! Matthias! Did you take anything?"

"Why am I suddenly a *thief*?" Max demanded.

Brand made a growling sound and grabbed the glass that I was holding. He sniffed it. He didn't smell anything that flagged his interest either.

Then his face went blank, the way it did that when he was mentally rifling through everything he'd seen and heard in an attempt to imagine the worst possible scenario. I heard him say, "Ice cubes."

"Ice cubes?"

"Oh fuck *me*. 'Cubic Dreams.' Clever—*fucking* clever." He looked over his shoulder toward the bar and said, "I need to have a word with that bartender."

Since he had his hands on his knives, I said, "Let's all go."

I gripped Max's t-shirt in a fist and lifted him upright. He squawked in alarm when the chair fell out from under him. The three of us moved to the bar. I watched the bartender's face as we approached, and looked for any sign of smugness or contempt.

"What did you give him?" I demanded.

"Give who? Cutie?" the bartender smiled nervously at Max, who grinned sloppily back. "Just the standard kick. He'll be fine. I thought you knew. That's what we do here."

"Define *standard kick*," I said.

"A little something-something. He'll laugh a lot, see some pretty colors, stuff like that. That's it. I promise."

"I'm a cutie," Matthias said.

The bartender smiled again, more confident. "Yes, you are. But. Um. I need to get back to work."

"Okay," Brand said. He reached out, slipped his fingers behind the bartender's neck, and slammed his head to the marble countertop. There was a crack, and I don't think it was cartilage. Blood from a split lip smeared an imperfect red circle as Brand put a hand on the back of the squirming man's head and pressed down hard.

Brand said, "You're lying."

"*I'm not!*"

Brand bent low and whispered in the bartender's ear for what felt like a very long time. The man's face went gray. He said, "Just a hallucinogen, that's it, I swear. I swear! He's a fucking Lovers! Did you know that? *Did you know that?* You're lucky I didn't reach for the rat poison!" Bubbles of blood popped from his nostrils. "We've got cameras! If you try to hurt me in here, you'll get into trouble!"

Now I bent low.

I made the young man strain to hear me over the music as I said,

"Where the hell do you think you are? This is New Atlantis, and that boy is under my protection. Harm to him must go through me. Break that law, and you become my legitimate prey."

"They're uppers! I only gave him some uppers! He'll just act goofy, that's all—I was just trying to, I was only—"

Brand pressed down harder. "Maybe he'll make a fool of himself. Maybe he'll get in the wrong stranger's car. Maybe he'll get in his own car and try to drive. Maybe he'll stumble across the path of someone who doesn't like goofy. Maybe you'll be waiting outside for him after closing."

"But he's one of *them*! Do you know what the Lovers did? Why they got their asses destroyed?" The bartender's eyes rolled from Brand to me. "*He was one of them!* I saw him! I went to some of the Lovers' *parties*." The word was steeped in spittle. "I went to them with my boyfriend, when he was alive, before they *took* him. This *boy* you're with—this *thing* you're protecting—he was always with his uncle, wearing a stupid dog collar, sitting in the corner while his uncle did *things* to the humans. He's *one of them*! Do you want to know what my boyfriend looked like by the time the Heart Throne was done? What they did to Joey's face? To his health? I—"

"Let him go," Max said softly. "This isn't fun."

He drifted away toward the door.

"Go with him," Brand said to me.

I looked at Brand's rigid arm and the bartender's pinned head.

Brand said, "I won't kill him. Go with Matthias, Rune."

That'd have to be good enough. I hurried after Max. He was lingering by the front door, picking at a loose chip of paint that crusted a light switch.

"Are you okay?" I asked.

"I thought I saw a saber-toothed tiger. But it was just a mophead."

"That'll happen," I said, gently.

"Maybe if we wait around long enough, it'll turn back into a tiger. I would like to see that. We could make it a pet! Maybe we should . . ."

He continued to chatter, completely unaware of the tears streaming down his face.

"Oh, Max," I said, "Come on. Let's get you home."

HALF HOUSE INTERLUDE

"Motherfucking horsefire shit!" Brand said. He hit the punching bag in the corner of the third-floor sanctum again. He had been hitting it ever since I told him about the Grim Omen, and that he'd need to stay behind.

"Getting shirty with me won't help. It wasn't my prophecy."

"Are you smiling? Is that a smile?"

Actually, it sort of was. I felt nearly stupid with relief. I knew the stages of Brand's anger better than my own. He was swearing a lot, which was good. It's when he stopped swearing that I worried.

Brand said, "If that kid turns out to be the bad guy, I will lose my shit on him."

I blinked. "Quinn? You think Quinn might be the bad guy?"

"I think everyone might be a bad guy. And look at the facts—if Quinn is behind all of this, then he's found a way to separate us. He also fell into a convenient coma just before the Dead Man attacked us. I'll have to go and visit his room with some flowers, or maybe an alarm clock taped to the end of a fucking baseball bat."

"Quinn as mastermind. Let's think about that."

"Don't fucking sass me," Brand said. He rubbed his knuckles and turned away from the punching bag. "I hate this, Rune. I'm your Companion. It's my job to go through the door first. Just because scary shit is waiting on the other side of the door shouldn't change that—if anything, it makes it *more* important that I do my job."

"Scary shit, I trust you with. A Grim Omen? No. *No*," I said, loudly, when he looked like he might raise one last objection. "You will not step through that door, because if you do, I might as well follow. You're not saving me from *anything* by dying."

"I'm not saving you from anything *period*," he said, upset. "You went after Lady Lovers without me. I left you alone right before the gargoyle attacked. I let Ciaran mind-fuck me. And now there's Matthias. Max."

"What about Max?"

Brand gave me a narrow look. "His uncle. Not a good guy?"

Shit. "I didn't want to say anything until I knew more."

"Yeah?"

I felt the oncoming shout vibrate through our bond.

"That is such *bullshit*," he yelled. "You were just avoiding the topic. How am I supposed to protect you—or him—when you keep details like this from me? How do I win here, Rune?"

"There's been a lot going on," I said, a little surprised, or maybe hurt. "There wasn't any time to talk. I only figured this out today, at the beach."

"You should have made time. He got dosed, Rune. That's the least fucking bit of nastiness that could have happened. If Max has a past, I need to know about it, or the next thing around the corner isn't going to be mopheads and magic carpet rides. Get your head out of your ass."

"You said that last part out loud," I told him in a rising voice. "Are you really mad at me?"

He started to say that, yes, he was really mad at me. Then his mouth shut so hard his teeth clicked. He had one of his Zen moments, where all of the volatile emotion got swept into pale wrinkles around his eyes.

"I'm upset," he said. "And I'm taking it out on you. That's pretty fucking crappy of me. I know . . . I know I can't go with you. I know. But . . ." He wiped his hands over his face. "At least tell me you have a plan. At least tell me you're taking some kind of backup."

"I have a couple thoughts."

"Then how 'bout we plan them tomorrow? You're tired. And you've been using your sabre too much. Why don't we just wait? Let's get the Tower on the phone. Let's get backup from him. Let's wait until tomorrow evening. You don't have to do this in the morning."

Dusk or dawn—those were my two options. They were very particular times of day, which would offer some extra, meager protection against the dangers of Farstryke. Problem was, I didn't think Addam could wait until dusk.

"You trust my instincts," I began.

"Rune . . ."

"You trust them, right? My gut is saying we need to go after Addam now."

Brand walked over to the draped windows. He parted the cloth with the tip of a calloused finger and looked out. There was only streetlight on the other side; dawn was still a few hours off. I didn't have much time to restock my sigils. I certainly didn't have time to sleep, or storm over to the Tower's penthouse and ask why he wasn't answering his damn phone.

When Brand turned back to face me, he looked resigned.

I went over, reached up, put my palms on either side of his face. It wasn't exactly a touch or a sign of affection—it was just shy a headlock.

I said, "Promise, no matter what happens, that you won't go in after me. *You promise me.*"

Even in shadow, he had the bluest eyes in the world.

Then he closed them against me and said, miserably, "I promise."

FARSTRYKE CASTLE

Farstryke Castle was the court of the long-dead Arcana who'd served centuries ago as the archetype for Time. It had been called, they say, the Hourglass Throne, and had been disbanded for crimes against humanity.

The castle had been one of the few Atlantean structures that could be translocated to Nantucket without legal concerns or court politics. The lands had been in a cultural trust, collectively owned.

Turned out, though, the translocation of Atlantean property was a bad idea. No one knew why. Within weeks of its translocation, it was a train wreck of hauntings. Dark spirits swarmed it like insects drawn to a rotting leg wound. Even on my best day, infiltrating it would be a challenge.

The best time for an extraction on haunted ground was dawn or twilight. Neither morning nor night, the minutes around sunset and sunrise had a way of unbalancing monsters both nocturnal and diurnal.

It wasn't a big advantage, but it was an advantage, and I'd take any I could get.

Ciaran gave me a red-lipped smile as I climbed into his front seat.

"I'm not sure what I love more," he said. "That you called me for help, or that you asked that we *carpool*."

"You don't need to love anything. You're getting paid. Are we going to be professional about this?"

"All friends," he said cheerily. "Professional it is."

Brand didn't even let us pull away from Half House's curb before he established a phone line. I spent the ride listening as he plowed through last-second research on Farstryke and its neighborhood. He'd accessed traffic cams, tracked crime reports in a four-block radius, even studied Doppler and multiparameter radar reports to see if there was any localized weather freakiness.

I woke up to Brand swearing loudly in my ear and accusing me of snoring. I said, "We're about to go into a tunnel. Are you there? Brand?"

"Fucking try me," he said. "Go ahead."

I slid my finger off the end button. I didn't need a Companion bond to feel his strum of tension.

I said, "I'll be okay. You know that, right?"

"How do I know that? We should have called the Tower, not hired backup off the island of misfit fucking toys."

"I have very good hearing," Ciaran said.

I sighed. "We're almost there, Brand. I've got to go, okay? Make sure Max eats all his vegetables. Talk to you soon."

I hung up, closed my eyes, and rested my forehead against the window. Its predawn chill revived me a little. When I opened my eyes, Ciaran was staring at me from across the seat.

"Your Companion mothers you," he said.

"Keep teasing him," I suggested. "You'll find out just what a mother he is. Do we need to go over the plan again?"

"You were quite thorough over the phone. Don't worry, Sun. Easy-peasy. Quinn will have his brother back in no time."

The car decelerated. The left front tire bumped over a curb. I got out and saw that we were at the mouth of a narrow driveway lined with beech trees. It was the only part of the property not surrounded by a low, gray wall covered in shining, coral wards.

A distant, crenellated roofline was outlined against a purpling sky. The tree-lined driveway cut through a ruined garden filled with terraced walkways. All of the garden's greenery was gone, choked under the advance of gnarled, native shrubbery, and trees spotted in fungal matter. I moved forward until the toes of my shoes were flush with a lip of dead grass.

I'd reluctantly traded in my boots for black leather sneakers that, while less substantial, had been imbued with wards very effective in graveyard-type settings. Any edge was welcome. I didn't have much hope for a lengthy element of surprise. Once we knew for sure the surprise was lost, our best tactic would be to become loud and ungrateful houseguests.

"Okay," I said. "So you know the plan. When I release the spell, we move. We'll have just under five minutes before the spell fails. When it does, I'd like to be off the lawn and in the building. If something comes at us, square up. If you hear me say 'Dead Man,' possibly accompanied by emphatic finger-pointing, it means that our plan is fucked. Scatter and start blowing stuff up. Be on the alert for when it rips up the floor and throws it at you."

I knelt down and touched the earth while releasing a sigil spell. For a second I couldn't tell where my fingers ended and the rock began, and then the spell stabilized. That was my backup plan. Next, I slipped a thumb under the top of my sock. My fingertip slid across the gold ankle chain. Its spell sprang free, a buoyant rush of energy.

Getting into a place like Farstryke isn't just about moving from point A to point B. You needed to think spatially. The garden grounds would attract earth and nature spirits that leaned toward the physical. At the turn of day, I'd hoped most of the garden ghouls would be bedding down, and most of the revenants and grave wisps would be barely stirring from their corrupted sleep. The best way to keep everything off our backs was to drop from their radar entirely.

"Like this," I told Ciaran.

I took a step into the air, tugged the levitation spell underneath me, and climbed an invisible step. Just like that, I was floating.

I shuffled to the left and right, showing off a healthy six inches between me and the sidewalk. I expanded the diameter of the spell until it included Ciaran. He mimicked my movements with the addition of a small pirouette, and hovered next to me. A Flight spell would have been faster, but Levitation was quickly stored and easy to spread among two people—and I'd had only a few hours to prepare.

I floated over Farstryke's soil.

My presence registered—I'm sure of it. The lawn seemed to flex, and the topiary rattled leafless, spear-like branches. But nothing attacked. No gleaming eyes blinked awake in the bushes. No fingers shoved up through the dirt. We headed across the garden toward a ruined, domed aviary, which I'd picked as our entry point.

At the bottom of the slope, we had to backtrack. A narrow moat there had thickened into compost and ooze. I didn't trust my spell over it, so we maneuvered onto the bleached planks of a walking bridge. We were on the other side, with the aviary maybe fifty yards away, when our luck ditched us. Ciaran stepped in a null thread.

Null threads are the tricky bastard children of null zones: tiny whip-lashes of void-magic that doused spells like cold water. Ciaran hit it and dropped onto the lawn.

There was no grace period. The haunted land began to shake and scratch beneath us.

"Ahead!" I warned, jumping onto the ground myself.

A ghoul had slinked from a briar thicket, curling its unnaturally lithe body around the bottom of a cracked birdbath. Its face, streaked with slick stripes of mud, resembled nothing so much as a beaten child. It gave us a chillingly sweet smile and ducked its chin against its shoulder in a parody of shyness. There were gray bits of gristle caught between its front teeth.

"Hit it hard, move fast—there'll be more!" I said, shaking my sabre loose. It scraped over my knuckles and hardened into hilt form. I cauterized the air between us with a firebolt. The ghoul shrieked and retreated.

Four more ghouls appeared, sniffing the air with the faces of mutilated adolescents. Two had been submerged in the foul brook—one came out of the briars—and a fourth rose from an unseen hole in the ground. Fuck us if we were standing on a nest node, because ghouls bred like rabbits, and we would be swarmed in minutes.

I curled a finger around my mother's cameo. The stored Shield released. I touched my white-gold ring and released Fire.

I was too tired to draw on my sabre for a salvo; so I instead extended the sabre hilt into a molten long sword, with a basket hilt that curled protectively over my knuckles. In my free hand, I drew on Fire, and wove a ball of crimson flame. I launched it at the two ghouls wading through the sludge. The surface of the moat caught fire—literally exploded into a sheet of tar-smoke flames. The ghouls wailed and swam away, their scabrous scalps trailing slipstreams of burning hair.

Ciaran extended his arm toward the ghoul in the briar patch. Magic swarmed his hand, potent enough to make his fingernails shine with friction. The ghoul began to leak—or sweat, or maybe bleed—rivulets of thick, sap-like liquid. The liquid began to glow. It flared into flame. Not just a powerful attack, but a tactical one—because the brittle nettles around the ghoul popped and sparked and began burning as well. The ghoul abandoned its ruined cover and raced for the hole in the ground.

I'd hoped for all of them to flee in the face of an actual threat this close to dawn, but the one that had crawled out of the hole stood its ground as its cousins slithered past it. It stared at us, arms akimbo, claws as sharp as casket splinters.

Then it froze, turned tail, and dove out of sight.

Instinct was already a syllable in my mouth. *"Incoming!"* I shouted.

The Dead Man stepped from behind a seven-foot cairn.

The full impact of the creature's arrival shut down my senses like a lungful of crematorium smoke. It was close, too close, and I could smell that awful combination of clean linen and moldering flesh. Its hood was pushed farther back than I'd yet seen, and the points of its face—the tip of the nose and chin, the top curve of its forehead—were the color of bruised fruit.

It held out its arms. I ran like hell. The world rumbled, and a great slab of reality severed loose with a thunderous crack. Tendrils of dead ivy, part of a hedge, and clipped bites of the cairn's stacked boulders began spinning around the Dead Man in a sharp, frantic sphere.

Since we'd made moving targets of ourselves, it had to pick—and

Ciaran was closest. The Dead Man launched the debris at him. Ciaran took a hunk of stone in the head and lost his legs. He skidded face-first down a gravelly embankment, out of sight.

I shot the Dead Man in the head with my sabre. Or I tried to—its head dodged the blast like a rearing snake.

It held out an arm. Ragged strips of crabgrass withered beneath it, tiny organic deaths that released flickers of black lightning that were drawn into the Dead Man's hands. I dove behind a hedge as the Dead Man flung the lightning at me. The hedge caught fire. A pall of smoke rose between us. I dodged to the edge of visibility.

When I could see again, I focused on the stacked cairn, on the thin spaces between the stones. I super-heated the air with Fire in a ferocious second. The loose rocks exploded outward, making the Dead Man stagger.

Then it spoke. "The levitation spell was a shrewd gambit."

I'd never heard of a recarnate speaking out loud. The words were rasping, slick on the *S*s, a wet vibration made from air forced through putrefied lungs.

The world flickered—a light switch turned off and on nearly too quick for the mind to follow. The Dead Man was now standing just in front of me. The lawn between where it had stood and us was brown and smoking.

I poured power into my Shield. Magic slid over my skin in a burst of fractal light. I swung my sabre blade at the Dead Man.

It raised its hand. Something whipped across me. I felt my Shield and garnet blade dissolve. A thin line of blisters rose along the back of the Dead Man's mottled hand, splitting and coating its fingers with pus, as if it had grabbed a hold of barbed wire.

The null thread. It had *grabbed* and *moved* a *null thread* over me. "Oh, screw this," I whispered. I flung myself down the tiered slope.

It was a practiced fall—head turned away to protect nose, shallow breathing, bent ankles and knees and hips. On level ground, I got up and ran. I didn't know how far the Dead Man could tug a null thread—which

K. D. EDWARDS

was sort of like asking oneself something as wholly fucking implausible as how far Santa's reindeer could fly before needing a nap. None of this should be happening. Only it had. Which meant I had to keep running, because I couldn't afford to lose any more sigil spells to null magic.

Cracked, leathery vines shot out of the ground and wrapped around my ankles. I cut them apart with a shot of sabre fire. A wall of thorny shrubs broke apart and unspooled toward me. I jumped over one thorny ribbon and fired at two more.

On the slope, the Dead Man rotated after me like a skater on ice, lifting both its arms.

The world began to shake. I had nowhere to duck. My Shield was gone; the Levitation was gone; my Fire was gone. I don't know where I got the idea, but I suddenly stopped moving and called, *"Must we be enemies as well?"*

It was an old, old greeting from the days of polite combat. It offered a chance of parlay between two puppet forces driven by the commands of corrupt generals.

The Dead Man hesitated. The rumbling faded.

"My name," the Dead Man said, "is Rurik. And yes, I must suffer the fools who summoned me. If you try to pass, I will kill you."

Recarnates don't use names. Which was just so many more napping reindeers. I asked, stalling for time, "Who summoned you?"

Rurik didn't answer.

I said, "Who the hell is mad enough at Addam Saint Nicholas, not to mention strong or nuts enough, to summon someone like you?"

"A summoning is a spell. A spell is words backed with willpower. Any willful, ignorant tongue may form the right words." Rurik paused. "It does not mean they will *hold* me."

"Can you tell me this? Is Addam alive? Am I wasting my time here?"

"If you try to pass, I will have to kill you. I do not—"

"Want to hurt me, yes, that's awesome. This might sound crazy, but I'm thinking we might actually have a common interest."

He laughed. Laughter from dead lungs was an awful sound. "I only said, sweet thing, that I do not want you *dead*."

He lifted an arm and brought his fingers into a fist. A steel vice crushed down on my throat. I collapsed to my knees and dug fingertips under my jawbone, but there was nothing to pry loose.

"Stay with me," Rurik said, walking towards me, pleasure drenching the sibilants. "Play with me. You are *filled* with games and nightmares."

I tried to marshal my scrambling willpower. I couldn't touch my sigils; I didn't have the concentration to access their remaining spells. My sabre began a transformation into a short dagger blade. Rurik clenched his fist again, and I convulsed. The sabre slipped through my fingers, and the blade crumbled out of existence in a flurry of fireflies. I let my muscles go slack so that I'd fall on top of the hilt. Rurik grabbed the collar of my shirt and pulled me up to him.

His cowl slipped back, and I got my first real look at his face.

He was a recarnate, or at least he'd begun as one, but he'd somehow reversed the rot. The reconstruction was imprecise. One eyeball had grown too big and bulged out of its socket; one nostril ended in folds of loose skin; one ear dripped wax that had hardened against his neck like the side of a candle.

He whispered, "I will lick your memories from my fingers."

"Not on the first date, dearie," Ciaran said. He stood about twenty feet away, his face a hash mark of scores and scrapes.

Then he threw, of all things, a rock. The aim was perfect. Rurik's head snapped backward and forward like he was nodding. He didn't go down, but he staggered, and my paralysis vanished in a cramp of pins and needles.

I grabbed my sabre and slammed the hilt into Rurik's ribs, then drew heavily on my willpower and generated a bolt of fire as thick as my wrist. The bolt tore through him and burst out the other side. I scrambled away as chunks of flesh fell from the chest wound, a nauseating mix of char and wriggling larval matter.

"And so," Rurik hissed. *"Enemies."*

He flicked a hand. Something flew out of a nearby bush and scratched at my face. I smelled death before I saw it: the corpses of hornets, squirming with necromantic energy. A stinger dragged a gash under my eye, another across my forehead.

I ran a thumb over the etched surface of Quinn's platinum disc and released its stored magic.

Light moved through me like spring water, clear and pure. It spilled out my fingers and eyes and nostrils, radiated from me like a child's drawing of a spiky sun. The hornets gave a high-pitched hiss and burst into flame. Rurik raised his arm in front of his face and staggered back.

It was called Bless-fire, a powerful and difficult magic, a holy magic. It was a spell to cower the undead. I'd sacrificed any hope of sleeping last night in order to store it.

Rurik held out his arms. Weeds browned underneath him; black lightning sang upward into his fists. He began to gesture at me.

Filaments of lightning arced from Ciaran's hands and turned Rurik's linen into black flakes. Ciaran drew on more power, scoring Rurik's dead flesh with glowing, molten marks. I let the Bless-fire loose in an almighty flood. It burst outward, turning everything into a silhouette. Flickers of orange light threaded through it—my Aspect rising, answering the call of Bless-fire with the purifying force of the Sun.

With a lingering screech, Rurik vanished.

I sagged to both knees.

I thought, *Down is good.* Lying down would be better. Lying down several city blocks away would be ideal.

But we'd bought ourselves a window, that's it. A window of opportunity. Plus, I was my father's son, and I did not kneel between battles.

I grunted to my feet and capped the Bless-fire that still burned through my skin. Bless-fire was a precious spell; I couldn't afford to expend any more of it than was necessary. I had no confidence that we'd seriously injured this Rurik. He'd been freakishly powerful. He had *moved* a *null thread*, which was the magical equivalent of picking up a river and slinging it over your shoulder.

Rurik. He had a name. I'd even started thinking about it as *he*. I'd never heard of a recarnate that had developed a personality, or at least anything more than the echo of its mortal life. I'd never heard of a recarnate that could channel magic like a living spell-caster. I'd never known a recarnate to heal its own decomposition.

None of that mattered now, though. Addam Saint Nicholas was still inside the castle.

Farstryke's aviary would have been beautiful in its prime: a two-story glass atrium designed to capture the east and west light. I used a cantrip to dislodge the few remaining teeth of glass that clung to one of the window panes.

"We can go through here," I said.

"The inside of the building will likely disrupt cell service," Ciaran said hesitantly.

"You've got someone you need to call?" I asked.

"You do. You must call Lord Tower and tell him about that creature. You must tell Lord Tower what it did."

"You know something," I said.

"Suspicions."

"Of?" I said when he didn't elaborate.

"Just call Lord Tower, Rune. He'll want to know." Ciaran turned and climbed through the window frame.

"Well, that's not like foreshadowing *at all*," I said after him. I'd never seen Ciaran so serious, which, in itself, was unnerving.

I pulled out my cell phone. I didn't have a signal out here, so I put the phone away and climbed after Ciaran.

Morning had enough trouble breaking through the cloud cover outside. It had no effect whatsoever on the rooms inside. I whispered a light cantrip, which pushed at the gloom, revealing broken statuary and long-dead trees. I sent the bauble dancing around the walls, illuminating the room's exits.

"Hey, Ciaran," I said. "Remember back when we were talking about your suspicions?"

Ciaran tutted me. He ran a finger along the grime of a worn angel.

"Any reason you're being so closed-mouth about this?" I asked.

"I don't want to be an alarmist. It's unnecessarily flamboyant."

"You turn things you touch into shades of pastel and fluorescence."

He gave me a pointed look. "Do we have time for this? When we spoke last night, you seemed to think finding Quinn's brother was urgent."

I blew a sigh out of my pressed lips, and dropped the matter.

Brand had quizzed me on blueprints he'd drawn up, based on a hurried internet search. The aviary abutted a music room and a conservatory, which opened to a great hall. We headed toward the conservatory.

As I stepped further into the building, the castle's *otherness* went from an itch to a vibration. I could feel the tense presence of spirits. From experience, I knew they'd be excited by my strong, fresh heartbeat. I let a little Bless-fire trickle from my hands. Its illumination was wildly disproportionate; shadows tripped over each other as they receded into corners and cracks.

The castle's restless energy retreated.

The conservatory was filled with big, clunky furniture covered in rotting sheets. One entire wall was a mural—stone inlaid with inscriptions, speckled with what looked like ash. When I wiped a finger across it, the flakes came away fine and greasy.

"How do you plan to find Addam?" Ciaran asked.

"Magic," I said. I focused on my thigh sigil. The spell released after a second's hitch. A ball of energy formed above my head, not unlike a light cantrip.

At my command, the ball broke apart and became a shining wind. It flooded away from me, through walls and floors, through doors and ceilings. It ignored ghosts and boggarts and paused only a moment above the scratching of rodents and insects. The spell finally swarmed over a large living creature—the only living creature inside the building. If it was Addam, then he was below me.

"This way." I headed toward the closed doorway on the other side of the conservatory.

My Bless-fire stuttered, then resumed its glow. It didn't have much duration left. It'd be worrisome to be stuck in the basement without it. The cellars of Atlantean castles were rarely used to store Christmas ornaments and lawn-care tools.

Ciaran hit me in the shoulder and shouted, "You are only my *face and voice*, not my *Will*, and I will have you remember that!"

"What the hell? Get off!" I shouted back at him, shoving him away.

He went still. He stared hard at the ground. His jaw muscle began to twitch.

"What's with the crazy?" I demanded.

"Something just happened. I was . . . I can't explain. I'm fine now."

We were in a haunted castle. I had no idea what to expect. Best advice? Walk softly and carry a flaming stick. I crackled my sabre into a burning, straight-edged scimitar.

"If anything comes at us, hit it hard," I said. "Shield your mind as much as you can."

I slashed an X on the closed conservatory door. The worm-eaten wood pattered to the ground. We stepped through the opening and into the great hall.

"Brand showed me all the routes from the first floor. This is the main hall—and basement access is somewhere over there." I pointed across a ruined landscape of wooded banquet tables and broken chairs. The doorway wasn't apparent at first until I spied the banner. It trembled as a faint breeze sucked at it.

Ciaran said, raw and loud, "She fooled us all, like Russian dolls inside Russian dolls inside Russian dolls. The canny bitch!"

"Ciaran, *shield your mind*!" I shouted.

He shook his head. One delusion slipped off, and another slipped in, turning his anger into grief. "Their bodies have been lost to the waves," he said. "There is no more cause for hope."

And because the universe is all about multitasking, the tapestry, at that moment, was ripped aside and four recarnates rushed out, carrying weapons. More guns in a magic fight.

"Ciaran, get behind me—you're compromised," I ordered.

"But . . . the Westlands is advancing on us, we must prepare."

"Get behind me!" I shouted. I let out the Bless-fire in a perfect ring. Table fragments skittered and smoldered under its energy.

I thought at first the recarnate soldiers were wary of the magic, but as they spread out around me in a semicircle, their most wary looks were sent upward.

It made sense when a rush of darkness ruffled my hair, leaving behind traces of frost.

I looked up and saw wraiths.

The hungriest of all ghosts, the wraiths came at us from a stairway at the other end of the hall. I sent another pulse of Bless-fire outward, strengthening the circle. The wraiths howled toward me, but they were old and corrupted beings, and the Bless-fire tore through them like a sword point. Three of them came apart entirely. Muted, colored memories flew from their bodies like ash. Pieces of the memories brushed past me, and I experienced starburst images from other people's lives. Maria's crooked smile, the cherry tree in my Atlantean orchard, Adeem's first pony being fed plums the size of coconuts.

The recarnates were not so well protected as I was. They were borderline energy—not precisely alive or dead—so the wraiths could still feed on them. I remember something Quinn had said, something about letting the ghosts eat first.

So I stayed put.

Two of the recarnates shot at the wraiths. Another aimed a pneumatic dart gun at me, and went down as a wraith bit his arm. A recarnate tried to jump across my ring of Bless-fire. His arm caught fire. He dropped to the ground and rolled. The wraiths dove on him and *ate*.

It took three minutes for the last of the recarnates to succumb. The wraiths howled and keened around my circle for another long minute, then whooshed back up the stairway.

My Bless-fire was now seriously ebbing. Even if Addam was downstairs with his coat on, I worried about having enough juice to get back to the castle gates.

"Ciaran," I said. "You need to turn back. The Bless-fire is the only thing keeping the castle from mind-fucking me, and I can't spare it on you without burning through it. If we both go nuts, Addam is screwed."

He gave me a sane nod. "My powers . . . are very similar to dreams and prophecies. I think that is why I am so susceptible."

"Addam's close—give me fifteen minutes, and if I don't report in, find cell service and call the Tower. And thank you. I mean that, Ciaran— thank you."

He inclined his head, then left.

I went across the great hall. As soon as I pushed through the old tapestry, I had a better understanding of why the recarnate guards had lasted this long.

The great hall, for them, was a killing ground. The stairwell and basement were not. Someone had warded it against spectral intrusion. I took a deep breath and felt some of the tension leave my shoulders.

Unlike the upper floor, the basement level was well tended. The ground was swept, hard-packed dirt. No cobwebs. The wraith wards had a strange effect on my light cantrip. It now cast a perfect circle of cartoon yellow around me, and did absolutely nothing to pierce the darkness farther away from me.

I walked down the hall. What felt like half a city block later, I came on a door.

It was in much better shape than its splintered cousins upstairs. My garnet blade bounced off the metal cross-braces when I tapped them. It was warded. Or maybe trapped. I put the palm of my hand just above one of the metal bands and concentrated.

Identifying spells was a dodgy business. Interpretation and a good gut meant everything. To me, the door felt faintly of static cling and sunburns. Some sort of shock or fire spell?

I had options. They lay in two familiar camps: smash or subvert. I went with the subtler option and released a sigil spell. It was called Opening. Once released, it sat ready in my brain, a little like a head rush from standing up too quickly.

I positioned myself on the side of the door and sent Opening into both the door and its trap. Gears turned and clicked inside the locking mechanism. The trap's magic parted, whole but untriggered.

I wasted no time in turning the handle to see what was on the other side.

Addam Saint Nicholas faced away from me. He had an MP3 player in one hand and was dancing.

There was a tray of food, a bottle of wine, a small stack of new-release paperbacks, and a camping cot. He wore only black suit pants. No shoes, socks, shirt, or sigils.

My first thought was that he danced like Brand.

Then, in an astonishingly fluid motion, Addam snagged the leg of a roughly-sharpened footstool he'd hidden in his waistline, and spun around to stake me. His eyes jerked from my extended sabre blade to my face. His fingers spread open and the stake clattered to the ground.

He said, "Ah. You're not dead. I am being rescued, yes?"

He had white teeth and a freckled tan. Tattoos covered one arm and one shoulder in an intricate Celtic sleeve. He was well over six feet tall. His hair, the color of sand, was tied into a short ponytail with a dirty rubber band.

He held out a hand and said, "Your blade."

I blinked back at him. "Um. No, thank you?"

He frowned. "Apologies, it has been a . . . long few days. Does anyone have a blade to spare? It would be better if I were armed."

It clicked. "Oh, I get it. You think this is one of them big, fancy rescues. Boy are you about to be embarrassed."

His burgundy eyes—a beautiful color—flicked behind me, then flicked back, filled with something not unlike approval. "You came into Farstryke alone."

"I had help outside." I retracted my sabre blade and stuck it in my waistband, and hopped around on one foot while taking off my sneakers. He watched me with an expression that swayed between amused and interested until I slapped my dirty socks against his stomach.

I pulled my shoes back on. While Addam put on my socks, I examined his tattoos. Most scions avoided them. Tattoos were uncomfortably close to runes, and sometimes they took on a life of their own.

I said, "Just to make sure I've got things right, this *is* a prison cell, isn't it? You're not just ducking your mom because you got drunk and woke up with a sailor?"

He barked out a surprised laugh. "It's a prison cell."

"Any chance you know who put you here?"

"I do not," he said, and his voice got a little hard. I heard the curl of an accent; heavy and Slavic, like his mother.

He said, "But I will."

ADDAM SAINT NICHOLAS

The Opening spell was waning. We needed to be on the other side of the door before the trapped wards reengaged.

"Let's go," I said to Addam.

He picked up his stake and joined me in the hall.

"Listen." I closed the door and released the Opening. The hairs on my arm stood up as the trap fell back into place. "The upstairs is lousy with ghosts. Worse, whatever that thing is that's raised those soldier recarnates—he calls himself Rurik—could come back. We need to move fast. If we can find a quick way out, great. If not, I have a . . . less comfortable option."

"There's a back exit," he said, pointing in the other direction. We began walking. "That's how they took me in. If we—"

I raised a finger. Noises—coming from the stairway. I tried to place the sound. A scratching or scraping, like mouse nails on plywood.

Down the hall, from the direction I'd come in, dull white sticks rocked back and forth in midair. As they neared our sphere of light, the sticks resolved into the ribs and ulnas of skeletons. They wore scraps of funeral shrouds, and stared at me through orbital sockets stuffed with gold coins and knuckle-sized gemstones.

Skeletons were down-and-dirty recarnate magic. It was far easier to raise the fleshless than it was the able-bodied recarnates I'd encountered upstairs. But while they were weaker, they could be summoned in greater quantity.

The corridor permitted four abreast, and I counted five bobbing rows of muddy craniums. "Get back," I said.

"Ten apiece," Addam whispered in a tight voice.

"*Shh.*" I called on the magic in my silver ankh sigil and held it ready. Its power rumbled through my fingers like a car engine.

The skeletons moved slowly into our sphere of waxy, yellow light. Several of them held rusted daggers. When they were even with the door of Addam's prison cell, one of them flipped its dagger back for a toss. Addam panicked and threw his stake. Neck vertebrae cracked as skulls followed its trajectory. The stake hit the closed cell door with enough force to trigger the trap. Streams of electricity arced from the ground beneath the first rank of skeletons. Charred bone and smoking rags scattered in a blast radius. It wasn't a bad tactic altogether—even if more than a dozen of skeletons were still coming at us.

I'd planned on piggybacking my own spell on the door trap. There was no use waiting now. I released Shatter.

The powerful magic hit them with a peal of thunder. The skeletons rained upward in pieces no larger than a child's tooth. When the pattering stopped, Addam came up next to me, so close that the warm hairs of his forearm touched mine. He smelled of sweat and faded cologne.

"Want me to go fetch your stake?" I asked.

He gave me a smile. "I am unaccustomed to being upstaged by a proper hero. That was *very* good spellwork." He winked, turned, and retreated. "This way, Hero."

I followed him, dividing my attention between chest and ground level, looking for both enemy and tripping hazards. We entered a large room. I pulled on Addam's elbow just before he stuck his foot into a rusting metal . . . bear trap?

I looked closer. It wasn't a bear trap, and that wasn't rust. I said, tiredly, "We're in a torture chamber, aren't we?"

"At the entrance to one. Ah—this is what I wanted to show you." Addam swung aside a tapestry with a flourish. A hidden granite stairway spiraled down into cold, black depths.

When I didn't comment, he said, "This is how they made their way into and out of the castle so easily. It leads under Farstryke grounds. We can use it to escape."

"Perfect plan," I said. "Let's go deeper into the basement of the haunted house. That won't go wrong at all."

"Have faith. How many more Shatter spells have you stored?"

I didn't feel like explaining that I had a limited arsenal of sigils. I'd already burned through every spell but two. "How about we go with plan B?" I asked.

"This would be the less-comfortable option?"

"It would."

I touched his arm and initiated the spell I'd released earlier, when I'd arrived at Farstryke.

It had been a while since I'd used a Slingshot spell.

Teleportation magic operated under the basic principle of establishing two or more reference points, and bridging those points with the instantaneous. A Slingshot was the shortcut version. It relied on a single point of fixed reference and used the spell-caster like a bungee cord. You couldn't return anywhere except where you started; the radius was crap; and you got none of those pleasant, cool tingles that real teleportation gave you.

The spell put our bodies through the sensation of being stretched far beyond any physical possibility, followed by a rapid collapse into a dense, carsick mess. We wound up next to Ciaran, tangled on our knees. Addam threw up. I managed to stumble over to a sewer grate. Our faces were beaded in something gelatinous and sour. It smeared orange when I wiped at it.

"Charming," Ciaran said.

"Ciaran?" Addam panted. He gave the principality a wobbly smile that was actually friendly. "I didn't know you were here. Did Quinn send you?"

Ciaran cut a look at me. I decided it was a bad time to tell Addam that his brother had been hurt. "We can go over the details later. I need to check in with my partner, then we'll move to a secure location. Ciaran, could you get the car started?"

"Your wish," he said, and swept me a bow. He offered Addam a hand up.

I called Brand. He answered with, "Are you hurt?"

"I'm fine. I've got him."

The line hissed as Brand released a deep breath. "Tell me."

I quickly described the events of the last hour. He asked a few questions, each one calmer than the next.

I said, "Anyway. I should be home in a couple hours."

"A couple hours," Brand echoed. His voice lost that calm. "And how does that fucking work?"

"I'm going to escort Addam back to his condo," I said. "I don't even know if we have a job past that point. I'll be home soon."

"The Dead Man isn't dead. He's not even incapacitated, not if he sent skeletons after you."

"Skeletons. *Phfft.* He's incapacitated enough, if he didn't come after us himself. You know, it *is* conceivable that I could survive on my own for another hour or two. And you skipped over the part where you complimented me on my derring-do."

"Yes, awesome job, thank you for not dying after you left me behind. I baked cookies."

"Chocolate chip or oatmeal raisin?" I asked.

Brand hung up. I tucked the phone back in my pocket and headed to the car. The phone vibrated. I pulled it out and saw that Brand had texted: "Dick."

Addam left me the front seat, while he sprawled along the length of the back. Ciaran pulled away from the curb before I even buckled my seatbelt.

"You must call Lord Tower," he said.

"Look at you, being all serious."

Ciaran spared me a pissy expression. "I am a principality. My obligations to the Arcanum are limited, not absent. Lord Tower must hear what happened."

"I know so little," Addam said from behind us. "I am not sure what *has* happened."

I turned around. "Do you remember anything about your kidnapping?"

"Just . . . that thing. Coming into my office. I only remember snatches after that, of recarnates carrying me through the tunnels under Farstryke."

"And you have no idea who ordered that recarnate, Rurik, to kidnap you?" I asked.

"The one who kidnapped me seemed much more than a recarnate. But no. Nothing was said. Do . . ." Addam's face was drawn with worry. "Is someone striking at my mother through me? Is my family in danger?"

"I don't know. But I think it may have been more personal than that."

"Personal," Addam repeated. "As in someone I know has done this to me?"

My cell phone vibrated. I pulled it out and saw Brand's name. I barely got a syllable out before he said, "Are you sticking to busy streets? Is anyone watching for a tail? Do you have your senses open to feel for power spikes?"

"What was the first one?" I asked.

"*Rune.*"

I thought about it for a second. I said, "Shit. You're behind me, aren't you?" I swiveled around. Brand's motorcycle trailed us by a half block. I felt a sharp, sudden surge of emotion—relief he was there, guilt that he always did a better job at looking out for trouble, and anger. Oh, there was anger. "Brand, so help me fucking gods, if you were standing outside Farstryke this entire time, it will be *war*."

"I wasn't!" he said. His helmet mic made the words crackle. "I just caught up with you. Damn it, Rune, Saint Nicholas is just sitting on his ass. Will you at least have him look out the window for ambushes?"

"I can hear him," Addam said.

"He's right," I said, nodding to Addam. "And blunt. Brand, we're heading toward Edgemere. I'll see you there. Addam, keep an eye on the left side. I'll watch the right. Ciaran, straight ahead. Stay alert, people. We're not out of this yet."

Addam lived in the Edgemere district, a wealthy neighborhood that straddled the financial and market districts. His building was a desanctified church, split into four large condos, each sharing a corner of a massive, circular stained-glass window. Addam had the upper right—a tip of an angel's wing against a sky the color of strychnine.

Brand was already off his motorcycle by the time we piled out of the car. My introductions were brief.

Ciaran left the motor running. He moved his chin to his left, inviting me to step aside.

"This is where I leave you," he said.

"I meant what I said earlier. Thank you. You didn't just do this for the money, did you?"

Ciaran paused, weighing his response. He came from a generation for whom gratitude was a vulnerability. "No," he finally admitted. "Quinn is a special young man. I am very fond of him. I will go now, and attempt to find him in dreams. Be sure to tell Addam about Quinn's injury soon, Sun. They are unusually close. He will not take it well."

"I will."

"And you will reach out to the Tower as well?"

"Still reluctant to share your suspicions?"

"For the moment. In part, I don't want to bias the Tower's own assessment. Make sure you tell him about the null line."

"Pretty hard to skip over that bit," I said. "Thank you, Ciaran. I'll make sure the Tower wires your fee as soon as possible."

Ciaran gave me a nod, lifted his hand in parting to Addam, and blew Brand a kiss.

As Addam, Brand, and I headed to the second floor, it occurred to me that Addam hadn't asked my name—I'd only introduced myself as the man hired to find him. He must have heard Brand use my name on the phone, though. And there weren't too many scion mercenaries on the market. I had a hard time believing he hadn't figured out who I was.

Addam's condo had no physical lock. It was completely secured by biometric wards. He said to Brand, "Would you be more comfortable standing watch out here?"

Brand just blinked at him.

"Brand's my partner," I said. "Not just a Companion. He comes with me."

"Plus," Brand said, "I hear all the cool bodyguards love to shut their clients in a strange room with a strange man. Extra points when zombies are involved."

"I meant no offense," Addam said, and gave a short bow. "Please, Brandon Saint John, join us."

Brand gave me an eye roll as he followed Addam inside.

As soon as we cleared the door, Addam restarted the wards, while Brand vanished down a short hallway into a dark room. Instead of blundering in his footsteps, I picked a direction he hadn't gone. Between the two of us, we turned on lights while walking off guest bedrooms, a master suite, a sanctum, a kitchen, and a living room that ran along an entire side of the condo.

When Addam rejoined us, I said, "Who else has access?"

"Here?"

"Yes. Your family? Any of your business partners?"

"Oh, no. Not them. Lilly Rose does, but not Michael, Geoff, or Ashton, or any of their assistants. My brothers and sister may enter. Lady Justice can get in. She goes where she wants, really."

"What about condo management?"

"In an emergency they can break the wards and enter, but I would know if they did. Do you think we are unsafe here?"

"Addam, Rurik got through your office defenses without any trouble." *Or someone helped Rurik through them.* "It'd be safer to stash you somewhere else while we figure out the next step."

Addam nodded grimly. He snapped the rubber band from his pony-tail and shook his dirty hair loose, frowning at the way it snagged between his fingers. "I will bathe first. Do you need to call Lady Justice? There's a phone on the kitchen counter."

"You want Rune to call your mom?" Brand asked in disbelief.

"To report in," Addam said.

I hadn't been clear before; he didn't know the Tower had hired me. It was an easy correction, but maybe he'd be hurt that his court hadn't been ripping the city apart in pursuit of him. "Actually, I'm not sure who your mother has looking for you. I'm here because of Lord Tower."

"Speaking of," Brand said. "I'm going to see if I can get Mayan on the phone." Mayan was Lord Tower's Companion and chief of security, the person Brand dealt with most closely at the Dagger Throne. "Maybe I can get him to start returning your fucking messages. Excuse me."

As Brand retreated back into the front hall, Addam said, "Lord Tower asked you to find me?"

"He was concerned."

The skin around Addam's lips and eyes pulled tight. "Quinn must be beside himself, as well. My brother. I need to call—"

"Addam . . ."

Addam went over to the island that separated the kitchen and living room. There was an old-fashioned phone mounted to the wall.

"Addam," I said. "Quinn's in the hospital."

Addam went dead still. "I don't—What? Quinn?"

"I'm sorry."

"Quinn? Quinn's hurt? What happened?" Addam's voice broke in honest panic.

"We were at the hospital where Christian is being treated, and some recarnates attacked us. He has a head injury. The recarnates were using concussive grenades—"

Addam began punching numbers on the phone. He started crying. Operator assistance connected him to an aide at New Saints Hospital, who connected him with the nurse's station on Christian's floor, whom he frantically bullied for information about Quinn's status. The nurse could only confirm that Quinn, while still unconscious, was resting and out of immediate danger.

When Addam hung up the phone, he stared for a long time at his fireplace. There were framed photos there. He wiped at his tears without shame.

And then ran over to his desk. Next to a tricked-out desktop unit was a tablet computer. He swiped it on and tapped into a mail program.

Whatever he saw made him go still.

Brand was at the edge of the room, watching us. As usual, he picked up on things quicker than I did. He said, "Did your brother send you an email before it happened, Addam?"

Addam gave him a sharp look. "You know about him, then. He . . . does this sometime. Usually when he's about to break his curfew or fail an exam. He . . . he apologizes in advance." Addam gave the tablet a small smile. The smile faded quickly. "It says, 'Most of the time I'm okay. Don't worry about me. It's after you.'"

"There's another one," Brand said, watching Addam closely. "You looked at two messages."

Addam's expression had given it away. He pressed a button and the screen went dark. "There was. He sent it right after the first. It said, 'No, it's after him now.'"

Brand's eyes snapped to me. And, yes, I was feeling every inch of all the shit I'd landed in.

Addam sighed and said, "I am very dirty." His Russian accent burned through the *very*. "I need to shower. I need fresh clothes. And then I need to find who hurt my brother, and kill them. There are coffee beans in the freezer if you'd like. Excuse me."

Brand and I looked at each other as Addam walked into the bedroom. Brand rolled his eyes. I went after Addam.

He was standing by a dark oak nightstand, head bowed. I said, "Quinn told you he'd be okay. He knows these things, right?"

"'Most of the time,'" Addam reminded me. "*Most of the time* he's okay."

"He was aware enough to speak with Ciaran through dream-walking. That's how I found you. That's a good sign, right?"

"There are no good signs here. This proves it, doesn't it? That someone is attacking my mother's throne?"

I blinked. "Honestly, Addam, I don't think so. Lord Tower believes that someone may be after you. That it's either personal, or maybe tied to your business."

"But why come after me with that *thing*? This . . . Rurik. Why come after me with a small army of recarnates? These are the sort of pieces put into play when courts invade courts."

"Or when a scion with more spell books than sense summons something too powerful, and then loses control of the summoning."

Addam just looked at me, long enough to have me fidgeting. He finally said, "You interest me, Hero. I'm fairly sure you saved my life, and a simple thank you seems so small. I don't know whether I should pay you handsomely, or invite you into the shower with me."

"We take checks," I said, before I could get uncomfortable or act stupid.

His smile brightened, just briefly, and then he vanished into the bathroom. The door clicked shut behind him.

Back through the bedroom door, I heard Brand either snicker or sigh. I couldn't tell which.

We waited a good two minutes before we began snooping.

Addam's condo was decorated in simple but sturdy fabrics. Lots of leather furniture against forest-green carpet and dark-red walls. The photos on the mantle were mainly of Quinn, but there were also some of Lilly, Christian, and one obligatory Crusader Throne press shot. His bookcase and entertainment center was an exact inversion of mine—the bookcase was an afterthought, while the CDs took up an entire wall. He had boxed DVD concert sets, vinyl records, cassettes, concert VCR tapes, concerts on beta max, even original record-sized laser discs. Atlanteans were a long-lived species. Our interests always outdated evolving technology.

The kitchen was a large alcove separated by a marble island. He'd painted the wall with chalkboard laminate. On it he'd drawn poetry, grocery lists, phone numbers, and song lyrics.

In a corner of the living room was the tricked-out desktop computer. Printouts from a laser writer lay next to an ergonomic keyboard. When I nudged the mouse, the screen hummed on. A web browser was open.

I studied both the laser printouts and the browser. "Zoinks. A clue."

"Zoinks?" Addam laughed. He came out of the bedroom, drying his hair with one oversized towel, while another was wrapped around his waist. The walls of the apartment were thick and probably soundproofed; I hadn't even heard the shower end.

He came over and stared at the computer screen. "What is that?" he said immediately. He pointed at the papers. "Did you print those?"

They were copies of tourist info on Brazil, along with local portal schedules. I'd already skipped ahead to the implications. From the look on Addam's face, he wasn't far behind.

Brand said, "New Atlantis doesn't ID people on their way out the door, they only track incoming travelers. Someone wants it to look like you used the portal station. You could have vanished in Brazil without leaving a paper trail."

"And," I said, "someone entered your apartment to do this."

Addam's family and Lilly Rose had access—they were the easy suspects. Supposedly none of the business partners did, but I wasn't ready to discount the idea that something or someone had gotten around his wards. Rurik had pulled a null thread, for gods' sake.

"They were going to kill me," Addam said softly. "Weren't they? They weren't going to ransom me. They were going to kill me and hide the body. Otherwise, why leave this? People were meant to find this and think I left on my own."

"It could have been a ruse to buy time while they planned a ransom," I said. "Don't make assumptions."

"Come with me," he said, and strode back toward his bedroom.

I gave his back an uncertain look, shrugged, and followed. I got to the door in time to see him shuck his towel and dig around in an oak dresser. He had a tan but no tan line. I lowered my flushed cheeks.

Addam tossed black cotton pants and a yellow t-shirt onto the bed, along with a pair of socks and a belt, but no underwear. As he dressed, he said, "While I appreciate what Lord Tower did, I will take over your contract myself now."

"Are you concerned about his involvement?"

"Not at all. But matters have changed. Will you help me?"

I wasn't sure I had a choice, not if Rurik really had developed a fixation on me. Having another scion at my side wasn't a bad idea. I said, "Okay. But I have ground rules."

He turned toward me after pulling the black pants over his hips. His lips quirked when he saw me fidget. "Rules. Such as . . . ?"

"Do what I say. Don't die."

"As you wish." The bright-yellow t-shirt was striking against his tan and the green-brown Celtic tattoos. He tucked it into the black pants, and then unlocked one of the dresser drawers with a key he kept in a nightstand drawer.

"I'm not joking," I said. "I'll watch your back, but you need to follow my instructions. My partner and I have a lot of experience with these things. We—*are those sigils?*"

Inside the locked drawer was a carved wooden tray that held twenty platinum discs. Coiled next to them was a slotted belt like the one that Quinn wore. Addam had sigils that *matched*. Twenty of them. And a decorative holder and holster. And this wasn't even his main residence, just a home away from home. I suffered a few second's worth of pure ulcerous jealousy, along with a strange sort of protectiveness for my own ragtag collection.

"Only four are charged," he said, a little abashedly. "Do I have time to charge more?"

"Do any of the four contain spells to make your teeth whiter? Your breath mintier?"

"Such a cleverly laid trap, Hero. Yes, please, allow me to admit being vain and vacuous." When I rolled my eyes, he added, "Telekinesis. All four of them. It's a very versatile magic."

"Well, okay. That's good. But let's pack up and move out. It's better if we don't stay in one place too long."

"I will follow your lead," Addam said, "so long as it takes me first to the hospital. I must see Quinn."

When I opened my mouth to object, I saw that Addam's eyes had gone glassy again at the mention of his brother. He added, in a tense voice, "Please."

"Okay," I said. "The hospital, then."

As the crow flies, it was only a half mile to the hospital. Addam had Brand move his motorcycle into a warded parking garage under his building. Brand didn't complain about us walking, which I took to mean he was happy to be unpredictable with our route.

We cut through a large square divided by a commonwealth garden. The fountain in its middle was filled with muddy river water, and I caught the corner of a white sleeve floating under the surface. If I remembered right, Jenny Greentooth had spent the season in it.

I looked around and spotted pixies in the wilting summer flowers. A dwarf in leg braces was smoothing the cracks out of the curb. There were a lot of portunes—small agricultural fairies—dispiritedly tending sickly trees and ivy stunted by car exhaust.

The streets became progressively more crowded as we passed the portal station. Long-distance portals were operated with proprietary magic from Lord Magician's Hex Throne. The massive stone building was as big as a football stadium, catering to all twenty-four time zones.

"Smell that," Addam said as a fisherman with a small watertight container pushed by.

"That's usually a question that doesn't end well," I said.

"Sturgeon roe. Caviar. Very likely pulled from the Caspian an hour ago. Have you ever been to the portal market?"

"Not since someone kidnapped you," I said. "Addam, we should really talk about this."

"I've . . . been thinking about it. Let's assume—for the sake of argument, Hero—that it really is about me and not the Crusader Throne. I've been trying to understand *why* it was done. If it's not ransom, then what? I'm not the richest scion. Most of my income goes into my business. I try not to make enemies."

"Jealous boyfriends or girlfriends? Jealous exes?"

"Is it possible to break off a relationship so badly that they send *recarnates* after you?"

"What about your family? You get along with your brothers, right?"

"Yes. Quinn . . ." Addam's face twisted. "Quinn especially. He is . . . I suppose you could say that he is mine. I was old enough to look after him when he was a baby, and my mother couldn't take time away from court. So he had me. He needed a lot of attention, when he was a baby."

"Why?"

"He almost died when he was born. The umbilical cord, it was around his neck. They were barely able to start his heart. He was premature, as well. When I first saw him, he wasn't any bigger than my palm. This. He fit in *this*." Addam held out a hand in wonder.

"You get along with Christian, too, I hear. You do charity work with him."

"Betimes. We run a nonprofit that arranges free concerts. I like music."

"Does Ella volunteer with you?"

He gave me a level look. After a pause, he said, "No, I do not get along with my sister. That is where this is going, yes? She treats Quinn like an embarrassment, which vexes me. But I did not kidnap *her*, someone kidnapped *me*. And she likes me. She has no reason to hurt me. She knows my company does well, which she feels increases her stature. She's very concerned with stature."

"So are most scions."

"Exactly, and most scions don't kidnap other scions. Kill them outright in duels, yes. But kidnap? Become involved with death magic? No, Hero."

Brand, who'd fanned out to keep watch, was rolling his eyes at this *hero* business.

I said, "You talk about your business a lot. It's a big part of your life."

Addam stepped aside to let a woman in a silk kimono pass. The back of the kimono fluttered in a sudden breeze, releasing a burst of cherry-blossom petals. Addam waved his hand through them, then came back to my side. "It is, yes. We're still making a name for ourselves."

"Of your three business partners, who's skilled enough to handle summoning magic?"

"This type of summoning magic? Necromancy? None. And why would any of them hurt me? There's no profit in it. There have been differences of opinions lately, yes, but—"

"Oh, for fuck's sake," Brand said. He gave me a plaintive look.

I sighed. "Addam. Sit down. Brand, can we have a moment?" Brand moved away.

We were close to a wrought-iron bench. Addam pulled an actual handkerchief from his back pocket and wiped the seat for me. When we were both sitting, I turned to him and said, "Can you do me a favor?"

"Of course."

"Get your head out of your ass. Stop being diplomatic. Stop speaking in hypotheticals. Put aside all of the sentimental bullshit that most people, as living creatures, use to convince themselves they really-really like their family and friends. Tell me—straight up—why and how one of these people would hurt you."

"Nothing in my life is worth killing over!"

"Walk down the wrong street in this city and you could be gutted for your shoelaces. You could have a dagger stuck in your eye because you used the wrong adverb. The inside of a person's head is a deep, dark place, Addam. No one really knows what another person is capable of, not until you're sitting in a big bloody mess. So why would Ella kill you?"

The topic had paled his tan. Just when I was about to harangue him, he said, "She'd advance in standing. Be closer to the heir scion position."

"Why would Christian kill you?"

"I . . ."

"Why?"

"I don't know!" Frustration boiled the accent back into his words. "He and my brother and sister would get my profits from Moral Confidence. But it's not that much—"

"Just the profit?"

"Yes. The shares, my actual interest in the company, would be divided among the founders."

"So that's a reason one of the partners might want you removed. Why would Quinn kill you?"

"He wouldn't."

"If you had to gue—"

"He wouldn't."

"Okay. Okay. How often do you disagree with your partners?"

"Not often. Some lately. Michael wants . . . riskier investments. Geoff is undecided. Ashton just wants whatever gets our name in print. Let's go now. Please? I want to go to the hospital. I need to see Quinn."

I hesitated, then gave in with a nod. I'd kicked some gears loose in his head, and that was enough for now. It was best to back off and let the suspicions gain their own momentum.

We stayed with Addam as far as Quinn's room. The sight of the sandy-haired teenager leashed to a heart monitor and IV, his small frame swallowed in sterile white sheets, was inexpressibly sad. When Addam's eyes filled with fresh tears, I stepped back into the hallway and gave them a moment alone.

Brand took watch, leaning casually into a snack machine as if browsing for choices. I paced down the corridor toward a large picture window. For a moment, the lack of sleep got to me. Was it really still morning?

"What are *you* doing here?"

I turned to see Michael Saint Talbot regarding me with suspicion. He was dressed in jeans and a rugby shirt, his face stubbled with yesterday's beard. He'd come out of the stairwell.

We were on the first floor. Christian Saint Nicholas was two floors above us. Had Michael been to see him? Why not take an elevator?

"Looks like someone beat the shit out of you," he said nastily.

I was too weary for banter. I just wanted answers. "What are you doing here, Michael?"

"You'll forgive me if it's none of your fucking business."

I blocked his path. Unlike most scions, Michael's polish was inexpertly applied. For a second, I honestly thought he was going to lose control and take a swing at me.

I said, "You might be interested to hear that I'll be hanging around a little while longer."

"What does that mean?"

"It means I'm working for Addam now. He wants to find out who kidnapped him."

"You talked to Addam?" Michael asked haltingly. "He's . . . okay? He's back?"

"He sure is."

"And that's what he said? That he was *kidnapped*?" His breath hit my face, clean and minty.

"He said a lot of things."

Michael reddened. "This doesn't make any sense. Why does he need you to find out who kidnapped him? Doesn't he know?"

"You'd think so, wouldn't you? I won't take up any more of your time. We'll talk soon."

"We've got nothing to talk about," he said.

"Oh, we really do. I'd like to ask you about those arguments you had with Addam just before he got kidnapped. I'm not a business major, and I have no idea what *morally gray investments* are, but—"

"You're out of line. And you're not needed. If Addam's in trouble, we can help him without you. Stay out of our way."

I waited a couple beats. "Are you going to say '*or else*'? It sounded like you were going to say 'or else.'"

"Keep talking like that and you're going to find yourself with a duel on your hands."

Brand had enough. He barked out a laugh, startling Michael, who spun around. "Duel you?" Brand laughed. "Look. I'm sure you were the shit on your frat's beer pong team, but we're past your pay grade."

"Who do you think you are? You're nothing. You're hired help. Neither of you are *anything*. You think playing detective makes you important again?"

I stepped into Michael's personal space and said, clearly, "Did you try to kill Addam, Michael?"

"*No.*"

"Someone sent recarnates after him. Spells like that always have a way of rebounding on the user. You know that, don't you?"

"It doesn't matter what I know, because I didn't do it. I'm leaving."

I stepped aside with a flourish. The shift in perspective gave me a perfect view of Ella Saint Nicholas, who was stepping off an elevator about fifty feet away.

"Oh, now *that*," I said, my voice as crisp as two puzzle pieces snapping into place, "is the easiest way to leave the building—and I was wondering about the breath mints."

Michael flushed red. His hands were fists. He took an angry step toward me, saw a knife already in Brand's hand, and just as quickly wheeled and stalked off toward the hospital's exit, in the opposite direction of Ella.

Ella had noticed me. One hand was up, covering her mouth. Her eyes grew bigger as Brand and I closed in.

She looked disheveled—smudged lip gloss, a fashionable blue hat tilted at an unfashionable angle. Her neck was bright with rash, the sort you got from bearded kisses.

"I was just telling Michael that a real gentleman would have escorted you to the door," I said with a large smile.

Her jaw dropped in slow motion. "Michael who?"

"Excellent," I said appreciatively.

She gave the nearby lobby a glance. "Please forgive my rudeness, Lord Sun, I know it's terrible of me, but I promised my aunt I'd join her for breakfast."

"There's nothing rude about breakfast at all. What brings you to New Saints at such an early hour?"

"I'm here to see my brother, of course."

"Just the one?"

Her face got pinched, as if she'd forgotten that her youngest brother was there, too. I said, "Now's a good time to visit Quinn, if you're interested."

"W-why is that?"

"I wouldn't want to ruin the surprise. And, by the way, you need to have words with your lady's servant, Lady Saint Nicholas. She's completely boggled the dress buttons in back."

"How kind of you to mention it," she whispered.

Then she froze. Her eyes went shiny and bright. She blinked as soon as they were full, which sent two fat tears racing toward her chin. I heard footsteps at my back.

"Ella?" Addam said.

"Oh, Addam! Addam!" She threw herself at her older brother, burying her face in his yellow t-shirt. "We were so worried! Why haven't you called?"

"I was . . . Something happened. I'm fine now. Why are you crying?"

"Oh, I'm not, not at all," she protested. She stepped back and looked away from us, dabbing her eyes with her sleeve. "It's just that Lord Sun had questions for me. I'm not sure I've ever felt so awful, even knowing I haven't done anything wrong."

"Rune?" Addam said.

I gave Ella a sharp smile. "Your sister was visiting Christian. I was trying to get her to stop and visit Quinn before she left. I thought it'd be a surprise to see you here."

Addam looked at Ella, his gaze weighed down by years of disappointment. "You weren't going to see Quinn? You haven't even seen him yet, have you?"

"I," she said, buying herself another second by dabbing at a tear. "I didn't want to disturb him."

"But you're okay with disturbing Christian? It's," he said, looking around for a clock, "barely eight. Why are you even here? Where's Aunt Diana?"

"I'm quite capable of going places without Aunt Diana."

"It's okay," I added. "Michael was looking out for her."

"Michael Saint Talbot?" Addam asked. "You're here with Michael?"

Ella realized she was trapped. She stopped wiping at her eyes and began to cry in earnest. When Addam reached for her, she ran for the front door.

In a genius move, she convinced the guard on the other side that something inappropriate was happening. He blocked our way. It took too long to pull rank. By the time we were outside, she was gone.

SOUTH STREET BRIDGE

I was thinking we'd head back to Half House, but Brand had different ideas.

He herded Addam and me into New Saint's public sanctum to refill some of our depleted sigils. The only spell I had left was Exodus, which was a pretty poor choice for anything except mass fusion.

Public sanctums did their best to offer as many crutches for spell storing as possible, given the unique way all spell-casters meditated over their magic. This sanctum, serving such a high-end clientele, was better supplied than most. There were dozens of cubbyholes stocked with bond paper, ballpoint pens, watercolor paints, hand weights, chess boards, lumps of coral and obsidian and dully colored crystals, wooden practice swords, and stacks upon stacks of soft porn.

In the corner were three antique phone booths paneled in oak and frosted glass, which offered the illusion of privacy for those who required solitude to channel their magic. Another wall was crowded with a mid-range sound system and a very eclectic collection of CDs. A line of earbuds—covered with tiny, disposable plastic slipcovers—were jacked into a multi-channel unit.

Addam went straight to the CDs. I sat cross-legged on a throw pillow. It was upholstered in a coarse, stain-resistant fabric, but after the day I'd had, it felt as soft as spider silk.

I closed my eyes and sank into a meditative fugue. The room's ambient energy hissed like static. It took time and patience, in a public sanctum, to build a link between my sigils and my willpower. I chose two spells that I could transfer quickly and competently: Shield and Fire. I imagined the spells as tiny nuggets of sand, and then slowly, slowly, slowly built pearls around them.

It wasn't until I opened my eyes that I realized Addam Saint Nicholas was dancing.

He held the earphone cord like a dance partner, twirling under its lariat arc. He'd taken off his shoes and socks. His feet, long and angular, were calloused with the wear of someone who didn't just dance for occasion.

I liked men who danced. It was something I was far too self-conscious to do well myself. Brand was a good dancer. Brand, who'd dragged a stuffed armchair to the corner so that he could keep an eye on the exits, and who was watching me watch Addam. I ducked my gaze.

When Addam stopped dancing, I said, "It'll ruin everything if that's Britney Spears, you know."

He gave me a tired smile, his right cheek caving into a dimple. "West Coast swing."

Brand dropped a boot from a crossed leg with a thud.

"So," he said. "Have you given any more thought to your sister and your business partner?"

Addam pulled on his socks and shoes. "Yes. I've thought that I should never think about it again." When Brand didn't crack a smile, Addam sighed and stood up. "Apparently my sister and my friend are romantically involved. Must that mean anything significant?"

"Yes," Brand said flatly.

Addam said, "They are young. Single. Neither has been promised into an alliance with an opposing court. There is no reason that they *couldn't* be together. It's strange, but it does not mean they tried to hurt me."

"Addam," I said. "They didn't want anyone to know they were together."

"Perhaps it is not as secretive as that. Ella has been taking day trips to our Westlands compound. I recall wondering about the sudden interest. They may have just been spending time together, privately—not necessarily secretively."

"In the Westlands?" I echoed. "On day trips? Addam, doesn't that seem a little extreme to you?"

"Ella's been . . . I guess the word is *chafing* under Aunt Diana's watch-fulness. We pretend that Aunt Diana is tutoring her, though we all know Lady Justice believes Ella requires caretaking. Ella's been demanding more independence lately—taking shopping trips on her own, taking these day trips out to the compound that the Moral Certainties share. I know the Westlands can be a dangerous place, but the paths there are secure, and the compound is very well protected."

"So are bear cages," Brand said. "So are nuclear power plants. That doesn't mean you step inside one to knock boots."

Addam's eyes, that unusual shade of burgundy, grew pinched. "She goes with an armed guard. Though . . . I admit I am concerned. She can be very impressionable. I wouldn't want to think Michael is taking advantage of that."

Brand said, "Rune gave you the speech. Aren't you listening? Don't you understand why seeing Ella and Michael together makes a lot of the pieces fall into place?"

"There are pieces?" Addam said, almost smiling. He saw the look on Brand's face. The smile failed.

And then a stinging spray of seawater splashed into my face. The ship's deck tilted under a wave and sent me stumbling into a pile of tarred rope. Brand and Addam weren't there, of course—which only made sense if one particular thing was happening.

"Whose memory am I about to tear my way out of?" I demanded furiously.

"Apologies," Lord Tower said from behind me. "It was a convenient way to talk."

My anger trailed into ellipses. Lord Tower stood at the prow of a ship, in this memory of his, which I'd been mentally pulled into. And he was young. Younger than I'd ever seen him, including after a rejuvenation treatment. He was dressed like an old-fashioned naval officer, under a punishing equatorial sun.

Barefoot Spanish sailors darted around us. On the horizon was an approaching crescent of land. Massive tropical trees teemed at the water's edge.

It was a very good memory construct. The sailors actually noticed me—or, at least, they noticed something *like* me that made sense in their ghostlike context.

"Be honest," I said. "Did it occur to you to try my cell phone? Even a little?"

"Matters are very serious, Rune," Lord Tower said.

I shut up.

"This is where I met its kind once," he said, and pointed absently toward land. "I was trying to see if I could recall anything that would help. You must come to the Pac Bell. Now. There is nothing more urgent."

"You know about Rurik," I said. "The recarnate that's been after me. Don't you?"

"I do."

"And you know what Rurik is."

Lord Tower said, "He's a lich."

"A lich." I shook my head. "Liches are a myth." Worry prickled my skin like a burn.

"Come to me," he said, and then he kicked me out of his temporal lobe.

The South Bridge in Edinburgh was built to span the thousand-foot Cowgate gorge. Completed in 1788, the nineteen-arch viaduct had extra floors and over a hundred vaults, making space for cobblers, smelters, milners, and cutlers.

It was, metaphysically speaking, cursed from the start.

First, they demolished three slums to make way for the project. Slums have always been a fertile ground for deep psychic residue. Then, the city rushed the construction and wound up with an architectural design that lacked sunlight, healthy air circulation, and sanitation. To make matters worse, the neighborhood's oldest resident was chosen to be the first to walk the bridge. The resident, an old woman, died days before the event. Due to political shenanigans she made the crossing in her coffin.

By the turn of the century, the vaults had become a nest of red-light districts, cheap taverns, and poor immigrants. A fire in 1824 killed dozens of Highlanders and Irishmen; and the infamous serial killers, Burke and Hare, allegedly murdered over seventeen people in the vaults and sold their bodies to a local medical college.

Eventually the vaults were abandoned and filled in with rubble, where they stayed hidden until the Arcanum bought and translocated them into underground paths beneath the busy traffic of the Pac Bell neighborhood.

I didn't tell Brand and Addam about the lich. They hadn't heard the conversation between Lord Tower and I—all of that had happened in thoughts, not reality. I only mentioned Lord Tower, his summons, and the Spanish ship. Past that, I was still wrapping my brain around the reality. It was not an easy task—not when you consider the number of real boogeymen that we already knew walked the earth.

As we crossed under the city's financial district, conversation was kept to a minimum. Brand gave a few terse instructions and settled into his hypervigilant bodyguard mode. Addam was still upset by our conversation.

Morning rush hour filled the South Bridge tunnels with all manner of people who didn't give a shit about my problems. There was something reassuring about that. A werelion and a were-dire-wolf in man-shift forms growled in each other's beard stubble. The crowd parted for a Minotaur laborer as he stomped his way to work. A businessman in a thousand-dollar suit sobbed openly into a cell phone while staring at a map directory and asking about street corners.

The tunnel was lined with restaurant shops and stands. They filled the moody stone arches with cantrip lights, roasting coffee beans, and the click of metal against porcelain. The sight of an espresso cart nearly filled my eyes with tears. I said, "Need it."

"You need sleep," Brand said over the muffled wail of emergency vehicles moving through the traffic above our heads. "You're dead on your feet. Why the hell couldn't the Tower just meet us at Half House?"

"Maybe he forgot the way," I said. "It's been ages since he's swung by for a barbecue or a ballgame."

Brand gave me a sour look.

"He's the Tower, that's why," I said. "I'm going to get a coffee. I love coffee. I miss coffee."

Brand pulled out his phone. "I'll check in with Queenie."

I walked away from them. Addam joined me at the kiosk. He said, "May I buy you an espresso, Hero?"

I sighed. "This *hero* business. Are you pretending you don't know who I am?"

"Am I?"

"Addam, you know who I am. You used my name with Ella."

Addam shrugged. "Lord Tower is my godfather. You are his protégé. It's not so unlikely I'd know who you are."

I almost laughed, because it was such a slick way of avoiding the fact that *every* scion knew who I was. I was a walking object lesson. I was what happened when a court wasn't strong enough to protect itself.

There was a young woman in line ahead of us. She had pale-blue skin and wings made of snow flurries. I brushed melting flakes off my cheek. Addam murmured, "Snegurochka. Russian snow maiden. Very rare."

"Is she part of your court?"

"No, her kind is from Kostroma. Russia's European plain. My family has Siberian connections. Irkutsk, mostly."

"Quinn doesn't have an accent."

"Quinn has only briefly lived outside the city. I was born in Irkutsk, and lived there for many years while New Atlantis was built. My older brother Christian sounds like me."

"I haven't met Christian yet," I said. "He's been in the hospital for a while, hasn't he?"

"And Ella may have put him there? Is that where this is leading?"

"Yeah," Brand answered from directly behind me.

Even I jumped a little. Brand gave me an angry look. "That's right, you didn't fucking see me. Coffee isn't sleep, Rune."

Addam gave Brand a look that, if not pissed, wasn't pleasant either. I moved up in line and placed my order, distracting them.

Addam said, a moment later, "You suggested that Ella and Michael being involved—romantically—made sense." Addam turned so that he was looking at me too. "What does that mean? What sort of sense?"

"I know your sister is manipulative," I said, "but is she cruel? Genuinely cruel?"

"*Manipulative* is a strong word," Addam hedged.

Brand made an exasperated sound. "Are you fucking interested in anything we have to say?"

"I . . . No, she is not cruel. She is . . . easily influenced, and she is very obsessed with her personal standing, but she is not cruel."

I said, "We've been trying to figure out what anyone would gain from your absence. We know that, with you gone, your interest in Moral Confidence goes to your business partners. That might seem like motive, but your interest in the company is nothing compared to your influence and court contacts, which they need. What we didn't ask ourselves was this: What if one of your business partners got your interest in the company but *didn't* lose the influence of the Crusader Throne?"

"Through a relationship with your sister," Brand said. "And think about this. Why keep you alive? Why go through the considerable godsdamn effort of using a small army of zombies to hold you captive? In comfort? You had wine and fast food, for fuck's sake. It's fucked up. It's two entirely different mind-sets."

"As if," I said, "Ella could only be convinced so far. Taking you? And increasing her standing? Sure. Killing you? Maybe she balked at that."

It was adding up.

Christian's illness and Addam's absence were both nonlethal ways of giving Ella a straight line toward the heir scion seat.

Michael Saint Talbot wanted to move Moral Confidence into a riskier direction, but Addam had resisted.

Addam had just told us that Ella was chafing under the excessive care of her family, much like Michael chafed under his.

I said, "For what it's worth, I really wanted it to be Ashton. He's such a douche."

"Ashton isn't nearly as indolent as he pretends," Addam said. His eyes lit as if this a better alternative. "Lord Strength is a stern man. He made Ashton train at a Wasteland camp. Ashton knows how to hurt people—he knows strategy."

"He did a pretty crappy job of it in the hospital. And anyway, they learn how to fight there, not summon recarnates," I said.

The barista cleared his throat to get our attention. Addam fetched my coffee for me. I started to follow, but Brand grabbed my funny bone in a pincer grip. He whispered, "What did the Tower say?"

"What do you mean?"

"*Rune.*"

"He thinks Rurik is a mythological monster. But you know Lord Tower, he's high-strung. I'm betting we just have an ordinary-sized monster after us."

"I hate when you're sleep-deprived. Everything's a bad fucking joke."

We stood by a circle of potted plants as Addam rejoined us, handing me my caffeine. At the table next to us, an ancient man—wearing the motley of the Fool's court—was reading the future with scalpel runes. As I watched, he accidentally laid open his thumb on one of the ceramic blades. He stared blankly at the blood and then fainted over his latte.

My nerves prickled. I didn't know why. But my instinct was strong enough to have me tossing my coffee into the trash, to free up my hands. "We need to move."

Magic surged. A rush of it, coarse and cold.

I turned in a circle, then twice, and on a third spin decided that it had come from behind us.

Another Revelry court member was shaking the unmoving prophet.

Noise above. More sirens on the roads overhead.

Had I heard sirens before?

And people. The flow of people . . .

Rush-hour foot traffic should have been moving in a predictably forward thrust. But I saw people standing in the middle of the corridor on phones, upset or excited. Members of the guarda were pushing their way toward the street exits.

"What's happening?" Brand demanded to a guarda officer who was rushing by us.

"Out of my way," the guarda said.

Brand grabbed the man's shirt and swung him into a nearby wall. The man's head bounced off stone. He said, "You can't do—" and Brand snapped his head back again.

"Tell me what's happening," Brand repeated.

The guarda were our police, but they weren't the city's real power, and they knew it. They respected force.

The officer said, "People are dying. All over the place. Just dropping. They say it's some spell, but no one knows."

"Maybe it doesn't have to do with us," I said weakly after Brand let the officer go.

"Maybe," Brand said. He gave both ends of the corridor a look and said, "Backs to the wall. Be alert. We're only two blocks away."

We moved. The taste of magic didn't fade. If anything, it now tasted like char. Brand saw the twist of my lips and picked up his pace.

"Can you feel that?" Addam whispered.

"Yes."

"What is it? Is it a spell?"

"I think so," I said, and then the sense of wrongness spiked, a kernel of god-awful flavor that had me gagging. I felt an awareness. No. More than awareness, more sentient than that. It was *recognition.* "Brand, I think Rurik's tracking us."

Addam said, "But the guarda told us people were dying. How is that tracking us?"

"I don't know. Brand, something's going to happen. Something's closing in on us."

Brand rammed through the crowd, shoving indignant, clueless people out of our way—people who had no idea they were bowling pins for whatever was rolling after me. Ahead I spotted the huge, modern stairway that led toward the Tower's block.

The lights overhead began to flicker, a five-second strobe made all the more dramatic by a keening wail that echoed off the pitted rock walls.

To our left, a woman screamed. She'd thrown herself to her knees. Next to her was a jaundiced man, coughing like he had pottery shards in his lungs.

The coughing stopped. The woman screamed louder. I don't think she saw the black air swirling from the man's dead eyes and slack mouth. I did, and I knew what it was.

A *spectre.* A violent, summoned spirit; a day-walking ghost. The spectre came together into a smoky humanoid shape and surged above the crowd.

I touched my mother's cameo. A fractal burst of light blazed around my body. I peeled the Shield off me and molded it into a ball. I hurled the ball at the approaching spirit.

The creature and my spell collided. The Shield slid around the spectre like a bright oil spill. I could see it thrashing inside the bubble, its phantom claws trying to bunch and tear the spell under gaunt, crooked fingers.

I focused on my wrist-guard. The metal became warm and malleable, and slid over my knuckles. Next to me, Addam released a spell from one of his own sigils. I felt the magic snap and push against us. Telekinesis. A very versatile magic, and completely useless against an angry spirit.

"Ten o'clock!" Brand shouted.

I hadn't even seen the second spectre soaring down the passageway.

I had three spells. One of them was tied up in the first spectre; the second would bring the tunnel down on our heads; and the third, Fire, had possibilities—if I could stall for the time it would take to release and shape it. Fortunately, my training had taught me this: *everything* was a weapon.

I said a simple light cantrip and anchored it to the flat of my sabre hilt. I swung the sabre at the rushing spectre. My arm sank halfway into the spectre's head. My skin shredded, deep furrows rimmed in gray frost. I forced my willpower into the light cantrip, which blazed within the monster's fleshless darkness. The spectre shrieked and shot upward, more startled than hurt.

That gave me time to run a thumb over my white-gold ring. The Fire flushed out—hot enough to make the frozen blood stream from my arm wound.

The spectre pinwheeled along the gothic arches, gathering itself for another dive. The crowd scrambled away. Addam, his hands and arms covered by a blurring rush of power, cleverly forced tripping hazards from our path with bursts of energy.

I shouted, to anyone listening, *"Cover your eyes!"*

The duration of a sigil spell is linked to the potency of its use. I could make Fire last over five minutes—nearly an eternity in a fight. Five minutes of Fire, though, wouldn't destroy a spectre.

But a fifth of a second?

I manifested Fire and shrank it into a space no bigger than the head of a pin. Just before the spectre dove into me, I triggered all of it, every bit of the spell. A small sun burned in my palm.

The spectre died in a roiling explosion. Smoke rose to the ceiling with an underbelly of flame.

"One o'clock, nine o'clock!" Brand snapped.

The first spectre was beginning to tear free of my Shield bubble. And

down the corridor, over the heads of the panicked crowd, six more spectres soared toward us.

I said, almost numbly, "Run."

We bolted for the stairway. Outside, we could alert the Tower, and
the people in the tunnels wouldn't die of bad timing.

Screams and hoarse shouts transitioned into the sounds of rush-hour
traffic as we emerged in the middle of a sidewalk. The Pac Bell was half
a block away. We made it as far as the next cross street when I felt the
tainted presence of the spectres behind us.

"Get help!" I yelled at Addam. He turned and ran for the Tower's
building.

Brand had knives in his hands. Both were made from volcanic glass
inscribed with coral. Behind us, six spectres—no, seven, my Shield had
failed—were circling above the South Bridge stairwell.

Farther down the street, a cloud rolled toward us. I didn't understand
what it was at first. My mind ran through a Rolodex of images: banks of
fog, the debris of explosions. Then it was close enough for me to see the
mob of spectres that numbered in the dozens.

Brand grabbed my wrist and yanked me across the street.

In front of us, the Tower's block was a frozen queue of pedestrians—a
window washer, a doorman, a woman with a dog.

They leapt into motion.

All of them, down to a man, rushed to the edge of the sidewalk. The
woman's dog vanished in a hiss of broken glamor. She put a hand on my
shoulder, grasped it, and tossed me behind her with inhuman strength. I
tumbled across asphalt and banged into a newspaper dispenser.

I could feel spells being released from over a hundred sigils. Fake
pedestrians—up and down the street—held out their hands and linked
together a wall of Bless-fire.

That was when I saw they'd left Brand on the other side of their
makeshift barrier.

I tried to run past the woman. She hip-checked me. I reeled back.

The spectres were nearly on top of Brand. I yelled something that wasn't even words. The woman moved to block me.

My Aspect flared to life, spilling from my eyes. It was brighter than I'd ever known it to be, brighter than it'd been in Cubic Dreams when I'd cowed Ciaran. Fire—actual *fire*—raced along my arms. The woman staggered to one knee. An opening appeared in the wall of Bless-fire.

I reached past her as the first of the spectres flooded over the opposite curb. Brand's hand grabbed mine, and I pulled him through the barrier.

The woman sprang up and rejoined the line, raising the barrier. The spectres drove themselves into it. They had as much of a chance as bugs on a windshield. The Tower's defense burned them into nothingness.

Brand and I collapsed to the ground in a tangle. Arms came into my peripheral vision, as Addam helped us to our feet.

I stared, dumbfounded, at the line of people. A six-year-old surrounded by abandoned chalk sketches. A bodega shopkeeper. Men in business suits. Women with now-empty baby slings against their breasts. Dozens upon dozens of fake-random people, loaded with powerful magic. The scope of the Tower's secret front-line defense left me staggered. A secret now compromised for me.

"Come on," Brand said tiredly. "Your arm is cut up."

I let him lead me toward the Pac Bell while giving my arm only a quick look. The flesh had been torn from wrist to elbow. It didn't even hurt yet.

"Maybe I do need a nap," I said.

Brand unsnapped the button over one of his shirt's ammo pockets. He pulled out a square of paper and handed it to me. It was a napkin, not a bandage. I unfolded it and saw an oatmeal raisin cookie.

I bit into it with a grateful sound and focused on the simple act of chewing. Ahead of us, the revolving door unlocked with a *kchunk* and began to spin, welcoming us inside.

The myth of liches is ancient.

They are allegedly the dead souls of powerful spell-casters

who'd turned their magic toward a perverted treasure hunt for true immortality.

Liches are supposed to be the antithesis of existence; the color negative of Nature. They suck the universe into them like a sponge, growing nastier and nastier, more and more powerful. Legend says that if they aren't cauterized early enough, they leave nearby nations as husks.

Legend says.

RURIK

The marbleized lobby of the Pac Bell was empty except for a man by the far elevator bank.

"My eyes itch," I said, rubbing them.

Brand clamped his hand on my shoulder to keep me in a straight line. "They were on fire."

"Ah." Then: "What?"

"Your eyeballs," he said. "Were on fire. When your Aspect took over."

I stared at Brand. He gave me a *you Atlanteans* shrug, which I'm pretty sure he was faking, because my eyeballs had been on fire.

"This is new?" Addam asked politely.

"It really is," I said.

We reached the man at the elevator, who I now recognized as Lord Tower's chief of security and Companion, Mayan. Mayan was the tallest person I knew, with long brown hair tied back in braids. All of Lord Tower's staff were trained killers, right down to the part-time bellhops, and Mayan was the head guard. It was enough to give one pause.

"Is Lord Tower expecting us?" Addam asked.

"Lord Saint Nicholas, with all respect, people in a five-block radius are expecting you."

Brand bristled—he'd been bristling since the moment he spotted Mayan. They had the complicated relationship of two alpha dogs. Brand said, "That was a great idea, not returning my fucking calls. It's not like you hired us to do a job or anything."

"We've been somewhat preoccupied," Mayan said dryly. He stepped aside and gestured into the elevator car. "Please."

He didn't follow us into the car, but turned a key in a console outside it. The doors slid shut. I experienced a moment of vague confusion at the lurch—vague enough that I didn't realize what had happened until Addam said, "Are we going down?"

"Oh," Brand said. "Mother*fucker*. We're going to his war room. Rune, we're going to the war room—what the hell is after us?"

I wanted to close my eyes and sit down. "Lord Tower thinks Rurik is a lich."

Brand's face went blank, and Addam's lips curled into an uncertain smile. "Liches don't exist."

"I think they do, Addam."

Brand's cell phone beeped. He took it out, rolled his eyes, put it back in his pocket. After a few seconds I said, "Anything interesting?"

"Max sent another text."

"Max is sending you texts?"

"Max is fucking flooding me with texts."

"Like what?"

"I need to do laundry. Is it okay if I try to fix the washer machine? Oops, I didn't fix the washer machine, where are the towels? I used up all the towels. Is it okay if I eat a Devil Dog? Oops, I ate all the Devil Dogs."

"He ate my Devil Dogs?"

"Go back in time and outrun the monsters without losing your breath," Brand said. "Then we'll talk snack food."

"I do not know what a Devil Dog is," Addam said. "Or a Max."

"Houseguest." I peered at the elevator console, which had no helpful flashing numbers on the panel. While putting more pressure on my arm wound, I said, "Are we going right *through* the center of the earth?"

The elevator slowed. I'd never actually been in the Tower's war room, and I hadn't felt the lack of it. Lord Tower was a man who ordered people's death from a chaise lounge. Anything that required his presence over an actual battle map was unsettling on a global scale.

The elevator opened into a narrow, stainless-steel hall. There were six-inch slits on either side of us. It was a type of decoration very popular in medieval castles, and it operated in much the same way as a slaughter ramp at a cattle farm.

We passed down the hall unchallenged, into another room. I wasn't sure what I'd expected, but there were no crackling walls of energy, no dragons flanking the entryway. It was just a simple, hexagonal room with a large tabletop monitor in the center. The fact that I couldn't even sense defensive wards indicated just how good they were.

Lord Tower stood by the monitor. He was barefoot and wearing a loose martial gown called a keikogi. His black hair was tied back.

Standing next to him was—

"*Ciaran?*" I said.

"Sun," the principality said. He gave me a wide grin.

"Godfather?" Addam interrupted.

Lord Tower tapped a button. Flashing red circles vanished from a digital representation of New Atlantis on the monitor. He came over and gave Addam a hug that was, I think, entirely genuine.

"Thank you for sending someone after me," Addam said.

"Addam," Lord Tower said, the word between a rebuke and affection. "Your mother would have, too, if she'd understood the level of danger you were in."

Addam gave him a rueful look. "She would have avenged me. It's not entirely the same."

"Are we supposed to pretend that Rune isn't bleeding all over the place?" Brand asked. "Because he is."

"Apologies," Lord Tower said, and brushed a hand over a sigil on his bracelet. Healing magic filled the air as he walked over to touch my injury.

My own healing magic was like sunburn; Lord Tower's was a cauterizing blowtorch. The moment my skin pulled shut, I yanked my arm away from him, saying, "It's like you mix your spells with horse cocaine."

Brand said, "What the hell is happening?"

I added, "What did Rurik do? What did he do outside?"

Lord Tower stared at me. He dropped a hand to the computer terminal and tapped a sequence of keys. The flashing red circles reappeared on the map. From where I was standing—from where anyone was standing—it was impossible to miss the symmetry.

"A grid," I said.

"Yes. The lich tracked you using fixed points of spectral observers. I can't say with any certainty whether it was searching for you or Addam, but it—"

"Not a tracking spell," I said. My voice was suddenly loud. "Not just. It was a tracking spell powered by a death spell. People—those—" I stared at all the red circles. I couldn't count all of them in a single glance.

"Yes," Lord Tower repeated in the same, level voice. "The lich used its own type of death magic, which preys easily on the old and weak. People died. More will. I'm afraid you have no idea how bad this is likely to get, Rune."

Brand was studying the expression on my face. His own was stuck between unhappiness and resignation. He said, "Are you sure it's a lich?"

"As the only living Arcana to have seen one," Lord Tower said, "yes, I am sure. It's a long story, but I'll tell it, if you'll indulge me."

I absurdly wondered where my coffee was. When had I lost my coffee? I couldn't even remember the last time I rested. When had . . .

I pressed my eyes shut, because the circles were still blinking and there were so many of them.

Lord Tower said, "The Dagger Court has always had concerns in Spain and Portugal. In my younger days, I would visit the older civilizations in Central and South America. By then, of course, many of them were in decline—we'd carried too many germs, both of illness and of ideas, into their cultures.

"In the mid-1500s, there was an explorer named Francisco de Orellana, of whom I was fond. A remarkable human. He'd been traveling since he was seventeen. In 1541, he joined an Ecuadorian expedition to map the Amazon—or what would become known as the Amazon—in search of the *Canelas*, the Land of Cinnamon, which they believed lay in the east. I went with him."

I wanted to ask question, but I didn't. The Tower almost never talked about his early years. I kept my mouth shut and learned what I could.

"Early on, Francisco was charged with gathering horses and left for Guayaquil. I traveled from Quito with the main body of the expedition. We were under Gonzalo Pizarro's command, and began with four thousand natives and over two hundred Spaniards. Expeditions in those days began as massive things—sprawling tent cities that sprang up around port towns, flowing with Spanish gold. But despite all the bodies and supplies and ships, the minute we entered the Amazon, we were dwarfed. We numbered over four thousand souls, and our insignificance was palpable. Once, I might have told you that a modern comparison was impossible. But now we have the Westlands. That is the closest I can come to describing the sensation of being consumed by nature.

"The expedition soon ran into trouble, as expeditions are prone to do. By the time Francisco and his horsemen met up with us, we'd barely left the region's mountains, and over three thousand natives and a hundred Spaniards were dead or had deserted. We were forced to camp, to build returning vessels for the sick. Francisco was charged with a second expedition in the meantime: to go and find the head of the Coca River."

Ciaran made an appreciative sound. "I've been there. In its own way, the Amazon and its rivers are as powerful as any jungle in Atlantis."

Lord Tower nodded. "It is an old place, as you say, with deep and strange magic. And I traveled, as you must imagine, without a sanctum. It took hours of meditation to restore the most meager spell to my sigils.

"When we found the head of the Coca, the urge to press on—to see what lay around the next bend—was obsessive. When Francisco broached the idea of returning to the main expedition, the crew nearly mutinied. So we pressed on, into the unknown.

"We were chased by the Omaguas. We found the Negro River, which took us in turn to the Amazon herself. We built a bigger ship to navigate the rougher waters. We were nearly butchered by natives, nearly starved. We saw a full turn of seasons. We spotted pigmies with heads growing from their spines; a race of blond and blue-eyed wizards; men with tails, and backward feet, and staves of living fire.

"And then, in June of 1542, we entered the lands of the people Francisco would name the Amazons—a race governed by aggressive warrior women.

"By the time we arrived, the lich had already rotted them at the core."

The Tower slid out a drawer, which held a sleek keyboard, and began to type a series of words that flashed across the bottom of the monitor. He put his finger on a glide pad and began to open documents from a file manager.

"Liches are associated with—" Images flickered across the screen: terrain maps, old papyrus pages, artistic representations. "The Antioch earthquake. Pompeii. Stroggli. But by 1542, liches were a myth, even among the Arcanum. Or—no, perhaps that's too strong. No, not a myth; they had become an extinct danger. Our records on them were antiques. We knew that liches were created using the inverse of creation magic. They are summonable creatures, and virtually immortal. They feed off death and annihilation; they draw strength from disasters on an epochal scale; and if they are not stopped they become, I promise you, a threat that can bring down empires."

He said, "All of these disasters followed the rise of a lich. In each case, one thing is clear to me: the lich, as a species, *changes*. As humanity ages, so do lich-kind's appetites. Look. We move from earthquakes and tsunamis, to plagues and pandemics, to . . . To what I saw among the Amazons."

The Tower stopped talking. He pressed a button, and the monitor went black. I could see the Tower's reflection appear beneath him.

"The lich called itself Yacam. It was accidentally summoned by the village's wise-women, and, at first, was revered. They fed it. They housed it. They let it grow. But unlike liches of antiquity, when Yacam's growth reached critical mass, it did not bury the land in rockslides. Instead, it ate their minds. It *played* with them.

"I hid my companions from Yacam's sight, and we watched as it possessed the population in segments. It would possess the men, and make them hunt the women. Then it would possess the women, and make them hunt the men. One hour, Yacam would have every remaining person tear apart the village in search of the eyes of old women; and the next hour, Yacam would have them rioting for the thigh bones of prepubescent boys. There was . . . more. But this is all I am comfortable saying."

Still, he lingered over this point. He finally admitted, "Between each routing, between each bout of lunacy and brutality, Yacam would lift the madness from the Amazons' eyes, so that they could see what they had done. That was worst of all, in its own way."

"Bloody hell," I said. "What did you do?"

"I retreated. I spent days meditating over sigils without sleep. And then I went back and ended it."

Lord Tower turned, to hide his expression, over the keyboard, pressing at keys that produced no visible effect.

The silence that fell was almost as uncomfortable as what Lord Tower had said. Addam finally broke it. "We need to rise up. The Arcanum must act. It doesn't matter how it began, or what happened to me. This is no time for secrecy, if—"

"No," Lord Tower said. He was looking at me as he said it. "We mustn't do that. Do you understand, Rune?"

I did. "It does matter who started it. Because that's how you reverse a summoning. Having the city panic would accomplish nothing. And I bet you'd need to spend time convincing the Arcanum that liches were even real. They're not all as old as you are." Lord Tower raised his eyebrows at the last part. I didn't care. I always got a little pissy when he tested me; he might as well hold up a sign saying "Future Arcana Training in Process."

"But if it's as serious as you say—" Addam tried again.

Ciaran said, "If the lich senses you're ready to move against it, it will run. We cannot afford the months it would take to root it out. It grows stronger with each passing day; though, fortunately, it is far from full strength right now. This is why I took my concerns to Lord Tower. He's in the best position to act quickly, given his past encounter."

"Which," Lord Tower said, giving Ciaran a narrowed stare, "I'd thought was known by very few." Just as quickly, he held up a hand, dismissing the curiosity. "Either way. Subtlety will serve us best here. I will alert Lady Justice. Given Addam's role in this, I am assured of her cooperation. Together we will figure out a way to approach the Arcanum. But now, for now, I need Rune to find the summoner."

"He—I mean, we . . ." Addam started to say. "There are suspicions that—Rune thinks—it's possible my sister is involved."

"I wouldn't doubt him, then."

"You have an idea where we should go next?" I asked Lord Tower, mainly to change the subject. I'm not sure Addam realized yet what Lord Tower was asking me to do.

Lord Tower dipped his head in a *yes*. "I've taken the liberty of gathering your houseguest and maid. You may—"

Brand said, losing control of his building anger, "You want Rune to expose himself to a threat like this? Did you know it's after Rune now? That it's fixated on Rune?"

"As it stands," Lord Tower said, "I'm counting on it."

Ciaran followed us to the tenth floor, where Lord Tower had arranged rooms.

"You're staying?" I asked him.

"Lord Tower is paying me *very* well," Ciaran said. He gave the Tower, who was standing behind us, a grave nod that was too respectful to be respectful.

"How is it that you knew it was a lich?" I asked, in retrospect maybe a little suspiciously.

Ciaran chewed on that. He said, finally, "It would be highly unproductive for you to suspect me of any involvement. Do you want my oath?"

I blinked. Oaths weren't small things, not to an Atlantean. "Godsdamn, Ciaran, how well is he paying you?"

"We're renegotiating," Brand said. He glared at Lord Tower. "This is now a new job."

"Have I ever slighted you before, Brandon?" Lord Tower asked.

Before Brand could *count the fucking ways*, or whatever else was coming out of his mouth, the elevator pinged and the doors opened.

The Tower said, "I've had the staff prepare the entire floor for all of you. There's a cold buffet in the living room if you want brunch, otherwise you should rest for an early dinner. We will make plans then."

After letting us know where Queenie and Max were, he excused himself and went in another direction. We headed to the common area, which was filled with plasma televisions, carpeting as soft as milk thistle, and plump leather chairs. Queenie and Max were watching a cooking show.

Max's face brightened. "You're here!" he said, and ran around the couch. There was an awkward moment when he wasn't sure if he could hug us. Brand solved the problem by putting him in a friendly headlock.

Exhaustion swamped me. I must have lost a few seconds, because everyone was staring at me. Queenie gave Brand a worried look and bustled everyone toward the wet bar for a drink, to give us a moment alone.

Brand said, "You need sleep. Come on, let's find our rooms. This is the safest place in the city. Take advantage of it while it lasts."

Five minutes later, Brand literally put his foot on my ass and shoved me into an empty guest suite. The door slammed shut behind me.

I stood in the middle of the room for a second, biting my nails, not knowing what to do. Then my teeth crunched on dirt wedged under my thumbnail. I decided to take a shower. After that, I collapsed into bed without dressing. My eyelids closed like a movie curtain, and I was asleep.

I awoke many hours later, just before sunset. The bed sheet had been pulled over me, and clean clothes were folded on top of the duvet. I pawed through them and recognized an old pair of my blue jeans, and a gray-blue button-down shirt that Queenie said matched my eyes. *Queenie.* It made me smile to think of the Tower's people descending on Half House to evacuate her and Max, only to have to cool their feet on the front steps while Queenie scuttled around packing overnight bags for Brand and me.

My mood brightened even more when I saw my best pair of boots by the door.

I dressed, pulled them on, and drummed the heels into place. I could feel the reassuring vibration of the recoil wards. I headed out to find the others.

The Pac Bell was very privacy-conscious; each suite had its own hallway entrance, and no two entrances were in eyesight of another. Since I had only a dim idea where Brand had settled, I went to the common room, which people had to pass to get to the elevator.

After a few minutes, I turned on the television set. I flipped the channel through two commercials and got a full-color shot of a New Atlantean street corner that looked as if a grenade had gone off. A red-spattered white sheet covered a body. The word *spectre* started scrolling across the bottom.

I shut off the TV, left the common room, and randomly started knocking on doors. On the third room I tried, Queenie answered. More surprisingly, Addam was in the room, too. He stood by a bed stacked with half-opened packaging and shopping bags, wearing only boxers, with a pair of scissors in his hands.

"I brought him clothes?" Queenie said to me. "That the Tower bought?"

"I am half-naked, Hero," Addam said. "And yet you have not taken your eyes off the scissors. Such a vigilant warrior prince."

"Thank you for noticing. And please tell Brand. So I'm guessing neither of you are ready to eat?"

190

"I'll see if things are ready, and you can help Addam clean up," Queenie squeaked, and hurried past me. She was too flustered to even phrase it as a question.

"I'm not really going to clean you up," I told him after she left.

"It might not be the chore you expect," Addam said. He sat down, crossed his long legs, and showed me a stretch of abdomen.

"How about I wait in the hallway while you clean yourself up?" I said, and shut the door behind me.

When he opened the door again, he was wearing a white dress shirt and gray slacks. Whoever had bought the clothes had gotten his waist wrong; he had a good three inches bunched under the belt buckle. Of course, that belt buckle now had a million dollars' worth of sigils strung through it.

"I just realized it may be a while before I can return to my condo," Addam said. "For now, I own neither toothbrush nor cereal bowl. It is a . . . clean feeling. Minimalist."

"That's the spirit," I said. "Don't you have rooms at the Crusader Throne?"

"Would it be wise to visit them?"

"I suppose not," I conceded. "Have you been in touch with your court at all?"

"I had no choice, as it turned out. Lord Tower came by and reminded me that the moment I left Farstryke, my mother would have been able to sense me." He grimaced. "She . . . monitors my well-being, one might say."

I remembered what Lady Justice had told me about the spells she'd placed on her children. She would, hypothetically, have been aware of the attack in the South Bridge tunnels. She would have been able to track Addam to Lord Tower's building. "I've got this image in my head of her bursting through the wall like the Kool Aid pitcher."

Addam smiled. "Perhaps not so dramatic as that. Either way, Lord Tower suggested I contact my agents at the Crusader Throne, and have word passed along that I was fine, yet out of touch. Lord Tower felt it would buy us time."

"Good idea. And is there—?" I hesitated, knowing it was a hard subject for him. "Is there any news on Quinn? Or Christian?"

"Christian is resting, but they have yet to identify the cause of his illness. Quinn is . . . asleep. Still asleep. It is kind of you to ask."

"I really think Quinn believed that he'll be okay, Addam. He's a seer. He's gifted enough to see his path."

"That's just it, though. From Quinn, I know now that there is no one true path. But Lord Tower has been in touch with Quinn's doctors, and offered his own medical resources. He tells me Quinn is stable, and the doctors are confident. That will have to be enough, for now."

I changed the subject. "Are you hungry?"

Addam's smile returned, though slowly. "Ravenous. Lead on."

It turned out Addam knew this floor better than I did. Instead of the elevator, he guided me to the southwest corner, where the ceiling had been knocked out to allow for the installation of a sweeping stairway. As we climbed it, Addam fell behind. I glanced over my shoulder to catch him staring at my ass.

He smiled at my raised eyebrows and caught up with me. "You are very handsome, Hero. May I admit something?"

"You know, you flirted a lot less when you thought your life was in immediate danger."

He ignored me and continued with his thought. "I would like to admit I am worried you have a poor impression of me."

"Why would you say that?" I asked, stopping short.

"I did not fight a spectre, as you and your Companion did."

"No, you just used Telekinesis to push bystanders from the line of fire. You pushed tripping hazards out of my way. And when I needed you to run for help, you went, without hesitation. You handled yourself well."

"So I impressed you?"

"You didn't not impress me," I said, a little nervous under the gravity of his stare.

He squinted at the ceiling and nodded. "An acceptable start."

The dining floor was divided into several kitchens and many different salons, from intimate settings to a ballroom that spanned half a
block. Servants guided us toward a room that faced the northern harbors,
its windows cleverly designed to appear as a solid wall of glass. New
Atlantis had gone several weeks without a Cleansing—the abrasive, toxic
spell that periodically scoured away the worst of city pollution. The smog
gave the sky a scorched appearance, almost pretty when viewed from the
comfort of indoor air-conditioning.

Lord Tower hadn't arrived yet, but Brand was there. He was doing
a circuit of the room, trying to find all the eavesdropping devices. There
were already three wireless transmitters in his palm.

"I'm not sure Lord Tower put those out as snacks," I said.

"He's testing me. It's fucking rude," Brand said. He looked up and
gave me a critical once-over. Whatever he saw made him nod. "You got
some sleep. You look good."

"I agree," Addam said, very politely.

Brand gave Addam a look. Then he went over to the wet bar and put
the listening devices into a bucket of crushed ice, which he then pounded
with a beer bottle.

When he was done, he popped the cap off the beer. He held it out to
me while giving Addam a flat smile. "Appletini?"

"A beer as well, if it pleases you, Lord Saint John," Addam said.

In the years since the fall of the Sun Throne, I'd had very, very few
romantic interests. I was uncomfortable with people flirting with me,
and usually let Brand growl them away. The fact that Brand was almost
speculative with Addam's interest was either really interesting or hor-
ribly unsettling.

Not long after, the others entered. A servant announced that Lord
Tower would be delayed and that we should begin dining without him. I
approached the table, and Addam, in a move that seemed entirely uncho-
reographed, stepped in front of me and pulled out my chair.

I caught Max staring at Addam with a look of minor outrage. "Max,"

I said carefully, while Addam sat in my right. More servants bled out of the woodwork and began swarming around us. "How're you doing?"

Max jerked into motion. He beat Brand to the table and slid into the chair on my other side. "I'm okay. How are you?"

Brand grabbed the back of Max's chair, lifted it up, and dropped it into the next place setting. He pulled another chair up for himself and sat down next to me.

Max, undeterred, wiggled forward so that he could look at me down the table. He said, "I tried to fix the washing machine, Rune."

"That's nice of you," I said.

"Um, it didn't work. I broke a mop, too," Max added.

"Least of my problems," I said.

"Fascinating," Ciaran said, speaking for the first time. His bright-red lips were pursed in Max's direction.

"Excuse me?" Max said.

"You're a Lovers. But your dreams make no sense. Just what on earth did they do to you?"

Brand went very still. I went stiller. I said, to Ciaran, "Back down."

Ciaran blinked at me in surprise. "You misunderstand. The Lovers were wretched people. The dreams in that boy's head are refreshingly kind. It's pleasant to see a decent branch in that family."

"I . . . Oh," Max said.

He wasn't sure whether to be pleased or mortified. But just the fact that he thought he ought to be pleased was, in a way, encouraging. I gave Ciaran a vague nod.

The table was laid out with steaming platters and frosted pitchers. A single covered dish was placed at each setting. Each guest had his or her own attendant, and the attendants waited until the table was fully laden before whipping off the silver domes.

"Are those . . . ?" Max asked curiously.

"Sundrop fish," Addam murmured with a pleased expression. "What a treat."

If I needed a reminder that Addam lived in an extraordinarily different tax bracket, it was right there. *Treat* was a poor way to describe a meal that I could never have afforded on my own.

The Atlantean homeland was abandoned in the wake of the Atlantean World War, but some of the more-profitable fishing grounds had been reclaimed. Sundrops schooled in only one location: a treacherous reef about a dozen miles off old Atlantis. They were tiny, minnow-sized fish—mostly scale and bone with just a morsel of flesh—that generated their own heat and light. Even in death, the slivers of meat emitted a warm, molasses glow. I hadn't tasted one in over twenty-five years, at my dead father's holiday table.

"Wow," Brand said. "This'll really give us the protein we need to fight monsters."

"I'm sure we could find something else for you, Brandon," Lord Tower said as he glided into the room. He waved off a servant and went to the bar. "Perhaps something simpler to honor your human roots?"

Brand waited until Lord Tower began to make a drink before saying, "You might want to use the other ice bucket. That one has bugs in it."

Lord Tower tilted his head down at the crushed listening devices. He *tsk*ed. "You only found three. I'm disappointed. Metaphorically speaking, the fourth you missed may get Rune harmed one day."

"I guess I'll need to be more careful who I let near him, then," Brand said stiffly.

"So there's this lich after us," I said. "Tall guy. Rurik. He may or may not destroy the world."

"I do wish you wouldn't personify it," Lord Tower said, walking to the table. He took a seat at the head, which we'd left free for him. "The creature is not a *he*."

"He speaks, he dresses himself, and he's pretty grabby with his hands," I said. "That's sentience."

"Can you tell us what happened now?" Max asked. "I was watching TV. There are . . . there're all these stories. They say a lot of people died. Are you okay, Rune?"

"I'm okay too," Brand said, leaning forward and planting himself in Max's line of sight.

"This is what you need to know," Lord Tower said. "A lich has been summoned. We suspect that one of its original purposes was to kidnap and hold Addam. I believe the summoner has since lost control of it. It used a very clever version of a tracking spell to find either Rune or Addam—it raised sentries in a grid pattern through the heart of New Atlantis."

"Like batteries," I whispered. "Rurik used vulnerable people like batteries to power-up the most evil motherfucking radar system in history."

Lord Tower said, "If nothing else, this development reinforces one fact. The lich is not without limitations if it needs such tactics to track or trap you. That will do nicely for our next move."

I could see that the royal *our* rankled Brand, who wasn't used to handing my well-being over to anyone else. He said, "How do we kill it?"

Lord Tower said, "The easiest way to banish it is to find either the summoner or the summoning circle."

This was the first he'd mentioned the summoning circle, which made my antenna twinge. "I thought you wanted us to go after the summoner? Or, at least, to find all of the suspects, until we know for sure who was involved?"

"Unfortunately, it appears that all of Addam's business partners have vanished. Michael Saint Talbot's rooms appear to have been the scene of an attack. Ashton Saint Gabriel was caught on a bodega surveillance camera one block from his house, running down an alley as if something was in pursuit. I have no intelligence on Geoffrey Saint Talbot."

"What about my sister?" Addam asked in a strained voice.

"That's unclear," Lord Tower said. "I have been unable to reach her through conventional means."

"We don't know who's behind this," I said. "We don't know if anyone's in real trouble. It could be a ruse."

"And, as such, things have changed," Lord Tower said. "I'll find the scions, assuming they remain in the city. I need to stay close to the Arcanum, in any event. I want you to find the place where Rurik was summoned."

"You want us to find a specific summoning circle?" I asked. "Maybe it's in a haystack. Next to a needle."

"The summoning of a lich is a significant endeavor. The ritual, almost certainly, would have required what we call an 'imbued' summoning circle. A very rare device. Creating one takes years of effort from dozens of magic-users. I suspect that whomever summoned Rurik used one of the two existing imbued circles on the island."

"Two?" I said. "I only know of one. It's at the Convocation."

I was rewarded with a slight nod of approval for knowing that much. "There is also one at the Magician's estate in the Westlands."

"*Is* there now," Ciaran said, eyes glinting.

"You will treat that information with discretion," Lord Tower told him. He continued, "The Convocation is heavily guarded—and subtlety is our opponent's best defense. It seems far more likely that they gained access to Lord Magician's estate."

"You're sending us into the Westlands," Brand said. About a thousand "fucks" sparked in his eyes.

"Not quite," Lord Tower demurred. He picked up his fish fork. "Let's finish our meal, and then we'll take a walk."

Later, Lord Tower escorted all of us, even Queenie and Max, toward a glass elevator attached to the outside of the Pac Bell. It hadn't been part of the building's original translocated design; he'd built it himself in a pique back in the eighties.

"I asked about killing it," Brand said, out of the blue, as we waited for the glass elevator to arrive. "How do we *kill* it?"

"With great difficultly and overwhelming force," Lord Tower said. "Which we'll apply if matters spiral further out of control. In the meantime, there are things that will injure or distract it. Bless-fire; graveyard amber; certain alchemical supplies lost to us with the fall of old Atlantis. I have my men trying to locate graveyard amber."

"Define 'overwhelming force,'" Brand said.

"I will," Lord Tower responded, "if Rune fails to reach the circle."

In my head I heard Lord Tower saying: "*I retreated. I spent days meditating over sigils without sleep. And then I went back and ended it.*" I had a strong suspicion that the Tower's version of *ending things* involved a whole lot of collateral damage.

The elevator arrived. As the doors started to open, Mayan strode up to us. He said, "Sir, may I?" and placed an enquiring hand near the Tower's shoulder.

Lord Tower raised both eyebrows when Mayan plucked a listening device off Lord Tower's back. Lord Tower cut his eyes to Brand. Brand pretended to be looking at the view outside the window, all but whistling. My fucking Brand.

We all moved into the elevator. The view was dulled by bulletproof glass. We descended to a balcony on the Tower's training floor. The balcony led to an Olympic-size lap pool, which led to a series of exercise areas for sparring, meditation, and weightlifting. We passed by several security measures—some of which I identified by sight, some of which I felt as a frisson of magic that raised the hair along my arms.

At the very end of a corridor flanked with ceiling turrets was a vault door. Next to the door was a black plastic panel. Lord Tower put his finger in an indentation and waited as it whirred in response.

"It's testing my DNA," Lord Tower said. "It will be a moment."

"Maybe we can talk about those next steps while we wait," I said.

"When you're unsure of the enemy's strength but suspect that it's greater than yours, and time is your friend, what is the recommended maneuver?"

"Divide, distract, deflect," I said automatically. Sun Tzu's battle theories were a favorite of his.

"We will divide the lich's attention by splitting into two groups;

and we will deflect our true purpose by crafting a distraction. I need you, Rune, to go to Rurik's summoning circle and perform a ritual. The best way to ensure your success is to prevent Rurik from following you. What's inside this vault will help do that. It's something I created many years ago for a purpose exactly like this."

"So you *do* want us to travel in the Westlands," Brand said.

"Not quite," Lord Tower said.

The black panel pinged. The steel door slid into a recess. I was the third person in the room, after Lord Tower and Brand. The air smelled like chlorine and climate-control. Whatever was in front of us made Brand's shoulders go rigid. The emotion that poured off him was so strong that I couldn't even tell what it was.

I stepped around Brand, and saw . . .

Me.

I was in the center of the room.

I was dressed in jeans and a long-sleeved t-shirt. Sunglasses peeked out of a breast pocket. My head was down. I was as still as a statue. Was I a statue?

"It's a golem, Rune," Lord Tower said.

I looked at him dumbly. A golem was a type of gargoyle, though with much less free will. There were other golems gathered around the fringes of the room, too. Lord Tower was there, in a black painter's smock. His children, Dalton and Amelia. Mayan. The mother of his children, Lissa, a woman who'd left the island many years back to settle in an exile community.

Lord Tower touched the golem's shoulder and whispered a couple words. Its—*my*—head lifted. Its eyes were obsidian, with hairline fissures that glowed from behind with lava light. I knew without checking that it would reek of my magical signature, too.

I looked back at Brand, hoping he'd say something funny and stupid that would make this moment less surreal. Instead, I saw that Brand's furious gaze had fallen on Lord Tower. Brand was in a *rage*. The bond between us was slowly igniting with his anger.

"Brand?" I asked quietly.

"How fucking dare you," Brand said to Lord Tower in a voice that shook.

"Brand?" I said again.

He wheeled on me. "Not *we*. *We* aren't going into the Westlands. Do you see my golem anywhere? Do you? How fucking successful a decoy will it be if I'm not at its side? He's going to make you go into the fucking Westlands without me!"

"But . . ." I said.

"Why him?" Queenie demanded, speaking up for the first time in hours. She planted herself in front of Lord Tower in a rare, if not unprecedented, show of fury. "Why must Rune do this *ritual*?"

"The ritual will contain the lich," Lord Tower said.

"Send Addam—he's the one who started all this!" Max cried.

"Max!" I said.

"I'll go," Addam said. "Of course I'll go, and do the ritual."

Lord Tower said, "Addam, as capable as you are, this will require a force beyond your experience. There are few magic-users I'd trust for a working of this magnitude. Rune is one of them."

"Don't *compliment* him," Brand spat in disgust. "Don't make this sound like a compliment!"

"You doubt his ability?"

"Of course I don't fucking doubt his abilities! He'll be greater than you one day, and you fucking know it! That's not what this is about!"

"Brandon," Lord Tower said. "This will be done. This will keep him *safe*."

"I'll go with him," Addam said. He gave me an anxious look. "You won't be alone."

"I'll go with Rune," Max added.

"Rune and Addam will go alone," Lord Tower said. "They must be quiet and quick, and escape the notice of our enemy. The others will assist with the distraction that will buy his safety. Ciaran will help me in my own preparations. Rune, you and Addam will travel to the Moral Certainties compound, which abuts Lord Magician's Westlands estate. By the time you reach it, I will have figured out a way to secure the Magician's cooperation."

"You always do this, you always try to separate us!" Brand yelled.

"And how, exactly, could you help in the Westlands? Overestimating one's own skills is a very sad trap, Brandon."

"Don't you patronize me! Don't you dare fucking patronize me!"

Storm clouds moved across Lord Tower's eyes. Literal storm clouds. In my entire life, I'd seen his Aspect only once. It'd been like standing before the end of the world.

"Hold your tongue," Lord Tower said softly.

"Or what?" Brand demanded. "You'll have me whipped? *Again?*"

"Oh, fuck." I grabbed Brand's shoulder and yanked. He was so upset that I actually caught him by surprise and made him stumble.

I dragged him out the door of the vault.

I backtracked through the exercise areas with Brand, leading him into an empty locker room. He was unsatisfied with that, and made us go all the way into the dry, tiled showers. He began to turn on all the faucets until we were landlocked in a single corner, unlikely to be overheard.

By then, his anger had drained into a watchful wariness.

"What are you thinking?" I said.

"I'm wondering how it feels, knowing the Tower has a blow-up doll of you."

"Brand," I said. "This isn't a joke. You *cannot* say things like that to the Tower. If he ever gets mad—really and truly mad—I won't be able to stop him. I won't be able to protect you."

"What, from killing me? He wouldn't dare. He'd never risk pissing you off like that."

"I'm not sure the Tower cares whether or not he pisses me off. Not really."

"Sure he does," Brand said flatly. "Who else would he buy Sundrop fish for?"

"What's all this about? Come on, talk to me. Do you think I can't handle myself?"

"Of course you can handle yourself. But he's talking about sending you into the *Westlands*, Rune. We don't have any experience going there—we haven't trained for it, we're not familiar with it."

"People go there all the time. Every throne has a compound there. Hell, technically *we* have a compound there."

"Every throne has a *compound* there, you're right, because it's suicidal to enter it without a fucking armed guard!"

"Addam and I will stay on the warded paths. Those are safe."

"That is such bullshit! There is no fucking *safe* in the Westlands, just *safer than*. Safer than fucking slitting your wrists with a rusty razor blade. Safer than using a rattlesnake as a cock ring. I don't want you going there!"

"But." I held out my hands to him in a helpless gesture. "This needs to happen. You know that."

"Then find a way I can go with you!"

"You . . ." I didn't know how to say what I needed to say next. "The Westlands is magic. It's, literally, a physical embodiment of magic. Between the both of us, you know it's something I'm better equipped to handle."

"Fine, then you get to stand in front, and I watch your back."

"No," I said. Then, louder, "*No.* I'm not going to have you hovering at my shoulder, waiting for the perfect moment to sacrifice yourself."

And he would. He would. I abruptly remembered the foyer of Farstryke, when I had barely enough Bless-fire left to protect myself from the advancing wraiths. *That* would have been the moment he died, if he'd been with me—that would have been the moment, when my magic wasn't strong enough to protect him. "I'll have Addam with me. He has an entire belt filled with sigils. You saw that he can handle himself in a bad situation. I'll be okay. I may even be safer than you. Did you think about that? You're the one who's going to be bait."

He said, in a strained and unhappy voice, "I stay behind when you go into Farstryke, and now I stay behind when you go into the Westlands. How am I supposed to react? What do you want from me, Rune?"

"Grim resignation?"

Brand's face hardened. "He's going to get his way, so fine, we'll settle this later. Do what you have to for now."

He whipped around and stormed through the spray of water, sure-footed on the slick tile. I stared at his back. I'd never responded well to the "we'll talk about it later" warning. It made me feel like a pendulum blade was scraping the back of my neck.

At the edge of the showers, Brand pivoted and strode back to me. He grabbed me in a wet hug. Into my hair he said, "You hate when I say that, I'm sorry. The last thing I want is for you to be distracted, to be worried about my shit. So, okay, I'm not mad. There's nothing to settle. I'll stay here and hang out with a golem and bang a lot of drums. I'll distract the *fuck* out of that lich."

My breath caught. I let him hold me for a while. When the damp clothing between us had cooled, I pushed away. His bangs had dripped into his eyes.

I wiped at them and said, "You look like you're in a wet t-shirt contest."

"The world should be so lucky," he said. He put his fingers on my chin and tilted my face up to him, studying me. "Damn. You're using your sabre too much, Rune."

"I'm just tired. One nap can only do so much."

"Don't fucking sass me. When you're tired, you get blue bags under your eyes. When you use your sabre too much, the bags get greenish. Every firebolt is a minute off your life, and you know it."

"A minute is a minute off my life. A minute fighting a lich is a minute off my life. I'll be fine. When this is all over, we'll take a week off, maybe go back to the Enclave and learn to surf with the krakens."

"I'll hold you to it," he said.

"Then we're good?" I asked. "No more threatening the Tower?"

"Oh, I'll kill him, if you get hurt without me. But I won't *talk* about it."

"I've gotten stronger reassurances from you before," I pointed out.

"I'm not feeling very fucking moved to provide one. But . . . Back there, with the Tower? I'm sorry I mentioned the time that . . . You know."

"The time I got you whipped."

"You did no such fucking thing and do *not* get me started. But I know you don't like thinking about it. I'm sorry I brought it up."

I shrugged and avoided eye contact. No, I didn't like bringing it up. It had been my fault, no matter what he said.

Things hadn't gone very easily in the early days of our living with the Tower. Something had happened. I hadn't handled it well. Brand had paid the price.

Brand punched my shoulder. "Come on. You're soaked. Maybe we can find you some clothes that don't look like a stripper outfit. Those jeans are shamefully tight."

"*Queenie* picked out the jeans," I said. "Not me."

He rolled his eyes.

I said, "By the way. When I walked in on Addam earlier, he complained that I only looked at the scissors he was holding and not him being naked. I was *vigilant*."

"You were naked with Addam? With scissors?"

"Addam was naked. Almost naked. Queenie was cutting tags off his clothes."

"And I'm supposed to pat you on the back because you kept your eye on a person you've known less than a week who had a weapon in his hand? Are you fucking twelve?"

"I really thought you'd be more impressed than this."

"Oh, absolutely," he said. "It's the same sort of pride I feel when you tie your shoes every morning, or when your spoon makes it all the way to your mouth."

I punched at his shoulder, and promptly slipped on the wet floor. He ended up catching me, like he always did.

I spent four hours in the Tower's guest sanctum, filling each of my empty sigils with the strongest spells I could most quickly meditate over—with the sole exception of the Bless-fire.

There was nothing easy about storing holy magic. More than half of the four-hour stretch was devoted to it. The version I used at Farstryke had taken me the better part of a night to craft; I didn't have the energy for that now, but I was comfortable with the results.

When I was done, I thought about taking a dip in the pool. It turned out I wasn't the only one with that idea.

A bored Max was sitting on one of the bamboo chaise lounges next to Brand and inking patterns on a piece of paper with a ballpoint pen and sticking them to his bicep to make a tattoo. Brand had commandeered a laptop from somewhere and was busy on the keyboard.

Addam, who did not appear to be wearing a bathing suit, did a back-stroke to the side of the pool closest to me. The motion turned his groin into a dark-blond ripple. I stared at my boots before the ripples could settle.

Addam said, "The water is nice, Hero."

"Why does he keep calling him *hero*," Max said sulkily.

"Zip it," Brand said.

I went over to Brand and Max, dragging an empty chaise the last several steps. "Where did you get the computer?" I asked.

"I borrowed it from Mayan."

"Is this one of those surprises I can look forward to, when he figures out you borrowed it?"

Brand smirked at me, and didn't say a word.

I peeked at the laptop. "What's the *Jamestown Press?*"

"Research," Brand said.

"Brand and I had an idea," Max added, a little proudly, or maybe possessively. "We're looking into the things that the Tower isn't discussing."

"What isn't he discussing?"

"Who are we fighting?" Brand counter-questioned.

"Ah. A teachable moment. Okay—we're fighting a lich."

"Is that all?"

"The person who summoned a lich."

"Who else?" Brand asked.

"Just . . . Oh. The recarnates." Our first problem hadn't been Rurik, it had been the recarnates. "And a gargoyle. Well, and spectres, skeletons, and wraiths. But lots of recarnates."

"Doesn't it seem funny that the Tower hasn't mentioned them? I get that some fuckhead scion might summon up a lich as a party favor— that's the sort of thing fuckhead scions do. But what are all the recarnates for? To kidnap Addam? No offense, but I don't think so."

"None taken," Addam said. He was still in the water, with his forearms folded on the rail. Underwater lights surrounded his torso in a deep-blue silhouette.

"So," Brand continued, "Max and I started researching tattoos."

The recarnates had tattoos. One in particular flashed across my memory: a red grenade in the shape of a segmented heart with letters under it. "USMC! Brand, I think these are soldiers. American soldiers. Isn't USMC the Marines?"

Brand gave me a look of long suffering.

I said, "Just to be clear, how many steps ahead of me are you?"

"Yeah, those are soldier tatts. And I knew the bodies had to come from somewhere. So we looked, and we found articles about desecrated soldier graves in dozens of American papers—*Pittsburgh Morning Sun*, the *Boston Globe*, the *Jamestown Press* in Rhode Island. None of them are so similar that you'd see a pattern unless you knew what you were looking for. A lot of times they even made it look like anti-war shit, not grave robbing. It goes back nearly a year, Rune. Some serious fucking deliberation went into putting this little army together. So . . . why?"

"Why indeed," I said. "Recarnates retain a sense of their physical skills and training. A dead soldier fights better than a dead accountant. That explains their firearms. There's a reason they wanted fighters."

"Brand had me do research on recarnates," Max added. "To find their weaknesses. Did you know that something about them being zombies keeps their dicks hard the entire time? And that their dicks fall off a couple days after being raised?"

Addam said, "Just what kind of websites have you been visiting?"

Max turned red. Brand stared at Addam and said, "Recarnates used to be alive, and a part of them remembers it. There's a part of them that hates what some sick necromantic fuck has done to them. And the more you make them aware of it, the harder it is for said necromantic fuck to hold them. You don't think it's good information that their dicks are about to fall off? Knowledge is a weapon. Knowledge informs *tactics*. Max did good work."

Max lifted his head and gave Brand a look like he didn't even understand what language compliments came in.

"My sincere apologies, Matthias," Addam said.

That just made Max scowl, and, damn it, when did he start being jealous?

I began to say something when a purple bird with a three-foot wingspan launched itself at my head. I yelled, tripped, and landed in a pile of steaming vegetation.

"You've got to be kidding me," I said, staring up at the parrot. I was back in the Tower's head.

The Tower—wearing his younger skin—curled his lips in amusement. I accepted his hand and pulled myself upright.

He said, "Would you please come to my office?"

"Really? I'm *right downstairs*. Forget a phone call, you could have just stomped on the floor."

"I thought you would appreciate the living memory."

"You have an odd understanding of the word 'appreciate.'"

Lord Tower looked back at the parrot, which had settled into a dead tree's hollow covered with hanging vines. The bird squawked and preened a pale-violet chest.

Lord Tower said, "I'll see you in my office."

He shucked me back into the pool room, where a naked Addam was shaking my shoulders.

In all the time I'd known the Tower, I'd rarely been inside his private study. I didn't know what to make of the invitation. Between the war room and the golem vault, I was getting one hell of a private tour today.

He met me at the door and waved me inside. He wore a long, silk bathrobe over pajamas, feet bare. It'd been a couple decades, though, since I was fooled by his sleepy handsomeness.

Once inside, I had a few seconds to form an impression of mahogany and green damask; of walls lined with bookshelves; of a black marble desk as imposing as a throne. Then my attention was drawn to the corner of the room, where the Tower was painting.

It was called jewel work. There were only a handful of artists in the world who even remembered the magic to create it. Jewel work used spells to melt precious gemstones into paints for only minutes at a stretch.

"It's beautiful," I said, standing before the painting. He'd finished half of it: a sunset sky dominated by the early appearance of a low, pale moon. Next to the canvas were hardened bowls of ruby and golden sapphire. As I watched, the magic in a bowl of liquid opals seeped upward like a sigh, and the surface hardened into crested patterns.

"Would you like to try?" Lord Tower asked from directly behind me.

"I don't know how to paint."

"Start the ocean for me," he said.

On a shelf above the easel were small copper casks. He reached for one and brought it down to the mixing table. Inside was a selection of blue gems. He swirled his fingers through them and picked two, so dark they were nearly navy, with white starbursts in their centers.

"Are those star sapphires?" I asked.

"Blue star sapphires," he said.

"Shit," I breathed. "I don't know why you asked me here, but I'm guessing it's pretty damn bad if you're going to melt down several thousand dollars and let me ruin your painting."

He laughed. It wasn't his public laugh—this was soft and questioning, as if the sound surprised him. "You won't ruin anything. Just a brushstroke."

He clicked the two stones into a shallow copper bowl. Mounted along the edge of the casket shelf were a series of sigils shaped like silver coins. *Seven* of them. *Mounted.* The sight gave my stomach a raw, familiar twinge. I imagined being part of a court that was so hale that I could toss away sigils for hobby magic.

The Tower released one of the spells. He traced a pattern with his fingers on the underside of the copper bowl. The blue star sapphires collapsed on themselves, effervescing into liquid. I took a paintbrush that the Tower offered, and dragged the bristles through the color.

As I painted a single stroke on the canvas, all envy faded. A reluctant, childlike smile spread across my face. The color was richer than anything I'd ever seen.

He took the brush from my hand and stared at the easel. I followed his cue. We stood there for a surreal minute and watched—literally—the paint dry.

I said, "You're leading up to something."

He gave me a sidelong smile and stepped away. He walked over to a corner of the room where a map of New Atlantis was carved into a wooden wall panel.

"There are things I'd like to tell you that must not leave this room. I would have your vow before I talk about them." I opened my mouth to say something smart, and Lord Tower held up a hand. "This is information restricted to the Arcanum. Do you understand what that means?"

I did, and it tied my tongue for a second. "Aren't I a little young for the missile codes?"

"You are, but needs must. Do I have your vow?"

"Can you imagine any circumstance," I said, "where your sharing this information with me could cause me or mine to come to harm?"

The Tower smiled. It wasn't humor; it was approbation. "You'll come to understand, Rune, that there are secrets which could, yes, cause great harm if shared. That is our responsibility and burden, as Arcana. If it makes any difference, I'm asking you to trust that I would not burden you unnecessarily."

"I'll hold what you tell me in confidence," I swore. A shiver ran through the air as my vow was realized.

The Tower turned so that I could see his finger on the map. He traced a square of land that spanned the border of the Westlands, all the way to the eastern shore, and all the way from the north and south shores.

"The Arcanum has laid several measures against certain emergencies. There is one in particular I would share with you. Buried along every street in this area is a network of wards and mass sigils, not unlike the safe roads in the Westlands. Upon activation, this defense would saturate the entire city in an aura of Bless-fire."

"Like what you had around the Pac Bell yesterday."

"The Bless-fire perimeter around the Pac Bell was raised by individuals. It was a controlled defense. The dormant Bless-fire network would have no such discretion."

Oh.

The consequences spiraled through my head like a domino pattern.

Bless-fire was a weapon against the undead and deconsecrated. It had crippled Rurik when we'd fought. Surrounding the lich in a field of Bless-fire would be an effective, perhaps terminal weapon.

But there were other things that walked this city that were undead and deconsecrated, that lived a peaceful coexistence within Convocation law. What would become of them?

Also, our translocated buildings were filled with dark, deconsecrated power. We often drew on this power. It was a massive magical resource. What would happen to it, if subjected to Bless-fire?

The defense that the Tower talked about was *sterilization*. A last resort. Not unlike my Exodus sigil—a stored spell of such potency that I wasn't sure I could stop how far the blast radius went.

"And here we thought you were just worried about the recarnate army," I said tiredly.

"I am. But my guess is that the recarnates serve a temporary purpose: to assist and protect the lich in its early stages when it's not entirely able to protect itself. As the lich grows, it will not need an army."

He turned away from the map and looked at me. "I told you earlier that I was concerned that the Arcanum would not believe me, about the lich. That was . . . misdirection. My real concern is that they *will* believe me. I know our brothers and sisters, Rune. Some would react poorly."

"So . . . we need to proceed as planned, before someone cuts off our nose to spite our face. I need to head into the Westlands and find where the lich was summoned."

"And I will continue to search for the scions. I needed you to understand the gravity of the situation. We must act without hesitancy. The people responsible for the lich must die, and they must die quickly."

"I understand," I said. "Ella. Michael."

I glanced toward the portrait. My mind jumped to another topic. There were unsettled things between Lord Tower and me, and I had to address them.

"I need to tell you something," I said seriously.

His stillness was his attention.

"I want to thank you for helping me outside, when the spectres were after me. You revealed one of your defense mechanisms to save my life. I know it wasn't an easy, or costless, decision. I need you to know that—that I am truly, truly grateful for your help and protection. I always have been."

"But."

"But if you or your people ever leave Brand outside that protection again like you did downstairs—when it would have been so easy to save him as well—I swear, on my name, by binding oath, that we are done."

The temperature in the room jumped with the force of the vow. The words coiled around us, and sweat popped along my hairline.

The Tower's gaze was steady and dark and so unblinking that his eyes must have been burning with the effort of it.

This is the thing: I didn't know—I honestly didn't know—what my relationship with the Tower exactly *was*. Brand seemed to think that Lord Tower was fond of me. Maybe Brand was right. But even if I couldn't put a label on the relationship, I knew I was important to him in a way that most people weren't. So this vow involved playing a card I couldn't easily play again.

Lord Tower said, "You've never forgiven me for hurting him, have you?"

"That's not what this is about."

"That's not what I asked."

"What's to be gained by talking about that? Have you changed your mind about what happened? Do you see your son more clearly now? Do you still think it was Brand who deserved to be whipped?"

"I've always seen Dalton clearly, Rune. That's not the lesson you needed to learn."

"That was no lesson!"

I'd never shouted at him before. But what he said hit a button that made me see red.

I did not want to think about it. I didn't want to think about those days after my father's death, when I was recovering from my injuries. From the rape.

Lord Tower's spoiled son had treated me like a new and vulnerable toy. Cornering me in empty rooms; touching my thigh under the dinner table; staring at me when no one else was looking.

Brand found out. He went after Dalton; he thrashed Dalton; and he was whipped for it.

In the aftermath, not even magic had taken the crook out of Dalton's nose, and not even magic had removed all the scars from Brand's back. It had been an untenable mess of a situation.

"You were sixteen years old and the last of your court," Lord Tower said. "You had *many* lessons to learn, and you had *no* time to learn them. You had *no* resources or protection other than what I offered; you had *no* margin for error. You needed to understand that *every* aspect of your life had consequences for those around you. You needed to understand that your response must be measured and cautious."

Tears gathered in my eyes. I was too angry to be embarrassed by them, too angry to hide them.

The Tower saw this and blinked.

I turned my back and went to the door, but before I crossed the threshold, he said, almost uncertainly, "It *was* a lesson, but perhaps one that was poorly planned."

I wasn't one hundred percent sure, but I think the Tower had just apologized to me.

"Brand shouldn't have spoken that way to you downstairs," I admitted. "I'm sorry about that. He's just worried about me."

"I know he is. There are times I wished I had such a dependable shield, as he is for you. Mayan and I are very different Companions. Rune, I cannot promise to extend the same protection to Brandon as I would to you, not if it comes to a choice between you. I think you know Brandon would insist on that as well. But in situations where I can protect him, I will. I will do that for you."

I let out a breath. "Thank you."

"Good night, Rune."

"Good night, Lord Tower."

THE WESTLANDS

In a gesture that short-circuited my sense of context—like coming home to find the mailman cleaning your pool, or your dentist burning leaves in your backyard—the Tower decided to personally drive us to the Boundary.

We left the Pac Bell via a mile-long underground tunnel just before dawn, in an SUV limo that was shielded with so many defensive spells that the buzz of them practically lifted my ass off the seat. Lord Tower and Addam were in the front, and Brand and I had taken the back. I hadn't even tried to suggest that Brand not accompany us as far as the Boundary. It had been messy enough saying goodbye to Queenie, who cried; and Max, who stared at me like the last bit of safety in the world was sinking out of sight. It occurred to me that my maybe going off and dying was one more thing he wasn't prepared to handle, not after losing everything in his life just days ago. I tried to tell him that Brand would remember to feed him if I didn't come back. It hadn't been my funniest moment.

The Tower had suggested that Addam and I cross the Boundary in the city's northwest corner, and that's where we headed. In the graying light, the downtown skyline slowly collapsed into the weathered, two-story buildings of a fishing port. The neighborhood had been settled by the last original Nantucket residents, one of the few human holdout communities left. Magic was scarce there, which worked in our favor. It eliminated some of the means by which we might have been tracked.

The Tower pulled into an alley between a fish-and-chips shack and a hand-knitted sweater store. He made us sit still while he studied a monitor built into the middle of the steering wheel. When he was confident that we were unobserved, he nodded and pulled out a cell phone. "Addam, I'm calling you now, so you'll have this number saved. It's a private line I share

215

with Rune. You'll be unlikely to have service in the Westlands, but one never knows." Addam's phone rang once. The Tower glanced in the back seat and said, "Brandon, I should send it to you as well."

He began dialing. Brand's eyes went wide. He blurted, "Rune already gave it to—" just as his phone began to breathe like Darth Vader.

Lord Tower gave Brand another long look. Brand had the good manners to look almost contrite.

We all got out of the limo, left the alley, and stared at the Boundary.

Stretching from the north to south shores, it was a ten-foot wall inlaid with coral and obsidian rods. Fresh coal dust was scattered along the base—another substance that did well against supernatural threat. There were no guards. Why would there be? If anything was strong enough to overpower the Arcana-level defenses built into the wall, there wasn't much a guard could do except die messily.

Lord Tower and Addam moved away from us to say their goodbyes. I went up to Brand and whispered, "I'll be okay."

Brand stared at me. After a very long minute, he dropped his gaze and started walking to the SUV.

"Aren't you going to say goodbye to Addam?" I asked, stalling for a few more seconds. I could feel his hurt pulsing through the Companion bond, could feel how unhappy he was, how much I meant to him.

"Don't worry," Brand said. "He and I already had a long talk this morning."

"Well, that doesn't worry me at all."

"You better come back to me," Brand said, without turning. Then he opened the door to the SUV's back seat and vanished into it.

As the door shut, Lord Tower said to me, "He'll be fine."

"I know he will," I said. "You made a promise."

"Pardon?" he said.

"You said you'd watch over him whenever you weren't watching over me. I figure that means if anything happens to me in the Westlands, he'll get your patronage for the rest of his natural life."

"That—" Lord Tower said. His mouth closed and opened. "I'm not sure that was the essence of what I meant."

"Maybe not, but oaths are tricky things. Just the other week I made one and got a teenager out of it."

"I see. I'll require you to survive this trip, then," Lord Tower said.

I couldn't leave things as lighthearted as that, though. It was too important. "At the very least, please, please watch over him if I don't make it back. Keep him from . . . following me."

Lord Tower dipped his head in a single nod.

"See you on the flip side," I said.

I backed away, turned, shifted the backpack's weight on my shoulders, and walked toward Addam. I felt Brand's eyes on me every second as Addam and I went to, and then through, the Boundary gate. I felt Brand right up until the Boundary's magic began crushing our bond into silence. At the last, I had the clearest sense of him grabbing his door handle so hard that he nearly tore a ligament in his hand.

And then the Boundary was behind us, and I was alone in my head for the first time since I was even capable of conscious thought.

Once upon a time, the Westlands was twenty-five square miles of dune, scrubby trees, field grass, and swimming holes.

Then my people settled in. In making New Atlantis on the eastern half of the island, the Arcanum expended centuries of stored power virtually overnight, teleporting abandoned human buildings from all over the world. While no one knows for sure what happened to the western half of the island, it's theorized that the backwash of all that translocation magic mutated it into Something Else.

It became a dangerous wilderness, filled with nightmarish monsters and spatial anomalies and, most unpredictable of all, wild magic. Wild magic was a primal, planetary force—nearly sentient, composed of millions of independent parts.

I remember a newspaper article from the 1980s about a man who went into the Westlands with a compass. He got lost, traveled northwest, and didn't hit an ocean until 1617. He died of a bacterial infection along with most of the Wampanoag tribe. His deathbed letter popped up in a museum of Native American history, a time paradox that made my head ache to think on it.

On the plus side, the pathways were safer than they'd ever been. The newest safety measures came after a highly publicized routing some twelve years back. Lord Hierophant, traveling in an armed party, barely escaped with his life after they stumbled into some sort of portal dimension where every shadow was filled with spinning shards of meteor glass. In response to the attack, Lord Magician pooled talent with other Arcana and beefed up the pathway's powerful wards.

Addam and I planned a route that would keep us off the main east–west thoroughfare, yet still safely on ancillary pathways. We would be walking, since vehicles didn't work in the Westlands, and renting the specially-bred horses would have drawn too much attention.

Unless we wandered into a particularly willful bit of wild magic, our route would be just under four miles.

On the other side of the Boundary was a grassy firebreak leading into a light forest.

Addam said, "Can you smell it?"

"I've had this conversation with you before."

"The *air*," he said with relish. "I love the way the Westlands smells."

I pulled a breath through my nostrils. The salt of the ocean was gone. Now I smelled sunbaked pollen and heavy vegetation. "You've spent a lot of time here, haven't you?"

"Every summer for a week when I was younger, up until the governess got mauled by a manticore. Her fault. The manticore was just being a manticore. Don't give me that look, Hero. It's very safe if you stay within the wards. Haven't you been here much?"

"Not often. Once or twice. It's my first time in about . . . thirty? Thirty years."

"Is it really?" Addam said, delighted. "It appears I am the subject-matter expert. I will be your tour guide."

"I want to see every place that doesn't have a manticore."

He favored me with a grin and picked up the pace.

The firebreak ended, and we were in the forest proper. The pathway alternated between crabgrass and trampled dirt, but wide enough for me to walk abreast of Addam.

We were silent for a bit. The day brightened, and rainclouds scuttled toward the sun. I smelled more of Addam's "air." All of the odors trapped against the city's concrete evaporated, leaving behind wholly natural scents. It wasn't altogether *pleasant*, but it was fresh, and it seemed to make Addam happy.

A fat, non-aerodynamic bug circled in front of my eyes and landed on my shoulder. I raised a hand to swat it, and Addam grabbed my wrist. He shook his head seriously. "Never kill a bug balloon."

"I was just going to give it a little move-on," I said. I brushed at my shoulder while Addam made a sharp sound of protest. The bug balloon had skin as delicate as wet tissue, and was filled with an implausible amount of gore. I stood there and stared as it dripped off my fingers in chunks. Addam fished a handkerchief out of his back pocket, took my hand, and wiped it clean.

When he was done, he gave me an assessing look. "My vigilant warrior prince is unused to these woods. The bug balloon was inconvenient, but harmless. However, you must assume that everything else in the Westlands, outside the wards, is filled with horrible, nasty, toxic surprises. Little bunnies have inward-facing fangs; butterflies can dust you with a paralytic; goldfish carry blood-borne pathogens. The most dangerous things in the Westlands aren't on the paths—they're the pretty baubles that lure people *off* the paths."

"Holy crap, are you giving me a lecture? Was that a lecture? I escape danger for a *living*, Addam."

"And you are very good at it," he said, but I knew by now his accent got pronounced when he was making fun of me.

We walked on. Overhead, a ghost zeppelin sailed through the clouds. There were woodpeckers the size of Dobermans. A tree with branches as wide as interstate highways. A pond filled with ocean waves. Nothing dangerous came close to the warded path, though, which gave us a measure of safety from which to gawk.

"I like your friends," Addam said out of the blue.

"I have friends?"

"I've known Companions before. And maids. And houseguests. Yours are much more than that."

I shrugged, pleased. He flashed dimples at me. "How long has your Queenie been with you?" he asked.

"Oh, she's been with us forever."

"And Max?"

"Since the business with the Heart Throne," I said. "He's a good kid. Been through a lot."

"And you are . . . fond of him?"

I stopped walking. "Addam, Max is my houseguest. My seventeen-year-old houseguest. He—holy *shit*, he said something to you, didn't he!"

"It's nothing," Addam said, reddening.

"What did he say?"

"I misunderstood," he insisted.

"I really doubt that. What did Max say to you?"

"He . . . may . . . He may have suggested that my presence was . . . *complicating* the early stages of your relationship. *May have!*"

I groaned and stared up at the sky. A swarm of bioluminescent bees were buzzing on both sides of the pathway, pulsing reds and blues.

"I feel bad," Addam said. "I think Max, in his own way, is being protective. He's watching your back."

"Oh, he is," I said in exasperation. "In a wholly inappropriate and awkward kind of way."

"For what it's worth, I don't think his attention is meant to be salacious. Or derogatory. He's young, and you are larger than life, and he has a crush."

I growled a bit, but didn't disagree.

"Have I upset you?" Addam asked.

"No."

He sighed. "I'm doing an awful job trying to get into your pants."

I barked out a laugh, surprised. "So that's what all this is about?"

"But of course. I was scoping the competition." He frowned. "I may be wrong, but I believe the ground is shaking. Is the ground shaking?"

"What? Damn it," I said.

There was a quiver in the nearby foliage, in the massive fern trees that were as big as buildings. The quiver became a thrashing, accompanied by heavy, rhythmic footsteps.

The spit dried in my mouth. I shook my sabre from wrist-guard to hilt form, and stepped in front of Addam. Addam drew a long sword he'd borrowed from Lord Tower.

We both swore as *something* lumbered into view.

It was huge. And shaggy. It had orange-brown fur and forklift-shaped tusks. It looked like it had chewed through the barbed wire around Jim Henson's workshop and fled into the wild.

It turned its head toward us, and I caught a glimpse of soulful brown eyes the size of hubcaps. Then it nudged the air above the pathway; gave a lowing moan when its nose sizzled; and ambled back into the giant ferns.

"Beautiful," Addam breathed, which was one way of looking at it.

"Do you know what it was? Or whether it was vegetarian?"

He gave me dimples again.

We kept walking. As we went deeper into the Westlands, nature became less exaggerated and more outright perverse. Frogs with hind legs made out of serrated feathers. Birds with wings formed from dandelion spores. Foxes with tails that bristled with storm clouds.

I said, "I wonder if the Westlands looks like Atlantis did. Does your older brother ever talk about growing up there?"

"Christian? No, not often. I think it is hard for anyone born in the homeland to speak about it without remembering the war and the plague.

221

So few of them made it out alive." Addam thought about it. "He has said a few things, I suppose. He once told me that, in Atlantis, magic was everywhere. He said sometimes the magic was so thick that you exhaled it like smoke. He talked about the Petal Sea, too. My family lived by it."

"I've heard about that. It's filled with flowers."

"It is. Or was. I assume it's still there. Christian said the waves washed crimson blossoms over you. Oh! And Christian told me about dragons, back when dragons lived in Atlantis. He saw dragons."

Dragonkind had been nearly wiped out during the Atlantean World War. What few remained were hidden, and they only flew to New Atlantis when summoned by Lord Chariot.

I started to tell him I'd seen a dragon during the Heart Throne raid, and noticed that my breath was misting in front of my face.

"So," I said. "Funny thing happened on the way to July." A puddle of water on the path made a brittle cracking sound as my boot went through it.

Addam smiled. "The Westlands has a mind of its own. Do not worry. It is not unusual for the seasons to change suddenly. Are you cold? Come here." He held up his arm, as if he expected me to scoot under it. He laughed at my expression and dropped his arm. "Look at the size of that cloud. Most impressive."

I looked up. The cloud was fringed in white with a pure-black belly, and heading right for the sun. It would kill whatever remained of daylight. "You're sure this sort of thing happens a lot?" I asked nervously.

"Yes. We could—"

The road buckled.

Something cracked—a loud, vibrating crack.

Addam gripped my forearms and leaned into me. His anxious breathing was warm against my cheek.

"What the hell was that?" I asked dizzily. It felt like I'd lost time, like my eyes had just open from a nap. "What just happened?"

I looked around, but didn't see any danger. We weren't under attack. *Were we?* My stomach churned with nausea.

"I don't know," Addam said. "I felt sick for a second. Is it—? It's snowing."

I stared up at the sky just as one meaty snowflake landed on my eyelashes and melted into a blink. There was already a fine layer of white on the ground. We weren't dressed for bad weath—

I froze. Just froze.

"Rune?" Addam asked.

I knew what I was seeing, but something in my brain actually tried to argue that it wasn't possible. "The path," I said. Addam let go of my wrists and looked down. "Addam, we're not on the path. We're off the road."

"Could—" he said. His voice broke. "Did we teleport? That's not possible. The wards should have—"

"Back to back," I said. I put my back to his and brushed a thumb over my ring, releasing Fire. In a practiced motion, I transmuted my sabre into a hilt again. I put half the Fire into the hilt to bolster its own magics. The other half went into an aura that warmed the air around us. Addam stopped shivering.

If we had teleported, it couldn't have been very far. The large cloud above our head had shifted only a little—the last fingernail of sun was about to get swallowed by it.

I spoke a light cantrip and pushed it away a bit so that it wasn't directly marking us. "Addam, we're going to move. Grab the back of my jacket. Don't let go. If things get bad, do *not* step in front of me. Give me a clear blast radius."

"I've never been outside the wards," Addam said in a shaky voice.

"It'll be alright, Addam. Stay focused."

Frozen blades of grass crunched under our feet as we headed westward. A light wind picked up. It sliced through branches and undergrowth, kicking up a hoarse sound. The skin on my neck crawled.

"It's getting darker," Addam said.

My mind raced. We'd been taken off the path—and it couldn't be a coincidence. I debated whether or not to unleash any of my other spells—maybe Bless-fire, or my Shield. But if something was smart enough to yank us off a warded pathway—if it was Rurik—than it was smart enough to outwait the duration of my spells. I didn't want to be caught with empty sigils, not here.

Behind me, I heard the hiss of metal against scabbard. Addam had cleared his sword. That was good; he was thinking.

Then, with chilling speed, a fog rose from the snowy ground.

It wrapped itself around our ankles, then calves. In seconds it was at our thighs. I could hear Addam's labored breathing. For some reason, that angered me more than anything else. He'd been smiling minutes ago. I liked when he smiled.

I stopped walking and shouted, furiously, "Only cowards use special effects!"

I pulled the Fire from my aura and flung it outward in a gush of flame. The flame burned away the fog and lit up the knoll. I banked the flame into a hot, steady glow around my right hand.

For a moment it was quiet—

—and then a burst of furious energy whipped through me. It doused my Fire. The light cantrip vanished. The wards in my clothing went dead.

I held out my sabre and swung it in a circle, looking for something to shoot. *A null thread.* That was a null thread.

Rurik.

I barely had time to shout a warning. Another wave of null energy lashed at us. I dove to the ground and rolled, screaming at Addam to do the same, but he was too slow. I could almost *see* the null thread sawing across him, writhing, bristling with an intensity that null threads just weren't supposed to have. Addam's belt—the sigils on his belt—began to smoke furiously.

Addam yelled and began struggling with the belt clasp. The null thread vibrated upward and vanished. I jumped up and went to Addam as he pulled the smoldering belt off and dropped it to the ground. The platinum disc sigils were bent in half like taffy.

Destroyed. The sigils were destroyed. Addam's sigils were gone; his magic was crippled.

"It's Rurik," Addam panted. "Isn't it? He's here."

The earth exploded to our left. A sapling, dirt, rocks mushroomed into the air. There was another detonation to the right. Then in front of us. Then behind us.

I shot a firebolt into a cloud of debris. The bolts momentarily lit up the glade, bright enough to reveal massive shadows prowling through the trees.

"Where is he!" Addam shouted.

"Calm!" I shouted. "Calm, Addam!"

The trees to our left began to tremble. I swallowed a *fuck me* and launched a volley of firebolts into the canopy. Something roared.

"Run—run!—don't let go!" I yelled. I picked a direction and set off, just under a sprint. When Addam started stumbling, I grabbed his sleeve to keep him close.

We ran over slick whorls of snow. Thin, wiry branches snapped against my arms. Every few seconds, I fired a bolt above my head, using the brief illumination to avoid trees or boulders. We plowed through a narrow briar patch. I lost skin to the thorns.

Then the ground exploded beneath us.

Dirt and gravel filled my cartwheeling vision. I hit the ground hard, stunned.

I looked next to me, but there were only dead leaves and snow. No Addam.

"Rune!" I heard him yell.

I tried to call out, but the most I could manage was a painful bleating sound.

Something cried, in my voice, "Addam, it's got me, help!"

I flopped on my back and fired a bolt into the air. It sizzled upward like a flare, until tendrils of darkness, with sentient precision, swarmed and extinguished it.

"I'm coming!" Addam shouted.

"It's got me! Help me!"

"*Rune!*"

Addam was moving away from me. Being lured away from me. I fired six times into the air. Each bolt was swallowed by the curls of darkness. If Addam saw it, he didn't come back. I heard him shout my name again, and the sound was so faint that tears came to my eyes.

"Ad . . ." I gasped, my lungs on fire. I braced my arms, shoved off the ground, stumbled in the direction I thought Addam had gone. My foot plunged into an animal hole. I twisted it while trying to keep from falling.

I shot more firebolts into the air, and ran on my hurt ankle. Branches whipped my face. The trees around me were shadows rimmed in an artificial twilight. I didn't see a rock, tripped into a tree, raked my palms raw against sharp, pus-colored bark.

"Addam," I said. My voice was back. I sucked in a breath and shouted, "Ad—"

An arm wrapped around my neck. I smelled rot and clean fabric. I jabbed my elbow backward into doughy-soft flesh. The arm around my neck went slack. I crouched, pivoted, balanced. Rurik stood there, recovering from a stumble. I touched my ankh, released its spell, lifted my arm, and hurled Shatter.

A tree next to Rurik splintered with a sonic boom. Broken rocks whizzed outward like bullets, and fog and snow blew clear. At the center of the maelstrom, Rurik stood unharmed. Not even his cloak stirred.

"Illusion," I whispered. *But I'd felt his arm around my neck.* "This isn't real." *But I'd felt his—*

Rurik came at me with long, sweeping strides. He bunched my shirt in one hand and swung me through the air. I came down hard on the fractured tree trunk. Jagged splinters stabbed into my back, sharp enough to cut skin.

Rurik reached down with his other hand. He splayed his fingers and pressed them on my face. He wore no gloves. His palm was moist and smelled like infection.

Magic surged from his touch. My mind first went blank, and then unfurled into blurs of color.

And then Geoffrey went off into the bushes with the girl. I stared hard at the ground and pretended I hadn't noticed, even as all the other scions snickered at my humiliation.

And then a black-haired young man backed me into a corner. He said, "You don't have a court anymore, you're no one, you live here on my father's sufferance."

And then the grass that covered my father's grave came away in clumps as I tore at it, howling with an emotion too raw and broken to be just grief. Brand's arms locked around me.

And then the underwear was torn off my body. Cold air pressed against my bare ass like an insult. I was shoved against a sofa that smelled like horse manure and hay.

"Ah," Rurik said. "There. *There.* That's where you live."

The metal of my sabre was cold against my palm. I angled it to shoot Rurik in the balls. I fumbled. The sabre was gone, its weight gone from my hand.

Rurik lifted me up, spun me, and slammed me face-first on the trunk. He twisted my arms behind my back. Just like I'd been pinned the night I was—

No. *No.* I would not be sucked into those memories. I gritted my teeth and grabbed for my willpower, but it slipped away like oiled marbles. Concentrate, I had to concentrate, without concentration or touch I had no hope of activating my sigils.

I pictured the emerald ring on my finger. Tried to imagine the Bless-fire stored within it. Tried to imagine burning the undead skin right off Rurik's rotting, smug face.

Long fingers, covered in white evening gloves, reached from behind me and brushed the hair out of my eyes.

The sight of those elegant gloves dissolved my connection.

Ahead of me, another man, this one in a hound mask, stepped right out of my nightmares and into the clearing's dim haze. He turned and examined the forest. "Dreary," he pronounced.

"No," I said. My heavy breaths sounded like sobs.

"It's been a long time," the Hound said. "Bet you're surprised to see us here."

I screamed, a full-throated sound, a terrified sound.

The Hound raised his masked face to regard whoever was behind me. "Just like last time," he said. "No need to shove. We have all night. Leave room for seconds."

"*NO!*" I screamed. Not again, not again, it couldn't happen, it couldn't happen–couldn't–it couldn't happen ag—

"You *did* miss us, didn't you?" the Hound said. He squatted in front of me and looked up into my eyes. Another pair of hands came at me from behind and dug into the waistband of my jeans. The button popped. The hands grasped the seat of the jeans and tugged them off my ass.

"*NO! FUCK YOU FUCK YOU FUCK YOU FUCK YOU!!*"

Memories fell on me like broken glass. I remembered how the blood would drip down my leg, how they would use it as lubricant, how they'd use knives on me, how they wouldn't stop, they didn't stop—they didn't stop for hours and hours and hours—

I frantically tried to concentrate, to feel the silver band on my finger, the sigil where I stored Exodus. I'd do it, I'd activate it, I would—I'd reduce this entire clearing to atoms, myself included, oh gods oh gods oh gods, I would, because in the darkest corner of my heart I knew this was why I'd created Exodus in the first place. I'd let the flames sing out and destroy me. I'd rather die than let this happen again, than be this helpless, than be this abased.

Hands squeezed the fleshy part of my ass and pulled at the cheeks. I screamed again and tried to press my thumb over the top of the silver ring.

Addam strode out of the shadows.

He wore glowing chain mail and wielded a giant sword. He strode forward as holy light, the power of his Atlantean Aspect, poured along the edge of his blade. The light cast razor-sharp shadows along an expression of righteous fury.

Addam swung the sword at the Hound. The Hound burst apart into clumps of dirt, dry leaves, and withered plant stems.

Whatever force held me in place vanished. I crawled off the tree trunk and collapsed into the snow. I reached for my pants only to find they were still on me, buttoned at the waist.

I grabbed the tree trunk and pulled myself up. Rurik stalked into view. Addam and he had engaged. Shimmering black gemstone ran up and down Rurik's cloak sleeves. He used it like a sword breaker, blocking Addam's swings. Each contact sent a shower of sparks into the darkness.

Addam circled to stand between Rurik and me. He swung at Rurik, but Rurik clamped the blade between his encrusted arms. I stepped toward Addam, thinking I'd release my Bless-fire and add it to the light on his blade. But my legs were still trembling, and I tripped. In the most amateurish move possible, I collapsed into Addam's back.

As my fingers touched him, power exploded between us.

Light—*sunlight*—washed outward in fast ripples. It covered Rurik, and orange flames tore from their touch.

Rurik gave a pained scream and teleported away.

I released my grip on Addam. The light vanished with a strobe-like flicker. I dropped to my knees. Addam was staring at me with an expression somewhere between astonishment and . . .

Joy?

The light faded from his sword. It fell from his limp hand. He crouched down and touched my cheek, staring at the point of contact as if expecting something. When nothing happened, he reached up with his other hand and cupped my other cheek.

"I think you're my . . ." he began to say, and then blinked. "Are you hurt?"

"Yes." I was close to tears. "I mean no. I'm not. Not hurt." Too much had just happened. I didn't know what it meant. That light; Rurik; the illusion of the Hound. Oh, gods, I almost unleashed Exodus. I almost gave up.

Ten seconds. Ten seconds was all it had taken to strip bare the realities of my present, and turn me back into the teenager who hadn't fought back as nine men burned his childhood to ash.

Addam said, "You're shaking."

Because I almost gave up. On me, on Brand, on everything. "I-I'll be fine," I stuttered.

He leaned in and hugged me. I didn't pull away.

After a bit, I said, "Rurik will come back. We should go. And the snow is getting worse. We need to find shelter."

"There's a house in the woods ahead. I saw it when I ran that way."

"A house?"

"In the woods. I didn't see any lights on."

"I see. And this doesn't worry you? Did it have gumdrops in its roof?"

He laughed. "We'll be very cautious."

While he picked up his sword, I found my sabre in the remains of the shattered tree. We took off in the direction of a gabled mansion.

THE MANOR

The bizarre wintry weather followed us across a snow-covered expanse—either a field or a lawn—and up to the front doors of a marble manor. The manor was in good condition, but there were signs of a homeowner's absence: overgrown ivy along the overhead portico, a debris-covered doorstop.

"This place . . ." Addam said. "Can you feel it?"

"Yeah." There were strong protective wards surrounding the property. That would have made me nervous if not for the fact that they hadn't identified us as a threat. "Someone's gone to a lot of trouble to keep this place safe but social. I wonder if it's an Arcana property."

There was a heavy brass knocker on the door. In the absence of a better idea, I banged it a few times. The metal had been cooled by the snowstorm.

"Let me try," Addam said after no one answered.

"Sure. Someone else pushing the button always makes the elevator come faster." I smiled at him. "With all these wards, I don't know how safe it would be to break in. The wards may decide we're a threat after all."

"Perhaps not," Addam said, smiling back at me. Then he faced the door and said, with clear enunciation, "I am a scion of Atlantis and mean you no harm. Will you shelter me?"

The heavy wood door swung open on creaking hinges.

"Oh, the *hell*," I said.

"There's a lot you never learned, if you haven't spent time in the Westlands."

Dumbfounded, I limped ahead while holding my hand behind me

in a "wait here" gesture. Addam snorted and followed, his abs, strikingly defined even through his shirt, deliberately pressed into my palm.

A bare stone foyer lead to a main hall that was dim with stormy daylight. Immense canvas tarps covered most of the furniture. There was little dust. I took a deep breath and caught the aroma of citrus-scented domestic wards.

Addam murmured a cantrip. Butterscotch light pushed at the gloom, revealing glimpses of color. The floor under us was a striking peach marble threaded with gold veins. The wood paneling was a warm cherry-mahogany. A staircase snaked along painted yellow walls and vanished into the upper stories.

I said, "Are you telling me you can go up to any house in the Westlands and get in by asking nicely?"

"The Westlands follows old rules—like Atlantis did. Atlantis had an entire etiquette built around travelers and guest privileges. It's biased toward the landed class, but I suppose that's worked in our favor."

"So it wouldn't work for bad guys?"

"It wouldn't work for anyone meaning the owner, or the owner's guests, harm. And I suppose it wouldn't work if the owner had anything to hide from unexpected guests."

"Like the bones of children in his oven?"

"Such a suspicious imagination," Addam *tsk*ed.

"Still . . . Rurik was able to smash apart the Magician's wards on the pathway. We don't know if he'll have any trouble getting in here."

"Do you think that's what happened to us?" Addam asked in a subdued voice.

"I don't know. Maybe the wards weren't broken. Rurik teleported us *off* the paths—he didn't attack us on them."

"Should we make a run for the Moral Certainty compound?"

I thought about it. Rejected it. "We have no idea where we are in relation to it. And we have no idea where the nearest path is. Let's wait out the storm and reassess. I think we hurt Rurik, at least. Last time I hurt him, he took a while until he came after me again."

Addam untied his belt holster. Melted sigils had fused around the leather thongs that had once held them. Addam gave the ruined devices an exasperated look, which reminded me, again, that he'd lived all his life behind velvet ropes. Because if that had been me? With all my sigils bent into slag? It would have meant the end of *everything*. It would have meant the end of my ability to make a living; to protect my household; to keep myself off the pointy end of a bad death. For Addam, it just meant a trek back to the family armory.

He said, "I'm sorry. I should have been quicker."

"It's kind of hard to dodge the impossible. How were we supposed to know he could destroy sigils? If Rurik can pull this sort of trick now, I don't want to see what he grows up into."

Addam tapped one of the melted sigils, quickly, in case it was still hot. When nothing happened, he balled the belt up and shoved it into his backpack's side pocket. "I'll be a liability to you now."

"You're far from a liability, even without sigils. You got us out of that trap, Addam. Thank you. You . . . I've never seen your Aspect before. I didn't even know you had one. It was . . ." *Magnificent. You were magnificent.* "Um, efficient. And tall."

"Is that what you think happened?"

I blinked.

"Is that what you think stopped him?" Addam asked. "My Aspect? That light, when we touched—that was not me. I think it was . . ." His voice trailed off. His eyes never left my face.

I didn't want to have this conversation now. I don't know why I didn't—I couldn't even explain it to myself—but I didn't. "Whatever it was, it stopped Rurik for the moment. Let's look around and try to figure out where we are."

I took a few deep breaths of the clean, unheated air while Addam wandered to an old-fashioned light plate. He pressed a button. Nothing happened except for a *click* that echoed across the hard floors.

He said, "Ah well. Too much to hope for. Maybe they have a generator? We should see if the water is turned on, too. You have many scratches on your face, Hero."

"The thorns didn't exactly bounce off you, either," I said. "Come here. I'm going to use a healing spell."

Instead of touching the gold chain around my ankle, I concentrated. In a moment, the spell released, and I felt the just-bearable warmth of healing energy. Before the precious spell could dissipate, I healed the scrapes on my face, my twisted ankle, and the puncture wounds on my back. I gestured to the red, raw hash marks on Addam's cheeks and, when he leaned in, touched him. He had the softest beard stubble I'd ever felt.

We stood there for a second, staring at each other. His breath was hotter than the air, damp against my cheek.

"Thank you," he whispered.

"You're welcome."

Hesitancy wrinkled his forehead. "Rurik was . . . doing something to you. Wasn't he? Tricking you with illusions. You were very upset."

I broke our gaze. "They were just illusions."

My arms dimpled with gooseflesh as the healing spell dissipated. I rubbed at them while turning in a circle. "Come on. Let's check this place out. I want to make sure we're really alone."

Addam sucked at searching.

He kept forgetting to be cautious or stealthy. He picked up anything that caught his eye, like a crow dive-bombing shiny coins.

Meanwhile, I went along as if something was about to jump at us from every corner. I cleared each room and hallway as we passed it, and walked on the balls of my heels to minimize noise. The first time Addam watched me fling open a door for a 180-degree pivot, sabre outstretched, he applauded silently. I got miffed and explained that slicing the pie was better than a button hook for possible hostile room entry. He added a deep bow to the applause.

"I'm not making fun of you, Hero," he insisted, catching the look on my face. "It is very impressive."

"Brand is better at it," I admitted. "This sort of thing is more his job. I'm just the firepower."

"Your Companion is also your business partner? Is that right?"

"Depends on how bossy he's feeling when you ask him."

Addam's gaze dropped. He peered down at the molding along the border of the floor. "You were very brave to go after him outside my god-father's building. Many scions wouldn't have compromised their safety like that. He obviously means a great deal to you."

It took me half a beat to read between the lines. I raised my eyebrows. "Are we doing this again? Are you trying to find out if I'm sleeping with Brand, too? I'm not good at these games, Addam."

"Perhaps my unsubtlety is, in fact, a clever and subtle tactic to introduce my interest."

"Let's try that hallway over there," I said, changing the subject and trying not to smile.

If I had any doubts that we'd stumbled on the compound of an Arcana, they were resolved when we entered the room at the back of the first floor.

It was a largish chamber, half a basketball court in length. The floor was hard stone scattered with pennyroyal rushes, and the walls were broken into alcoves filled with man-sized clay statuary. The statues, though old and worn, were a strange mix of soldiers, jugglers, musicians, and mounted cavalry.

I said, "Mother*fucker*."

Addam raised his eyebrows at me.

On a hunch, I went through an archway at the far end. The adjoining room was a cluttered maze of equipment and tables. Aside from a few safe paths, the ground was studded with spikes of volcanic glass. So were the tables, and desks, and cabinets. Next to the doorway were wicker baskets filled with oversized boots and mittens, all of them sewn with a lining of obsidian thorns. It looked like a pod of serial killers had gotten together to throw a yard sale.

"I have no idea what I'm looking at," Addam breathed from behind me.

"It's a training ground for a very, very rare type of summoned construct. Those," I said, and pointed back through the archway, "are from China. They're part of the Terracotta Army—statues from about two thousand years ago that were buried for the first emperor of China, so that he'd have an army in the afterlife. I have no freaking idea how they got here—I can't even imagine how priceless they are. And if you know the activation codes, they come alive."

"Like the Tower's golems?"

"This is on a whole other scale. The clay army is nearly indestructible, but obsidian and coral can slow it. They're strong as hell, too. They can glamor themselves to appear human, and they've got the mental aptitude of an eight-year old—which is more than you can say for most constructs. That's why they have this room."

"I still don't know what I'm looking at. What is *this* room?"

I stepped—carefully—along one of the paths to a cluster of tailor dummies. The cloth torsos were barbed with small spikes of obsidian. "You can't turn them loose in public without training. Otherwise they'd be tearing off people's arms during a handshake, or driving rib cages into lungs when they're just trying to haul their owner out of danger. They train the soldiers in rooms like this, forcing them to pay attention to every single move they make."

Addam marveled at it. "Which Arcana lives here, do you think?"

"The Hierophant. I'd bet money on it. He's the best summoner on the planet, and he's got an Asian fetish. Damn, I wonder what else is in the manor."

We went back to the room with the clay soldiers. Addam pulled off his backpack and settled it by a wall, then slid down to the ground. "Your Queenie packed us sandwiches. Are you hungry?"

"Maybe later. I wouldn't mind sitting for a while. Are you going to think less of me if I have a cigarette?"

"I may even join you."

I rifled through my backpack. The only thing that remained of the cigarettes were broken filters. Since I'd snuck them in there just before leaving the Tower's, I wasn't sure whether to be impressed or irritated with Brand.

I sighed. "Did I mention he was bossy? It's not even worth arguing the point with him, either. It'll be all *blah-blah lung capacity, blah-blah fighting for your life.*"

Addam rolled his head along the wall and gave me a wry smile. "When Quinn was younger, he'd smash up onions with a hammer, and take pictures of his eyes watering. He would paste the pictures to my cigarette packs."

My laughter filled the air with puffs of frost. Addam laughed along with me, until the humor dropped off his face like a rockslide.

I said, "He'll be okay, Addam."

"He has to," Addam said. "If you're right . . . if Ella is involved . . . then she's responsible for hurting Quinn. I'm having a very hard time accepting that. As would Quinn. He would be so distraught."

"I didn't think he and Ella got along."

"They don't. Ella treats him with indifference, at best. It's a very sore point between us. But for her to—" His voice shook. "Quinn is sensitive to how others view him. If he thinks his own sister is capable of hurting him, he'll take it hard." Addam closed his eyes. His light cantrip bobbed and flickered. "I know I didn't cause this—I know. But *if* it's true, if Ella is involved, then I'll still be a man whose own family turned on him. I'll still be a man who's lived his life in such a way that such a thing was possible. Does that make sense?"

"It does, but you're stupid."

Addam opened his eyes and stared at me.

"You are," I said. "Trust me. I'm pretty well versed in the shitty things people are capable of doing. In some families you can see why things turned wrong—the people who hire me are just as bad as the people I'm being hired to stop or investigate. But I've met Quinn, and I've met you, and you're not shitty. Addam . . . I'm really sorry I wasn't able to help Quinn more. I'm sorry I left him behind."

"As you tell it, you had little choice. In a strange way I'm . . . glad? No. Reassured. *Relieved*, maybe, that you took his warnings so seriously. Some people disregard Quinn and his gifts. Many are afraid of him. It's why it was so difficult to leave him when I was stationed in Russia." Addam smiled. "Not that it quite turned out that way. I'm not sure if it's because he's a seer, or because he's a Quinn, but he has a remarkable tendency to get his way."

"I sense a story," I said. "Possibly with wallet photos."

Addam gave me an uncharacteristically shy look.

"I'm teasing," I said. "What happened in Russia?"

"It was my mother's idea, that I spend time in Russia. Irkutsk. Quinn was only five years old, and we'd never spent a day apart. When Quinn found out I was leaving, he cried for days. On the morning I was to go, he hid, and refused to see me off. We finally gave up looking for him, and I drove to the portal station. Quinn waited until the guards were looking the other way, snuck off our estate, and began running through the city after me. He made it twelve blocks before security caught him. He'd wrapped a cheese-and-pickle sandwich in his bedroom drapes, tied them to a curtain rod, and had it slung over his shoulder, like a little boy in a Norman Rockwell painting."

Addam shook his head. "Over the next seven days, he ran away a dozen times. When I found out, I called and tried to explain to him that I'd return, that the assignment wasn't forever."

"Did he understand?"

"He understands far more than people realize. He told me precisely how many people on the estate were scared of him. How many of his guards would ask for a new posting since I wasn't around to scowl them into being polite. He told me how many times he'd cry himself to sleep if I didn't come back, and how many times he'd get so sad that he'd throw up. He said . . . Ah, you have to know Quinn to understand how he sees things. He sees the future like it's the past—*futures*, really. He said if I didn't come back, then one time he ran away and got lost in a bad section of town. He said sometimes a man in a white van pulls up and offers him candy."

I burst out laughing. "Oh, he's good."

"Indeed. So I signed away a tenth of my trust fund to have a private portal constructed between Irkutsk and the court. I'd spend the week in Russia, and weekends with Quinn. Or at least I tried. He didn't have much respect for the concept of *here* and *there*. I lost track of the number of times I'd come back from meetings in Irkutsk and find him curled up in my bed, having snuck through the portal because he'd gotten it in his head that I mustn't wait until Friday to know about his new toothbrush, or the frog he caught. He brought the household guards to tears on a weekly basis."

He smiled for a second, and then the smile faded, weighed down by the present. He clapped his hands together and rubbed them. "Let's have a snack, and then continue our search, Hero. There must be a generator or fireplace somewhere."

We completed our search of the first floor.

I was on the lookout for anything that would help us communicate with the city or pinpoint our exact location. Technology was notoriously unreliable in the Westlands, but Arcana usually had people on their payroll smart enough to ward phone and internet lines.

The only thing I found of practical use was a large, rough sketch of Nantucket's northwestern shores. It was thumbtacked to a corkboard in a downstairs office. The Moral Certainty compound was labeled, which was great, but I wasn't sure how much we could rely on the map of a forest that ignored geography depending on what mood it was in.

"They are *moving*," Addam said.

"What's moving?"

"The lines on the map. Look, there. The tree line is now thicker between here and the ocean."

"Damn," I said with a low whistle. "Do you have any idea how much a map like this is worth?"

"Careful, Hero."

"Yeah, I know. Wouldn't want the wards to think we're ungrateful houseguests." I pointed to a spot on the map. "Look there. I think those double lines are safe roads. Here's one that goes near the Moral Certainty compound."

"I recognize this," Addam said. He tapped an oval outline. "Peat's Swimming Hole. It's just outside the compound wards."

"There's about a football field's worth of unprotected ground between us and your compound's wards, then. Filled with snowstorms, liches, and huge Muppet monsters."

"Will we risk it?"

I nodded slowly. "But not until my sigils are swapped out with some different spells."

We went back to searching.

On the second floor were guest rooms, sealed up for an extended absence. One of them had a marble fireplace and a bin filled with seasoned logs. I thought if worse came to worst, maybe we could camp there.

At the end of a west-wing hallway, we had another stroke of luck.

Against a stretch of eggshell-colored wall, my senses began to tingle. I put my hand on it and felt a vibration. It was a steady, grounding power—unmistakably a sanctum. But the doorways on either side of the wall led only to bedrooms, and neither bedroom had an entrance to the sanctum.

In one of the bedrooms, Addam went over to the balcony doors. The glass was crusted with thick frost and he couldn't get a decent view out of it. He said, "I think there's a loggia here. Perhaps there's an entrance from it to the sanctum?"

We both had to pull on the handle to crack the seal of ice. As the door opened, winter shoved in. The weather tantrum had worsened: the sky now spat ice and long streamers of sleet.

As I stepped onto the long loggia that ran along the side of the house, I tried to stare through open archways, looking for any signs of ambush or aggression, but everything around the manor was lost in a churning grayness.

We made our way down the unprotected balcony. There was, as Addam suggested, a middle balcony doorway. The glass panels had been cracked by a loose tree limb, spilling snow drifts into a bare, diamond-shaped sanctum. He shouldered the doors open and went inside just as hail began to pelt from overhead, bouncing and skittering across the flagstone.

Once we were inside the sanctum, we closed the damaged door as best we could, and took stock. There was no doorway on this level other than the one we'd entered, but a wrought-iron stairway spiraled up to the third floor. I climbed the stairs high enough to peek into the room over-head. It was a few square feet shy of being a master bedroom. Maybe the consort quarters, or close family.

Addam pulled his ruined sigils from his backpack and spread them out on the floor. After a long minute of staring at them, he shook his head. "I do not think these will function at all. I sense no magic in them. It shouldn't be possible."

"Welcome to the story of my life. The impossible things that get shoved in my face are never like winning the lottery or digging up Spanish doubloons in my vegetable garden. Impossible things are liches and melted sigils."

That got me a wan smile. I was playing it light for Addam's sake, but inside, I was worried. Sigils were the bedrock of a scion's power. They were the irreplaceable product of a dead art. I'd never heard of one being destroyed before. Lost? Sure. Won in conquest; pawned; even dropped between the sofa cushions. But not destroyed.

The cracked windows of the balcony stole whatever warmth the manor offered. I took off my crusted jacket and shook the sleet into a corner, and laid it open on the ground to dry.

While Addam reluctantly returned his sigils to his backpack, I went to stand in front of him. When I had his attention, I touched my two necklaces: a cameo and silver ankh. The ankh needed cleaning; it had begun to tarnish.

I lifted it and said, "I got this when I was seven. It was one of my first sigils—a gift from my father's seneschal." I unwound the necklace and pooled the chain in my hands. On my hands were three rings. I pointed to the gold and emerald band. "Elena Lovers gave this to me. Long story. Well, not so much long as not reflecting too well on my sense of self-preservation." I took the ring off, then leaned forward and stuck out my leg while tugging up my pants. The glow from Addam's cantrip caught my gold ankle chain and made it slick with caramel-light. I bent, undid the clasp, and palmed it.

Addam said, "This has the appearance of a strip tease, but usually strippers remove the articles of clothing without describing them."

"Funny." I cradled the three sigils and said, "I give these sigils freely. Your Will is now their Will."

"What are you doing?" he asked in surprise.

"You have a better chance of protecting yourself with sigils. I trust you to give them back when you're done."

Addam regarded the sigils I dumped next to him in wonder. "Rune . . ."

"And if you break them, you get a visit from Brand."

"You'd lend me these? Knowing I could not even protect the ones I had?"

"I could just as easily have lost mine to Rurik. Plus, I'm not doing anything Quinn didn't do for me." I tapped the platinum disc on my belt. I would have given Addam that one as well, but I didn't have time to recharge the spell I'd stored within it.

"True," Addam said, "but Quinn's a remarkable young man. I don't often find people who measure up to him."

I took a deep breath and pushed out the one question I hadn't wanted to ask. "Addam, what do you think happened when we touched in the forest?"

"You want to know?"

"I asked."

"I think," he said, "that you're my *talla*."

Surprise first made my face go cold, and then warm as a flush rose beneath it. In a voice far gentler than I'd thought I could manage, I said, "We're not *tallas*, Addam. I'm sorry."

"How can you be sure?"

"I just am. It's not possible. It has nothing to do with you."

"Is . . ." He chewed on his bottom lip. "Is Brandon your *talla*? Is that why?"

"That's not why," I said.

"But when we touched . . . what I felt . . . didn't you feel it too?"

"It could have been another part of your Aspect. Or maybe it was part of mine—it looked like sunlight, didn't it?"

"Or maybe it came from both of us. Don't such things happen between *tallas*? It's a mysterious bond. Powerful."

Would that it were so easy, I thought tiredly. "We should get some rest. We head out at first light."

He stared at me, hard, for a good ten seconds.

Then he nodded and said, "You can run, Hero, but you can't hide."

Right around midnight, I accepted that we were stranded for the night.

Tactically, I didn't want us splitting into separate rooms. Logistically, there was only the one bed in the suite I'd picked earlier. I tried to avoid any future awkwardness by making appreciative comments about the fainting sofa in the corner.

Addam gave me a small smile and went into the adjacent bathroom to see if the pipes worked. They did. I won the coin toss and got to take a quick, lukewarm shower to clear the worst of the dirt off me. Addam headed downstairs to scrounge for food.

When I was done showering, I cleared the mirror with the side of my hand. I hadn't packed a brush, so I had to finger-comb my hair into respectability.

I got dressed and left the bathroom. Addam had returned from foraging and dumped a pile of packaged food on the bed. I poked through it and saw olives, digestive biscuits, animal crackers, and water chestnuts.

Addam said, "We may possibly come to blows over the animal crackers."

"Digestive biscuits?" I said in disgust. "What kind of man leaves million-dollar golems in the open and can't even stock microwave popcorn? Just see if I break into the Hierophant's house again."

"To be fair, there was plenty of food in the pantry, but it was behind a sealed vermin ward. I didn't want to tamper with it. We've intruded on the house's good will enough as it is. But at least we'll have a fire. Behold my industriousness!"

I walked over to the wide marble fireplace, where Addam had stacked a pyramid of logs.

"It is soft pine," he said. "It will smell very nice. Do you have a lighter?"

I transmuted my wrist-guard into a sabre hilt and shot the pyramid with a firebolt. I kept on shooting until flames roared out the jumping logs.

Addam leaned against the wall, pulled off his boots, and dropped into a heap. He wrapped his hands around his toes to squeeze warmth into them. As the glow in the room grew steadier, he allowed his light cantrip to die.

While I tore open the waxy lining of the animal crackers, Addam said, "Was the shower pleasant?"

"It's not my fault all the hot water is gone," I said quickly. "There wasn't much of it."

"Suspiciously defensive," he said.

"Sorry. I'm used to fighting about hot water. Brand has more knives than you, though."

Addam got up and came over, briefly touching the side of my head.

"Your hair is cute when it's wet. I will shower now. Must I dress in these clothes afterward? Will my vigilant prince require us to sleep in battle gear in the event that Rurik comes calling?"

"I can honestly say Rurik will have no bearing on my decision to keep my clothes on."

He winked and vanished into the bathroom.

I split up the food, skipping the water chestnuts and olives, but sampling a digestive biscuit. It tasted like sawdust and cough syrup. I put the box in Addam's pile, palmed some animal crackers, and went over to look at the hardbacks on the bookshelf.

When Addam came out of the bathroom, he was in a towel. As he sat down by the fire, the towel parted over his muscled thigh. The flames made his leg hairs glint like bronze.

He saw my attention and stretched a smile over his lips. "Do my tattoos really look like I got drunk with a sailor?"

"Oh. Um. No. Did I say that?"

"You did. Do you like this one right here?" He touched the side of his stomach, where the tattoos feathered out at his waist. "Or this?" He touched his hip bone, nudging the towel loose.

"Stop that, or I eat the last giraffe."

He laughed and knotted the towel closed. He held out a hand for the crackers.

While he ate, he studied me, his wine-colored eyes narrowed into a crescent. I tried not to react, but he was half-naked and wearing my sigils, and it was distracting. My ankh was against his chest, the emerald ring wedged between the knuckles on his index finger, the gold chain loose on his ankle and reflecting firelight in a dancing glimmer.

He was, truthfully, one of the most handsome men I'd ever laid eyes on. The reality of that filled me with regret. I always felt a sharp sense of regret when I stared at a truly beautiful man.

"So," Addam murmured. "Do you want children?"

"What an awful pickup line."

"And what are your views on group marriage?"

"Even better. You want to knock me up *and* see other people. You know, I was led to believe you were good at this sort of thing."

"Perhaps I am sly. Perhaps I am overreaching in my negotiations, in hope that I end up with a simple kiss."

"I don't think there's a single thing about you that's simple, Saint Nicholas."

He gave me a slow grin and leaned back. His arms were braced behind him, his body spread into something like a pose or an invitation.

Things stopped seeming abstract and started seeming like a real and present danger. I started fidgeting.

And then, to my surprise, the grin faded from his face. He pulled his legs up against his chest. "You are such a good fighter that I was . . . surprised. In the forest. To see you at a momentary disadvantage."

Since he was being oblique, I responded in kind. "Hmm."

"You've been skittish since then."

"Skittish?" I repeated. "No one's accused me of being skittish since I was a pony."

"Perhaps I am not expressing my concern as well as I'd like. I am asking if you are well, Rune."

I gave him a slow shrug. "I know you are. Addam, Rurik fucks with people's heads. I told you that before we headed out. He was messing with my memories, trying to get me off-balance."

"He . . . had your memories? He read your mind?"

"No, he," I said, and stalled by taking a bite of cracker. "He can make you relive things. He makes you relive the things that hurt you. He feeds off dark thoughts and—"

Addam drew in a breath. I saw it in his eyes: it clicked. Maybe it was because I'd been thrown over the tree trunk when he arrived. Maybe he'd seen me scrambling to button my jeans. Maybe he'd noticed how doggedly I protected my personal space. But, either way, it finally clicked for him. "You relived your . . . assault."

"Sort of. A little."

"But . . ." To my utter astonishment, tears filled his eyes. "Oh, Rune. I've been so forward. I have been awful. I am so very sorry, I didn't—"

"Addam, it's okay."

"It is not. I've been boorish and insensitive. I didn't mean to act in such a way. I didn't mean—"

Before I could think better of it, I lifted my butt off the ground and scooted over to him. His mouth closed in surprise. I leaned in gave him a quick, aimless kiss on the cheek and scooted back the way I'd come.

"If you still feel bad, though, you can give me the best side of the mattress." I thought about it some more. "And the rest of your animal crackers."

His discomfort broke apart, and he recovered his smile. He had a nice smile. It was a good thing to watch.

Later, I returned from a bathroom break and caught Addam slipping out of his towel and back into boxer briefs. He sensed my presence and turned. I expected a quip or a double entendre, but his cockiness had been tempered by the talk we'd just had. He gave me a small smile and tugged the briefs up over his pelvis.

He'd already removed the protective covering from the mattress and remade it with sheets he'd found in a linen closet. He slipped under the covers, then stilled and watched me cross the room.

I took off my socks and shoes, and unbuttoned my jeans. I thought about stripping down to my own underwear, I really did; but the idea was met with a near mental shutdown.

I got under the bed sheet and sunk low, hiding my flushed face in the pillow. Addam slid down so that our eyes were on the same level. Heat stirred the scent off his skin: sandalwood soap and fireplace smoke. I got lost in it for a moment.

"Thank you for the sigils," he whispered. "I am humbled that you trust me with them."

"They're a little more raggedy then the ones you're used to, but they'll do the trick."

"I like your sigils. They say something about you."

"My cameo necklace says something about me?" I asked.

"It is unique," he insisted.

"And a woman's emerald ring? That says something about me?"

"You're teasing," he said.

"A little. It makes your accent sound funny."

"A lot of things make my accent sound funny. And it was a genuine compliment—I like your sigils. The quartermaster only gives me and Quinn platinum discs."

"Ah, yes, my grass is so much greener," I said. "Know what's funny? I used to hate this cameo sigil. It came from my mother, who died when I was very young. I was embarrassed to wear it, though. Gods, I was such a shit. I put it in a cubbyhole in my room and never took it out. . . . The thing is, that's exactly why I have it now."

"How so?"

"I scavenged most of my sigils from Sun Estate after the attack. The people who—killed everyone, they took the armory and ransacked the rooms. If I hadn't hidden this along with my ankh, they might have been taken too."

"*Scavenged* is a strange word to use," Addam said. "Sun Estate is yours."

"No. It's not. Sun Estate belongs to the dead. It's very haunted. I don't walk into it unless I'm armed like a tank. Or if I need money for the cable bill."

He laughed, and we lapsed into a comfortable pause, punctuated by the crack of tar and sap from the burning logs. Addam had been right. It did smell nice.

Addam said, "You're lovely in firelight. You really are as beautiful as I've always heard."

"For the record, the seer was drinking eggnog when she made that prediction."

"I was not speaking in terms of prophecy. I was speaking of this real, breathing moment."

"You need to stop complimenting me," I said. "You've already talked me out of my shoes. That's a good start."

"Do you not think you are a beautiful man?"

Maybe I was tired. Maybe the firelight really did make things prettier than normal, including words. Either way, I said what I thought. "I think people make themselves beautiful. I think everything on our outside is a line sketch, and whatever's on the inside blows those lines into three dimensions. It's like with Brand. Now, there's a man who puts no effort into looking good. There's not an ounce of vanity in his body. Yet he walks into a bar, and people drop and gasp like drowning victims."

"Your Companion is very handsome," Addam agreed. "But I've yet to have him step in front of me, in a dark Westlands forest, without the sanctuary of safe paths, and burn away a lich's self-important theatrics with a wave of fire."

"Oh," I said, and laughed. "Oh, you are so full of shit." I pushed at his shoulder, turning him on his back. "Go to sleep, Lord Saint Nicholas."

He propped back on his arm long enough to kiss my eyebrow, and then withdrew into a burrow of sheets.

Between the fire's stupor and the aftermath of a long day, he grew drowsy quickly. His breathing went from calm sighs, to the fits and hitching of someone wavering on the point of sleep, and finally to a loud, dragging rasp that was just shy a snore.

When I was sure he was asleep, I slid a little closer to him. He'd gotten a sunburn on his neck during our walk. The heat of it warmed my cheek.

Life magic was one of the strongest forces known to Atlanteans—the twin of wild magic, potent enough to be nearly sentient. And within the constraints of this rare and powerful magic, *tallas* were considered its most seldom occurrence. *Tallas* were a pairing of souls; a joining of Will and way. It wasn't exactly true love, though certainly lovers have become *tallas*. But there are also stories of mortal enemies developing a bond: soldiers on a battlefield, warring Arcana, court rivals. Hatred and conflict can be as strong as love and intimacy.

Still, whatever the relationship, *tallas* gained strength and magic from their forced union. I had heard of *talla* bonds curing cancer; bridging unwanted distance with spontaneous acts of translocation; folding time with a kiss.

Even though Addam couldn't be my *talla*, my tired mind played around with the idea. I wondered what it would be like to be metaphysically duct-taped to another human being.

Eventually I tired my brain, and fell asleep to the metronome of Addam's breathing, even though I'd planned on keeping watch.

I dreamed of creatures the size of skyscrapers, and necrotic flesh that turned healthy and pink under waves of white sunlight. I dreamed of a long, teasing conversation with someone who I knew to be both Brand and Addam at the same time. I dreamed of doing cartwheels through a field of bioluminescent bees and kicking up clouds of monochrome butterflies. While some of these dreams had the markings of nightmare, not once did I feel threatened or scared. In every scenario I was *contained*. By a warm jacket. By a tight belt. By humid summer heat.

Much later, I opened my eyes, and found myself in Addam's arms.

He was still asleep. His breathing made the hair around my ear hot and damp. I went still, very still.

As quiet I was, though, I woke Addam up. The arms around me tensed.

In a flash of insight that felt like panic, I realized I didn't want him to pull away. And I think he knew it. Because, tentatively, he moved a hand up my chest until it covered one of my own hands. I curled my fingers through his. He pulled tighter against me, his knee slipping just through my legs, his chest against my shoulder blades.

I moved back into him as he pressed forward. My breathing slowed, a rasping sound. His fingers tightened around mine, once, before snaking free and trailing down my abdomen. He traced a pattern down the front of my underwear. When I ground back into him to signal my willingness, he outlined my hardness with his fingertips and circled the tip.

And then I felt my orgasm, a sudden, unstoppable surge. I made another sound, this time horrified. Whatever muscles or willpower were supposed to stop something like this from happening failed me. My cock jerked three times, shooting warmth. I tried to push Addam's hand away as if that could hide anything.

Addam said, "Rune, *shhh*," but I struggled until I was free, until none of his body touched mine. I sat up in the bed but kept the sheets over my lap.

"It's okay," he said.

"It's not." Tearing the sheets away, I retreated into the bathroom, the humiliating, wet cling of my underwear making bile rise up my throat.

I shut the door behind me, turned on the shower, and undressed with clumsy, angry movements. I threw the underwear against a wall. While the shower heated up, I unspooled toilet paper and cleaned myself.

As soon as the shower was passably warm, I stepped into it and put my head under the stream. I kept it that way until I was gasping for breath. I punished myself by replaying the scene again in my head, over and over, like grinding a toothache into your soft, swollen gums.

I put my arms against the tile, and hid my face in them. Sometimes, my life sucked. It was so much easier to fight the monsters outside my head.

"I'd like to shower," Addam announced from the other side of the curtain.

I wiped the water off my face. "Um. Okay. I'll be out in a minute?"

There was a short pause. Then Addam said, "Hero."

"Oh. Now. Come in?"

The shower curtain parted and Addam stepped in behind me.

It was a large shower, and he didn't need to touch me. He didn't try to reassure my ego or soothe my feelings, which was pretty damn insightful of him. He just stepped around me and nudged me back, and bowed his head in the shower until his dark-blond hair was wet.

Then he opened his burgundy eyes and just stared at me.

"Would you let me touch you?" he asked.

"I'm not . . . I'm not very good at . . ."

"If my touch is unwelcome, or unwanted, you must tell me. I will respect that."

"It's . . . I do. Want it. I do—I'm just not good at—"

He braced his hands along my body and slid to his knees. He touched my thigh with his lips, kissing my hip bone. He continued to kiss his way upward, tracing each inch with the roughness of his tongue. He was very patient, and it lasted a very long time. By the time he took me in his mouth, I was hard again.

If the shower stall hadn't been right behind me, I would have fallen. Addam reached up and kneaded my thighs, encouraging them to do their job.

He was skilled, and gentle, and very determined. He kept going until my world was his warm mouth and the cold water, until another orgasm shot out of me. I think I screamed along with it.

He kept me in his mouth as I softened and then kissed his way back upright. When he was standing, I put my chin on his shoulder so that he couldn't see the look in my eyes.

Was I supposed to do something to him now? I'd forgotten the rules.

I cleared my throat and asked, "Should I . . . ?"

"No."

"No?"

"No, Hero. Not right now."

"Why did you come in here?" I asked stupidly.

He smiled into the side of my face, drank water from my neck. After a while, he said, "I needed *this* to be the memory you remember, from tonight."

"Addam," I said, closing my eyes against the conviction in his words. "I wish you could be my *talla*. I do, I swear I do. I wish it were that easy."

"I don't think it will be easy at all, Hero. I think what would be easy for anyone else is a very great challenge for you; just like I think you routinely do things that would be impossible for others. Now. Take a moment for yourself. Then make the fire hotter and come back to bed. I am very sleepy."

A kiss on my forehead, and he was gone. I heard him rummaging through the linen cabinet for a towel, and the bathroom door clicked shut.

Later, I went to bed naked—with only brief hesitation—and squirmed backward into Addam's embrace.

He said, "You rest now. I'll watch."

Using the crook of his arm as a pillow, I surprised myself by falling asleep in moments.

THE SWIMMING HOLE

In my dream, the manor was neither abandoned nor snowbound.

The drapes were thrown wide to thick summer sunshine, and servants, scions, and children raced through waxed and dustless corridors. The dream-people moved faster than I did, leaving vague tracers of light behind them.

I walked along the edges of the main hall to avoid the swift traffic. At the stairs, I paused, and then started upward. At the second-floor landing I decided to climb over the banister and sit on a wide decorative ledge.

"You don't really think this is a normal dream, do you?" Ciaran asked. I heard him sigh. "I detest explaining the difference. It's tiresome."

I looked up. The principality had his hand on the banister, which turned from walnut to tarnished copper. He blinked at me with irises that moved with vague, rippling light.

He said, "Hello, Sun."

"Hello, Ciaran. What a surprise. How in the world did you know that I liked people invading my sleeping mind?"

I dropped my smile and pulled hard on rational thought, on my inner Will. The blurriness of the dream hardened.

"At ease," he tutted. "I'm doing you a favor. A costly favor. Do you have any idea how hard it is to dream-walk at this distance? I'll be at sixes and sevens all day."

"Start making sense," I suggested.

He smiled at me with bright-red lips. "Someone would like a word with you. I'm simply making the connection."

A connection. The last person I knew whom he'd made a connection with in dream was . . .

"Quinn," I said.

And then Ciaran was gone and the young, blond, cowlicked teen was next to me. He sat cross-legged, in blue jeans and high-top sneakers.

I felt a weird blend of emotion—a jarring overlap of my distrust of seers and my unexpected affection for the person Addam had been telling me stories about.

"Wait!" Quinn said. He struggled up on his knees, and ducked in to kiss my cheek.

He leaned back and gave me a satisfied look. "Hah. You never get mad at me when I did that first. Well, one time you kicked me off the stairway, but *everything* can happen once, even meteors made of soy beans."

"Verb tenses aren't usually a suggestion."

Quinn laughed and clapped his hands. "Most people would have asked about the soy beans. I made that up. We never get hit by a meteor made of soy beans, not really."

"Quinn," I said. "Can Ciaran pull Addam into this dream? He's very worried about you. He needs to see you."

"I want to see him," Quinn said, and his smile broke apart. "But Ciaran said your mind is better at this than most people's. But he didn't say it like it was a compliment. And I don't think we have much time. I just wanted to let you know that I've been trying to help. You *do* need to go off the safe path by the swimming hole, like you saw on the map. It's the quickest way to the compound, and Rurik won't be able to break into the compound, not yet. But, most important, there are no null threads nearby, and he likes those. So you need to go there. Everything important starts to happen there."

"But he's expecting that," I said. "Right? Rurik is expecting me to go off the safe path at the point closest to the compound."

"He expects everything," Quinn said. His face hardened. "But so do I."

I settled back against the bannister and calculated sigil spells. Had I done enough yesterday in the sanctum? Was it a fight I could win—at least long enough to break for safety?

I said, "Can I at least tell Addam you're okay? He'll focus better if he's not worried."

"I'm . . . trying to wake up. The doctors and nurses are very nice. There's a lady who rubs my hair and whispers to me. But it's hard. I'm trying."

Quinn suddenly threw back his head and screamed. I just about shit myself.

He stopped and scratched his nose. "That didn't work," he said. "Maybe you can pinch me? Or slap me. Try to slap me."

"I don't think Addam would want me to slap you."

"But you don't care what he thinks yet," Quinn said, and then his face puckered like he'd tasted a lemon. "Oh, you *do*, and that's not what a shower is for *at all*. I need to go now and dream about battery acid. *Feh!*"

He vanished and Ciaran reappeared, still at the railing. The texture of the banister changed under his hands again, now a spreading pool of velvet green moss. Ciaran had always had an unpredictable impact on reality, but this was the first time I noticed that the impact was not unlike the unpredictability of dreams. It made me wonder about the source of his powers.

Ciaran arched an eyebrow and plucked his fingers off the railing. "Don't give me that look."

"What look?"

"The look a butcher with a chainsaw gives a cow." He gave me a *shoo* gesture. "Be off now. I need to go."

"Ciaran, wait! Can you please get word to Brand and Lord Tower? Tell them I'm okay. Tell them where I'm headed."

"That would never have occurred to me. I'd actually been planning on keeping Lord Tower in the dark. I hear he appreciates that sort of thing."

He started to say something else, and a smile flitted across his lips. He stared upward. "It appears that Lord Saint Nicholas is being rather . . . enthusiastic in his attempts to wake you. You should—"

"Oh," I said as my eyes shot open.

The sights and sounds of the dream blurred into the physical sensation of Addam, from behind, squirming against me. Which made me say, again and with feeling, "*Oh.*"

When he realized I was awake, he wrapped his arms around my stomach. "Good morning, Hero," he yawned against my shoulder blades.

"I had a dream," I said.

"I see. And you want to share it. Is this something I can expect every morning?"

"No, smart-ass. Ciaran brought Quinn to me."

I felt Addam's entire body go still.

"He's going to be okay, Addam. He's trying to wake up now."

Addam didn't move, didn't speak. I started to turn, but he tightened his arms and kept me facing away. A few seconds later, I heard him clear his throat and sniffle.

I gave him a moment to collect himself, and enjoyed the expiring warmth of my pillow.

Outside, the freakish winter weather had given ground to something more like spring. It turned the lawn into boggy turf and mud puddles.

As we trudged toward the nearby safe path, Addam looked like he had something on his mind. It took him a couple dozen yards to work up the right words.

"Do we need to talk about last night?" he asked.

"Absolutely. That's how I always get ready for battle, talking about my feelings."

"That's settled, then," he decided. "Very well. Matter at hand."

A minute later, we transitioned from one ward to another. I felt the frisson of the estate's protection yielding to the stronger defensive spells of the safe path. I was relieved; at least Rurik hadn't broken past these wards yet.

Of the three routes that led off the estate, the one closest to the Moral Certainty compound was much, much narrower than the road we took yesterday. The forest was close. Thin branches crossed the air in front of

258

us, and shadows fell across our bodies like ash-colored whip marks. I took the lead, pushing the branches to the side and holding them for Addam.

We walked for a half hour, hands near weapons. Clouds slid across the sun by eight o'clock, dulling the sunshine. Eventually the woods opened up into a field of yellowing grass. It was scattered with shells, sand, driftwood, and dried starfish. We were a good mile from shore, but this was the Westlands, and stranger things had crunched underfoot.

"We're close," Addam said. "That's Peat's Swimming Hole, past those trees. We need to get to the other side."

The safe path veered north. The swimming hole was straight ahead.

"When we leave the path," I said, "release your spells, and move fast. I'll scan left and forward, you scan right and behind. Look up and down, not just eye-level. Be prepared for an ambush at any moment."

"We're going to empty our sigils? All of them?"

"We can fill them again at your compound. I want to cross that hundred yards like gods, Addam. I want our footsteps to be like thunder. I want to show that miserable creature what it means to interfere with an Atlantean scion. Are you with me?"

His lips curled into a sharp smile. The thought didn't scare him, which was good.

I touched my white-gold ring, then Quinn's platinum disc, and then pressed a hand against my thigh. The Shield and Fire came first, a fractal, pulsing high; followed by the release of Bless-fire. For a moment, until the spell equalized, globules of white, holy light drifted up from my lips and nose, like underwater air bubbles.

I felt the push of Addam's own released magic. A veil of distorted air appeared around his hands and sank into his fist. The dirt near his feet trembled and distended, as if fingers were pushing from beneath. He pulled out his sword, and a thin rim of Bless-fire licked up the edge. He'd created his own abbreviated version of a Bless-fire spell after asking my advice, which made me proud. It was not an easy magic.

"Ready?" I mouthed.

He stared at me and dipped his chin. His knuckles were white on the sword pommel.

"Showtime," I said, and ran toward the swimming hole.

Rurik sprang his ambush immediately.

Fog rose from the ground with unnatural speed, fast as steam from a hot skillet. In the near distance, bruised shapes formed in the face of the mist, metastasizing into a small band of skeletons led by Rurik himself.

I spotted the animated bones of a bear and a wolf, and two upright human skeletons with rusted rifles in their fleshless arms. Behind them was a wyvern made of tree bark—a gargoyle-construct not unlike the one that had been set against me days ago. It reared above the other skeletons and thrashed its head. Its rotating neck sounded like falling logs.

"You have no idea," Rurik said loudly from his linen cowl, "what forces are marshaled against you. I will bring everything I have to bear on—"

"Fuck that mastermind chatter," I said, and hit him with a surge of fire that blackened the grass under his feet. "Addam, take the summonings! Rurik is mine."

I flung myself forward, using my Shield like a scythe and bringing it hard against Rurik's ankles. When he staggered, I launched a barrage of fireballs. Rurik windmilled back into the fog.

I raced forward to keep him in sight. Passing under the ring of elm trees, I saw the swimming hole. It was a perfectly round, gray-green body of water the size of a small house. Lily pads and rotting vegetation floated across its surface.

I'd already transmuted my sabre from a wrist-guard into a hilt; now, with a burst of willpower, I formed a garnet blade in a molten flurry. I infused it with Bless-fire, making the blade brighten with searing orange-white flames.

Rurik recovered from the stumble. I went at him with the blade. Diamond fire crystalized into armor up and down his arms, which he used to block my swing. It created a shower of sparks so bright that, even in daylight, we both flinched.

Reality shimmered around Rurik. I knew that trick, and had no desire to see another parking garage pulled down on my head. I threw a blossom of Fire at his eyes and slammed out with my Shield. He went sprawling.

He spun up from the fall—not a movement, but an adroit display of levitation. He hovered above me with his diamond-encrusted arms outstretched. Reality shimmered again, but instead of pushing his willpower into the world, he pulled the world into his willpower.

Grass withered under his feet in a ten-yard radius. A sparrow dropped from the sky with a twig in its mouth. Where the decay touched the swimming hole, frogs and eels bobbed lifelessly to the surface. The stench was appalling, like sewage and burning compost.

I didn't wait to see what he'd do with the energy. There were small patches of fire on his linen cloak from my fireballs. I sent Fire into them, twining the spell among the flames. The threads burst into bright lines and spread to his chest and hood.

Rurik growled and ripped the cloak from his body, revealing rotting, old-fashioned undergarments. I had a glimpse of his fun-house mirror face, and then a wash of fog came between us. I lost sight of him.

In my peripheral vision, Addam whirled into sight with sword extended. The bones of the bear and wolf were at his feet. He lifted a hand, and sharp mineral spikes erupted from the earth, shattering the manlike skeletons.

I turned back to see Rurik leap from the fog and point to the forest behind us. Earth and wood groaned and splintered as he pulled on the environment for more ammunition. I lifted my burning sabre blade and threw all my Fire into it. The garnet blade turned into a solar flare.

I lunged and brought the blade down on Rurik's outstretched hands, severing them at the wrist.

Rurik laughed. Power exploded from him. A wave of unfocused telekinesis threw me off my feet. I soared backward into the swimming hole.

My sabre blade hissed as foul-smelling water closed over my head.

I sank a good ten feet without hitting bottom, flailed, stroked upward. Weeds hung over my ears as I spit and spun on the surface.

Addam was surrounded by pieces of wet bark. He'd engaged Rurik, keeping the lich's attention from me.

Rurik's entire body danced with glittering, black gems. He'd formed dagger-like blades where his hands had been. He caught Addam in a stumble on the uneven ground, and Addam cried out as a dagger laid open his cheek. He fell to his knees.

I reached for the vegetation-choked edge of the swimming hole, pulling myself toward it so hard that I tore a muscle in my shoulder. I slapped the elbow of my sword arm onto the ground and brought the hilt into aim. Rurik spared me a glance, and as I fired, a wall of mud rose between us. My firebolt thudded into its side and sent boiling muck back in my face.

I grabbed the shore with my other hand and pulled myself from the water. Rurik had done something to Addam. Addam wasn't defending himself; he was on both knees, head thrown back, throat exposed. Rurik's arm went up, then sped down for the killing blow.

I heard the crack of a bullet breaking the sound barrier.

Rurik's head snapped sideways.

Two more cracks. Rurik's head jerked again. Addam trembled and broke free of whatever spell had him immobilized. He rolled to the left, braced, sprang up.

Brand—my Brand—was lying on the other side of the swimming hole, his rifle on a bipod in front of him.

He caught my eyes. We had a moment. He said, thoroughly exasperated, "Get the fuck up and hit it!"

Triumph flooded my arms and legs like a drug. I strode from the water's edge and sent my willpower into my sabre, manifesting a garnet scimitar as bright as sin. Whatever Brand had shot Rurik with weren't normal bullets; the edges of the entry holes glowed like lines on burning paper.

My Aspect ascended, a predator's response to weakened prey. Flames began to lick at my bangs.

We threw everything into the moment that Brand bought us. Addam reached an arm toward the ground under Rurik. Water frothed to the surface, turning the dirt slick and muddy. Rurik lost balance and went down on one knee. I sent Fire into the mud and made it boil. Rurik screamed, fell back on his hands-less forearms, danced from stump to stump. Addam called mineral blades from the earth. A stalagmite went through Rurik's chest.

The lich's power surged outward, a gasp of dying energy. Addam and I were lifted off our feet and tossed away. I ended up in the water again. I flailed back to shore just in time to see Brand walking up to Rurik with a short, bulky gun. He didn't waste breath on a quip; he simply aimed and pulled the trigger.

A flare arced at Rurik, slow and brilliant. It broke into powder burns on impact. Pinpoints of savage light appeared on Rurik's body—first dozens and then hundreds and then thousands, and then Rurik was a single, roaring mass of flame.

With a final wail, Rurik exploded. Chunks of him shot outward. One landed on my cheek. It smelled wretched, and there were moving, worm-like pieces in it. I ducked clean under the water, and then shook my head like a wet dog.

None of us talked for a good ten seconds. The only sound was the crackle of flame from Rurik's empty clothing. Finally, Brand stepped up to the edge of the swimming hole. He said, "Looks like them Duke boys have done drove Roscoe into the pond again."

"I was standing in a bad spot," I said. "This could have happened to anyone."

"And yet, twice," Brand said.

I stared at him until he held out a hand and pulled me out.

I got my footing and hugged him as hard as I've ever hugged anyone in my life.

THE COMPOUND

In soaked clothes, I was cold enough to make my teeth chatter. Brand took off his coat and gave it to me.

My smile was filled with pure, stupid pride. "Let's play a game. Raise your hand if your name begins with a *B* and you killed a lich today."

"Killed it?" Brand snorted. "In our fucking dreams. It's just decorporealized. We still need to go to that imbued circle so it doesn't get summoned again. We're supposed to wait at the Moral Certainty compound until the Tower gets permission from the Magician to enter his estate."

Addam stepped up to Brand. His face was covered in bloody scratches, a deep cut, and pieces of dirt. He held out a hand and said, "Thank you. Thank you, Brand. You saved my life."

Brand shrugged and shook Addam's hand. "We lose our bonus if you get gutted," he said, but I could tell he was pleased. "We need to go. The lich isn't the only thing that could fuck us up. Let's get behind the compound's wards; it's not far."

"I still can't believe you're here," I said as Brand went to retrieve his rifle. "Quinn set this up, didn't he? He came to you in a dream?"

"He came to Max in a dream," Brand said.

I realized, then, that Quinn couldn't have come to Brand in a dream, because Brand hadn't slept at all since I left. He had dark bags under both eyes.

Brand went on. "He told Max—who apparently Quinn has been famous friends with, and I quote, '*for many years in the future except that one time we were mortal enemies and you rubbed a ferret in my hair*'—that you'd stopped off at the Hierophant's compound last night."

265

"We got stranded," I said. "We fought Rurik, and then got caught in a blizzard."

"Which makes absolute sense," he said, staring at the allegedly summer sky. "I fucking hate the Westlands."

"Brand, did Max say Quinn was okay?" Addam asked anxiously. "Do you know if Quinn is awake yet?"

Brand hesitated. "I got the idea that he might have woken up already if he didn't feel it was so important to be in people's heads."

Addam closed his eyes. With a grim look, he set off for the nearby compound.

We followed. At first, Brand asked me questions about everything that had happened in the forest yesterday. I didn't want to talk much about the fight with Rurik, though. And I was more interested in how Quinn had arranged this.

Brand's eyes, bodyguard-serious, were moving between eleven and one o'clock, a trick to increase the width of your peripherals. He said, "So, Quinn told Max that you and Addam were going to step off the safe paths this morning. That's smart stuff right there, by the way."

"We did not have a choice," Addam said from in front of us. "Rurik broke the road wards. We weren't safe anywhere."

"Just busting your balls. Quinn told us that. He said you were going to step off the paths, and that there'd be a fight. He told Max where I needed to be. He said first I had to go see the Tower and get a bunch of ingredients from a cemetery—cemetery salt from old gravestones, cemetery rainwater, cemetery grass, and . . . do I really fucking need to go into the recipe? Mayan helped me put the paste into bullets and the flare."

"And then you walked here?"

"It was just three miles," Brand said with a shrug. "The Westlands didn't go bat-shit crazy and make me walk through 1989 or anything."

"Three miles is still a decent hike."

"Sure it is, and I run ten of them a day in that murky period you sometimes call morning. Rune, you better fucking not be *thanking* me. I'm exactly where I'm supposed to be."

"Yeah," I said. "Yeah, you are." I smiled at him.

The climate changed again as we crossed the warded boundary onto the Moral Certainty grounds. Late winter leapfrogged into spring, where flowering trees and plants were releasing thick, noxious waves of pollen. It was so pervasive that caretakers were swarming the lawn with leaf blowers, their sweating skin caked gray-green.

The compound's main building rose above us. It was a sprawl of marble and stained glass, topped with a massive pitched roof. Defense magic hummed through the ground underneath me. It was much stronger than what I had felt on the Hierophant's estate—not surprising, considering the compound was jointly owned by the power bloc formed by Justice, Strength, Temperance, and the Hermit.

Addam led us toward the closed doorway of a glass-walled solarium. "Maybe we should clean off first?" I asked, peering at the stretch of glistening white marble on the other side.

"There are showers outside the pool area, if you wish," Addam said.

"We should have someone tell Max and Ciaran we're here," Brand said.

"Max is here?" I asked, startled. "*Ciaran* is here?"

"Quinn told us to bring Max. And Ciaran volunteered, once he was done shipping Quinn around people's heads."

"Ciaran has been a good friend," Addam said. "He is fond of Quinn. True seers are not so common a community."

"Really?" Brand said. "Rune can't swing a dead cat without hitting a fucking prophecy."

"But Quinn said to bring *Max*?" I persisted.

"Quinn said a lot of things," Brand said. "Some of them were about tactics, and some of them were about weird seer shit, and some of them were about bubblegum. And he also said you'd need this—though he specifically said not to use it until you really need it."

Brand lowered his rifle bag to the ground and pulled out a small, handkerchief-wrapped bundle from a vinyl pocket.

"A cookie?" I asked hopefully.

Brand stuffed it into my hand. It was round and palm-sized, but hard. I folded back the checkered plaid and saw the edge of a clay disc.

I sucked in a breath. "*Brand.* This is my mass sigil."

"Good eye."

"This was buried. In the foundation of our house."

"On the plus side, the girl at the hardware store where I rented the jackhammer is real fucking cute, and she said cement mix is going on sale next week."

I gaped.

He rolled his eyes. "It doesn't pay to argue with *true seers.*"

I folded the handkerchief and, almost skittishly, put it in my jacket pocket. My imagination tripled its weight. Mass sigils were very, very powerful devices. They were flamethrowers to a standard sigil's blowtorch; and it wasn't every magic-user who could easily wield one. I used my mass sigil—the only one I had; the only one that had survived the fall of the Sun Throne—for an emergency defense of Half House. I'd been charging and recharging its stored spell for years now.

Brand said, "Look. There they are now." He tilted his chin to our left.

And there they were. Max was eager and vibrating, like a young hunting dog. Ciaran sat on the waist-high branch of a chestnut tree, swinging his legs idly. His reality-shifting powers had turned the grass underneath him a shining yellow, mimicking a sphere of stage light.

I set my eyes on Max, remembering that he and I were due a talk. When he caught my expression, he gave a guilty start and ducked his gaze.

"Hullo, hullo!" Ciaran said. He slipped a cigarette from his breast pocket and began to field strip it. "I see our intrepid young Quinn was right. You *did* venture off the safe paths. Risky tricksy, Sun."

"It's been that kind of morning," I said. "We—"

"That's Rune's," Max said, pointing at Addam's neck. "That's his sigil. Why are you wearing his sigil?"

"For the love of—" Brand said.

"Max," I warned.

"And that's my grandmother's ring! You *gave* it to him? The one you took in exchange for me? You gave it to *him*?"

"Godsdamnit," Brand said. "No arguing. We just fought something that even Lord Tower calls a monster. None of us are in the mood for giving each other shit. Addam, who's that?"

Addam followed Brand's finger. A man was hurrying across the lawn with a wooden box in his hands. "I believe it's the compound chiromancer. To heal us, I assume."

"Well, I'm assuming my rifle in a firing position. It's a bad day for people to come running at me."

Addam beat a path to the man who was, in fact, the compound healer. The box was filled with antiseptic, bandages, pain-killing ward stones, and two sigils loaded with healing spells. The sigils were made from Victorian cravat pins in the shape of caduceus staves.

Addam insisted that the chiromancer tend to me first. I insisted that he move fast enough to heal both of us with a single spell. I wasn't entirely convinced we wouldn't need the second healing spell later.

While my various cuts itched closed, the chiromancer turned and ran pale fingers over the gashes on Addam's face. He lingered at a slash that ran from Addam's ear down the back of his neck. The blood had clotted Addam's hair into a dreadlock.

"I must use the second sigil," the man said in a strained voice.

"No, it's healed," Addam said, touching his neck.

"But there's a mark. Perhaps another spell will remove the mark."

"Come, man," Addam said, embarrassed. "It's fine."

"But it will scar, Lord Saint John."

"It will," Max said, in a voice that dripped with fake concern. "Behind his ear, too."

I grabbed the collar of Max's t-shirt and yanked him away from the group. Over my shoulder, I said, "Is there a shower by that pool over there?"

Addam blinked.

"We'll meet you over there," I said.

I dragged Max to, and then around, the corner of a nearby maintenance shed. When we were out of sight of the others, I pinned him against the stucco wall with a forearm.

"Matthias," I said.

"You're mad at me," he whispered.

"Did you tell Addam that we were involved?"

Max lowered his eyes so far that the lids nearly closed. "We . . . talked. He might have gotten the wrong impression."

"I can assure you that lying to me, right now, right here, is the wrong, wrong tactic. You are seventeen years old. We will not become involved. Your behavior toward Addam is unacceptable."

"I—"

"We will not have this conversation again," I told him.

I released pressure and swept back, causing him to stumble; and then waited out his sullen silence until he was forced to look at me. I said, "Until I say otherwise, stay by Ciaran. He'll keep you out of trouble. Go."

Max's face scrunched up in misery. Without another word, he turned and walked back to the others. There were pollen stains up and down the back of his pants.

I sighed and rubbed at my eyes. Tough love was more Brand's style, but I could manage it in a pinch.

The pool was crystal-blue water locked in by a half acre of black, porous stone. Attached to the outside of a three-room pool cabana was a large shower area. A servant was already waiting for us, in that mysterious way that good servants do. Addam asked for three sets of clean clothes and a platter of crackers and cheese. Max and Ciaran had been sent inside, so

Addam asked them to be fed as well. The servant squinted at our shoulders and waist, perhaps for measurements, and hurried off.

"Shall we share the shower?" Addam asked me. Only he said it like he was saying, *Shall we share a shower AGAIN*, which had Brand's head snapping up. I hid a flush by pulling my soiled shirt over my head.

"Would you like to go first?" Addam offered Brand.

I saw the wheels turning in Brand's head. "It's big enough for all of us."

Addam shrugged, like it was nothing. Most Atlanteans had no taboos about nudity; and from what I'd observed, Addam had even less.

Brand went over to the shower and fiddled with the faucets. Water shot from six separate showerheads, scattering like marbles against the peach-colored stone.

"This is okay, Hero?" Addam whispered.

"I just want a shower," I said.

"But he's testing me, yes? This is a form of competition?"

"It really is," I said. "But not for my attentions. I told you, it's not like that with Brand and me."

"I see," Addam said. He unbuttoned his pants and let them slither down to his feet. It was too graceful to have been anything but practiced.

Addam laughed at my expression and walked over to the shower. Brand was already under the water. His back was to us, and puffy clouds of steam slid up his heavily-exercised body. When he heard Addam approach, he turned and stretched his arms upward to bring his front into the best definition.

The trap was sprung.

I couldn't see Addam's face, but his shoulders actually sank as he caught sight of Brand's endowment. Addam turned and gave me such a comic expression that I started laughing.

"Again," I reminded him, loud enough for Brand to hear, "not a competition for my attentions."

I got undressed, spooling my torn and bloodied clothing into an untidy pile. The only items I kept for later use were my warded boots and coat. As I stepped into the rain shower, Brand threw a bar of soap at my head. I whispered a cantrip that gave my hand added friction and caught it without a fumble. Brand sniffed his approval and went back to shampooing his hair.

I picked my own corner of the bath, standing under one of the rain-forest heads. The steam and hot water began to soften the muscles in my often-reinjured shoulder. Grimacing, I reached up to knead it. Brand knocked my hand away and began to do it himself. He'd once spent six weeks training with a professional massage therapist as a birthday gift for me.

"I'm not making a move," Brand said to Addam. "He has a bad shoulder."

Addam said, "What's the best way to help it?"

They started to talk about my bad shoulder and the best way to unknot it without worsening the injury. I decided to let them bond, because it felt too good to complain.

When Brand's hands finally fell away, I reached for one of the shampoo bottles in an elevated niche. Through a cover of suds, I peeked at both of them. Addam was combing his loosely-braided hair with curled fingers. Brand had tilted his face toward the high-pressure stream. He was standing at an angle, and the scars down his back were pale against his pinkening skin.

Emotion lodged in my throat. All of his worst injuries had been because of me.

Brand turned around quick enough to catch my expression. "Stop with the look," he said.

"What look?"

"Like you're about to burst into song or hug me." Brand glared at Addam. "He wasn't like this when you left. I told you not to break him."

"You have my word, he did not burst into song once while we were together," Addam said.

Brand crossed his arms over his chest and kept staring at Addam. He said, finally, "Rune likes you."

I opened my mouth. Brand pointed at me. He said, "Addam, you don't have to hide how you feel about him. It's not a contest. But just know—he's mine to watch. That will *never* change. Whatever happens between you is going to include me."

"I can accept that," Addam said.

"Too fucking right you can, and it wasn't a question."

"He is very lucky to have you," Addam said diplomatically.

"Your mouth to God's ear. Okay. You're done here. Give us some time alone."

Addam only laughed and bowed. He shook water droplets from his hair and moved up the stone steps. Grabbing a towel from a stack the servant had left, he wrapped it around his waist and vanished into the pool house.

"That was a little abrupt," I said.

"My manners are completely misunderstood."

"Why do we need time alone? You're not going to yell at me, are you?"

Wrinkles appeared around his eyes. His controlled, unhappy expression. "Do you want to talk about what Rurik did to you?"

Despite the edited version I'd told him on the walk back, I should have known Brand would catch on. He read more into my pauses than most people would from a handwritten note.

"It was all in my head," I told him. "That's it. I promise. He . . . They were just bad memories. Rurik made me relive bad memories. He made me think it was happening again. That's all."

"That's *all?*" Brand's blue eyes got bluer, glowing with a sheen. "Rune. *Fuck.* I promised myself that I would never, *never* let anything like that happen to you again. You—Rune, you—you can't do this to me again. You can't leave me behind like this again. Do you have any idea how hard it was to stay behind? I should have *been there.*"

I could have gone through all the reasons why we made the decisions we did, or all the reasons I hated putting him in harm's way, but it wasn't what he needed to hear.

He must have seen some of the hesitancy on my face, because his own, against expectation, softened. "Rune," he said. "You understand that being a Companion isn't just a job, right? Just because we call ourselves partners now, the Companion part of me doesn't go away. I can't turn it off like a light switch. It's not a choice; it's not a lifestyle; it's my *purpose*."

"You're right, it's *not* a choice. You never had a choice. You—"

"Don't tell me what I fucking did or didn't have," Brand said. "Do you remember the first time I protected you?"

I felt my forehead crease.

He said, "That motherfucking stableboy, what's his name? Gregor. He liked to bully you when you were a kid, real clever-like, so that he couldn't be called to task for it. He tried to make you feel small because he felt small. . . . Remember that time we rode on the beach, and Gregor made some shitty comment about you needing to ride a pony instead of a horse? That look on your face killed me—you'd been so, so proud that you'd finally just learned to ride a horse like a grown-up, and Gregor knew that, and used it to *hurt* you. He made you feel less than you were. So I broke his nose. And it felt *so fucking good* to be a hero to you."

I blinked a few times. More than a few times. "That wasn't the first time. You've always protected me. You've always been my hero. You ate my broccoli. You told my father that you were the one to run out on the ice when the pool froze over. You made me drink my stupid juice when I was sick. Always. You've always been there, and I don't know why I deserve it. Because of my DNA? Because of whom my father was? Because—"

Brand grabbed the sides of my face. He stared in my eyes and said, firmly, "Rune of Sun House, I believe that you are meant for great things. I truly, truly do. Your story has *barely begun*. It is my honor to be along for what has been, and is, and will be one hell of a ride. So don't leave me on the bench again. That's all I wanted to say."

He gave me a rare smile, untouched by anything except pleasure, and leaned forward to kiss my forehead. Then he shoved me back to my side of the shower.

I ran my palms over my eyes. "We just covered a lot of ground, didn't we?"

"Fucking emotions. What's next on our to-do list?"

"We search rooms and question people. Did you know Max told Addam that he and I were involved?"

Brand shrugged and said, "I told Addam I'd kill him if you got hurt."

"Well, okay, and now I have another point to make entirely."

"Finish up, princess," he said, throwing a bottle of conditioner at my gut. "Let's just do the job and go the hell home."

Ella's small suite was on the second floor.

The compound's majordomo was waiting at attention in the hallway, dressed conservatively in a charcoal suit and navy blue tie. When I tried to step toward the door, he slipped in front of it. "My lords," he said.

"McAllister," Addam replied, frowning.

"I was told you requested I meet you here," McAllister said. "If it's not too presumptuous, may I know why?"

"Seeing as how you just blocked my boy from walking in the room," Brand said, "I'm guessing you've got a clue."

Color rose under the man's collar, mottling his lower jaw. "Lady Saint Nicholas's room is locked, Lord Saint Nicholas."

"And now we approach the portion of this conversation devoted to the past tense of *is*," Brand said. "Step aside."

"I'm afraid we have strict protocol in place for accessing a scion's personal space," McAllister said, continuing to speak only to Addam—or, rather, a spot in the middle of Addam's forehead. "Perhaps if I knew you were here with your mother's authority?"

I transmuted my sabre into a hilt and shot out the lock. Sparks jumped and landed on McAllister's sleeve. He slapped at them with a cry. The door creaked open.

"Deal with him," Brand told Addam, and pushed past everyone.

The bedroom was a narrow space, narrower than even the width of Half House. It made sense, given how many family members each of the four courts supported. Space would be at a premium.

Ella had decorated in searing shades of pink and purple. The bedspread was crowded with stuffed animals and fuzzy throws; a waist-high Victorian dollhouse overwhelmed an entire corner; and a box of condoms poked out of a nightstand drawer that had been slammed shut crooked on its tracks.

"Are we tearing the room apart?" Brand asked.

"Let's keep it intact for now," I said. "There're only so many places she could hide anything."

"Intact like the door lock?" Brand asked. When I shot him a look, he held up his hands. "No, it was very cinematic."

We began to search—or at least Brand and I searched, while Addam, who'd ordered McAllister to stay out of the room, watched with mounting apprehension. I had to remind myself that it was his sister we were investigating.

The only locked object was a hope chest, stenciled with unicorns. The flimsy lock vaporized under the force of my firebolt. I opened it and unpacked a stack of photo albums. Brand began to flip through them.

The first photo album detailed Ella's infancy. The second aged her until her early teens. The third book hinted at a young woman's interest in men of status—all were of Addam or Addam's older brother Christian, or other male Moral Certainties scions. Most of them looked bored or boorishly polite. There was more than one expression of exasperation at the camera flash.

In the back of that third album, Ella had hidden a photo in the cover flap. It was of her and Michael Saint Talbot at a carnival. Ella was kissing

Michael on the cheek; Michael was looking away from the camera with a frown. A balloon bobbed out of sight, trailing a curling blue streamer.

"Not exactly a smoking gun," I said. "But it proves what we already suspect. There's a connection between them."

"But it doesn't mean that she and Michael were behind what happened," Addam said. He met my eyes. "I'm not being naïve. I just need to be sure. What they did to me is nothing. Summoning something like Rurik? They'd be executed for that, Rune."

"I know," I said, not unkindly. "We won't act until we're sure. I promise."

"We need to get a look at Michael's room," Brand said. "Let's—"

"He's not here?" Geoffrey Saint Talbot pushed past McAllister. His forehead and cheek were covered in hash marks of dried blood.

When no one answered, he said, "Did I beat him here? He's supposed to be here! We're . . . we're meeting. We . . ."

He trailed off. His eyes were bloodshot and glassy. He looked at me and said, "I need help. Please help me."

We hurried to the rooms that Geoffrey shared with Michael. As we went, McAllister insisted, and not for the first time, "I would know if another scion was here! We take their arrivals very seriously!"

"Look," Brand said in exasperation. "A hundred scions with the right spells could have wiped your fucking nose without you knowing. Just stay quiet and let us do our job."

"Wait!" I shouted as Geoffrey reached for the closed door. I grabbed his sleeve and jerked it back. He was in a panic, though; he grabbed out with his other arm, trying to get by me.

Brand snagged his collar and threw him behind us.

"There's a ward on it," I said, pointing to a small, clay octagon that had been affixed to the molding. "Does that belong there?"

"I've never seen that before," McAllister said.

"Is that a . . . domestic ward? Some type of stasis, I think," Addam said, peering at the carved glyphs.

"I think it is," I said grimly.

"But why?" Addam asked.

I had a very bad feeling about this. I had a similar ward in my own home. It was a domestic ward, like Addam said. Used to trap odors.

I turned my sabre hilt around and thumped it against the ward. The clay cracked and fell away, and its magic faded out like radio static.

"Stay back," I said, and reached for the handle.

"Sure," Brand said. "Just do me a favor first and go to bodyguard school for fifteen fucking years." He shouldered me aside and opened the door at an angle. Nothing lashed out at us, except for the smell.

"Geoffrey, stay out here," I said.

"What is that?" Geoffrey demanded in a shaking voice while holding his hand in front of his nose. "What is that?"

Brand and I exchanged a look. We stepped into the suite together.

Inside, the drapes were drawn, but sunlight was filament-bright along the edges of them. The plush beige carpeting was speckled with gore that radiated out from Michael Saint Talbot's torn body.

He was in the middle of a summoning circle made of flexible copper strips nailed into the floor. Michael's body was so badly desecrated by bites and claw marks that he was recognizable only by one eye and his sandy hair.

In the doorway behind me, Geoffrey started making low, choking noises. I said, "McAllister, take Lord Saint Talbot somewhere close by. Get him a drink. We'll be along shortly."

"I can't leave him," Geoffrey moaned.

"You can," I said. "Go and calm down, Geoffrey. I need you calm so you can tell us how you got your little brother killed."

It was a merciless bull's-eye. Geoff's face caved on itself. He started to cry "*I never, I never wanted, I never wanted,*" so I stepped up to him in a quick motion that made him stumble back. "Go with McAllister. But if you try to leave, Geoff, so help me, I will hunt you down."

"I never wanted . . ." he repeated.

His whole body started shaking. McAllister wrapped Geoff's arm in a surprisingly firm grip and began to pull him down the corridor. The majordomo had a small two-way radio in his other hand, and began speaking instructions into it.

Addam gave me a lost look, not sure who he should follow. I said, "You go with them."

"No. No, I want to stay with you. This is all because of me."

Brand went over and poked a finger in Addam's chest. "This is *not* because of you. This was done *to* you. We don't need you standing there, wringing your hands; we need help searching the place. Can you handle it?"

Addam pressed his lips together, nodded, and stepped over the threshold. He gagged a little, and squeezed his eyes shut. I didn't blame him. I was taking shallow breaths myself.

"Let's look for summoning paraphernalia," I said.

"What more do we need to see?" Addam asked. "Isn't that paraphernalia right there, that circle? That?" Addam pointed at a bowl near the body. Michael had dribbled his blood into it at the start of the summoning. Or at least, that's the way it looked.

"Trust me," I told him. "It's what isn't here that's interesting. Don't disturb anything yet, just look for more summoning tools."

The suite was bigger than Ella's. A studio kitchen was separated from the bedroom by a half wall, and there was a small bathroom. The bathroom was clear of gore, so I sent Addam in there to look.

I took the dressers, wardrobe, closet, and wastepaper baskets. We failed to find what I was looking for. I couldn't find the hammer used for nailing the copper strips into the carpet. No open box of chalk; no knife sets; no receipt for the bowl, which still had a sale sticker on the bottom. No herb crumbs in drawers; no nail holes in the floor under the carpeting other than the ones that had just been made; no healed bloodletting scars on Michael's wrist or fingers.

"This," I said, "is staged as hell. Which means . . ."

"It's Ashton," Brand said.

Addam made a sound from the bathroom and stepped into the doorway. "Ashton?"

"Addam," I said, "there's nothing here to show that this room has ever been used for a summoning before today, or that Michael was a practiced summoner. It stinks of a setup. Call it a gut feeling, but I'm betting Ashton doesn't have a dead brother or road rash on his face. I'm betting Ashton isn't lying in a pool of blood."

"Ashton, Geoffrey, Michael," Brand said, his eyes lit by his uncanny intuition. "*All of them.* We're going to find out that they were all in on this, and either they've started turning on each other or, more likely, Ashton was Lead Douchebag all along." Brand glared at the room around us. "And bet your fucking life, each of them hid something that incriminated the others because they knew they were all untrustworthy bastards. Luckily, Michael was an idiot. If he hid something, it's either in one of those sports trophies or in the place he stashed his porn when he was a kid. Fuck not disturbing anything, let's tear this place apart."

"Should . . ." Addam started, and then gagged. He looked away from Michael's body. "Should we be worried? If it was Ashton—could he still be here?"

Brand went over and crouched next to Michael's body. His knee hit the ground between blood splatters. He pulled Michael's torn shirt away from his chest and jabbed a finger deep into one of the knife wounds. Addam gagged again.

"He's been here a while," Brand announced. "The body has cooled. Now tear this place apart. I want answers."

Brand picked the trophies. I went for one of the two mattresses. I didn't know whose bed was whose, but there was a racing journal on one of the nightstands, so I picked the bed nearest it first.

In the edge of the mattress facing the headboard, there was a jagged slit. Inside was an electronic storage device and a couple of ancient *Dear Penthouse* magazines.

"It's an SD memory card," Brand said.

"That's what I was thinking," I said in what I hoped was a wise voice.

He snatched it out of my hands and plugged it into an adaptor he had in one of his vest pockets. He stuck the adaptor into the side of his smartphone.

The memory card contained a bunch of images. Brand swiped through squares of blue-and-white diagrams. Blueprints?

"Can you tell what they're for?" Addam asked.

"They're screenshots of a GIS overlay," he said.

"What's GIS?" I said.

"Rune, when I plugged the memory card into my phone, it looked like your head was going to explode. I'm not fucking explaining what GIS is. Just take my word—it's a really high-tech map."

"Okay, then what's it a map of?"

He frowned at the phone. "A building. Security system. Air ducts, sewer lines, marked exits. Damn, I think that's a secret passage." He swiped to the bottom corner. "Here . . . You can see the cross streets outside the building. Nazaca and Hyperion. What's there?"

"Arcana compounds," I said. "There's a string of Arcana compounds on Nazaca Road. The road is built over the island's main ley line. Can you access city records?"

"No cell service," Brand said.

His nose wrinkled, and his gaze shot to Addam. He took in what he saw faster than me, because he started swearing first. Addam had picked up a tiny, stoppered bottle from a nightstand and opened it. The smell was foul—fresh shit mixed with gardenia. It was also familiar, and *that* was the reason Brand was swearing.

"I'm a fucking idiot," Brand said. "That's how he did it—that's how he tricked us!"

"Ashton," I said. "That's the cologne he was wearing at the hospital, when we got attacked."

"I discounted him, just a little, because he was there when we got attacked. He had to *fight* with us—and it looked like he was in just as much danger. I had all the pieces right *there*! We know Ashton trained at one of the Wasteland camps. He knew how to fight. And yet there he was, with us, fighting the recarnates, and using all these fancy fucking flourishes that would have gotten a normal person killed in a fight. And I fucking ask you: Why would someone who knows how to fight use fancy fucking flourishes in a life-or-death battle?"

"When he knows he's not in any real danger," I said.

"I'll bet you everything that this," Brand said, and pointed to the bottle, "acts like a scent marker. This kept Addam's fuckhead business partners from being attacked by the recarnates that they're *working with*. We—"

"*Sh!*" Addam hissed, holding up a hand. Brand's teeth clicked shut. His response to caution was much more developed than my own.

Addam cocked his head. I heard it, too. A shushed murmur, a repetition of the same syllables. The sound resolved into words: *"Doesn't work doesn't work doesn't work doesn't work doesn't work . . ."*

Brand began knocking on the wall. Six inches to the left of where he started, the bang went hollow. He felt around for cracks in the whitewash, and gave me a quick look.

I opened my senses to the unseen, one of my gifts. I immediately spotted the spells that kept something hidden. I went to where I thought the handle was, and, as easy as anything, opened a secret door.

Inside was a closet filled with coats, board games, and a desiccated old bong covered with rugby stickers. Curled on the floor was Ella Saint Nicholas. Her thin face was lined with tear tracks. Emaciated hands were pressed over her mouth. She had bitten down on her fingers in a bid to keep quiet; the half-moon teeth marks had filled with shallow blood.

Addam went down to his knees and pulled her against his chest. "It's okay, don't look," he whispered, keeping her face against his shoulder. "Just hide your eyes. I'm going to pick you up now."

"It d-doesn't work," she stuttered. "It doesn't work anymore. They came for us, came after us. They didn't stop. They didn't stop when

Michael told them too. We ran in here, and he hid me. He told me to hide. He told me I'd be okay if I hid. And I did, and they came, and he screamed, oh, he screamed, he screamed, and he *won't stop screaming!*"

Brand went to the room where Geoffrey was being held, presumably to loom menacingly over him. I followed Addam to Ella's bedroom.

Once there, Addam laid her on her bed, on a girlish quilt of pink-and-purple yarn. He pulled the quilt over her. Without the glamors I'd seen her use previously, the true scope of her self-starvation was laid bare. It was a hard sight.

Addam's face had filled with despair. He wasn't stupid. He knew that not only might Ella not recover from this, she might not be allowed to recover. The things she was involved in carried death sentences.

I couldn't stop thinking about one thing: Michael had hid her. Bad things at the door, and his last thought was to keep her safe? It was an unexpected mercy. There was something about it that made me want to cry.

I went back into the hall. A servant materialized. "Can you stay with her?" I said. "Keep her in her room? Someone should be with her at all times. Give her a light sedative, if you have it, but nothing that will knock her out. We'll need to talk with her later."

"Yes, my lord."

"Rune," I said.

"Yes, my Lord Rune." The woman hurried past me.

After a minute or two, Addam came into the hall. We walked in silence to the room where Geoffrey was being kept. I juggled half a dozen platitudes in my head. Finally I said, "Because smelling a sealed vial in the room of a dead man is *such* a good idea."

His face inched into a tiny smile. "We did learn something from it, Hero."

"Nice spin control," I said.

Ahead of us, Brand slipped out into the hallway. "How do you want to play this?" I asked him.

"With patience and compassion," Brand said. "What do you fucking think? I took away all his sigils. We should beat the ever-loving shit out of him."

"I think I should go in alone," I told him.

Brand's face went neutral. "No."

Speaking to Brand as much as Addam, I said, "I have a . . . prior relationship with Geoffrey. Let me see what I can get out of him first. As much as I want to know why they've done what they've done, I'm more interested in finding out where Ashton is now. We need to lock him down and make sure Rurik isn't brought back."

"'Prior relationship'?" Addam asked.

"Oh, for fuck's sake," Brand said. "Rune, talk to him, but we're standing in the doorway."

He shoved me into the room.

Geoffrey was in the process of standing up. His footing was already unsteady, and I got the impression that the half-filled tumbler of liquor on the table next to him wasn't his first. The whiskey bottle sat in a puddle of splashes.

"He's dead," he said. "My brother's dead."

"Geoff, did Ashton try to kill you?"

"He did that to Michael, didn't he? He did. Of course he did. I think he tried to kill me, too, I . . . There was a car. A car jumped the sidewalk and almost ran me down. I knew, I knew, I *knew* it was Ashton. Everything went wrong. This wasn't what we set out to do. This wasn't how it was supposed to end. You've got to believe me, I—"

"Geoff, I need you to start from the beginning. It's time to come clean. You realize that, right? As bad as things are, they can still get worse. Do you have any idea what you'll be held responsible for if Rurik gets summoned again?"

"*Again?* Does that mean . . . It's gone?"

"So you know about Rurik," I said.

Geoff gave me a tired look. "You don't need to trick me. I'll tell you everything."

I topped off his whiskey as he settled in the chair. I sat on the sofa. Geoffrey didn't speak as he lifted the tumbler in a spasming, two-handed hold. After a fourth coughing sip, he set the glass back down and looked at me.

"We wanted more out of life. Michael and me. The Temperance Galley . . . Well, all of them, all of the Moral Certainties . . . they're so *slow* to change. They're all so *careful* in their projects. Michael and I wanted to follow in the footsteps of men like the Tower and the Chariot—men who embrace the human business world, who've become financial giants. We thought Ashton wanted the same thing. That's what he told us. I think even Addam agreed with us, at least up to a point, but he never wanted to go far or fast enough. Right, Addam?" He looked behind me. I don't know what expression Addam gave him, but Geoffrey quickly dropped his eyes.

"In the beginning, the idea was to get Ella into a . . . leadership role. She was sweet on Michael. All he had to do was tell her he was interested, and she was hooked. He—" Geoff stopped talking and went, if possible, paler. He was looking at Addam again. I didn't have to guess what look was on Addam's face this time.

"It wasn't supposed to turn out like this. It wasn't supposed to be about harming you or Christian. We just wanted Ella to get more contacts. Then she could take your place in our business. She wanted the same things we did. Or at least she wanted whatever Michael wanted. That's how this all started, I swear, it was just a . . . a . . . a shifting of power, of getting Ella on our team instead of you."

Geoffrey looked back to me. "I didn't know about the kidnapping or Christian's poisoning until they were done. And by then, Michael and I were in so deep, we couldn't go to the guarda without implicating ourselves. And . . . and all of the sudden, Ashton had that Rurik, and those recarnates. He had an *army.* It was scary, so bloody scary."

"You poisoned my brother," Addam said softly.

"Ashton did," Geoffrey stammered. "He used some sort of rare herb.

285

Something the doctors wouldn't figure out right away. It was supposed to keep Christian weak. Sickly."

"Is it reversible?" Addam asked.

It was the darkest tone I'd ever heard from Addam. I knew that Geoffrey's life hung, possibly immediately, on his answer. I swiveled around and saw that Brand was putting a hand on Addam's shoulder, more to give me a chance than to restrain him. Brand would have no problem with Addam putting a sword through any part of Geoff's body.

"It's reversible," Geoff said. "It is. We never intended to kill him, just inconvenience him. At least, that's what we all said, but now . . . Now I don't know what Ashton intended."

"Geoff," I said. "What's at the corner of Nazaca and Hyperion?"

He sank back into the sofa cushions, eyes wide. "I only found out later," he whispered.

"I don't care when you found out. I want to know who lives there."

"Lord Hermit. It's the Hermitage. I think . . . I think Ashton wanted to destroy the Hermit. Then all of Lord Hermit's assets would get absorbed into the three other Moral Certainty courts. With Ella as the acting heir scion for Justice, and between the three of us, our resources would increase. I think Ashton wanted to take the Hermit down. He said it would be easy."

Easy? I wasn't sure about easy, but as far as courts went, the Hermitage was far less protected than most. By his very nature, Lord Hermit didn't surround himself with others.

And while this was interesting, it didn't address the biggest concern of the moment. "How did Ashton summon a lich?"

"I didn't know it even was a lich! Not at first. They're not even supposed to *exist*! I didn't know . . ."

He lifted the tumbler to his mouth. I stood up and slapped it away. "Geoff, *enough*. Stop telling me how you're a victim. Start telling me *how Ashton did it*."

"I don't *know*! He said he had friends who owed him favors. Powerful friends. I don't know how it was done, or where it was done, or when it was done." Geoff looked past me. "They'll go after Ella now, Addam. She'll be in danger, too. And he hates you, Rune. Ashton hates you; he says he won't let you ruin his life again. He's going to keep trying to kill you."

"When the hell did I ruin his life the first time?" I demanded.

"That's what he said. I don't know what he meant. It doesn't make sense—no one knew you were going to get involved. The recarnates were never meant to be used on you. Rurik was never supposed to go after you. But when you began looking for Addam, everything started falling apart, and Ashton committed more and more resources to stopping you. Now his plan is ruined. There's no way he can go after the Hermit. I think . . . I think he's snapped. I think he just wants people to suffer. He tried to kill me. He killed my . . ." Geoff stopped talking. Fat tears slid out his eyes.

"He didn't snap," Brand decided. "Michael's murder is too calculated. He's tying off loose ends. I don't like this."

Geoff grabbed my hand and started to say something, but I pulled it away with such force that he fell out of the chair.

Geoff let out a low moan and hunched into a ball.

Something about that pathetic display made my conscience twinge. I'd cared for him once. And he'd as good as lost everything. I knew what that felt like.

I crouched down to say something not entirely awful, but Geoffrey cringed. He said, "You don't have to hit me. You don't have to send *him* to beat me up again. I've told you everything. Michael's dead. What else matters? My life is over. My . . . Oh, gods, my mother, I have to tell my mother about this."

And that? That about summed Geoffrey up. I decided I didn't feel much sympathy for him after all.

I started to get up when his words penetrated. "What do you mean, 'beat you up again'? Brand? Brand didn't beat you up."

Something sullen broke through the tears. "Back *then*. That night you saw me go into the bushes with Lydia, you sent him to beat me up. You're lucky I didn't have him arrested."

I got up and joined Brand in the hall. He avoided my eyes.

I whispered, "You beat Geoffrey up for me."

"I didn't like him," Brand said. "It's not like I needed an excuse. Get that smile off your face."

"You defended my honor," I said.

"This strikes you as a good idea," he said. "Teasing me."

Whether I did or not became irrelevant, because the hallway lights went dead.

Which wasn't half as bad as what else had happened.

"The wards are down," Addam said in shock. "The estate wards just went down."

SIEGE

While everyone began to talk at once, I whispered a cantrip. A sphere of light appeared above my head and burnished the dark hallway.

McAllister was saying, "We have backup energy sources; the lights should have—," while Addam was saying, "They're not coming on, the backup wards should have come on immediately!"

"What other defenses are there?" I said. I raised my voice over theirs. "Addam! Quickly!"

"Let me think," Addam said, and squeezed his eyes shut.

He didn't understand. Brand did, judging from the leathery rasp of a blade being pulled from its holster. So did McAllister, who hovered behind us with a terrified expression. We had moments. It didn't matter if Ashton was moving against us or not—we were open to the Westlands, and we had moments.

Addam braced his hands against a wall. His willpower surged. After a few seconds, he sagged. "There are mass sigils in the foundation of the compound. But they're gone, or empty. It's . . . Geoffrey! Geoffrey, try with me!"

Geoffrey, pale-faced and wide-eyed, stood in the doorway. At Addam's shout, he closed his eyes and tried, uselessly, to establish a connection with the defenses.

"Don't waste your time," Brand said. "Ashton has access to the same wards. Oh, I love it when family turns on each other. They know all the dirtiest tricks. Rune, what can we do?"

Addam's words echoed in my head. *In the foundation.*

An idea clicked into place—or, if not an idea, then an understanding of a chain of events that Quinn had stacked in place like dominoes.

"How many people are on the estate?" I demanded.

"Thirty-two," McAllister replied. "Plus your associates."

"Are they inside? Are they all inside the house?"

"Unlikely," the majordomo stammered. "We have groundskeepers. They—"

The handheld radio in his belt began screaming. Not static or shouts: people on the other end were screaming. We were out of time.

I pulled the clay disc out of my pocket and exchanged a glance with Brand. He swore, pressed his back to the wall, and braced his legs. I pressed my thumb into the center of my mass sigil. The released spell hit like the back of God's hand.

Ceramic shattered; framed portraits skidded away in a blast wave; everyone but me was knocked off their feet.

My mass sigil had spent over a decade buried under the foundation of Half House. I'd been building up the same stored spell the entire time.

The release of magic lasted forever, a private eternity stretched between one adrenalized heartbeat and the next.

I'd barely ever used a mass sigil and didn't know what to expect. The power . . . It was immense. The boundary between me and all the energy in the world became thin. For a moment—for an unending moment— there were no aches, no pains. My old shoulder injury did not hurt. The tired grit was gone from my eyes. I didn't doubt anything: myself, my ability, my course of action.

I released the spell. Its radius raced along ceilings and floors, along carpets and window frames. I felt the magic slide around mice and termites, over dead organic matter—old wood, woven cloth, fingernail clippings, dried flowers. There was a terrified child hiding in a dumbwaiter; there was a mummified body behind a wall on the first floor. The spell considered these and every obstacle as it stretched and bent. So many details, impossible to absorb, but the magic didn't need my understanding; it needed only my instinct.

It flowed until, finally, I reached the hard boundary of the outer

K. D. EDWARDS

walls. A building's outer walls have meaning. They separate the primal concepts of Inside and Outside, a basic tenet of hearth magic.

This was the moment of decision. If I kept going—if I tried to stretch the spell across the estate grounds—I'd diffuse the magic. I'd shorten the duration. It wouldn't work as well, or protect us for as long.

So I snapped the spell closed, and the walls of the compound became the edges of my defense. Anyone trapped on the other side was lost to us.

Brand picked himself up off the ground. "An hour," I told him hoarsely. "Maybe more. The barrier should hold at least an hour against anything outside the building walls."

McAllister scrambled to retrieve his radio. Before he reached it, the screaming ended with a wet gurgle. McAllister, stunned, held the radio toward me like an offering. He said, "I can contact anyone caught outside. They can gather in one spot, and we can lower the spell—"

"We can't," I said.

"But if they gather, all together—could you extend—"

"I can't," I said. "It doesn't work that way."

McAllister dropped his gaze. He went into a corner and began to speak on the radio. His footsteps crunched over a broken mirror.

"Those are my people," Addam said. He'd hit his head when he fell; blood pooled over an eyebrow. "We need to find a way to get to them."

"No, we don't," Brand said. "Not now. Now, you save who you can, because in an hour we'll be right back where we started. Do you have any idea how little time that is? How isolated we are? We are in *trouble*."

Whatever ground Addam had gained with Brand, he lost when he turned to me for confirmation. I said, "Trust my Companion."

"Tell . . . tell me what to do," Addam said.

Brand said, "Rune, can you tell if the compound was breached before the spell went up?"

"I'm not sure. There was so much area to cover. I had to stretch it past its design, use it like a barrier." At Half House, in such a small space, I'd

291

have been able to turn every square inch into a killing ground. I wasn't sure how the magic would work as a barrier.

Brand snapped his fingers at McAllister. The majordomo turned down the radio volume on snatches of panicked words. "I need a central location, midlevel, lots of space."

"I've asked everyone to gather in the ballroom on the third floor," McAllister said. "Is that acceptable?"

"That's great," I answered for Brand. "And—oh, I think there's a little girl hiding in a dumbwaiter. I don't know more than that."

"Let's move," Brand said. "You too, Geoffrey. You stay in my fucking sight. If I find out you had anything to do with this, I'll kill you."

"I don't know what's happening! I'm not lying!"

"Brand isn't lying either," I said.

We began jogging. McAllister and Addam shifted into the lead. I half-expected Brand to pull them back, but he paced himself close to me instead.

"Do we have any way of contacting New Atlantis?" Brand asked.

"Very few," McAllister huffed. "The Westlands interferes. There are indicators tied into our defense system that would alert the city residences—but I don't know if they've been tampered with as well."

"How big is your armory?"

"It is significant."

"We need vulcanized-coal weapons. Anything with obsidian or coral. Do you know how many people are inside the building?"

McAllister said, "I've asked radios to be distributed to everyone. We'll know soon."

By the last sentence, he'd run out of breath. We hurried on. The plush carpet underfoot became marble, and our footsteps ricocheted as we ran down a sweeping flight of stairs.

Max was lying flat across the bottom step. Ciaran was sitting on top of him.

"Lord Sun," the principality said.

"I don't want to know," I said. I ran by them, into the doorway of a ballroom. Inside, staff members moved in loud, frantic eddies, crying and begging for word on loved ones.

I expected Brand to step inside with me, but he was still in the antechamber, frowning at the ground. I went back to him as he crouched low and laid his hand on the marble.

"What?" I said.

"Vibrations. Is it your defense spell?"

"I feel it, too," Geoffrey said. "Why would a defense spell make the building shake?"

It wouldn't, but the already-scared people we'd caught the attention of didn't need to hear that.

A woman came up to us and said, "My son? My son?" Her chapped fingers knotted in Addam's sleeve. Addam bent over her and said something soothing, and took her off to the side.

McAllister's face fell. "Her son is a groundskeeper."

Brand caught the expression on my face. "Don't you dare," he said in an undertone. "Don't you dare start blaming yourself. Stay with me, Rune."

He was right. I took a deep breath, then clapped my hands for attention. Conversation stopped and eyes turned our way. "Ladies and gentlemen," I said loudly, "the estate wards have failed. We've erected a temporary barrier, but our situation is critical. We must prepare for the worst. My Companion, Lord Brandon Saint John, has studied siegecraft. You will follow his instructions as you would those of Lords Saint Nicholas or Saint Talbot."

"My son is outside," the old woman said in a trembling voice. Addam was still holding her arm.

"At present, they are unreachable," I said. "The best way we can help them is to be in a position to provide aid once the danger is past."

I was about to pass their attention to Brand when the mansion groaned around us.

It was a low, rolling sound that raised the hair on the back of my neck. Slowly, my eyes tracked to the crystal dome overhead. Clouds had churned afternoon into an artificial, sudden twilight.

"He wouldn't," Geoffrey whispered from behind me. "He wouldn't dare. Weather magic is forbidden."

"You need to stop saying such dumb fucking things," Brand said. "Rune, we need to get these people organized."

Weather spells were slow, deadly, and incredibly easy to foul up. The environment overlapped like tectonic plates; you couldn't easily interfere with one section without shaking apart another. It was such an illegal act that, if I hadn't been convinced of it already, I'd have now realized Ashton had no intention of letting anyone leave here alive.

Brand raised his voice. "McAllister, get someone to the highest point of the building with a two-way radio. I want to know what they see. Then start splitting people up—those who can fight, those who can move fast, those who need to be put somewhere safe."

McAllister raised a hand to a thin young woman with blue hair and said, "Emma, the tower." She took off like a shot, skinny legs barely hitting the ground.

Overhead, lightning turned the world white, silhouetting the veins of rain that spread across the dome. Two beats later, thunder flexed like sheet metal.

"This doesn't make any sense," Geoff said under his breath. "If he needs the imbued circle like you said, why waste time coming after us?"

"Without Rurik, I'm not sure he'd be able to break through the Magician's estate wards," I said.

"Which means he may have changed tactics," Brand said. "Maybe he's trying to get rid of witnesses. That would explain why he killed Michael and tried to kill Geoff and Ella."

"Ashton doesn't know that Lord Tower is onto him," Addam said.

"Big damn deal," Brand said. "It's not like we can throw open a window and shout, 'You're already fucked anyway.'"

"Maybe someone will notice our danger, if the alarms aren't working," Addam said. "Lady World lives in her Westlands compound. She'd sense the storm—she's a nature mage."

"*Maybes* aren't going to do us much good," Brand said.

McAllister had been following Brand's instructions as we spoke. The room was more or less split by the elderly and very young, and anyone who could hold a weapon. Seeing that, Brand raised his voice again. "McAllister, lead a group to the armory. Coal, coral, and obsidian weapons go in the hands of the best fighters. Pair them with people who know the layout of the mansion best and can move fast. Patrols on all main points of entry: basement, each floor, the biggest unit on the top floor. Ranged weapons go in the hands of people upstairs. If patrols find a breach, do *not* engage, just alert. And I need a space like this, but smaller and with limited entry points. High up. Pick someone competent to lead the noncombatants there."

"There's a conservatory on the fourth floor," McAllister said. "Main wing."

"That'll do. No one—"

The marble shook under my feet, and my eardrums popped.

I threw my hand toward the ceiling, sending my light cantrip racing toward the dome. It highlighted a web of cracks spreading from the metal rim.

Brand started to shout commands, which barely drew lines around the spreading panic. If the dome had given way, it would have been a bloodbath. But it held. McAllister funneled the household servants in one direction, while Brand grabbed my sleeve and dragged me in another. He said something I couldn't hear, and pointed to Addam and Ciaran. *Spell-casters.* We split wide, and began to herd Addam, Geoff, Ciaran, and Max into the corridor with us.

Brand lingered at the rear of the group to make sure the staff had evacuated without injury. When the ballroom was clear, he came over. "We don't know what Ashton has planned. The barrier won't hold forever. One way or another, you scions are the firepower in a fight."

"Our sigils are empty," Addam said. "We used them against Rurik."

"That's why we need to go to the sanctum," I said, picking up Brand's thread of thought. "We'll take thirty minutes to store what spells we can."

Addam took a breath. "The sanctum is one floor down, one wing over. Follow me."

We started out at a brisk pace. I touched Brand's shoulder and pulled him close. "It would make more sense for you to help the noncombatants," I said quietly. "There are elderly and children—they could use your direction. I'll meet up with you after we're done in the sanctum."

Brand said, "I appreciate your thoughts on the matter," and twitched my hand away. He stepped up to take the lead from Addam.

I sighed and pointed at the two-way radio Ciaran had managed to snag from somewhere. He handed it to me while weaving around a potted plant. I pressed the button on the side and said, "This is Lord Sun. Emma, are you there?"

"I'm here!"

"Do you see anything yet?"

"Oh!" There was a bang and a crackle, as she either gasped or dropped the radio. "Oh, there are so many of them. And they look . . . sick. I can see them through a lens cantrip. They're dressed in black, and they look pale and sick."

"How many," Brand said over his shoulder.

"How many of them are there, Emma?" I asked.

"A hundred. More. They're gathering in front of the north courtyard, outside the gate."

"Please continue to watch them," I said. I lowered the radio to my side and took a second to get my breath. We turned a corner and swept down a large stairway.

Black and sickly-looking. I said, "You were right, Brand. Back at Lord Tower's, you said we'd forgotten about the recarnates. You were right."

Brand shot me his silent *do-I-even-need-to-say-I-fucking-told-you-so* look, the one he used when we had company. A burst of lightning flashed through a window and, a moment later, I felt the thunder in my ankles.

We picked up our pace and entered a double-wide hall. Portraits lined the walls like a string of unsmiling dominoes, our bobbing light cantrips animating their displeasure. Addam said, "Through that green door ahead."

On the other side was a hallway—a loggia, actually—with closed floor-length windows. Lightning flashed as the storm bore down. The massive lawn strobed from a grim darkness to a surreal, acid green.

At one end of the corridor, only a few yards away, was a double door gilded with both gold and silver. "Brand . . ." I said.

"Don't even," he said.

"I'll be fine in the sanctum. Go organize the barricade, then come back with armed staff."

Brand's jaw set mulishly.

"Please," I whispered.

Geoff was looking back and forth between us. "You can't be serious. He's a Companion, he should stand guard while we meditate. Have the majordomo handle the servants."

"Geoff," I growled. "Brand, you should take Max, he doesn't have any sigils. It makes sense."

Max immediately opened his mouth to protest. Brand's eyes snapped in his direction. Max closed his mouth and lowered his eyes.

Ciaran said, "My sigils are topped off. I'll go with them. Best to stay in groups, eh?"

"Thank you," I said. "Brand?"

"You won't leave the sanctum until I return," Brand said.

"We won't," I said.

"I'll be back in twenty minutes."

"You'll actually go?" Geoff demanded. "You would leave scions unprotected?"

"Rune is never unprotected," Brand said. "And shut the fuck up."

If there was an expression between pale and red-faced, Geoffrey was going for it. "I'm a *scion*."

"You so fucking are," Brand agreed.

I said, "Brand. You should go now."

"Twenty minutes," he told me, and then he began retracing his steps with Ciaran and Max in tow. Max looked at me over his shoulder as he went, stumbling twice.

I waited until they'd gone through the green door, and then I punched Geoffrey in the nose. He doubled over, spurting blood. I grabbed his arms and spun him into a wall. He went down. I pressed my sabre, shifted into hilt form, against his temple.

"You have harmed me and mine. Under every rule of Atlantis, that gives me right to retaliate. Do you not understand that I may decide to *kill you*? You need to start showing a sense of self-preservation, and you need to start showing it soon."

I left him in a heap, and went into the sanctum.

It was the height of arrogance.

For a few moments I could only stare at the glass windowpanes with rising temper.

They'd built a sanctum in a greenhouse. We were surrounded by glass and storm and dead protective wards. This space—a sanctum, the very *heart* of sigil magic—was now so indefensible that it could be taken down by nothing more complicated than a big rock.

"There are usually spells protecting it, of course," Addam said uncomfortably.

"Of course," I said. A tree limb the size of a Volvo sailed by outside. "Godsdamnit."

"You look as if you want to give your *stupid scion* speech, Hero." He stepped up behind me. The greenhouse was cool, and his presence against my back was warm. He lowered his voice. "Are we unsafe here?"

"My defense spell won't keep the storm out—or anything that doesn't actively mean us harm. We need to move quickly."

Geoffrey made an irritated sound from a nearby sitting area. He'd smeared blood all over his face in an effort to stop the nosebleed. "Where are the wretched towels?" he asked.

"Ask a maid," I said. "I bet they'll climb over each other to serve you."

"You've already made your point," Geoffrey said coldly.

"And I'll keep making it." I picked up a blue shop rag that was lying next to a garden trowel. I balled it up and chucked it at Geoffrey. He caught it, unfolded it, stared at the dirt, and tried to fold it back into the cleanest square possible. He didn't complain, though, which made me think that he was catching on.

"Let's get started," I said. "Pick a corner. Move quickly. We're standing inside a bloody lightning rod."

"They didn't return my sigils," Geoffrey said. "I only have this and this." He tapped his eyeglasses and a tiny diamond earring almost hidden in the folder of his earlobe.

"Do you have any useful spells in any of your other sigils?" I asked.

"I have Shield in this," he said, tapping the earring again.

"Do you have any useful spells in your other sigils?" I asked again.

"They are . . . noncombative."

Which meant cosmetic or eidetic, knowing Geoffrey. *That* is what made me give *stupid scion* speeches. "Empty whatever is in your eyeglasses and fill it with something combative. We're not going to have time for anything else. Move, Geoff."

Geoffrey went into a corner. Literally into the corner—he stood and faced it. I'd forgotten how his method of storing spells reflected his punishing lack of confidence.

I picked the corner closest to the main building, which at least put a stone wall on one side of me. The area was canopied by giant fern fronds that smelled like fresh dirt and old water. Overhead, a sheet of rain gusted across the panels.

Addam followed me. His accent thickened the way it did when he was upset. "I am . . . unaccustomed to sigil work under these conditions. I do not want to let you down. It makes me very nervous."

"Do you know what happens to your body when you're afraid?" I asked. "You sweat, your heart rate increases, your adrenaline level spikes. Do you know what happens when you're angry? Sweat, heart rate, adrenaline. And when you're exhilarated? Sweat, heart rate, adrenaline. It's all fuel, Addam. It's all energy and willpower. Use it. Dance and be afraid. Dance and be angry. Dance with me."

"You meditate. You don't dance."

"I can do both," I said.

He lifted his eyes to mine. Some of the tension lines went smooth around his mouth.

I pulled the ancient clay disc out of my pocket, and cupped it in a palm. Addam put his arms around my shoulders. He began to move. It was less a dance than a sway, but rhythmic enough that I was able to fall into the fugue I needed to store spells.

The world closed in on me in stages: Geoff's muttered deprecations, then the dancing, and finally just Addam's closeness. Then I became lost in the gray haze of my meditation. My willpower unfurled and I sent feelers into the disc.

I'd found the mass sigil years after the fall of my father's court, when I'd first started making forays onto Sun Estate's haunted ruins. Rather than sell it for a small fortune, I'd made the decision to bury it in the foundation of Half House, to protect us against invasion. In all that time, I'd never used it for anything else. I had no idea how it would feel to fill it with a more aggressive form of magic.

For a few seconds, the cavernous potential of the artifact filled me with despair. The close confines I normally associated with sigils were gone. I couldn't even feel the borders of this empty device. Easier to fill a lake with a fire hose, or build a snowman by catching flakes as they fell from the sky.

I'd told Addam to make use of emotion. It was good advice. I took my doubt, balled it up, crushed it into a fuel I could use. Normally, to craft Fire, I imagined putting my arms around a bonfire. Now I imagined the bonfire putting its arms around me. I imagined the whiteness of a bomb blast; I imagined floating in the heart of the sun.

A minute may have passed, or a hundred of them. When I finally returned to a blinking awareness, the mass sigil was ready, and Addam was still holding me.

Trying not to disturb him, I slipped my cellphone from my pocket. Fifteen minutes had passed. The defense perimeter was still holding strong, which left time for another spell. Excepting Fire, my most common sigil spells were Healing and Shield. I decided on Shield, and spent minutes crafting and storing it. I could have done it quicker, but it was harder to work magic in a strange sanctum.

When I was done, I noticed that Addam had stopped swaying. "Did you fill a sigil?" I asked.

He leaned his head back so that we made eye contact. His eyes glinted with satisfaction.

"Nice work, Saint Nicholas," I said. "Geoff! We need to head back to the others."

I stepped past the giant ferns and into the center of the greenhouse, just as the wall exploded.

It happened in gunfire-fast movement. Something vaulted toward us in a glitter of water and glass. Geoffrey screamed. Hot rain splashed across my face.

Then adrenaline slowed my reaction time, allowing me to put the images into a narrative. One wall of the greenhouse had cracked and shattered. A horned deer had jumped inside and clipped Geoffrey with a hoof. Its jugular had been severed, and it was covered in circular, lamprey-like bite marks. The beast thrashed on the tile and sprayed us with arterial blood.

I held up my forearm to keep the splatter away. Addam ran over to Geoffrey, who scrambled backward on elbows and feet.

"What did that!" Geoffrey cried over the wet roar of the storm, staring in horror at the bite marks on the deer.

I transmuted my sabre from its wrist-guard form. It glowed a dull garnet as I rotated and aimed—ceiling, waist, floor—in a stop-start motion like Brand had taught me.

"Move to the hallway," I said. The deer trembled with slowing spasms. The bite marks had a bigger spread them my splayed palm. "Addam, get him up!"

Geoffrey grabbed at Addam's arm and was pulled to his feet. His hand reached for his eyeglasses, and I yelled, "*No!* Save your spells! The deer can't hurt us—and whatever hurt it can't pass the defense barrier." *I think.* "Just get to the hallway."

I covered them while they stumbled from the sanctum, then slid around them, aiming my sabre at the darkened end of the loggia outside. A stuttering flash of lightning turned my shadow into a marionette against the wall.

After a few seconds, I let my shooting arm drop but kept the elbow loose.

Geoff said, "Which way should we go? We should avoid Lord Strength's wing."

"Agreed," Addam said. "Rune, the main hallways will take longer, if we want to rejoin the others, but we'll have more space to react."

"Let's check with Brand first," I said. I turned up the volume on the two-way radio. For a second I thought I'd caught someone mid-conversation, until realizing that Brand was repeating my name.

"I'm here," I said, pressing the button.

"What the fuck happened?" Brand demanded, because of course he'd have felt my alarm when the glass broke.

"A deer jumped into the sanctum. It looks like something attacked it. I'm pulling us out of here."

"You fucking think?"

His sarcasm was a front, but . . . something else. Something else was wrong. I could feel it, through our bond. "Brand, what is it? Are you okay?"

"Two units aren't reporting in," Brand said after a pause. "The defense perimeter is still active, right?"

"Yes. But we could have been breached in the minutes before it went up."

"I sent a patrol your way. Ciaran's with them."

I looked unsurely at the loggia's window-wall. "That's fine, but we're not in a safe area. I want to move into an interior room. I'll call when I know where."

"Patrols are on channel five—I'll try to raise Ciaran for you."

"I'll switch over as soon as we're clear," I said, and then I hooked the radio on my belt. "Geoff, can you alter the shape of that?" I pointed at the squirming light cantrip that he'd manifested above his head.

"I . . . think so. Into what?"

"A big glowing bull's-eye?"

Geoffrey actually started to transmute the cantrip, before scowling at me and extinguishing it.

I sighed. I felt like I'd been sighing a lot these last few days. "If the compound has been breached, we need to assume ambush. Throw the light ahead of you. It'll reveal or flush out ambushers. Like this." I blended words and willpower, and tossed them away. A ball of pale amber light appeared at the far end of the corridor, illuminating an additional length of exposed hallway. "Addam, what are our routes? We need to get away from these windows."

Addam pointed as he spoke. "That corridor leads to a solarium. Over there is the servant hallway we entered from. That opens into some sitting rooms."

"Sitting rooms," I said, moving toward a double door gilded in lace-like silver. I waited until the next round of thunder masked any noise, then spun into the room at a crouch. I ran my sabre in a semicircle over sitting chairs and a floral-print fainting sofa. When nothing stirred, I sent a light cantrip across the room and edged along the wall, to make sure nothing was using the furniture as cover.

Geoffrey invoked another Mobius of light above his head. I was about to call him an asshole when he snuffed it out, saying, "I can't make it move like you can."

"Maybe now isn't the best time to practice," I said. There were two other doors leading from this room. I realized, uncomfortably, that I was going to be wholly dependent on someone else's sense of direction.

I switched over to channel five. "Brand, we're in the sitting room closest to the sanctum. We'll give Ciaran a few minutes, but I don't want to wait."

"Just fucking wait. He's close."

"Copy," I said.

I lowered my arm, and Geoffrey stepped up to me. He said, "What if Ashton is inside the house? Brand said people are missing. Maybe they've been attacked. We should find somewhere nearby and barricade ourselves. I have the Shield, I can help."

"Barricade ourselves," I repeated.

"And a Frost spell. I have a Frost spell in my glasses. I could use that for a barricade as well, I think."

"That's just brilliant, Geoffrey," I said, and my nervousness flipped over to show a belly of dark anger. "That's just *great*. Screw everyone else upstairs."

"They're building their own barricade!" Geoffrey said.

"We went to the sanctum because we're their best defense. You know what? Let's forget the fact that we have a responsibility to stand between them and harm. Let's forget that they're your people. Instead, let's just remember who pulled the fucking lich out of the ether and started all this in motion in the first place."

"*Ashton* did that! He fooled me just as easily as he did you!"

"Not as easily," Addam said quietly. He walked over to an ornamental fireplace, and hefted a brass poker. "I was fooled most of all. Go ahead and stay here if you like, Geoff. I'll find you afterward."

Geoffrey's face went pale around the purpling hoofprint on his forehead. He crossed his arms over his chest and turned away from us—right into Ciaran, who dropped his Camouflage. Geoffrey screamed and fell over a footstool. The principality's upturned lips were bright in the scarce light.

"Made you flinch," he said.

"Camouflage spells still cast shadows," I said. I wiggled my sabre at him; I'd lifted it to aim even before he'd materialized.

Ciaran tutted. "You're always so stingy with compliments."

"Did you see anything on your way here?" Addam asked.

Ciaran wore a necklace made of knucklebones, each one a sigil. It was an old magical device, from the days when magic's packaging needed to be as grim as the magic itself.

There was fresh blood across the bones. Ciaran said, "Indeed."

"Were they recarnates?" I asked. "Inside the manor?"

"They were. We were surprised, but we handled it. Boys?"

From the corridor, three armed servants stepped into the doorway. That drew my attention to the windows behind them; the sky was a sinkhole of spinning grays.

My ears popped.

"Your hair," Addam said. Wisps of his own hair—whatever wasn't bound into a sandy braid—lifted off his forehead.

Ciaran began yelling for everyone to move just as I grabbed Addam and threw us across the room. We went down in a tangle as lightning struck the side of the mansion.

My senses got scrambled for a second—screamingly loud whiteness; a yellow clap of thunder—and then one of the guards was on fire. He windmilled around in a tight circle, which only fanned the flames. I ripped a wall tapestry off its hangers and tried to smother the man in a hug. Bright points of heat bled through the fabric under my fingers. Finally, the man's knees gave way, and I was able to roll the flames out.

I pulled the tapestry aside long enough to see that most of the man's face was gone, and his life with it. I yanked the cloth back.

"We . . . need to get away from these windows," I said over the wind. Most of the nearby loggia windows were gone, and rain whipped across my bowed head. "Addam, find us another way."

"There. Down the corridor on the other side of that door," Addam said numbly.

We moved out in shocked silence. The two remaining guards took the rear. They whispered to each other in fear, and, really, I didn't blame them. If they'd thought nothing could go wrong because they were surrounded by scions, they were mistaken. We were one-trick ponies. Our power was limited by the very instruments of our magic. How the hell was I supposed to protect anyone, if we had enemies both outside the barrier and within it?

I pushed through a swinging door. I pumped willpower into my light cantrip and sent it flying ahead, lining a stretch of glossy, dark parquet.

"This way," Addam said, pushing ahead and opening a door on one side of the hall.

I got a glimpse of moss-colored carpet and then Addam's boot was squishing down on something wet. I yanked him back just as spores, firefly-bright, puffed into the space he'd been standing.

"Gods' love," Addam hissed as I lit up the room with a light cantrip.

From the shin up, it was a richly-appointed reading area; but the carpeting seethed with mushrooms. They were slick and fawn-colored, their gills fleshy and swollen.

"We were open to the Westlands." I turned and looked at everyone else, almost angrily. "It was only for a minute, but we were open to the Westlands, and there's no telling what the hell got in before the barrier went up. Don't touch *anything*; I don't care how normal it seems. If you lean against a desk and it eats you, I'm not fucking responsible. Any questions?"

"They'll be in oilskins," Ciaran whispered.

"What are you talking about?"

"I can see some beasties," he said, and shook his head. His eyes—

always a bit shimmery—now glowed. "I'm afraid we're running out of time, Sun."

"We can go that way," Addam said, pointing to a door farther down the galley.

We passed through it into a library, and from there into a musical conservatory. Decorative glass doors faced another dark hallway, which Addam urged us into.

My light cantrip, thrown ahead of us, drew the first ambush.

Dead men leapt from a corner. Two of them dropped to their knees, rifles braced against shoulders. I jerked my hand. My light cantrip split and flew into their eyes. The recarnates were startled; one stumbled sideways into the path of the second rifle.

Ciaran swept in front of me and barked, "*Remember!*"

One of the dead men staggered back from the others and shouted a woman's name—an actual voice, something that shouldn't have been possible. Another began to tear at the funeral stitching on his face. A third pulled a knife from its belt and stabbed it into its neighbor's chest.

"Not in the heart. Here. Here." Ciaran touched the back of his head. "It can end."

The recarnate reversed the knife and stabbed the other recarnates in the brain stem. None resisted. In the end, the dead man turned the knife on its own neck.

Like most types of violence, it was over before your brain had time to add in the subtitles. Someone dry-heaved. Addam was breathing fast.

I had no idea what Ciaran had done. I'd felt no sigil release.

"You forget that I traffic," Ciaran reminded me, "in dreams."

"The fuck kind of dreams you have?" one of the guards blurted.

"Not mine," Ciaran said. "Theirs. I gave them back their dreams, so they'd remember they'd once been alive. Don't forget that, in their own way, they are victims of your Ashton as well."

In the distance, a woman screamed.

The armed servants looked at us. On a normal day, they'd have gone running. This was not a normal day. These were no longer familiar hallways.

The screaming stopped.

"Jesus," one of the servants whimpered. "What's *happening to us?*"

I said, "We still need to get to the others. Just focus on that. Let's go."

We moved. Up a narrow stairway to the second floor. Through an open archway, into the residential part of the mansion. I wasn't sure which Arcana claimed this area, but it was spartan. Wooden boards were covered with rushes from fir trees. Petrified berries crunches under my feet, cracking into a swirl of resin.

Somewhere close by, a man began yelling. One of the guards shouted "*Peter!*," and took off like a shot. I ran after him. The man disappeared around a corner. Bright jugular blood arced back in his wake. No scream, no sound of struggle, just the heavy patter of blood as it hit the white walls.

I ducked low, roared a battle cry, and brought up my sabre hilt. There were two bodies on the ground, one of them moving but bleeding badly. A man stood over him, wearing dull-green oilskins. He had the slack, bloated features of a drowned man.

Wide-spaced eyes, flesh as gray as sharkskin. Teeth like hypodermic needles. *Draug.* A godsdamn *draug*—a water spirit, a riptide vampire.

I roared again and fired. My firebolt took it in the shoulder. It shoved its victim away and stumbled over the prone body of my own guard. The guard's throat was torn, his life seeping out in spit-bubbles of blood.

The rest of our party rounded the corner. Geoffrey released a spell, and faceted light brimmed over his skin. It distracted the draug long enough for one of the armed servants to stick a sword in the creature's ribs.

Draugs were not undead, not the way recarnates were, so vulcanized coal wasn't a special threat. The draug spun around and caved in the guard's head with a backhand. The man barely twitched for a second before dying.

Since Geoffrey had made himself so nicely invulnerable, I grabbed him by the shoulders and shoved him at the draug. The draug swatted Geoffrey away. I funneled willpower into my sabre hilt, making it blaze with garnet light. The hilt boiled outward into a blade as long as my forearm.

"Save your sigils!" I shouted, while bringing one foot back and my hip forward. I took two quick jabs at the draug's eyes. It stumbled, buying me room for a cross punch. The blow made its head snap back. I shrugged up my shoulders to protect my neck against its flailing claws, and stabbed it through its arm. It tripped and went down on one knee. I hacked downward and tried to behead it.

Its skin was too tough. The draug dropped to all fours and shrieked. Then it realized it was next to a bleeding food supply, in the form of the guard that had run ahead of me. Quicker than thought, it had its claws in the man's throat.

I saw the servant die. Saw his spirit shudder free. Three men entrusted to me for a simple walk upstairs; three men dead.

My Atlantean Aspect rose at my command. In a way I'd never done before, I *called* on it. I brought it to my skin, let it flare like fever. I became the brightest thing in the hallway. The brightest thing in the world. When I opened my mouth to speak, my words were like the flame of a blowtorch.

I whispered, "*Burn.*"

The draug's face began to smoke. Patches of skin peeled away from jawbone and incisors. Its hair clumped and curled into tight, foul nubs.

It died into a blur of smoldering darkness.

Everyone went quiet.

As the light dimmed—*my* light, the light that was me—it took conscious effort not to sag. "Just curious," I said in a shaky voice. "Were my eyeballs burning?"

"Yes, they were burning," Addam whispered in awe. "You were burning."

"Very impressive, Sun," Ciaran said. "More interesting, however, is that draugs travel in *shoals.*"

I said, "Shit," and pulled out the handheld radio. "Brand?"

"I'm heading towards you. What happened?"

"No, don't come, stay there. We fought off a draug, it must have come in under the cloud cov—"

The penny dropped. It wasn't a coincidence that the storm blocked the sunlight. Cloud cover allowed draug to move in daytime.

I said, "This must be part of Ashton's move. He's working with draugs, too. If there's one draug, there's a group of them. Pull the patrols back, we'll sweep the building when this is over." *If there is an over.* "You pull back, too. I'll meet you at the barricade."

Brand said, "McAllister, recall basement patrols. Rune, switch to channel four."

I switched to channel four.

Brand said, "Shut the fuck up and start yelling 'Polo.' I'M COMING TO YOU."

I smiled and said, "Meet you in the middle."

We ran for a long time, behind the bobbing blades of cantrip light. We slipped on wet tile, squished over wet rug. Broken windows hissed and spit rain. An office smelling of stale cigar smoke transitioned into a room ringed with barre bars and mirrors. A trick of the cantrip lighting turned our party infinitely smaller in the facing mirrors.

"Rune, you're close," Brand said through the radio. The words were tight with tension. Before I could reply, I heard him suck in a breath. "There are six of us. I don't think we're alone. We're on an outside patio— your spell cut across the mouth of it. The flagstones look orang—"

The reception cracked. Through the Companion bond, I felt vibrations of surprise and adrenaline.

"Addam, where is he?" I said. "*Where!*"

"It sounds like the rear patio of this wing. It faces the back lawns. That way."

I spotted the door from his finger-point and bolted for it. It opened into a rotunda, a wide, octagonal space done in starburst tile. A shallow dome, only a single story overhead, revealed a writhing sky.

Halfway across the rotunda, a full-sized tree shot through the dome. Everything became a roar of falling glass and metal struts. Sleeves were grabbed, arms were yanked. I was pulled out of the path of a crystal shard as long as my thigh bone. Someone shoved me into a hallway, and his body plowed on top of me.

Through all of this, Brand's alarm sang through me. He was fighting.

"Where—where are we?" I said as the noise died. I snarled a light cantrip and pumped it with so much willpower that my eyes ached. There were only two of us—only Ciaran and myself. No Addam. The mouth of the hallway was blocked by what appeared to be the roof.

Brand was fighting, and now Addam was gone. The sensation of being pulled in two directions was exquisitely painful. But Addam was closer, for now.

"*Addam!*" I roared. I ran up to the blockage. Through gaps, I saw rainfall and darkness. As I started yanking on a razor-edged length of metal, Addam shouted, "We're okay! We can go around this way. You go through the storage rooms. Look for a window that opens onto the rear patio."

"Are you okay to move?" I asked Ciaran.

"I cut myself when I saved your life," he said, examining a deep gash on his wrist.

"Sure, yes, thank you, now *move*. Please, Ciaran! Brand's under attack!"

The dust-choked hallway led to a service area, and from there to a huge storage space as long as the entire wing. The room reeked of dust and disuse, and was crowded with tall objects under canvas tarps.

I came to a stop in the middle of the room and stared at a wall. There were no windows or doors in eyesight—just this wall. "He's there," I said. My voice shook in anger. "He's on the other side!" With a wordless cry of frustration, I shot off a firebolt, powdering a marble frieze and setting cobwebs aflame.

"Doors and corridors and corners," Ciaran said in disgust. "Rats. They have us as *rats* in a *maze*. Enough."

He touched a link on his bone necklace. Magic snapped free and surrounded us like a freeway rumble. He lifted a hand toward the wall, and a length of it shuddered and buckled, grinding against itself. When the thunderous shaking stopped, the wall was still there, but it looked different. Less substantial.

"Take a swing," Ciaran said. I lifted my sabre to fire at it, and Ciaran grabbed my wrist—which turned the cuff of my godsdamn leather jacket into corduroy. He repeated, "A swing."

I shook him loose, strode the three steps, and snapped a side kick at the wall. It cracked through. The stone had thinned to shale.

A spindly table was overturned on top of a nearby shroud. I yanked it down and used it to batter the wall. After my third swing, the storage room opened into shouting, into a drizzle of rain.

Through the ragged hole I spotted Brand. He and five household servants had formed a loose circle in the middle of a rainswept patio. Recarnates in muddy urban camo were coming at them from every side. At least two layers of corpses surrounded Brand. Blood had turned one of his sleeves red.

As I watched, one of the servants was run through by a recarnate's blade.

I shouted, "*DOWN!*"

Most of the men followed Brand's immediate lead as he dropped. He yanked the rest off their feet. Not wasting time climbing through the wall, I brought my shooting hand up and sprayed the area with a chest-high barrage of firebolts. Brand didn't wait for an all-clear. He spun his leg out and broke the ankles of a recarnate who tried to dodge between the blasts. When it staggered, Brand hooked his hand in its waistband while stabbing the back of its neck.

I turned my strafe into precision shots, going for recarnates on the other side of the defensive huddle.

Revitalized by my appearance, and following Brand's tactic, the rest of the servants began stabbing at legs and ankles with their blades, pulling the recarnates into killing range. It was over in seconds.

Ciaran said, "Budge up," and shoved at the small of my back. I grabbed the edge of the fragile hole and pulled myself onto the orange-colored terra-cotta. The rain made the stone slick, so I watched my footing as I ran to Brand.

"There'll be more," he said, and glared when I tried to pull up his sleeve. He gave a pointed look toward the household worker who'd been stabbed, as if I was supposed to worry about anyone else first.

"Why are you out here?" I asked.

"Shortcut."

"Through an exposed outdoor patio in a lightning storm. You should make maps."

"The storm's ending," he said through his teeth.

I looked up while ripping his sleeve to the elbow. The sky still churned with layers of gray and black. "No, it's not. That's just the eye."

Brand had a six-inch cut on the outside of his forearm. It was bleeding freely and would need to be sealed, but he'd had worse. He kept super-glue in one of his belt pouches, which would hold it for now.

"How is he?" I asked Ciaran, who was crouched over the servant who took a sword in the gut.

Without lifting his head, Ciaran shook a *no*.

"Let's get everyone back to the barricade. And reload those." I pointed to the two crossbows the servants had dropped.

Across the patio, a French door opened so hard that it cracked. Addam and Geoff spilled into view. Addam had drawn his sword, and Geoffrey, the little fuck, had wasted another sigil spell. An icy nimbus of light surrounded his outstretched hand.

A window on the other side of the patio shattered. A hat rack stabbed back and forth through the opening and cleared away the glass. Max's blond head poked out.

"I have the healing kit," he called. "I heard you were attacked. I want to help."

"Then kick yourself in the ass *really fucking hard*," Brand said. "I told you to stay put."

As he stomped to the window to drag Max out, Addam crossed the patio toward us. He stared at his fallen man, and went down on one knee before the body.

I would have joined him, but Ciaran hissed in a breath. The principality lifted a hand into the air, fingers splayed, questing upward toward the roof, and then down toward the storage room we'd broken through. He said, "More coming."

"Recarnates?" I said. "Brand, form up!"

Ciaran shook his head slowly and said, "And draug." He repeated the word with a drawn-out *Z*. "*Draugs.*"

"Get those crossbows loaded!" Brand shouted. "Geoffrey, use that damn spell before it runs out—Addam, anyone injured goes inside a circle!" He pushed Max in the circle too.

That was as much time as we had for strategy. A mass of bodies reached the hole I'd made in the wall of the storage room. Three recarnates jumped through. Behind them I could see pale faces and oilskins.

"I've got this," Geoff said. As crossbows twanged and took down the recarnates on the patio, Geoffrey flung a squirming ball of Frost against the building. A wall of wavering mist stretched across the hole.

A recarnate, trapped behind the barrier, charged. Its face blackened and split. It fell out of sight in heavy, frozen pieces.

Geoffrey poured his willpower into the subzero defense. But it was a futile effort. Ciaran's spell had weakened much of the wall. More and more stone began to chip away under the pressure, forcing Geoff to expand the surface area of the barrier and weaken its efficacy. Worse, the draugs grabbed the recarnates in their midst and tossed them into the spell.

The barrier overloaded and vanished with a *whumph*. The draug swarmed. Four of them—five—more than half a dozen. *Too many.* No matter what tricks we had up our sleeve, there were too many.

The two last crossbow bolts twanged, tearing into the draug with enough punch to stagger them. Behind me, I sensed Ciaran and Addam unloading sigil spells. Addam's sword flared with a rim of Bless-fire, while Ciaran created a shuddering maelstrom of force around his entire body. He took three steps away from us and held out his arms. Patio furniture and walls buckled as he pulled loose the bolts and nails and pointed a hand at a draug. The nails snapped forward. Impaled through neck and chest, the draug dropped.

I saw Brand's eyes jerk upward a half a second before the next prong of the attack hit us.

Five recarnates vaulted from the roof. I hadn't expected them, and I should have, because recarnates wouldn't care about broken legs or sprained muscles, and because Ciaran had already indicated danger might come from above as well.

The dead men hit the ground, stood on splintered bones, and ran at us.

Brand took the first. He slashed it across the eyes with a knife, pivoted, and punched the point into the recarnate's neck. The recarnate hadn't even hit the ground before Brand spun to stab at another. I lifted my sabre and shot three firebolts at the circling draug, the greatest threat, hoping to keep them at bay. I took one in the eye at the same moment five carpenter nails stabbed through its jaw.

We lost a man, taking a dagger in the cheek from a recarnate. I glimpsed teeth through a gaping tear as he went down. Addam positioned himself in front of the servants and engaged with his sword. One of his swings cut off half of a recarnate's face. Black blood splattered me, cold to the touch.

I shot at the draug. Another recarnate dropped when Max leapt forward and stabbed it in the neck. I ran, grabbed the back of his shirt, and hauled him into the center of the circle. I shot firebolts into the wounded recarnate's head until it stopped moving.

Another recarnate took advantage of Addam's defense parry to slip by and charge us, claws extended. Geoffrey ducked behind the household staff, leaving an open path to me. My sabre shot went wide and scorched the second story. I sent willpower into my sabre, transmuting it into a punch-blade. Before I could use it, Brand spun past and took the creature down with a cut.

"Sigils!" he barked at me.

"Not yet," I said.

"Draug!" Ciaran shouted as the first real wave of draug attacks began.

I dove forward and met the first riptide vampire. The rotting oils on its bloated cheeks gleamed with reflected light. I ducked one blow, and a riposte, and then a fake lunge put me in front of its twist. I stabbed it in the chest. My punch-blade hooked inside the creature's brittle ribcage. Rather than pull it out, I dissolved it into flaming sparks. The thing died in a screaming fit.

One of the draug had pulled a servant from our midst and was feeding on it. Another was locked in battle with Brand. As fast as Brand was, he was already bleeding from cuts on his face.

"Reload the crossbows!" I shouted while jumping at the draug. Max tried to follow, so I spared a second to whirl back and shove him into the relative safety of the huddle. Geoffrey grabbed him and held him for me, which was nice, except for the fact that Geoffrey was a bloody coward probably just using Max as a shield. I moved in front of them.

Addam passed me with his Bless-fire burning sword and killed the draug that had cornered Brand. The last of the recarnates were dead behind him.

Still too many.

I touched my thigh and sent willpower into the sigil there. The released Shield shimmered across my body. Before it sank into my skin, I pulled it into a wedge-shape. I lashed out with it, sending two draug flying to the edge of the patio. One of them lost precious seconds in a scramble back toward us. The second hit my defense barrier and began to smoke and burn.

"Force them to the edge!" Brand yelled as our eyes met. He disengaged from the draug he was fighting, ducked, spun, caught the draug in the center of its gravity with a round kick. Brand kept at it, trying to force it into the defense perimeter.

A draug leapt over our heads and landed in the center of our circle. Another raced up to Brand to outnumber him. A third jumped over Addam and flanked him.

Too many.

Max had moved in front of the remaining servants—in front of *Geoffrey*—and was fighting the draug with a kitchen cleaver. Before I could race toward him, Ciaran caught the draug on the side of its head with a table leg, and the draug collapsed.

Brand was down on one knee, blood all over his leg. I started running toward him. Then a draug came out of nowhere and nearly raked claws across my face. I lost balance on the slick tiles and stumbled. Ahead of me, Brand twisted out of the way of one attack, but took a horrible swipe against his neck. I reached for my mass sigil. The draug grabbed my collar and yanked me off-balance. My mass sigil scattered to the tiles, out of reach.

"You waste our time," the creature hissed through swollen, drowned lips. It had breath like seaweed. "You don't have the sense to lie down and bleed."

I shouted in its face and smacked it with my palm. I called on my Aspect, but I'd drained too much of my willpower reserves. The creature opened its jagged, broken teeth in a soundless smile and tried to bite me. I punched it. Its head snapped back. It lifted a hand to swipe me with razor-sharp nails.

Max ran up from behind and tried to block the creature's swipe with his cleaver. The draug's thrust skated up Max's arm. All five nails went into Max's neck.

A pressurized burst of blood jetted out of the teenager. I stared numbly as Max's body started to slide downward. I yelled and moved,

317

THE LAST SUN

and then the draug was flying off me, as Ciaran threw it toward the defense barrier.

I stood there looking at Max's unmoving body—looking at one of the last servants, dying on the ground—looking at Addam, throwing himself between Brand and a sword thrust—looking at Brand, unable to put weight on his damaged leg—looking at four more draug, fresh to the fight, scrambling onto the patio.

There were no words that could describe what I felt. There are no words to describe the feeling when the battle tide has turned against you, and you are drowning in your own loss.

From that space in my heart where desperation lived, my Aspect finally answered my need.

My arms burst into flame. Fire raced up my chest, covered my face, my field of vision. I shook with power, stronger than any I'd ever tried to channel. It clawed up my throat like a diamond-sharp scream, begging release.

I fell to my knees and howled at the sky.

A bolt of magic—a bolt of visible, brilliant magic—shot into the clouds with strobe-bright intensity. The eye of the storm boiled. It began fraying first into snatches of indeterminate color, and then into vibrant shades of blue.

Afternoon sunshine poured down. Shadows ripped wide.

The draug—creatures of night—burst into fire. They screeched and attempted to fall back to the building, but the survivors fell on them and hacked them to pieces.

It was over in a moment.

ENDGAME

By the time I dropped to the ground next to Max, the power had left me. I was shaking and exhausted and feeling very, very mortal.

I pressed my hands over the fast flow of blood. He'd lost so much already; my knee slipped sideways in a pool of it.

"Max," I said hoarsely, wiping at the pink froth at the corner of his lips. When I looked up, everyone was standing around me. "Where's the healing kit Max brought?" I demanded in a panicky voice.

"Look for it," Addam said, grabbing Geoff by the neck and throwing him toward the pile of dead men. "Look!" Addam himself went down on both knees and began rifling through the corpses.

Brand crouched on Max's other side. He was covered in blood, and one of his legs was splayed out. He held out a hand to me. Cupped in his palm was my mass sigil.

"What happened?" he asked me in a whisper. "What was that?"

I angled my eyes toward the sky. Gray clouds were drifting back into the hole I'd torn, but the sun was still bright. *What had I done?*

"I don't know," I said softly.

"Whatever it was, it worked. Are you okay?"

I didn't want to talk about that. I didn't know what any of it meant. I felt a . . . a hollowness inside me, like I'd emptied something that wasn't ever meant to be emptied.

Max coughed. The foam on his lips deepened to scarlet. His eyes opened. "Did I do good?" he gasped.

"Save your energy, Max," I said. He grimaced when I pressed my hand tighter over his wounds, his life pumping through my fingers.

"But I did good?" he asked.

"You did great," I said. "You were so brave."

"And stupid," Brand added. "So stupid."

"Oh," Max breathed. He smiled. "What Rune said."

His face screwed up in a spasm of pain, and he tried to swallow a scream. I shouted, "Find that fucking kit!"

"It's here," Ciaran said from my left. He passed the kit to Addam, who went to Max's other side. Addam banged it open against the orange patio stone, spilling bandages, wards, ointments, and the small gold caduceus we'd saved from earlier.

"It should be keyed to me as well as our chiromancer. I should be able to use it," Addam said. There was a frisson of magic, and the spell surrounded Addam's hands like sunbaked rocks.

I tore open the first few buttons of Max's shirt with my free hand. Addam put his hands along Max's neck. Through the smear of blood, I watched sunburn spread from Addam's touch. The ragged skin went shiny and began to inch closed. Patches of it peeled away in sodden, red curls.

Addam leaned back and rifled through the kit. He picked out two flat stones and laid one on Max's forehead, and one on his chest. Max didn't like that at all, but I held down his hand when he tried to swat them away. His eyes grew heavy.

"Pain wards," Addam said. "Rune, he . . . There is much blood loss. We need more healing spells."

Patio doors banged open. My hand was half a heartbeat from grabbing at the mass sigil Brand held when I recognized McAllister. The majordomo, along with three other servants, hurried onto the patio with armfuls of towels and bandages. Another two men carried a table with the legs broken off. It took me a second to realize they planned to use it as a makeshift stretcher.

I watched as McAllister realized that the only one who needed carrying was Max. All of his people were dead. All of them. All of the staff who had stood with us. It was a delicate work of guilt, to be admired later in obsessive detail.

"Stay with Max, please?" I asked Brand. After he nodded and handed me my mass sigil, I stood and stretched, and walked through pins and needles over to Geoffrey. I pocketed the mass sigil and transmuted my sabre from a gladius to a dirk.

Geoffrey saw me coming. "Rune," he said when I was in earshot. "What did you *do*? Did you—" Geoff glanced around us. "Did you use weather magic?"

I hadn't. I didn't know why I was so sure, but I was, and fuck him for complaining about the way his miserable life was saved.

I stared at him without comment until he began to fidget. Then I said, "This is what you're going to do. You're going to *run* back to the sanctum. McAllister will have someone retrieve all of your sigils. You will fill no less than four of them with healing spells, and when that's done, you will *run* to wherever Max is, and you will make sure he survives."

"But . . . but the sanctum has been breached."

"I don't care. It's still a sanctum."

"It's *breached*. Anything could get at me!"

"*I*," I whispered, "*don't*," and pressed my face right into his, "*care!*"

He surprised me by pressing back and hissing, "*I'm not you!* Do you think I'm not aware of that? Do you think I'm not aware how useless I am in a fight? How much longer do I need to apologize that I'm not as good at killing things as you are?"

"Oh, take another step along that high ground. Go ahead. One more step."

"I'm not doing it! The sanctum has been breached; it's suicide!" He pointed a finger into my chest.

I grabbed the finger in an overhanded grip, twisted it around, and stabbed my sabre through the center of his palm. The heated blade slid through bone and tendon with only a small, jerking resistance. When Geoffrey started to scream, I grabbed his jaw in my free hand and shoved him backward. He windmilled four or five steps before losing his footing. As soon as he hit the ground, I pinned him with my knee, and waited until he stopped screaming.

When I had all of his attention, I yanked my sabre blade loose. More screaming. I didn't have to wait long this time for him to subside to a dog-whistle whine.

"If I find out you used a healing spell on yourself before everyone else is healed," I told him, "I won't just kill you, I'll kill you slowly."

I got off him. He scrambled to his feet and ran toward the patio doors.

Addam, with a shocked expression, tripped over a dead body on his way over to me. I held up a hand to stop him, because I wasn't ready to talk to anyone else yet. I stared down and focused on my breathing.

A mottled, gray face stared back. One of the recarnates. A photograph had slipped out of the dead man's pockets. I bent, picked it up, saw a gap-toothed girl. On the back of the picture were a couple misspelled words written in crayon, the sort of thing a kid might slip into a coffin.

My decision came quickly. I let out a breath I hadn't even realized I was holding.

I wondered what it said about the life that Brand and I led, that of all the emotions we shared through our bond, it was this *relief* that made Brand's face go pale with fright.

"Rune!" he shouted, limping over. "We need to go. We've got to get behind a barricade. It's been almost an hour since you set the defense perimeter."

"I know," I said. "I can feel it fading."

"But you'll have to help me upstairs. Okay? My leg won't hold. You can bandage it for me."

I reached up, wiped at the blood on his cheeks, and said, "Nice try."

"Rune . . ."

"You know I need to go out there."

"No," he said. "No, I don't."

"I have a loaded mass sigil. I have Exodus. It's the best plan."

"That's *not* a plan; it's the absence of *options*. No."

"If I'm alone—if I don't need to control myself, if I can just let the magic flow—I'll have a chance. I can surprise them where they're gathered, before the barrier fails. I'll have a chance to save us *all*. It's not a suicide gambit, Brand—I may be able to save us *all*."

"Don't ask this of me," Brand said, and his voice cracked. "Don't ask me to stay behind again."

The faint crows' feet next to his eyes were twitching. My fingers were still lightly pressed against his bloody cheeks. I said, "This is my story . . ."

"Rune," he whispered.

"And it's barely begun."

I was close enough that when he bowed his head, his forehead rested against mine. After a few seconds of hard breathing, he said, "What spell did you put in the mass sigil?"

"Guess."

He opened his eyes and tried to smile. "I guess I'd like to see Ashton's fat fucking face when the Day King heads his way with a mass sigil filled with Fire."

"You can't be serious," Addam said loudly.

Brand and I turned as one. Addam was standing there. His expression was red and getting redder.

"You cannot go out there alone," he said.

"Addam, I have a mass sigil filled with Fire magic. And I have something else—a spell I call Exodus. It's stored in a sigil that I've been charging and recharging for years. Trust me, I've got aces up my sleeve."

"And you think you need to do it alone? This plan makes you happy?"

"It's not crazy enough by half to make him happy," Brand said.

"I am a scion, too," Addam insisted. "These are my people, my duty. You will not go alone. I forbid it."

In a way, it was the perfect thing to say—because there was no better way to get Brand rallied behind me than to question my competency. Sure enough, he bristled. "Who the fuck do you think you are? Who do you think *he* is? Didn't you know what his father was like—what kind of ability Rune has inherited? Those aren't just shoes to fill, it's the whole fucking shoe factory. Don't you *ever* doubt whether he can do what he says."

"But—" Addam said. His eyes watered with frustration. "I feel . . . I should . . . I should help. I feel very useless."

"The support group meets on Tuesdays," Brand said.

"You're not useless," I told Addam. "And, like you said, these are your people. Get them somewhere safe. I can hold off the worst, but you'll need to be ready for whatever gets through. And stop writing my damned eulogy—this isn't a grand gesture. I'm coming back."

The barrier. I felt it flutter like a torn sheet. It was weakening fast. If I didn't move, I'd lose the element of surprise entirely.

"I need to go. Help Brand upstairs?" I asked Addam.

"Don't you fucking dare," Brand said when Addam offered a shoulder.

"Just," I said, and waved at Brand, "wipe him off and superglue everything shut."

"I can take care of myself," Brand said through a scowl.

"More than anyone I've ever met." The barrier was now buckling. "I need to go. Hurry, Brand. Get everyone inside, I'll give you as much of a head start as I can."

His worry crested into a single flare of panic, and then all emotion flattened into his cool sense of professionalism. Brand gave me a sharp nod, turned, and barked orders to McAllister and his men. Nearby, Ciaran gave me his own nod and grabbed one end of Max's makeshift stretcher to help carry it.

"Hero," Addam whispered shakily.

"Not like that," I said. "Not like a good-bye."

Addam's eyes glittered with emotion. He bent forward and kissed me. I'd already forgotten how warm his lips were. Were other people's lips so warm?

He turned and went to help the others.

In under a minute, I was alone on the patio.

There is a trick to lying to Brand.

Although the Companion bond isn't telepathic, Brand is very good at gauging my sincerity. He knows when I'm not being honest. So the trick is to not think about anything except the certainty that I'm telling the right lie. That way, what he senses is only the truth that I have decided I'm going to lie and tell him that it will be okay.

I was scared as hell. My heart wasn't just pounding; it stabbed at my ribs like it was picking a fight. I was alone, and wading into a battle I wasn't sure I could win.

Had my father ever done this? He was older than New Atlantis—he'd been born in a much more violent time and place, when spell-casters settled differences with small armies. How often had he carried this sort of responsibility on his shoulders? The odds seemed so precious and unreal. It didn't matter how good you were—eventually everyone zigged when he should have zagged. How did you recover from a mistake, no matter how slight, when an army was piled around you?

With a grimace, I shut down those thoughts. Doubt would only crack my determination. The people who'd died today deserved better than that. The people who were still alive inside the mansion deserved better than that. Every second I wasted increased the chance that Brand would face a mob on a slashed leg. That Addam would face a mob with empty sigils. That Max would bleed out before Geoffrey got to him with healing spells.

I experienced a moment of total clarity. The adrenaline before a fight. The world became drawn in dagger definition.

In front of me was a high, white-stone wall topped with metal spikes in a fleur-de-lis pattern. A swinging wooden gate, two stories tall and carved with dulled, dead runes, separated the compound from the Westlands.

Through the gate's slats, I caught glimpses of motion.

I reached out with my willpower and brought down the defense barrier.

No time to waste.

A fresh breeze tugged at my hair as I pulled the clay disc from my pocket. Swallowing spit, I circled my thumb a few times above its worn surface, and pressed down.

The Fire spell, magnified by the power of a mass sigil, rose up around me.

It smothered me in wave after wave of energy, whipping dirt and brittle leaves off the ground in a circling wind. My skin flushed red; the blood in my shirt collar heated to body temperature.

I started laughing. It wasn't stopping—the euphoric release of the spell wasn't stopping. It continued to build and boil. My ears were muffled by a sound, like the *whump* of a helicopter's blades.

This. This is what it meant to be Arcana. Using the mass sigil for a defense spell had been an awesome exercise in power. But using a mass sigil for offensive magic was the difference between being witness to, and the cause of, awe.

As the Fire continued to crescendo, I raised my hand and blasted the massive gate off its hinges. Past its enormous, somersaulting slats, a hundred dead men teemed in regimented rows across the outer lawns.

Charred corpses—draug, maybe, fried by the sunlight—grave-marked each line.

The dead men turned toward me. The ones with guns dropped to their knees. Bullets flowered into orange petals as they hit the heat shield that I raised with a flick of my finger.

I stalked toward them. They stretched at least a city block in either direction. There was no sight of Ashton. No sign of a command tent or post. *Too spread out.* Mass sigil or no—Exodus or no—I didn't have the range to level them all in a single blast.

I gathered the heat shield as loose armor, and sprinted at them.

Camera-flashes of bullets flared across my vision as I plowed into the first ranks, denting their neat formation. I let a fraction of my Fire pulse away from me, turning the nearest recarnates into torches. The other recarnates came at me, pulling knives and short blades from their waistbands. I ran to the left and pulled the mob tighter. Every few yards, I made a soft pivot, threading the recarnates in a loose *S*.

Greasy hair. Scars and pre-mortem burns. Funeral makeup, plain service daggers, tactical black camo. Their hatred and presence engulfed me. I used only enough magic to clear a path and deflect damage.

The lawn dipped into a gully. I fell face-forward onto a dead man's mud-stained boots. The boots, and the dead man, caught fire as my heat shield consumed it. The flames spread in a chain reaction. By the time I reined in the hungry magic, I was in a forest of flailing, screeching arms.

I scrambled up and ran left, went a few yards, hooked back toward the right. Any time I saw a break in the crowd, I ran for it, hoping to get a clearer view of the field, to see if I'd pulled enough of the army toward myself.

On my left, recarnates had trampled each other into a mound. I expanded my heat shield to force a path between it and me, and got a running start. I took huge, staggering steps up the pile of bodies, and flung myself forward.

As I crested the heads of the tallest of the dead men, I saw at least fifty nearby recarnates trying to tear toward the center of the circle I'd made.

I held my arms wide and let the Fire have its way.

The magic *exploded*. I became an inferno, a nuclear reaction. I became a sheet of unending flame.

The pressure of released souls sang against my face as they rose upward.

I had never experienced this much power. It was almost too much. I . . .

"*I am,*" I said, or laughed, or screamed. "*I am Arcana. I will be Arcana.*"

In seconds, it became impossible to make out one recarnate from another. They were simply flames cut into the shapes of men, pulling each other down in a frenzied bid to escape.

The last of the mass sigil's Fire died in a curtain of silence. Here and there a body part twitched. The smell of cooked, rotten flesh was nauseating. I was surrounded by blackness. Blackened grass, blackened bodies, blackened clouds of ash.

My clothes were in tatters—in shredded, crisp strips. As I stumbled backward, my shirt fell from my chest.

I turned in a slow circle to see if I'd succeeded.

The nearest recarnate was a football field away. *But they were there.* On either side of me. Dozens, still, on either side.

For a second, I thought I was laughing, but I wasn't.

I was crying. Because I'd failed.

The insight—the awareness of what I'd just done wrong—squeezed my breath into gasps. I should have held onto the heat shield and used Exodus. Then, after Exodus leveled as many recarnates as the Fire had, I would have been able to repeat the tactic and draw those two groups of recarnates together.

Now, without a shield, I'd fall quickly. There was no way I could destroy them all before I was pulled down.

I had no choices. I just stood there and let them come toward me. Their strides kicked up flash-fire clouds of resin and ash. I transformed my sabre into a hilt and took potshots at the front lines. How many knife cuts could I endure before I'd need to use Exodus? How long could I last? Every recarnate I didn't take down would turn toward the compound.

The nearest recarnates was close enough that I made out dirty-blond hair and gray teeth. I turned my sabre hilt into a gladius, letting the garnet sparks of the transformation shower me.

I thought about the time I'd made Brand ride a big wheel down the stairs.

I thought about my father standing with me on the roof of the house, pointing out the edges of our little kingdom.

I thought about how warm Addam's lips had been.

I thought about what had happened in the carriage house, and how I'd spent twenty years ready for this moment. Ready to close my eyes without the weight of knowing they'd reopen.

A dark shape hurtled through the air. I raised my blade as a man slammed into the earth, his fist digging a furrow into the torched dirt.

Lord Tower rose and released magic from a necklace of mass sigils.

Balls of liquid formed around each hand. They glimmered like huge beads of mercury, showing a warped reflection of the forest around us. Lord Tower threw the magic at the advancing lines. Both were perfect strikes. They detonated into asterisks of energy—not fire or lightning, just pure energy. It was a stunning use of power. Each burst took down nearly a dozen recarnates.

The Tower filled his palms with two more spheres, and decimated the recarnates on the other side of us.

I smeared ash out of my eyes, which made the claw marks from earlier sting like a bitch. "Admit it," I told him. "You were peeking around the corner, waiting for the last possible second to make your entrance. You Arcana are such drama queens."

"Unfortunately," he said, "you're wrong. This is not the last second."

Apprehension pulsed.

Lord Tower said, "Ashton Saint Gabriel is nearby, and he's resummoned the lich."

I'd be lying if a small voice inside me wasn't saying, *Lord Tower is here, he'll take care of everything.* But it wasn't like his presence was going to result in a nap. I was still needed.

"You can take him?" I asked.

"It," Lord Tower clarified. "And, yes, I'm prepared to unmake it. Are there any wards left functioning at all?" He'd shifted his attention back to the mansion.

"Ashton tampered with them. I set a boundary, but had to pull it down to meet the enemy."

"So I saw. A nice bit of magic." The Tower pulled a piece of jewelry from his belt. It sparked in the dull light. As the Tower set it on his head, I saw that it was a diadem, filled with six large gemstones. Each of the gemstones was a mass sigil. Lord Tower had come to the Westlands ready to fuck people up.

"No tiara jokes?" he said under his breath.

"Not a one," I said honestly.

The multiple release of mass sigil spells knocked me off my feet. I spun in the air and gouged my chest on a charred thighbone, and had to brace arms and knees to steady myself.

When I looked up, I saw that the mansion was glowing. "Did you . . . just *recharge* the wards?" I asked.

"Just the ones in the house. Tricks of our trade, Rune. You'll grow into such secrets one day."

The Tower reached a hand to me. I thought it was to help me up, but when our skin made contact, adrenaline slammed into my body with such force that it had me seeing rainbows for a full five seconds. When I could finally speak, each word came out as an individual breath. "Are you serious?"

"You were sagging. I need to find the lich's location. Keep watch over me." He released another spell and closed his eyes. His body went still as his spirit brushed past me.

I spent a few seconds self-consciously pulling the last of my burned shirt off my shoulders. It wasn't a good look on me. I nudged at the recarnate bodies for a replacement, but I'd burned everything in sight.

A sound made me glance toward the mansion. A small group of people was heading through the shattered courtyard gate. My eyes went right to Brand and Addam, and widened when I saw that I was with them. Or my golem was, at least.

"He doesn't talk as much as you do," Brand said when they were in earshot.

"Should I feel bad that everyone felt it was safe to come outside as soon as the Tower showed up?" I asked.

Brand snorted. "If you want. It has nothing to do with the fifty zombies you turned into nuclear shadows."

"I did do that."

"You did," he agreed.

We stared at each other for a second. It was one of those times when the Companion bond was a good thing. Then I nodded respectfully at the Tower's Companion and said, "Mayan."

"Lord Sun."

Addam was staring at the bodies around me. His eyes scrolled all the way to the left, stopped, and then scrolled back to the far side of the carnage. He shook his head softly, and gave me a measuring look.

I ran a quick gaze across their faces and saw shiny, red skin. Brand wasn't limping, either. I was about to ask if Geoff had come through with the healing spells when Ciaran said, "Lord Tower brought gifts. The compound's chiromancer is healing anyone who needs it. Max is stable."

"Gods," I breathed. "That's good. That's great. Did anyone tell Geoffrey he can rejoin the group?"

"Fuck Geoffrey," Brand said. "He's lucky I'm not hiding outside the sanctum, making ghost sounds. What's happening now?"

"The Tower is far-seeing for Rurik," I said. "Ashton resummoned Rurik."

"Saint Gabriel used the imbued circle on the Magician's estate," Mayan said. "He's nearby now—we know that much."

Ciaran had an odd look on his face. "And how did your Ashton get past the Magician's defenses?"

Lord Tower made a sound, then blinked away his fugue. He gave a quick look past us—away from the mansion—and then faced our small party. "That is a question," he said. "There are an uncomfortable number of questions." He spared Brand, who was fiddling with the knives on his chest harness, a glance. "We know that the recarnates were a feint. They pinned you down and distracted you from the real threat. You were right, Brandon. We shouldn't have discounted them."

Brand looked up from his knives and said, "What?"

Lord Tower started repeating the sort-of apology, then realized that Brand was trying to get him to say it twice. He closed his mouth and pointed toward the woods. "There's a church there."

"It's a basilica," Addam said. "A memorial to former Moral Certainty Arcana."

"Ashton has taken shelter there," the Tower said. "The lich will be damaged and weakened. We must find it before it can go to ground. We cannot let it escape."

"Ciaran," I said. "Lord Tower has . . . reinvigorated the wards, but we can't be certain the interior is completely safe. Would you watch over the staff while we find Ashton?"

By doing this, I was, in a way, stealing command from Lord Tower—or at least keeping it as my own. The Tower's expression didn't give anything away, but he didn't contradict me. That was good. His first thought was rarely to protect bystanders; and collateral damage followed him around like a drunk puppy.

"If you think best," Ciaran said. He gave us all an exaggerated head bow and spun back toward the mansion. On the way, he slapped my golem in the ass. The animate's sunglasses skewed, showing lava-bright eye holes.

"Thank you," I said to his retreating back. "For everything. Brand, maybe you should—"

"I will *cut you*," Brand said.

"I will not cut you," Addam added, "but I will not turn back either. Please do not ask."

"Then we move," Lord Tower said, and he began striding toward the tree line. "Rune, a word. Mayan, watch our rear." He hesitated. "Brandon, the golem's control phrase is *fail-safe five*. Please keep it oriented."

"*Five?*" Brand said. "Does that mean you have four more Runes?"

The Tower set off at a pace that had me skipping to catch up. When I was even with him, he nodded a chin at the mangled sky. "Ashton Saint Gabriel used weather magic."

"He did. To bring draug in undercover."

"There were draug," the Tower murmured. "Our little villain appears to have some unexpected connections. Why did he break the storm, though?"

"He didn't. I did."

Lord Tower's next step hitched. He recovered in a long swoop over the last of the recarnate corpses. "You used weather magic as well," he finally said.

"I didn't. I—I don't know. I needed the clouds to go away, and they did, and the draug burned. But it wasn't a spell. I didn't use a sigil."

The Tower's head snapped toward mine. For a moment—just a moment—there was an expression on his face that I entirely mistook for pride, only wondering in hindsight if maybe it had been triumph.

Any question I may have asked was lost in a sudden *whoosh* of damp, spiced wind.

A harpy dropped from the sky and landed with a resoundingly loud crash. She had the body of a lion and the face of a crone, with a wingspan as wide as a small truck. Her talons reeked of frankincense. They were highly poisonous; one scratch would turn a man's flesh to water and make his bones fall apart like clattering dice.

She threw back her head and cawed. "Lovelies! Squirming, soft-bellied lovelies!"

The Tower said, "I am the Dagger Throne."

She shuddered, twisted her head, and trailed claws across the soil in huge, smoking furrows. With another screaming caw, she launched back into the sky, her massive body rising and falling in heavy jerks.

"Not everything in the Westlands is a thinking being that responds with common sense," the Tower said. "We don't have time for distractions. Take a step back, Rune."

Since it was the Tower asking, I took five.

One of the stones in his diadem winked as its spell released. A halo of blue light appeared around his hands, thick as fresh paint. He waved an arm in front of us and ripped a bloody safe road from the earth.

It was a long and uneven path, the dirt fused into glass, covered in flaking vegetation ash. It radiated defense magic as strong as most wards I'd ever felt.

"Addam," the Tower said, pushing a sleeve past his elbow. His upper arm was nested with armbands of different metals, each a sigil. He flicked hidden catches and opened four of them. I got bronze and brass; Addam, gold and platinum. As each went into our hands, he tapped it. "Frost and Bless-fire, Addam. Rune, Fire and Shatter. I lend these freely. Your Will is now their Will."

I fastened them, relieved to have useful spells again, even if they weren't my own.

We began moving down the ad hoc safe road at a fast clip, passing into an orchard. As we went, we changed positions. Mayan maintained his spot in the rear, Addam went abreast of the Tower, and I hung back with Brand and my golem.

"You're being very well behaved around Lord Tower," I complimented him quietly.

"Do you think he has four more blow-up Runes?"

I swallowed a smile. "I think he has a golem for himself, his wife, and his two children."

Brand muttered, "I am the Dagger Throne. *And court is now in session.*"

"Go on," I said. "Get it all out."

His eyes landed on mine for a full second, which, when he was in bodyguard mode, was as good as a hard stare. "What was it like?" he whispered. "When you went outside and used the mass sigil, I felt . . . through our bond . . . I don't know. What was it like?"

I rolled down my sleeve, covering the borrowed sigils. "I'm not sure it'd be good for me to rely on mass sigils. I think . . . I think I want to bury it again." It was an inadequate response to an emotional reaction, but I just didn't have the words yet to describe the temptation of that power.

Brand thought about it. "And at what fucking point did it seem like a good idea to tear your shirt off? Were you actually standing on a mound of bodies when you did it?"

"It *burned* off."

"I'm cancelling Cinemax."

"I was on fire. It *burned*."

"I can already hear you using this excuse for the next hundred years. We—Look. There," he said, pointing suddenly.

Through a lattice of bare tree branches—this bit of the Westlands was still stubbornly fixated on autumn—I saw the white-blue, arched walls of a small, multi-domed basilica. Doves fluttered along the cornices and turrets. That seemed a bit too precious, until I saw that they were covered in bristling brown mange. The Westlands had been at work here, too.

The Tower saw it as well. He stopped us with an upraised hand and released two more mass sigils. I was ready this time and braced, leaning forward to grab Addam. Brand and Mayan kept steady in a low-gravity crouch.

Lord Tower sent a defense spell forward in a tidal surge. It flared along walls and domes with a melting-glass glow. As it covered a tool shed attached to the building's west side, the shed imploded in a burst of powdered stone. I didn't even want to know what had infested it. Visible Westland enemies were bad enough.

"Stay on guard," the Tower said, leading us toward open, twelve-foot-tall doors. The lower half of the right door was scored by gouges that dripped black gelatin.

Next to me, Brand flipped two vulcanized-coal daggers into his flexing palms.

We passed into a large entryway ringed by a mezzanine. Ashton hadn't even attempted concealment. He stood at the far end of the hall, dressed in a bright silk shirt. Fashionable metallic snake scales were sprayed along his cheekbones. He was hunched over a bleeding gut wound.

A dozen recarnates flanked him. Rurik stood off to one side. All of the facial reconstruction the lich had achieved was gone. He—*it*—was once again misshapen, and shaking with inchoate emotion.

The Tower walked to the center of the vaulted room and tapped his foot against something that sparked. I relaxed my eyes and called on my willpower until I could see the wide barrier that stretched across the chamber.

"Ashton Saint Gabriel," Lord Tower said.

The lich threw back its head and wailed. Unchanneled power rolled outward in a frostbitten wave.

Ashton gasped a laugh. "Forgive me if I don't bow. My associate behaved poorly during the summoning."

"How do you expect this to end, scion?" Lord Tower asked.

"I'm not sure yet. Interesting things can happen in corners. Shall we negotiate?"

Lord Tower toed the barrier again, considering Ashton for a long moment.

"No," he said.

He shoved at the barrier with both hands while releasing a sigil spell. Cracks spread along the walls that anchored the barrier. A second slam made dust rise. The third strike shattered the spell into invisible, hissing wisps.

"The lich is mine. Handle the rest," the Tower said.

Rurik sprang at the Tower. Its scream shook the ground. Ten feet apart, they each jerked into stillness, linked by a clash of Will that made the dust floating between them catch fire.

Other spells popped loose—me, Addam, Ashton. One of Brand's knives somersaulted at the closest recarnate, taking it through the brain stem. It hadn't even dropped when Mayan took down a second recarnate with a knife of his own.

Addam and I both held Fire—my orange flame to his white Bless-fire. "Take the recarnates, Addam. Ashton is mine." I narrowed my attention to the wounded scion.

Ashton grinned through bloodied teeth. One of the spells he'd released scissored toward the ceiling. A gold chandelier broke loose and plummeted to the floor. Just before it hit, its gas-style arms turned into legs. *Gargoyle.* Another spell shot past my head, into a mural. The mural began to peel itself from the wall with a spine-cracking wrench.

"Blunt weapon, blunt weapon!" Brand warned while taking aim at another recarnate.

"Or," I said, and touched the brass armband. The Shatter spell vibrated through my fingernails. I hurled it at the plaster gargoyle, and the creature exploded before it had even fully formed.

I shook bits of wall out of my hair and turned my attention toward the golden gargoyle. I needed to move quick, because Ashton was taking advantage of the attack to slip into the corridor behind him.

"Hello, you beauty," I said, slipping my sabre off my wrist. The gargoyle turned in a heavy, thudding circle, lifting finial-studded arms toward me. It was flowing and reforming into a manlike appearance, its footprints rimmed in molten metal.

I shot a firebolt. It ricocheted off the gargoyle into the charged space between the Tower and the lich, causing a small explosion. I shook the sabre hilt while it changed into a mace, and then studded the end with barbed protrusions. When the gargoyle entered striking distance, I bashed one of its arms and crouched under its counterstrike. Before it could lumber into another striking position, I hit it from behind, making a sickle-shaped dent. The metal was still soft, which gave me an idea.

I danced to its other side while gathering Fire in my free hand, molding it from a kernel of flame to a softball-sized sphere. I pitched the fireball at the gargoyle. The gargoyle flew backward, right into the space between the Tower and Rurik. It fast-forward evaporated in seconds. Lord Tower interrupted his trance long enough to flick me a glance that definitely wasn't approbation.

I took off after Ashton, who'd run down the corridor. Brand and the others caught up with me.

"The fountain room is down there," Addam said, pointing. "That's it—he can't be anywhere else."

"Is there a back door?" I asked.

"Just windows."

"I need to watch Lord Tower's back," Mayan said. "I'll make sure nothing takes you from behind. Be careful—the scion isn't our main target, so don't take any risks."

"Don't tell me my fucking job," Brand said. "If we let Ashton get away, what's to stop him from summoning the lich again? *Fail-safe five*, take point."

My golem bounded into the lead. It had lost its sunglasses somewhere, and its eyes left orange tracers in the air.

The four of us moved down a short hallway lined with marble busts. I scuffed my foot in a blood trail, wondering how badly Ashton had been hurt. I didn't have to wonder long. The hallway opened into a huge, circular room with a fountain in its center. Ashton stood on a raised dais opposite us, recarnates spaced in front of him.

"So it comes to this," he called to us.

"Your last fucking soliloquy?" Brand asked.

"Perhaps. But, like I said, interesting things happen when you find yourself in a corner."

Sigil spells flared free. Ashton lifted a hand toward the fountain. Pipes ripped upward in a geyser of water. Ashton waved a hand, and the water spun toward him in a cyclone. He ran his fingers through the blood on his belly, then shook droplets into the water. The swirling funnel darkened and steamed. Death magic.

"Freeze it!" I shouted as Ashton sent the cyclone at us.

Addam threw his Frost spell at the cyclone. It glanced off the poisonous water, which spun to a sluggish, then frozen, halt. I sent a lance of Fire forward and shattered it.

"Kill them!" Ashton yelled.

"*Fail-safe five*," Brand said.

Recarnates and golem leapt at each other. Brand swapped glances with Addam and me, trying to get us to approach on one flank while he went to another. I swapped a glance right back at him. Brand glared at me, but nodded. He and Addam took the far approach.

I was crossing to the other side of the hall when Ella Saint Nicholas ran into the room.

It was not a graceful run. She wore a dirty, white shift, and a cracked mirror was clasped in her hand like a Disney witch. I tried to grab her, but she wrenched free. She had three silver necklaces around her gaunt neck, and she headed straight at the recarnates while touching one and releasing a spell.

There are things all Atlanteans know how to do. Bad things. Like burning ants with magnifying glasses, but on the scale of young gods. Most kids grew out of that phase before their parents beat it out of them, but in the back of our minds, we all remembered.

The spell Ella let loose tore a hole in reality. It unraveled the souls of the recarnates. She didn't kill them, or release them. She *shredded* them. It would take decades before they found the cohesion to properly die. It was their final desecration.

Across the room, Addam watched it happen, and his cry was filled with genuine despair.

"*FACE ME!*" Ella shrieked at Ashton. "*FACE ME!*"

Brand and Addam ran at her. Ashton released another spell. I aimed my sabre at Ashton's head and fired. He scrambled from its path, and the loss of concentration interrupted his spell.

Just as Addam reached his sister, Ella activated a second spell and turned to face the golem. Air whistled as something sliced through it. My golem's face was ripped apart in great, bloodless strips, from eye to jaw.

"Get him down!" I shouted to Brand, terrified. "Get Addam down!"

A golem is forged from the deepest fires of the earth. Cutting it open compromised the safeguards, meaning that Ella had more or less skinned a grenade.

Brand tackled Addam and rolled him behind the broken fountain. I dove behind a pillar. The golem detonated. The blast wave nearly bowled me over. Through our bond, I felt Brand's sentience snuffed—alive, but knocked out. A quick glance showed that Addam wasn't moving— I'd have to hope he was okay; I didn't have time to check. I climbed unsteadily to my feet but couldn't see them through the cordite haze.

Ella was crouched behind a Shield. Ashton was, as well. My sabre wasn't in my hand anymore. I turned around in a dazed circle to find it, dimly aware of my concussion.

Ella stormed toward the dais. Ashton pulled pendants from under his shirt and wrapped his fist around them. The flash-fire release of sigil spells made the air steam. A heartbeat before they began to fling magic against each other, the ground shook.

An inhuman shriek came from every direction at once. I covered my ears and watched as a whipcord of energy raced across the floor. It washed over us, and in its wake my Fire was snuffed out. We'd been hit with a moving null line.

Ashton and Ella hadn't figured it out. They stood there, pantomiming useless arm swipes, looking puzzled at the lack of response. I picked up a length of rebar that had been severed from the destroyed fountain.

"No," Ashton said in a small voice. He ran his hands frantically over his emptied pendants. *"No."*

Ella had cut her forehead open, and blood covered one of her eyes. "Why did you do it, Ashton?" she begged.

Ashton touched the rings on his fingers; the bracelet on his wrist; a broach on his chest. He was making a desperate, stuttering sound.

"Why?" Ella said, in a voice filled with lucid grief. "I loved him. He loved me. Do you have any idea what that meant? How long I've waited for someone to want *me*? Why did you take him away?"

"You stupid bitch," Ashton said. There were tears in his eyes. "Do you have any idea what's happening?"

"Michael's dead, and everything is over," Ella said. "I know exactly what has happened. Why did you do it? We would have gotten away with it!"

"You would *never* have gotten away with it," Ashton said.

"We would have! My mother wouldn't have punished us. She would have been *impressed* with me. She would have *approved*. She would have respected my strength and resolve and cunning. She didn't try to stop me, did she?"

"Ella," I said, and coughed up dust. I couldn't be sure that all her sigils were empty. "Stop this. It's not too late for you."

"It is." She looked at her feet. "There's nothing left to care about."

"*TAKE REVENGE!*" Ashton yelled. "If you want to honor Michael, then rip that man apart! If he hadn't interfered, we wouldn't be here!"

"He didn't kill Michael. You did." She looked back up at Ashton, and the craziness was gone. "Why don't *you* tear him apart? You don't have any sigil spells left, do you, Ashton? I do. I can do *awful* things to you."

"Ella, listen to me," Ashton begged. He swept down the dais stairs and, when he was close enough, punched her in the collarbone. It sounded like a bag of branches being swung against a cement wall. Ella grunted and hit the ground. She didn't get up.

Ashton spun toward me, and I saw it on his face. Ella was right. He had no more spells left.

I stalked toward him. Ashton lifted his arms to protect his head. I prodded the end of the rebar into his gut so that he tumbled backward. I said, "There was a household servant who heard his friend being hurt, and ran toward him, right into the arms of a draug."

I stabbed at his gut again. "There was another who caught fire, and died while I put him out."

Now I swung, and took out Ashton's knee. He crumpled with a howl. I spoke above his shouts. "And there's a woman whose son worked in the gardens and who probably died when I trapped him outside my defense spell. Do you think there are any remains? Do you think she'll have anything to bury? Do you feel *anything* for these people you've destroyed, you miserable, useless inbred?"

Ashton started laughing through gasps of pain. "Just you wait until I tell you what I *feel*."

I hauled back, ready to crack his head open.

"They planned this," he yelled quickly. "I think they always knew this was going to happen. I think they put a leash on my neck, and tied it to a post in the ground, and then I went and swung myself full circle."

"What the hell are you talking about?"

"They wanted you involved. They weren't helping me—they weren't repaying an old favor. This was never about my plans with the Hermit, not for them. This is a game board within a game board. This is about *you*. They *knew* that *you*, of all people, of all *fucking* people on this island, they knew *you* would get involved."

"Who are *they*?" I demanded.

Tears washed clean, hot lines down Ashton's dirty face. "This is all about you. And that's why you're going to do what I ask."

"That is very fucking unlikely."

"You're going to kill me," he said.

I hefted the rebar, balancing the weight in my hand. "Don't worry; you'll die. For what you've done, every Arcana will turn hand against you, even your own father. You will not survive this, Ashton."

"If you don't kill me now, right now, they'll get to me. This will never go to trial. They won't risk my spirit being called back to confess. They'll send the Sorrowful Mothers after me. They will destroy my soul. Do you understand what I'm saying? They will erase me."

"You can't play with my head. Whatever this is, it won't work."

"I wore the cat mask," Ashton said.

I froze.

"I wore the cat mask," he repeated.

"This is bullshit," I said, but my voice shook.

"I wore contacts so you wouldn't be able to describe my eyes. We all wore cheap, black clothing from an American department store. There were nine of us. Everyone seems to get that wrong—perhaps you intend it that way. But there were nine of us, in that carriage house. And I was in the cat mask."

I almost dropped the rebar. I shook my head.

Ashton gave me a bloody smile. "I was the one who dipped the broom handle in a barrel of road salt, and then fucked you with it until you screamed yourself unconscious."

My vision filled with black fireflies. I took a deep, noisy breath, but the automatic breathing reflex didn't kick in. I had to force more air into my lungs.

"Now kill me," Ashton said.

"This isn't happening."

His smile cracked. "I was just as much a tool as you were. We were all just tools. You have no idea what's at stake. You have no idea who your real enemy is. *Kill me!*"

"I . . . It . . . *tools?* What are you . . . ? I was fifteen years old," I said. The words were hoarse and raw. "*I was only fifteen years old.*"

There were noises in the corridor. Lord Tower was calling my name.

Ashton said, "Kill me or I'll tell *everything*. Have you forgotten what I saw? What I know? I was there. I know what happened. I know the secrets you keep. What will happen when he finds out?"

Just like that, my anger became terror.

It was a very specific fear, one I kept buried in the farthest corner of my brain. It came out like a weed, trailing noxious roots of memory.

"Kill me!" Ashton hissed.

Across the room, Lord Tower called out.

"Gods," I whispered, and I didn't know what to do. Lord Tower was here. Lord Tower would find out. I could not trust Lord Tower with this information. I'd lose everything.

"Kill me or—"

"No," I said. "No, no, you—"

He raised his voice into a shout. "On the night—"

I touched my white-gold ring and unleashed Exodus.

A woman's voice.

"People say white is a peaceful color," she tells me. "The color of silence, and rest, and emptiness. People lie. Ask anyone who's ever been caught in a killing blizzard. Or watched the static on television screens following a nuclear blast. Or stood in the path of that spell of yours. That Exodus was quite the loud, blank mess, child."

All around me, whiteness. It flows and groans, a current of sensation leading into the ineffable distance.

"You're enjoying oblivion far too much," she says.

I ignore her and let the River pull me.

"Stop," the woman says, and she pins me in place with a force of will.

"Wake," the woman says, and she throws me back the way I came.

I was in Addam's arms. He cradled me and whispered my name, and ran fingers through my hair. My bangs were heavy with dirt and oil.

One of my ears wasn't working. My chest hurt. I looked down and saw that blood had dried to a tacky mess alongside deeply sunburned skin. I'd been healed recently.

My Companion bond stirred sluggishly. With unerring accuracy, I turned my head so I could see Brand. He lay in the dirt not far away, dazed and barely conscious. Addam's jacket was wadded under his head.

"You're back," Addam whispered.

I opened my mouth to ask him why it was so dark, and coughed up blood. Addam rubbed his hands over my chest in small, smoothing circles until I gagged myself silent.

I tried again. "Where's Ashton? . . . Why is it so dark?"

"Ashton is gone."

"He got away?" I rasped.

"No," Addam said. "He's . . . gone."

"You vaporized him," Lord Tower said. "Along with several rather important pillars."

I craned my head back. The room was dark, except for someone's cantrip light. The roof seemed so close that I could touch it. "Are we in a crawlspace?" I asked, confused.

"We are not," Lord Tower said. "My Shield is holding the roof from our heads. I'll need your help to get it off us, once you catch your breath."

"Well, shit," I coughed.

Lord Tower whispered a cantrip, and three more balls of light lit the space between us. I could see the Tower's face now, and I knew that look. He wanted to see my reaction for himself.

"What happened?" he asked.

"I already told him," Addam said. "Ashton was about to use forbidden magic. You saved us."

Not only was Addam a very bad liar, but the fact that he even tried to lie made me think he hadn't been all that unconscious in the end.

Before I had time to worry, Brand began coughing, too. He said, "I had the weirdest fucking dream. You were swatting a fly with a sack of nitroglycerin."

"Nitroglycerin the heart medication, or nitroglycerin the explosive?" I asked.

"You really want me to come over there and explain my metaphor?"

"Yes," I said, and I was being honest, because I wanted to see him move and know he wasn't hurt.

His gaze softened.

"I'm okay, Rune," he said. "We're okay."

EPILOGUE

A week passed.

I was still jumping at shadows. Battle adrenaline had a way of working itself into your muscle memory. It was tough to let it go, even in the narrow comfort of Half House.

Ella Saint Nicholas was in custody. I was called to give carefully edited evidence to the Arcanum. For reasons which were my own, I protected Geoffrey and Michael from the worst of it. Michael would be remembered as a dumb bastard manipulated by Ashton. Geoffrey was required to offer the Arcanum a Vow of Redemption. He'd be watched for the rest of his life, but he wouldn't be executed.

Ashton's minimal remains were buried in a potter's field. I hadn't heard from Strength's people, which made me nervous, since I killed their heir scion. But I heard through Addam that Lord Strength was accepting the shame of his son's actions, not excusing them.

Could Ashton's spirit be raised for questioning? I didn't know. One crisis at a time.

I hadn't heard from Lady Justice either, but, then again, I'd gotten her daughter arrested, had dragged her son into the Westlands (where people died, and he lost about a million dollars' worth of sigils), and wasn't able to keep another son out of a coma. I wasn't holding my breath for a gift basket.

Addam spent nearly every waking moment by Quinn's bedside until Quinn woke up. Addam's other brother, Christian, stabilized. With Geoffrey's help, they determined that Ashton had poisoned him with a rare herb, and they were able to develop an antidote.

Brand and I went to a mass funeral in the Westlands for the Moral Certainty staff who lost their lives in the siege. I held an old woman's granddaughter—the little girl I'd sensed in the dumbwaiter—while the woman keened over her son's coffin.

Ciaran faded back into the woodwork. Our partnership had been strange and brief and wholly unexpected. I made sure he was compensated by Lord Tower, and hoped I'd have a chance to thank him personally.

Addam's assistant, Lilly Rose, baked cookies and offered to give us a kitten. Brand told her I'd once killed a cactus, but baked goods were acceptable.

Lord Hierophant sent me a water bill for my emergency stay in his mansion, along with a politely worded threat not to mention anything I saw. Such as a clay soldier? I tucked *that* tidbit away against future need.

As for my own golem, there was no word if Lord Tower replaced it.

Lord Tower himself had been quiet. A large check was messengered over, but he hadn't spoken with me personally, or raised the question of what happened with Ashton. As far as Lord Tower went, that meant he was on the hunt. But there were some secrets I'd kill to keep. I had to trust that Lord Tower would respect that boundary if I confronted him with it.

There were a lot of other remaining questions. The events of last week hadn't left me with loose ends, so much as a hundred different knots.

But such was life. I'd cope.

"Max," I said from the doorway of the guest room.

He squeezed his eyes shut and pretended to be asleep.

"Brand hasn't made you listen to the recording yet?" I asked.

Too curious for his own good, Max cracked an eyelid. "What recording?"

"Of you sleeping."

"Why does Brand have a recording of me sleeping?"

"It's one of his training exercises. He'll make a recording of you sleeping, and then you have to practice breathing like you do when you're asleep. That way, if you get kidnapped, you can fake being unconscious."

"I think you're joking," Max said uncertainly.

"Not even a little. Wait until the final test. I won't say that you'll wake up half-drugged in a Warrens bazaar wearing only a loincloth, but you will."

I went into the room and sat on the edge of the mattress.

Max had recovered from his injuries, thanks to lots of rest, several loaves of banana bread, and liberal doses of healing spells. But the better he seemed to get, the more he withdrew from the household. Something was scaring him, and Brand and I hadn't yet been able to broach the issue. I decided on the direct approach.

"You look well enough to talk," I said. He tried to shake my gaze, so I waited patiently until it was too awkward for him not to look at me. "We need to talk, Max."

"You're going to make me leave," he said. He turned his cheek into his pillow.

"No," I said.

"You don't want me to stay," he said.

"No again."

"You don't," he insisted. "This isn't real. Me staying in this room, like it's mine. Feeding me. Buying me clothes. This isn't real. It's all going to end."

"Who says?"

"It . . ." He gave me an aching look, a painful mix of adult knowledge and a teenager's confusion. "I don't understand what you want from me. You're supposed to want something. Everyone wants something. It doesn't make sense otherwise."

"You're wrong. I wish I could explain it to you, but it's something you'll need to learn for yourself." I paused, but not for long. Kindness wouldn't make the next bit any easier. "Max, who's after you?"

The question moved across his face like a slap. He shook his head.

"Brand and I can't protect you if we don't know who it is. Is it your uncle? I know he hurt you. Are you worried he's after you?"

"Protect me?" Max said. His eyes watered, even as he laughed.

"You've never been alone, have you? You've always had a *Brand and I*. It must be so incredible to have a Companion."

"Incredible? I think I'd pick a much more neutral adjective than that."

"You joke, but you don't mean it. He'd do anything for you. He always has your back. He'd kill to protect you. I think he literally sits around waiting for you to ask."

"He's protective about people he cares for. And he's begun caring about you too, Max. You're important to him now, too."

"Am I . . . Am I important to you?"

"Max."

"I want to be important to you."

"We talked about this. You're seventeen years old."

"We are a long-lived race," Max said. "I'll live for hundreds of years, and I won't be seventeen again for any of them."

Brand jumped down the stairwell and landed in the hallway. I'd known he was listening, and he'd known I'd known he was listening, but he'd apparently wanted to prove a point by sneaking past me to the third floor. It had a better vent for eavesdropping.

"Beautiful job getting to the bottom of things," Brand said.

He came into the room and slid onto the mattress next to Max. After bunching the pillow to support his neck, he jabbed Max in the back and said, "What's wrong with you? He's so old."

Max ducked his blush until he could shape-shift it into a consistent pale.

"You went about it all wrong, anyway. If you really wanted to catch Rune's eye, you should have stood outside his window in the rain and held a boom box above your head."

"Brand."

"What's a boom box?"

Brand snorted. "And how stupid do you think we are? You've dodged every question Rune asked. Do you think we're not going to get answers?"

His gaze traveled between us. "I . . . In the beginning, I was so worried you'd figure it out. When I first came to Half House, you thought I cared that my family was gone. That I blamed you for being a part of the raid that brought the Lovers down. I didn't know how to tell you the truth, that . . . That it was an escape. But now I'm not so sure I escaped anything." His voice broke. "The other day, a messenger came to Half House. I don't know what to do."

"Who came to Half House?" I demanded.

He shook his head.

Brand jumped up and swung in front of Max. Max's gaze was pinned by Brand's advance, a deer in headlights.

Brand said, "Who is after you?"

"The . . . person. The person who I was being . . . married to."

"Max," Brand said. "Don't make me ask twice."

Max said, "The Hanged Man."

I stepped back, hit the wall.

"The Hanged Man sent someone to our house?" Brand asked Max in a dangerously quiet voice.

"A messenger. He said . . ." Max stopped talking.

"He said the Hanged Man still has a claim on you?" I asked.

Max nodded.

"Won't happen," I said.

"He's the Hanged Man," Max whispered.

"And I'm me," I said. "It won't happen."

One crisis at a time, I thought.

Later that day, I told Brand I was going to see Lord Tower, and I left Half House by myself. It was my standard lie when I needed to get away. It wasn't as if Brand would willingly call there to check up on me.

I took the underground to LeperCon, to a scruffy street several blocks away from Addam's business offices.

The studio apartment was a rent-controlled gift from a client who couldn't pay cash. Brand didn't know about it. If I had my way, he never would. I kept my name off the lease, utility bills—anything that could be tracked back to me.

The first thing I did was putter around the tiny corner kitchen to make a pot of coffee, a small ritual of mine.

When the knock came, I froze. No one had ever knocked on the door before.

I was not unarmed, of course. I'd tailored my sigil load for the unexpected, a blend of aggressive and stealth magic. Wiping a thumb across my mother's cameo—which Addam had long since returned, as I'd returned their house sigil—I let its stored spell shiver loose. The world briefly flashed in sepia hues.

When the spell balanced, I used the Vision spell to mentally peel layers of wood and plaster away from the wall. It took a moment to moderate the sight, from solid material, to bones and tissues, and then back into very two recognizable forms standing in the apartment hallway.

Before I could decide what to do, a voice said, "I like it when you make the candygram joke. The Avon joke isn't very funny when you tell it, and maybe a little sexist."

I disengaged the ward and deadbolt. Quinn Saint Nicholas stood on my shabby welcome mat with his aunt, Diana.

"Addam didn't tell me you'd been released," I said.

Quinn scratched his cheek and said, "Um."

"We'll be returning to the hospital shortly," Diana said, fixing a firm stare on her nephew. "We made a deal."

Quinn was craning his neck around me in obvious interest. He was about to squirm past me when Diana cleared her throat and said, "Manners."

"My manners?" Quinn asked.

"Nephew."

"Oh, the gift! I have a gift!" Quinn dug into the big, wicker-handled purse that Diana was carrying. She gave him a look of exasperation as he yanked her arm back and forth while rooting. He triumphantly pulled out a belt, then held it up for inspection.

It was beautiful: hand-worked black leather with braided, decorative slots.

One of the slots was filled with a small platinum disc.

"Is that . . . ?" I asked.

"The sigil you returned. Addam told you that you could keep it, didn't he?"

"I can't accept that."

"You always accept it," Quinn said, rolling his eyes. "Why wouldn't you? You saved Addam's life over and over. You saved so many people. Don't you know what would have happened without you?"

"It's too much," I said hesitantly.

"It wants you. You used it more than I ever did, and for better ends. It recognizes you now. It sings for you."

I'd already accepted that Quinn was no ordinary seer, so the statement didn't surprise me nearly as much as it might have. Why shouldn't he talk to sigils?

"May Quinn wait inside while we speak?" Diana asked politely, taking the belt from Quinn.

"This isn't a place for kids," I said, somewhat stupidly, but it was true.

"I'm not a kid," Quinn said. "Is that a lava lamp?" He squeezed past me and trotted over to it.

Diana sighed.

I gave the older woman a glance. The matronly polish from a couple weeks ago was tempered by lines around her eyes and lips. I think I understood. She'd given her life in support of her sister's reign. She'd been Ella's caretaker. She had her own consequences to contend with.

I gave Quinn a speculative glance and wondered who was really accompanying whom.

Diana saw my glance. She said, "We were awful to him."

"We?"

"Myself and . . . Ella. We were never kind to Quinn."

I didn't comment. I wasn't very good at sweetening the truth.

"It's an irony," Diana said. "Of our entire family, Quinn is the only one who has visited Ella in captivity. This isn't the first time he's snuck out of the hospital in the last few days."

"What did . . ." I wasn't sure how to phrase my question. "I mean, does Quinn know what will happen to her? Can he see her future?"

"She won't be executed. She'll be exiled. Quinn says it won't be easy, but—" Her lips quirked. "But most of the time, she has many opportunities for happiness. Once she even got married, and he'll make her eat lots of food."

"She did awful things," I said.

"She is a foolish, damaged girl, who did foolish and damaging things. And we enabled her. *I* enabled her." She pressed her lips together.

Across the room, Quinn made a satisfied sound as he found the lava lamp's on switch. Diana smiled faintly. "I am accustomed to being the attendant to my sister's children. And Quinn needs . . . friends. I'd hoped Addam wouldn't mind if I offered my time."

"Addam did a very good job raising Quinn, didn't he?"

"He did at that." Diana held the belt out to me. "You will accept this."

"It's a *sigil*."

"Manners," she said, and shook the belt. I took it. For the sake of form, she added, "I give this family sigil freely. Your Will is now its Will."

And just like that, I had an eighth sigil.

"Quinn would like to speak to you alone," Diana said. "I apologize for any imposition. May I leave him with you while I sit outside? There's a nice breeze in the park across the street."

"I'll talk to him," I said after a pause. "I'll bring him outside in a few minutes."

Diana left.

"You're looking good, Quinn," I said, closing the door.

He tapped the side of the lamp, trying to get the blob to split.

"You had something to say to me?" I asked.

Quinn looked up. In five or ten years, his expression may have passed as guarded; but he was too young to keep the facial tics from betraying his tension. "Sometimes you need to talk to me," he said. "Sometimes I just get to give you the sigil, and we're both happy."

"Sometimes I need to talk to you," I echoed, and mulled that over. "About the fact that you tried to kill Max?"

His face crumpled. Just crumpled.

"After things settled down, I had a lot of time to think," I told him. "There are so many unanswered questions. And one of those questions is about Max. I couldn't get it out of my head. Why did Max come with Brand to the Westlands? Brand said that you told him—via dream-walking with Max—that Brand had to come to the Westlands with Max and Ciaran. And Max swears that that's the truth. So I thought to myself, *Why didn't Ciaran come to the Swimming Hole with Brand?* They knew I'd be facing Rurik. Why would Ciaran stay behind? And Brand told me that you were clear about that as well. Ciaran had to stay behind with Max, to keep Max from following. And *then* I started wondering why Max was so important. Why was his presence so important?"

"To take the knife thrust," Quinn whispered.

"To take the knife thrust instead of me," I said. "You used Max like a pawn, Quinn."

"I . . . it's not . . . It's not like that." He swallowed jerkily, causing tears to spill from his eyes. "He always had a good chance of being okay, but *you* didn't. Time after time after time, *you* didn't. You don't understand what it's like. You don't know what it's like to *see.*"

"So you let Max get stabbed so that I wasn't taken out. So that, what, I would still be able to save Addam?"

"No! That's not—I'm not that selfish! I let Max get stabbed so that you could part the clouds!"

I blinked, surprised. "And that was important."

"It was the most important thing in the world," Quinn whispered.

My skin crawled. I rubbed at the goose bumps and said, "Why?"

"I can't tell you. Won't. Can't. It's hard to explain."

"Why? Why can't or won't you tell me?"

"Because it's not my role."

"Whose role is it, then?"

"Time," Quinn said sadly. "Time will show you."

I turned away from him in a slow pivot and walked to the other side of the apartment. More than one emotion squared off in my head. Addam made everything messier. Addam made this complicated.

"*Prophets*," I said angrily.

"I didn't ask for this," Quinn whispered.

"No, you didn't. But you're too godsdamn young to make these decisions. You're fifteen, Quinn. You don't have the life experience. You don't understand consequences."

"I see nothing *but* consequences," he argued.

"I'm not sure you understand them, though. Ashton Saint Gabriel summoned a storm. He used weather magic. When I broke the cloud cover, I sheared the storm in two. One half dissipated in the Westlands. The other pulverized two homesteads before heading out to sea. It swamped a fishing vessel, and two lives were lost. It's a small hurricane now, heading north."

"But it could have been so much worse! If you hadn't been there, it could have—"

"There is no longer any *could have*! It's happened. It's fixed in amber. People are dead, and they aren't coming back."

Quinn was five or six breaths away from actual sobs. The look on his face tugged on something deep in my heart, a very personal and private place. I'd been fifteen once. I'd been drawn into adult events far beyond my control.

"Quinn," I said, and I walked back over to him. I dropped to my knees and looked up into his face. "This will kill you. You know that, right? Most people with your gift don't die in their bed of old age. They get lost in their visions and die of starvation, or have heart attacks, or get into avoidable accidents. Or they go mad. You are *too young* to be playing with this gift."

His lips worked around a few words. But he just shook his head.

I said, "I know that this isn't the sort of gift that can be returned, but you can choose not to use it in the fashion you do. And there are ways to help you with that choice."

"Ways?"

"We can talk with Ciaran. Maybe Lord Tower. There are ways."

"You mean drugs," Quinn said.

"Yes. And alchemy. We need to look into it."

"You keep . . . saying . . . *we*."

"Yeah," I said. "I do."

A fresh batch of tears swam out his eyes. "I scare you."

"I scare people, too," I said.

I made a decision—one of those weird, impulsive calls that you're fairly sure is going to change everything, one way or the other. "What time are you coming to the barbecue tomorrow?"

"The barbecue?" he asked.

"The barbecue. What time are you and Addam coming? You should bring your aunt, too."

"But . . ."

"Didn't Addam tell you?"

"He said he was going. I didn't know . . . I mean, he didn't say you wanted me . . ."

"So it's settled."

Quinn's eyes went unfocused for a second. "I remember the barbecue. I have three hot dogs, even though Max drops one of them on the ground a lot."

"Yeah, okay, do you remember that time we talked about the responsible use of your gifts?" Then, against my better judgment, I said, "And now that we know he drops the hot dog, I can stop it."

"You try, but Brand usually gets mad that you're hovering next to the grill and punches you in the funny bone."

I slapped him on the knee and got up. "Tell Addam that if he brings a thousand-dollar bottle of wine, I'll hit him with it. Make him buy something a non-ridiculously-wealthy person would bring, like a watermelon."

"We'll bring a watermelon," Quinn promised, the start of a grin on his face.

"Good. Now let's go find your aunt."

I caught him staring behind me, and I turned around to unplug the lava lamp. I handed it to him. "One more thing. This place is . . . it's where I go when I need to be alone. It's a secret."

"I won't say anything."

"You shouldn't track people down in places where they don't want to be tracked down. If we're going to be friends, we've got to have ground rules."

"I understand," Quinn said, nodding at me gravely. "And thank you for the lava lamp."

I walked Quinn outside. Once he was safely pawned off on his aunt, I went back into the apartment, secured the door, and poured a cup of coffee. I stood there for a long time, staring into the sink, letting my mind wander.

When the coffee was gone, I rinsed the mug, put it back in the cabinet, and walked to the far side of the room. I focused on my gold ankle chain. A spell flowed loose. It surrounded my hands like static.

I waved a palm toward the wall.

The smudged plaster vanished. In its place was a nine-by-seven collage of notes, newspaper clippings, Post-Its, photographs, guarda reports. Thumbtacks were dull points of color in a violent black-and-white representation of a twenty-year investigation. At the top were nine large squares drawn in black permanent marker.

I pulled a torn magazine page from my pocket and unfolded a publicity shot of Ashton Saint Gabriel.

I tacked the picture into one of the nine squares with painstaking care.

Half House's backyard was wider and deeper than the rest of the house. Queenie's one-room cottage took up a large chunk of the northwest corner, but there was still enough room to squeeze a large amount of people into it. Well, "large" by our antisocial standards, at least.

Addam; Quinn and Diana; Lilly Rose. I'd invited the Tower and Ciaran, to be polite, but neither had shown. Addam brought a strange, black watermelon, and he was carving it up on the picnic table. He handed me a slice on his way to the grill, which he'd politely commandeered when Brand started getting too free with the lighter fluid.

I took the watermelon to the cherry tree, and eavesdropped. Lilly Rose was whispering to Queenie about dental plans. Max and Quinn were sizing each other up—and this after Quinn pointedly warned Max that he would tolerate no ferrets in their relationship. Max was even laughing, which was a nice sound to hear.

"See," I said, when Brand came over. I held up my watermelon. "This is a normal, everyday gift. He'll fit in."

"Sure he will," Brand said. "I've lost fucking count of the times that someone's brought a densuke watermelon to our house."

I stared at it. "I'm not sure what that means."

"It means that your everyday guy is a really rich smart-ass."

Half an hour after the grill's last yield, the doorbell rang. I waved Queenie off and went inside the house myself.

I checked the peephole first, which Brand had installed through the woodwork, about five feet from the fake peephole. A small smile crossed my lips. I went over to the bookshelf above the sofa and pulled down an old book with a broken spine.

"Why hello, Geoffrey," I said when I opened the door.

Geoffrey gave me a deeply suspicious look from the front stoop.

"Thanks for coming," I said. "Sorry about the short notice."

"What's going on?" Geoff asked. He sniffed. "Are you barbecuing? Did you call me here for a *barbecue?*"

I went out on the stoop, nudging him aside when he didn't step back. I shut the door behind me.

Geoffrey didn't look good. It had been a hard week for him. If there'd been a funeral for Michael, I hadn't heard about it; and the Arcanum's investigation had been taxing.

"Do you honestly think," I said, "that I'd invite you into my home?"

Geoffrey reddened. "I don't need to take this from you anymore. I've made my peace with the Arcanum."

"Because I protected you."

Geoffrey gave no response other than grinding his teeth.

"I protected you," I said.

"You protected me," he spat. "But even if they knew what you knew, I'd have survived this. I wasn't the real villain, Rune. You know that."

"It's a bad practice, telling me what I know. It makes me want to ask all sorts of questions."

"Enjoy your barbecue," he said, turning to leave.

"Not so fast. I bought this for you." I turned the book faceup and held it out for him.

His face ran through emotions like a child's flick book—annoyed, puzzled, shocked, scared, and, finally, a forced blandness. Geoffrey would never make a good poker player.

"What is that?" he asked.

"A copy of the book you were holding when I first met you at Moral Confidence." I tilted the binding. "Rare herbs and their history. Fascinating shit."

"I read a lot of books, Rune."

"Sooner or later, we'll get to the part where you poisoned Christian Saint Nicholas."

"*Ashton* poisoned him. It was *Ashton's plan!*"

"Do you honestly think that lie would stand, if the Arcanum put the right questions to you?"

Geoffrey took a step back and stumbled on the edge of the landing.

"This is what I think," I continued. "I think Ashton *was* the real villain. And I think you're greedy and stupid. I think you saw a chance to become important. But, either way, you were much, much more involved than you've admitted."

"What are you going to do?" he said.

"I'm going to blackmail you, Geoff."

"I . . . I gave the Arcanum a Vow of Redemption. I can't—"

"You're going to swear a greater vow to me. I'll set up the ritual this weekend."

"Why?" Geoffrey demanded. "Why would you do this?"

"Because a man who knows poisons now owes me a favor. Think of the possibilities. Now get the hell away from my house, Geoff. We'll talk soon."

I went back inside and shut the door. The look on his face was something to be cherished.

I was in the process of sliding the book back into place when I noticed a man sitting on the other end of the sofa. He wore a brown cowl and had a large and dripping nose.

"So," I said. "This is happening."

"Brother," he greeted me.

"Lord Hermit." I went over to the armchair and sank heavily onto the cushions. "How much of that did you hear?"

The Hermit made a dismissive sound. "Don't flatter yourself with your schemes. You still fail to see the larger picture, child."

Considering I'd never so much as exchanged a word with the man before, his presumptuousness seemed cheeky.

"There is," the Hermit said, "a prophecy about you."

"Oh, don't *even.*"

Something that may have been a smile flashed white inside the cowl. "It's too soon to tell you. One day, not too far from now, you'll come to me for answers. And I'll tell you the truth. I'll tell you what I know. I will do this, for the service you provided me."

"Ashton was an idiot. A raid on the Hermitage would never have succeeded."

"Maybe so. Maybe not. Nevertheless, I will discharge my debt."

He stood up and folded his arms under his sleeves. "Be cautious, brother. Coincidences will draw closer, and the current will become deeper. Be cautious."

He vanished.

Fucking Arcana, I thought.

I surprised myself by having fun. It was a fun afternoon.

We ate and drank and laughed. It was unspeakably normal. Even Quinn fit in—relaxing into his age, acting like a real teenager. When he found out Brand had considered him a suspect in Addam's disappearance—however briefly—he was ecstatic. He spent the rest of the barbecue jumping around with his hands on his hips, waxing a fake mustache.

As the failing sun seared the horizon, I retreated to the elevated patio with a bottled beer. Addam joined me after a few minutes.

"Densuke," I said. "Really?"

"I know a guy."

I shook my head through a smile.

Addam stared over at his younger brother, who was telling Max a story that involved wide, exaggerated arm gestures. "You are saying something with this."

"With what?"

"Inviting Quinn. Do you know how many barbecues he's been invited to? How many birthday parties? How many opportunities he's had to be . . . For this . . ." His voice went tight, and he cleared his throat. "For this alone I will love you, Hero."

"And yet," I said in a shaky voice, "you're scared of me."

He raised his eyebrows.

"Don't lie, Addam. I saw the look on your face back at the basilica."

To my surprise, he laughed. He wiped his eyes and laughed.

"Of course I am scared of you. You brought a church down on our heads. You scare the sainted spit out of me, Rune."

"We're both scions. We're both powerful."

"I am a scion. You are Arcana. I accept this."

"It's that easy?" I asked. I stared at him, not sure I wanted the answer to the next question. "And that's the only reason you're scared?"

"Ah. What happened at the end, with Ashton, is . . . It is blurry. I did not hear as much as you seem to suspect. I simply know that it was a very, very hard moment for you." He looked at me. "You have secrets. I will not ask questions. I respect your judgment. I *do*," he added, seeing the look on my face.

I opened and closed my mouth, and then opened and closed it again.

"You will not convince me you're not my *talla*," Addam said softly. "You will not convince me that we're not important."

Addam kissed me on the forehead. "Tomorrow, I will begin our courtship."

He walked away.

The railing under my hands was moving. I looked down and saw that branches were growing out of the wood. One of them was studded with buds, and the buds bloomed into powder-blue flowers.

Brand came over. We stared at the railing. After a suitable period of reflection, he said, "You are such a freak."

He slapped the bottom of his beer against the neck of mine so that foam shot out of it. I laughed and held it away, while he walked off.

There are moments in your life that are so impossibly large that it's difficult to even comprehend them. They make your very bones vibrate. Standing there, it was like my future spiraled outward. Waves of possibility crashed on each other, bound by the insane certainty that everything could start.

That everything could finally start.

ACKNOWLEDGMENTS

For the best agent in the known multiverse, Sara Megibow of kt literary; for my awesome editor, Rene Sears of Pyr; for the Writer's Cramp and its exceptionally talented authors; for the fantastic friends I made in the Emerging Leaders Network . . . There are, quite literally, a million thank-yous I need to make, starting with Miss Hubbard and going straight through to the amazing folk at Pyr (Rene! Jade! Jake! Hanna!); the talented cover artist, Micah Epstein; and the barista who made my iced mocha at Open Eye this afternoon. But Sara? Rene? The Writer's Cramp? ELN? These people helped nurture and shape the book you just read. I am so grateful for their skill and support.

ABOUT THE AUTHOR

K. D. Edwards lives and writes in North Carolina but has spent time in Massachusetts, Maine, Colorado, New Hampshire, Montana, and Washington State. (Common theme until North Carolina: Snow. So, so much snow.) Mercifully short careers in food service, interactive television, corporate banking, retail management, and bariatric furniture have led to a much less short career in higher education, currently for the University of North Carolina system.

And feel free to follow K. D. Edwards on Twitter, @KDEdwards_NC! (Except for parents and coworkers and anyone else who thinks K. D. is polite and mild-mannered. Seriously. Save him from that reckoning.)